Howard Carter Saves the World

A Novel by Scott Perkins...
...with Robots!

CROOKED CAT

First Purple Line Edition, Crooked Cat Publishing Ltd. 2015

Discover us online:
www.crookedcatpublishing.com

Join us on facebook:
www.facebook.com/crookedcatpublishing

Tweet a photo of yourself holding
this book to @crookedcatbooks
and something nice will happen.

For Kristin, who always knows
when to say
"Tell me a story"

About the Author

Scott Perkins was born and raised in rural Missouri, dreaming about turning his grandfather's tractors into giant robots. His parents' house was more library than anything else and he grew up tromping through the woods with his cousins and absorbing the classics. Despite an early fondness for mysteries, he was most enthralled by the sort of science fiction and fantasy stories that were fundamentally silly and held out some hope for humanity. Scott wrote his first novel when he was nine and never looked back.

At some point, he got a bit older and accidentally become a graphic designer and illustrator (which are just another way of telling stories after all) and now spends his time helping run a college writing and tutoring center in Tacoma, WA. His short story about the clash between Daylight Savings Time and Armageddon was a finalist in the *6th Annual Writer's Digest Short Short Story Competition.*

His secret island lair is located somewhere in Washington State, where he lives with his wife and assorted feline lifeforms. You can connect with Scott online @Pages2Type on Twitter, on Facebook, and Tumblr, as well as his website: www.pagestotype.com. Dr. Villainous Deeds, PhD has a life of his own and you will find him @LaughManiacally on Twitter.

Regarding Footnotes

As everyone knows, all works of Great Scientific Import™ must be heavily footnoted, cross-referenced, and otherwise [1]annotated. Where your humble chronicler has something additional to say that might deepen your understanding of the story (or in some cases befuddle you in a pleasingly scientific manner) you will find an endnote. To access the note, click on the superscript number (like the one you probably ignored up there by the word annotated) and you will be taken to the corresponding annotation. Once you have read and either understood or been pleasantly befuddled, click the number again to be returned to your place in the story. This should work on most currently-available electronic reading [2]devices.

---

[1] Okay, we freely admit that this is not a work of Great Scientific Import but we did it anyway. See how this works? Easy peasy lemon squeasy, as they say in all the finest scientific publications.

[2] For those of you participating in our special limited-time beta test of direct cerebral upload, just locate the footnote in the area we call *Wernicke's file cabinet* located on the left side of your brain. Press and hold for three seconds. Once you have regained consciousness, please log the duration of your dream state, plus any strange visions on the provided bug-reporting sheet. Thank you for participating in Arkham Technical Institute's "Negotiable Neuroanatomy" research and always remember our motto: "This is awful, taste it" constitutes a valid disclaimer of medical liability."

Acknowledgements

I want to thank my parents, Ted and Patricia Perkins for telling young Scottie it was okay if I became an author as long as I got my homework done first. Mom, your encouragement and love is boundless and the reason stories exist to be told. Dad... I just wish you'd lived to see this. Thanks to my sister, Tammy, her husband Doug, and my wonderful nephews and fellow mad scientists Jared and Morgan for boundless inspiration.

Thanks to my publishers, Stephanie and Laurence Patterson at Crooked Cat who found something in Howard worth taking a risk on and my editor and cheerleader Andy Angel. Thank you Treehouse Writers Joel Reid, Deirdre Sargent, Maggie Secara, Thena MacArthur, Valerie Fredericks, Kristen Francis, Kathleen Bartholomew, Charles Cowan, Christine Butler, Sharon Cathcart, Ari Berk, Gabrielle Kirouac Byrne, Mary Elizabeth Wine, Kory Doyle, Penelope Dreadfulle, and Steve DeWinter. Some people have writing groups; I just keep a treehouse full of writers out back.

This book was written before a live studio audience... or at least a blog audience. Thank you to all my readers to followed along and offered helpful suggestions and inspiration along the way. And thank you to the Office of Letters & Light for your annual "NaNoWriMo" event, which helped provide the imaginary deadline I needed to finally sit down and write Howard's story.

John & Hank Green don't know it, but they and the Nerdfighters helped me through a dark time. Their efforts to encourage peace and empathy in the world and to form a support community for those who are not chosen first, kids who are mocked, scared, or live in fear of themselves are laudable and should be supported. In recognition, a portion of the author's proceeds from this novel will be donated to their *Foundation to Decrease Worldsuck*. Learn more about how you too can support their efforts at fightworldsuck.org and

<u>projectforawesome.com</u>. Don't forget to be awesome.

Lastly, I must thank my wife Kristin once more for putting up with so much and making so much of this possible. She is my lifeline to the real world, my consulting engineer, my ballast when fancy flies too high, and my balloon when it sinks too low. With all my heart, I thank you for everything.

Scott Perkins
September 2015

Howard Carter Saves the World

Prologue

Bob Engels had been a farmer his entire life. He had never known anything except the smell of tractor exhaust fumes and the pleasant sight of acres and acres of the green and growing.

It began as a normal morning of mumbled pleasantries around the breakfast table as he and his family tried to chase away the phantoms of sleep with coffee and flapjacks.

The doorbell rang and they glanced at one another and then over at the front door. No one who knew them ever came to the front door; friends and family entered and exited through the kitchen as was right and proper. They lived too far from town for salesmen or missionaries to bother -- the world left his family to fend for themselves for brushes and salvation.

Then the tractor walked past the kitchen window.

Lumbered, he supposed was a better word for it. Sort of a slow, ponderous march across the back yard. It took Bob a minute or two to get past the 'Oh, that's odd' and all the way to 'Tractors aren't supposed to do that.' The family rose as one to watch the big green tractor step almost daintily over the back fence and strike out across the fields in big loping strides.

The doorbell rang again.

"Zeke, get the door," Bob mumbled to his eldest son. "Mabel, fetch my shotgun."

"What good's a shotgun going to do?"

Bob didn't know. He only knew that was what his daddy would do and somehow he felt like it was the right thing to do when your farm equipment was trying to make a break for it. His hands ached for the smooth surface of the walnut stock.

He heard voices from the hall and turned to find Zeke leading a younger boy into the kitchen. The kid was dressed in a suit and tie but looked like he'd been sleeping in a ditch for a week. He had a copper trash can tucked under his arm that had been fashioned into a sort of helmet.

"Who is this?"

"I'm Howard Carter, sir," the boy stuck out his hand. The fingernails were dirty with axle grease and Bob Engels had the feeling he was about to find out why his tractor was running away. His hands itched for that shotgun. Or a hickory switch, teach the little hooligan a lesson...

The first flying saucer shattered the front window as it roared over the house. Everyone ducked. Everyone except Howard Carter. He stared up at the shaking ceiling with the look of someone facing an algebra test that they'd stayed up all night studying for: resigned but ready.

"What was..." the second flying saucer drowned out the rest of Bob's question. He looked up to find the boy watching him.

"I'm sorry about your tractors, I promise I'll try to get them back to you in one piece." The boy led the way out into the garage, the Engel family falling in behind him like soldiers behind a general.

Outside the sky was alight with a sickly green glow and one of the neighbor's big red harvesters was tapping its foot, waiting impatiently for the boy as more flying saucers lit the sky with their sickly glow.

"When the government gets here, tell them to keep their distance," Howard Carter shouted over the whine of the spaceships. Bob Engels nodded dumbly. What could he say to this odd boy and his robot army?

"What is this?" Bob shouted. "What are you going to do?"

The boy glanced up at the sky and gave Bob a resigned smile.

"I'm going to save the world."

The giant robot bent down and plucked the kid off the driveway and raised him to sit on its mighty shoulder. The Engels family waved as Howard put the copper helmet on his head and pointed his robot across the fields in the direction of the glowing woods.

Bob turned to his family. He caught a glimpse out of the corner of his eye of the battered old farm truck watching him from the shadows of the garage.

"Well? What are you waiting for? You might as well get after him!"

The truck flashed its headlights and sprinted off down the driveway and across the culvert while overhead, the saucers began to circle and land.

PART I
A ROBOT TOO FAR

1. For Want of a Fridge Magnet

Humanity's attempts to understand the universe have produced countless theories to explain how their world and the universe operate. Beautiful, elegant theories about things you can't see like quantum mechanics and things like gravity that make anvils fall on cartoon characters.

Along the way, they've also found places where the math and theory are sound, but reality refuses to cooperate. For instance: in an infinite universe other life forms beyond Earth are inevitable. Everyone knew this, but put it on their list of Things Not To Think About until a physicist named Enrico Fermi leaned over to someone at a dinner party and asked, "If that's true, then where is everybody?"

This is called a paradox, which in this case means *"Yeah, we don't know what's happening either. Weird, huh?"* The scientific community named this one after Fermi, whether as an honor or punishment depends on who you talk to.

Just as important, perhaps, for our story is a somewhat lesser-known Deeds Paradox, which states that you cannot find anything until you either stop looking for it or don't need it anymore.

Fermi came up with his idea at a fancy dinner party. Deeds didn't get invited to fancy parties. He came up with his in his living room one day after spending several fruitless hours searching his home for a pen, only to find one in a desk drawer where he'd already looked more than a dozen times[3]. As a result, Deeds posited that your odds of finding anything were inversely proportional to your need for it.[4]

While it's not as disturbing as the grandfather paradox and doesn't sell as many tee shirts as Fermi's paradox, it is still on the list of things that are pretty useful to know if your job is to watch for approaching alien invasions. People who routinely ask secret government appropriations committees for $2 billion dollars to build giant telescopes try to downplay Deeds and his hair-brained theories. It's hard to persuade a senator you need $2 billion to *not* find something[5].

Honestly, a refrigerator magnet in the break room would've been enough, but no one bothered. No human eyes spotted the incoming flying saucer that warm spring night.

The only pair of eyes that did spot the saucer-shaped spacecraft were not human. They belonged to a robot standing atop a trash heap on the outskirts of a small American city called Sedville.

The robot hadn't been looking for aliens that night -- it was trying to find a hat that had been knocked off its head and carried over a fence into the junkyard by the wind. The metal man wasn't all that surprised to see them, though.

It had been that kind of day.

---

[3] For some reason, keys, pens and socks defy the usual solutions used to find your car in a parking lot. (That is to say a simplified Bayesian analysis of known quantities followed by a grid search that usually ends with running in circles whilst whimpering pathetically.) Automobiles are softies, but socks, pens and keys are immune to our pathetic cries.

[4] In an often overlooked addendum, Deeds states that the amount of time it will take to overcome this problem is exactly the amount of time anyone will be willing to wait on hold for you to do so, plus one minute. If his initial paradox caught on in the tee shirt market, Deeds planned to spin this off and name it after one of his cats, but it never did.

[5] Unless, of course, you're asking him for money in return for not finding out why he bought all those flowers and chocolates last February when his wife says he forgot Valentine's Day...

Technically, the robot didn't have eyes. In their place it sported a handful of photo-receptors embedded in wads of modeling clay shoved into holes punched in the upended wastebasket that served as its head. The robot was an odd-looking creation, not the finest example of engineering or design, festooned with exciting wing-bits and blinking lights. The lights didn't do anything except blink. Its maker liked blinking lights and when they weren't mostly burned out, it glittered like a Christmas tree.

It was tall and roughly man-shaped with a torso made from an old vacuum cleaner. Its original function had, in fact, been to clean, but its current occupation was *pirate*[6].

The image of the flying saucer was reported promptly to a brain that had been cobbled together using a computer program designed to run a large model train set. The robot wasn't scared of the aliens or even all that curious about them. The most the robot was able to muster was a sort of temporary giddy excitement that model train sets specialize in.[7]

The robot watched the flying saucer coming toward it with a detached certainty that humankind was doomed. Which was unfortunate. Not because it liked the humans, but because it would get bored if they weren't around.

It glanced down and noticed that the missing hat had turned up next to its foot. It reached down to pick it up just as the departing saucer roared overhead, the wind of its passing sending the hat skipping and skittering away to dance across the fields of debris.

---

[6] The robot, I should note, was a little vague on the specifics of being a pirate. It lived in Missouri, a state that sits smack in the center of North America, about as far as it's possible to get from an ocean. Near as it could reckon, without an ocean, being a pirate had mostly to do with wearing hats and having a peg leg. It tried wearing an eye patch for a while, but it kept tripping over things.

[7] Model railroads in general are only capable of mustering four emotions, Sunday afternoon melancholy, weepy nostalgia, childish excitement, and annoyance when the thing doesn't work like it's supposed to for no reason at all. This robot specialized in the last one.

The robot was so busy chasing the runaway hat that it didn't see the saucer land briefly and leave behind a passenger. By the time the pirate hat was back in place atop the waste basket, the saucer had taken off again and rocketed back into space with a green flash of light.

The government men tracking the robot didn't see the saucer. By all rights, they should have since they weren't looking for it, but no one had told them about Deeds or his paradox. They found the spectacle of the robot chasing its runaway hat too funny to concentrate on much else. The sight of the metal man stumbling, hopping and hobbling around the piles of junk on a peg leg had sent them into hysterics.

The green flash caught their attention too late to spot the alien spacecraft and distracted them just long enough for the robot to catch its hat and slip away into the night.

Frustrated and annoyed, they spent an hour coming up with elaborate lies to tell their bosses about why they lost the robot they had been sent to capture. They eventually decided to claim the robot had vanished into thin air, evidence of some super-science they couldn't be expected to anticipate and therefore should not be blamed for

As is often the case, the lie was not nearly as incredible as the truth. Which is just as well, because though everyone knows that truth is stranger than fiction, no one is actually willing to admit when it happens.

***

The alien waved at the departing saucer to display thanks and reassure the rear-facing laser turret that it wasn't going to shoot them down.

One of the few truly universal gestures is showing friendliness and thanks by displaying that one's hands, claws, pincers, or tentacles are empty because shooting someone with small and easily concealable weapons is also a universal gesture. This has led the inhabitants of even the most marginally civilized worlds to develop the habit of waving hello and goodbye.[8]

It kept waving until the saucer disappeared behind the planet's only moon and turned to its task.

Readings were checked on strange instruments that would have been of profound interest to the government men still squabbling in the nearby van. Once the alien was certain it could breathe the moist atmosphere, the clear dome of the helmet retracted.

Alien lungs inhaled and exhaled, savoring the air. To the annoyance of biologists and science fiction fans everywhere, the alien was in no way inconvenienced by the millions of viruses and bacteria in the air. Life forms of all sizes instinctively avoid hostile environments and even the common cold was smart enough to steer clear of alien nostrils.

The planet's natives viewed their galaxy edge-on as a thick band of stars stretching across the darkness. It was pretty, in its way. And it told the alien all it needed to know about where it was and when.

Humans are noisy creatures and even so late at night the air was alive with information and voices broadcasting inane chatter from a mouth in one place to an ear in another and back. As it listened, the alien body began to shift and elongate into what its research said would be a new and locally pleasant form.

It took the visitor a moment to get used to going about on only two feet and manipulating instruments with the long extremities that extended from the end of each of its two upper appendages (the information stream informed him that these were called *fingers*) and wiggled the similar but shorter lower extremities in the cold grass (which the locals apparently called *piggies*).

Its soft bare feet carried it as far as the edge of a paved causeway leading toward the distant lights of the city. Transports of varying sizes whizzed and roared along the paved

---

[8] Though, it's worth noting that 'doing the wave' is a uniquely human behavior, as is having two entirely different sports, both named 'football'.

thoroughfare, painting the new body with their lights. Alien lips pursed to whistle a happy alien tune as it hooked an alien thumb toward the distant city in the other truly universal gesture.

Humans roared past the odd little pink visitor with its thumb stuck out without a backward glance. The oral history of their people had taught them to believe that no matter how small and innocent-looking, the figure alongside the road was a vicious serial killer with a hook for a hand. They averted their eyes and accelerated away without a backward glance.

If someone had stopped to pick up the strange little hitchhiker, it's possible that a good deal of what follows might have turned out differently or not happened at all. But no one did and the alien visitor reached the city at morning's light, footsore and in a foul mood.

***

Doctor Deeds rolled over in his sleep, ignorant of the fact that the theory for which he was most often mocked was currently being proven correct .

We'll get back to him later.

2. The Mummy's Curse

When you ask adults what they think of children, the responses tend to revolve around the theme that their generation was more imaginative, more productive, more inventive, and more obedient than the new one[9]. When adults who know Howard Carter are asked the same question, they fall silent. If pressed, they'll admit that he's too imaginative and they wish he could be a bit less productive, *far* less inventive, and a lot more obedient.

Howard is a bit too inventive for just about everyone's comfort.

On the first day at a new school, Howard's mother always writes a letter to the principal explaining why her son is changing schools (*again*[10]) and so soon after the last one was damaged in that freak accident. And how, Howard certainly could not possibly have had anything to do with that fusion reactor that was found in the basement. The one that was powered by candy in a manner that the authorities are still trying to understand.

Any indication that he might be to blame for these things is a

---

[9] Handily ignoring that their parents thought the same of them as did their parents and theirs all the way back to the first caveman telling his son off for tracking mud into the cave and drawing on the walls. Humans, as a rule, are bad at the 'historical perspective' game.

[10] Careful examination of the letter will reveal to the alert school official that it is a form letter of the sort with blanks ready-made to be filled in as events warrant. School officials who are not alert do not fare well with a student like Howard in their school.

vicious lie.

And on what I assure you is an unrelated note, could you please see to it that my son does not get any sweets?

Howard had to change schools a lot and in fact his family recently left Ohio entirely after what the city of Dayton still refers to in awed whispers as "The Lawnmower Incident".

It's not entirely Howard's fault. He goes home crying from a bad day at school and locks himself in his room and before he knows it, there's a robot that used to be a Volkswagen standing in the middle of the playground asking the kids why they keep choosing Howard last for baseball[11].

And off his family goes to the next town.

The latest town was the smallest yet; Sedville, Missouri sat in the middle of miles and miles of rolling farmland at the intersection of two major highways. "Perfect for a quick getaway" his dad quipped as they drove into town.

He was only sort of joking.

The major industries seemed to be growing corn and making metal toolboxes.

It was the perfect place for the Carter family to lie low as their names and descriptions faded into the dim memories of the authorities back in Ohio. Howard's parents lost no time getting comfortable in their new town. His mother got a job designing machines to make better tool boxes and his dad set up an art studio in the attic. Howard wished he had choices like that, but he didn't -- he had to go to school.

James K. Polk Middle School looked exactly like his old school. The kids looked just like the old kids and the principal exactly like the last one. Howard wondered if there was a mold somewhere in a factory where kids and school officials were turned out on an industrial scale.

His science teacher gave him some glimmer of hope. Dr.

---

[11] Howard stopped doing that after he realized that even though the kids chose him first under the watchful gaze of his giant robot, it was inevitable that the robot would be chosen next by the other team. If there's anything more humiliating than being chosen last, it has to be getting beat by the other team after they recruit your robot to bat cleanup.

Deeds looked like Albert Einstein's long-lost son, his hair prematurely white and left to do whatever it wanted, his cheeks fuzzy and his clothing wrinkled under a crisp white lab coat.

Howard felt an affinity for the man if only because his hair was also prone to sticking out in every direction in spite of the layers of goop he used to tame it. His affection for the man ended when he asked everyone in the class to stand up and introduce themselves.

Kid after kid stood up and told a little about themselves. At some point, a kid named James who said he was named after President Zachary Taylor (it's a long story) and everyone who followed tried to one-up the person that came before them.

By the time it was Howard's turn, he was doomed.

"My name is Howard Carter and I was named after the guy that found King Tut." He could have stopped there. A famous archaeologist was perfectly respectable. Cool even. But the kid before him had been named after a fighter pilot and the girl before that was named for someone who marched with Martin Luther King Jr. So he added: *"Howard Carter was killed by the mummy's curse."*

Well, *he* thought it was cool.

With his classmates' taunting laughter still ringing in his head, Howard sat back down and stared at his desk, waiting for it to end. When the class's attention finally turned to the next student in line, Howard pulled his history book and a pencil out of his backpack and turned to the timeline of world history at the back of the book. Above the most recent entry, he wrote *"May 25, Howard Carter ruins his life"* and drew an arrow to roughly the point on the line where he was stuck.

New town, new school, new life and he'd already ruined it.

If his classmates and teachers had known him longer, or if his mother had been a bit less vague in her letter, someone might have had the good sense to worry.

***

As he dug through the boxes, Howard palmed the tears out

of his eyes and told himself it was the dust. Except that the garage wasn't dusty. Their new house really was new -- it had only been built the year before. There hadn't been time for it to build up a good layer of dust.

He pushed aside the last box and there it was, the object of his greatest desire, the solution to all of his problems.

"Um... hello?"

Howard turned around to discover he had an audience. In the doorway of the garage stood Ericka Platt, the girl whose aunt had marched with Dr. King, and a skinny boy he didn't know with a mop of curly brown hair and skin so pale that Howard was pretty sure that if he had a bright enough light behind him, they would be able to see his insides.

He wondered how long they'd been standing there as they picked their way through the boxes toward him.

"Wow, you guys have a lot of books for one family," Ericka said. "Are your parents librarians?"

"No, we just like books."

"I do too!" The boy pointed back at the backpack slung over his handlebars. Howard spotted King Tut on the cover of the one sticking out of the top. The boy rounded the last pile and spotted the time machine. "Wow! Is that how you're going to do it?"

"Do what?"

"You were muttering when we rode up," the boy said. "You said you were going to go back in time."

"I was just playing," Howard lied. "You know... pretend."

"I don't think so." Ericka was watching him with an odd look in her eye. "I think you really want to."

"Wouldn't you?"

"I guess so." She shrugged. "Those kids were pretty mean to you."

"Was it true?" the boy blurted.

"Was what true?"

"About the mummy's curse."

"Did you follow me all the way home just to make fun of

me?"

Howard glared at the new boy.

"N-no! I just wanted to know more about the mummy!" Howard saw Ericka nudge him. "Oh! And to give this back to you." The boy dug in his pocket and produced what looked like a man-shaped bundle of white tape.

Howard took the bundled action figure and turned it over in his hands. It had been wrapped head to toe in tape; like a mummy. It took Howard a few minutes to realize it was the GI Joe he thought he'd lost. He felt the tears well in his eyes and looked away, blinking furiously.

He was too old to cry over toys.

Ericka and her friend were polite enough not to notice the tears that were not spilling down his cheeks. Howard shoved the mummified toy in his pocket and sized up his new allies. He turned to the boy.

"What's your name?"

"Gary Parker."

"Want to help me travel back in time, Gary?"

"Are you going back to fight the mummy?"

"You watch a lot of movies, don't you, Gary?"

Ericka said "Yes" at the same time Gary said "No" and Howard couldn't help but laugh.[12]

"No," Howard shook his head. "I can't go back that far -- I just need to stop myself from saying anything about the mummy at all."

"Oh!" Gary blushed. "I guess that makes sense."

"No it doesn't," Ericka said. "Doesn't that cause problems with the..." Ericka waved her hand to indicate the entire universe. "I've seen movies where this kind of thing causes the world to fall apart."

---

[12] Gary Parker, in fact, doesn't watch "a lot" of movies. Gary watches "too many" movies. If m is the amount of movies a normal movie fan watches, Gary watches m^3 movies. And he memorizes them. He can turn down the sound and recite entire movies in perfect sync with the actors without facing the TV.

"Those are just movies."

"You can time travel?" Ericka sounded incredulous.

"We're all time travelers, moving down the road to the future every second of every day," Howard said. "The real trick is finding reverse gear."

"Have you done this before?"

Howard's shrug was a bit too casual for her but out of curiosity she helped him stand the time machine up and wheel it out of the garage. With Gary running along behind, they pushed it around the side of the house where it would be hidden from the street.

Gary and Ericka stood back and marveled at the contraption as Howard turned wheels and flipped switches. It was made entirely out of brass, several large concentric rings as tall as they were sat atop a base that looked like it had been made out of an old Radio Flyer wagon. As Howard made adjustments, the rings rotated inside one another, numbers and symbols glittering in the late afternoon sun.

"That thing doesn't look like it'll ever get up to 88 miles per hour." Gary took a step back as the time machine began to vibrate and hum.

"That was just a movie," Howard muttered as he watched the gauges climb to the READY line. "And I'm not allowed to drive the car anyway."

"How is it powered?"

"Cold fusion," Howard said.

"So now what?" Gary asked.

Howard stood up and planted his hands on his hips, trying to gauge how much he could ask of his two helpers. He was about to ask more of them than he might be willing to give to someone he'd just met.

He took a deep breath.

"We need fuel rods," Howard answered. "Frozen Funtime Pops to be precise."

"Funtime Pops?" Gary said. "Your time machine runs on Funtime Pops?"

"I tried penny candy, but it gummed up the works and caused... problems." Howard finished vaguely. "The reactor needs cold sugar and I've found that pops work the best."

"You built a time machine that runs on Popsicles?"

"Funtime Pops."

"And you need us to..." Ericka looked like she already didn't like the sound of what came next.

"Bring me as many of them as you can find," Howard said. "We just moved in and my parents haven't caught up on the shopping yet."

For a few minutes, he thought they might mutiny rather than surrender their frozen treats to the whims of the space-time continuum. Finally, they glanced at one another and shrugged.

"I think we have some, but you're going to owe us," Ericka promised. "Big time."

An hour later, they had rounded up enough frozen sweets to get the machine humming and spinning.

The time machine shuddered and whirred and shot random beams of Berry Blue and Cheery Cherry light out of the gaps in its fuselage. Howard donned his helmet and settled his goggles over his eyes as he approached the wormhole[13]. Gary handed him the timeline torn out of his history book that he had marked *"May 25, 9:35 a.m. -- Howard Carter screws up his life."*

Howard rolled the page into a tight tube and used it to salute them both as he stepped across the event horizon and went hurtling through the stuff of time and space.

***

If you were bored enough and had some free time on your hands, you could dig through the receipts in the Federal Receipt Vault located in an unassuming bunker below Cheyenne, Wyoming and add up all the concrete that the United States

---

[13] The safety equipment wasn't necessary, but his mom worried and made him promise to wear it.

government has purchased since 1900. It would take you a while, but you could do it if you put your mind to it.

Then (assuming you were still bored and/or crazy enough) you could wander down the road to the Federal Repository of Triplicate Forms and add up all of the forms required when the government paved a runway, built a building, laid the foundations for a monument, built a receipt vault or did any of the other things concrete was good for.

At the end of your fun, you would be astonished by how much concrete one nation can use and might even wonder if the military poured it on their breakfast cereal. You would also discover that the government buys more concrete than it admits to using.

A *lot* more.

Some of the missing concrete built things like missile silos and bomb shelters. Some of it's missing because there are people who like to get paid for things that they never delivered. If you dug deep enough, you could figure out which government contractors had fudged their numbers or when the missing concrete went into something obvious, but only someone who was determined enough to decode a filing system devised at great expense to keep people from finding things, would discover that most of the missing concrete really was missing.

And almost all of it had been signed for by someone named "Ward".

Roughly a thousand miles from where Howard and his friends stood watching as the time machine shuddered and juddered its way through the calculations necessary to create a rift in space-time, a machine began to beep. The beeping machine was located in a vast underground chamber made from purloined concrete and filled with machines whose main functions were to beep urgently and often.

This was WARD... or more accurately: WARD[14], which originally stood for *Wartime Advanced Research Directorate*, though most of the people in the room no longer knew that. A lot of them made a game of guessing what the name stood for, if anything (currently in favor among the younger Suits was "Wickedly Awesome Research Department" which was at least sort of close.) When the secret agency was created by President James K Polk in 1841, it was intended to fund the sort of oddball research projects that the eleventh president thought would help in the looming war with Mexico and the dispute with Britain over the Oregon Territories.

WARD had outlived its original intention and was wiling away the decades in a forgotten corner of the US Federal Budget, eating concrete and computers and giving precious little in return.[15]

"There it is again." A technician pointed at the blinking light on the beeping machine. "It's coming from somewhere in Missouri."

Behind him, an old man in a dark suit made a thoughtful noise and inserted a toothpick between his teeth. He wasn't allowed to smoke in the underground bunker, a fact he blamed on the whims of the technicians.

Something about smoke being bad for the machines.

Half of the people in the room were technicians, wearing tee shirts and blue jeans and making a point of knowing how to make the machines work. The other half of the room's inhabitants wore suits and knew how to make the technicians work.

"Bring it up on the big screen," a younger suit ordered.

---

[14] It used to be W.A.R.D. but the periods were lost in a tragic accident involving a devious sentient spellcheck program that attacked government agencies and stole away all their periods, leaving us with the CIA, FBI, and WARD.

[15] WARD actually enjoyed a brief resurgence during World War II when the idea of advanced weaponry was suddenly important again. But after what came to be known in whispers as the "Rosie the Riveted Incident" they were ushered back into the shadows and advised to remain there.

The suits stood back as technicians flipped switches and typed incomprehensible techie code until one of the walls lit up with a map of the lower 48 states[16]. Every suit in the room turned to face the map as the map zoomed-in on a blip at the center of the central state.

"Is that where we caught that robot last year?"

"No, that was Ohio, I think."

"You mean the one you lost last night?"

"That was not my fault."

"I hear one of our teams have caught up with it again."

"In Missouri?"

The suits nattered among themselves as their leader moved his toothpick from one side of his mouth to the other and then back. He didn't like technicians or states that weren't nice and square. He had a genuine soft spot for Wyoming and Colorado. Nice, *square* states. John Wayne states[17] full of men who could wear big hats and cowboy boots without looking like fools.

How he envied men who could pull off a cowboy hat.

The old suit cleared his throat and the young suits fell silent. The technicians squirmed and exchanged wary glances. They didn't like it when the suits were silent; it usually meant they were thinking of new ways to make technicians miserable.

"Time travel?" he growled.

"There was a huge energy spike on the outskirts of Sedville, Missouri at 1630 local time," the technician reported. "It didn't come from any licensed reactors and was too big to be caused

---

[16] The man in the suit also didn't have much use for Alaska and didn't really believe Hawaii existed. His mind didn't have room for places with pristine beaches, tanned surfers and lots of sunshine and more importantly his government salary didn't allow him to go see for himself. (He was a little skeptical of California and Florida too, but since his mother in law lived in Key West, his wife insisted that he accept Florida's existence. The jury was still out on most of California.)

[17] For the record, John Wayne was born in *Iowa*, which isn't really square. It's a bit bulbous along the sides, as if Minnesota is too heavy and has started to squash it.

by fluctuations in the local electrical grid. It was followed by a gravitational disturbance caused by the creation of an artificial wormhole..."

"Cut the techno-babble and give me the bottom line," the old suit interrupted.

"Yes, time travel," the tech finished. "Someone in central Missouri just traveled back to this morning."

"I *hate* time travel."

"Yes sir."

The suits broke into excited babbling, giving the smirking tech an unobserved moment to collect his winnings. (A favorite pastime was betting on how far they could get into a technical explanation before the suits lost patience. A bonus was paid to anyone who could get them to say 'techno-babble'.)

"Do we have any teams in the area?" a younger suit asked.

"Team Epsilon is nearby," another young suit answered. "They're in the area, tracking that missing robot."

"That's quite a coincidence," the old suit mused. "Dispatch a backup team to Missouri. It sounds like we have a rogue scientist out there somewhere and I want this guy secured before he attracts any more attention."

Technicians and Suits alike lunged for phones. The suits called airstrips to arrange flights for their agents and other secret repositories of lost concrete to tell them to be alert for more strange energy signatures. The techs called their bookies to alert them that the next twenty-four hours were going to be profitable.

3. Late for School

The trouble with time is that it doesn't really exist, at least not in any sense that makes sense to most of us.

From where we stand on the surface of planet earth, time seems to move forward, always forward and always at the same rate. But in reality, that last part is only true because we're sitting in the same gravity well on the same planet. This gives us the illusion of time being constant. It is not. For instance, satellites orbiting the planet have to constantly make tiny adjustments for their speed and their distance from Earth in order to stay in sync with the planet below, or they wouldn't be able to give us accurate GPS data and inaccurate weather reports. Mass and gravity also change how time moves in alarming ways -- if Earth's mass suddenly increased, the stronger gravity would make time move slower. If you are traveling at the speed of light, *your* mass increases until time moves even slower still.

Explanations like that one are the reason that Old Suit hates time travel.

It's just important to remember that time is relative and like most relatives, talking endlessly about it can be tedious and boring. Let it suffice that Howard Carter built a machine that could poke a hole from the present into the past and allow Howard to step through.

Howard's like that; don't worry, you'll get used to it.

On television and in movies, time travel is all about the special effects: flaming tire tracks, whirling tornadoes, arcs of lighting, explosions. To the disappointment of time travel researchers everywhere, it turns out that it's more like turning a corner to find you wandered into yesterday. The time machine hums, you experience some mild discomfort as your mass and personal gravitation sort themselves out and you're then.

If you want lightning and firestorms, you have to add them.

Howard appeared on the edge of the playground and rolled as he hit the grass, rising to his feet dramatically backlit by the whirling vortex of lightning and fire. It was too bad there wasn't anyone around to see it because it looked incredibly cool.

As the wormhole evaporated, he surveyed the empty expanse of the baseball diamond behind his new school and sighed. It would've been awesome if he'd arrived in the middle of baseball practice. He pictured himself stepping out the whirling light of eternity to smack a baseball into tomorrow.

Literally.

Except that he wasn't very good at hitting a baseball and it would be embarrassing to step through a time portal and strike out.

"Oh well." Howard pushed the goggles up and tucked the helmet under his arm as he ran toward the school building. His calculations had been off by a decimal point and he'd arrived later than planned and about three feet to the left.

His mom was right: even with a time machine, he would be late for school.

The original plan had been to drag himself aside before class and explain things, but he had misjudged his entry point. Either the time machine had been knocked around by the movers or Ericka's load of sugar-free treats had been a mistake.

He took the stairs two at a time and ran flat-out through the empty halls, his sneakers squeaking on the polished tiles as his mind raced for a new plan. What was he going to do, burst through the door and tackle himself before he could speak?

That would certainly be a different kind of memorable.

Mr. Deeds had already called the class to order and Ericka was in front of the class talking about her aunt meeting Dr. King. Next would be Kenny the fighter pilot's nephew and then he would step up in front of his classmates and ruin his life. Then the humiliation would start all over again.

He scanned the hallway for ideas, his eyes finally falling on the fire alarm. White letters spelled out his only option: *In case of emergency...*

Before Howard could decide whether or not this counted as an emergency, he caught movement in the corner of his eye. Turning his attention back to the classroom, he spotted Billy Wexler, the popular kid who sat behind him, leaning down to pick up his pencil off the floor. On his way back up, a hand dipped into Howard's bag. As the larger kid sat back, some of his cronies snickered and leaned in to see what he had taken.

The GI Joe.

Billy had taken the GI Joe before Howard had spoken a word. Nothing he said would've made a difference, Billy's crew was planning to pick on him regardless. The mummy tape was an afterthought.

He watched the other Howard get up and walk to the front of the room, passing Ericka in the aisle and knocking a notebook off Gary's desk. He watched himself bend down and return it to the smaller boy's desk with an apologetic smile. He didn't remember doing it, but the grateful look on Gary's face stayed the hand reaching for the doorknob.

"My name is Howard Carter and I was named after the guy..."

He stepped back from the door and kept backing up until he was in the library across the hall. Howard couldn't take watching the kids laugh at him again.

His hip knocked something off of the librarian's desk and Howard looked down as something hit his leg. It was a book on King Tut with a pink hold slip sticking out of the top bearing Gary's name. Gary had the book on hold long before Howard said anything about his namesake finding the tomb.

He had friends in that room and just didn't know it yet.

In his mind's eye, he pictured his two new friends bringing him every Funtime Pop they had access to. A kid they just met, a complete lunatic who told them a crazy story about time travel. He unrolled the time line and stared at the arrow scrawled on it to indicate what was happening across the hall where he could already hear the echoes of mocking laughter.

Howard reached into his pocket and took out the mummified GI Joe and closed the pages of Gary's library book around it so he'd have it to bring to Howard later. He didn't want to think of what the gangly little kid would have to do to get it from Billy any other way[18].

As he walked out into the hall, he almost got hit by the classroom door as his other self flung it open and ran out into the hall. Howard pulled back just in time to keep himself from getting run over. Not because anything spectacular would happen, but because it would hurt to get run into by a crying kid running pell-mell down the hall.

He'd blocked-out that part from his memory too.

Howard stood watching his own retreating back and contemplated following himself to the boy's room. He decided not to -- it was probably better to let this one play out. It was time to find some place to hide until the second Howard stepped into the portal.

Then he was going to take his new friends down to the corner store and buy them a soda. Howard stuck his hands in his pocket and walked off in the opposite direction, oblivious to the fact that the teacher was watching him through the open classroom door with an odd look on his face.

***

Howard's science teacher threw his briefcase into the back of his car and glanced around at the departing cars of the other teachers. He smiled and returned waves and as soon as the last car was out of sight, the smile faded into a sneer.

Fools.

Deeds pulled a smartphone out of his pocket and called up an application he'd created for just such an event. Holding the

---

[18] The alert reader will note that there are now two of the mummified GI Joe figures in the world. Time travelers create these odd little hitches in reality all the time and things have a funny way of sorting themselves out for themselves. The universe is a strange place and duplicate toys are the least of our worries, believe me.

phone before him, he wandered around the corner and onto the practice fields beyond. Luckily, none of the teams were practicing that afternoon, so his greatest danger was getting hit by a lawn sprinkler.

The science teacher let the beeping phone lead him, pointedly keeping his mind blank. Not looking for anything was a difficult skill to master, but Deeds knew better than anyone what sort of disasters came of seeking too hard for what he most desired. The trick was to not desire anything, simply keep the mind open and accepting of whatever happened to come his way...

The phone began to beep.

Deeds almost lost the signal as he focused on the blip and momentarily thought of the boy. He forced himself to ignore the phone and it started beeping again. *Deeds Paradox,* he thought sourly, *if you're looking for it, you'll never find it.*

The boy nagged at him. Howard Carter was not a twin, he'd checked, but there had been another Howard in the hall with goggles on his forehead and a helmet under his arm. Deeds forced the boy out of his thoughts.

The beeping grew louder as Deeds crossed the grassy expanse and came up against the chain link fence surrounding the baseball diamond. The science teacher jumped the fence and continued down the third base line, the signal growing stronger as he reached the outfield. He slowly circled the burn he could already see ahead.

As he'd suspected, the signal was strongest above the burn. A perfect circle of grass five feet wide was charred and ripped-up. Small charred craters surrounded the circle as if a tiny lightning storm had ripped across the outfield.

Only a rank amateur would make a mess this big.

He glanced down at the smartphone in his hand. The needle on the screen was buried in the far right end of the monitor. The strongest signal he'd ever seen.

An amateur... or a kid?

The small hairs on the back of his neck began to tingle and he turned and ran back toward his car. As he ran, he hit the button to close the application and hit number one on his speed dial.

"This is Doctor Deeds," he said as he opened his trunk and began to unpack his equipment. "I need an appointment with the Professor."

4. A Robot, A Robot, Oh Yes, a Robot He...

"HOWIE! HOWIE! WAKE UP, HOWIE!"

The shaking brought Howard up out of his favorite recurring dream about swimming in ice cream to find himself inches from two glowing holes cut in the side of an upended wastebasket. The tarnished copper wastebasket didn't startle him nearly as much as the plastic pirate hat perched on top.

That was new.

"HOWIE? ARE YOU AWAKE?"

"Robot?"

"YES! YOU'RE AWAKE!" The metal man clapped its interactors[19] together in glee and hobbled back away from the bed. "YOU NEED TO COME WITH ME."

"What are you doing here?"

"COME WITH ME IF YOU WANT TO LIVE."

"What?"

"I'VE COME TO SAVE YOU."

"Save me from what?" Howard pushed the robot away with one hand and sat up to get a better look at the strange figure in his bedroom. "Why are you wearing a tiny pirate hat?"

"DO YOU LIKE IT?" One interactor went up to tilt the hat to a

---

[19] Howard called them 'Interactors' instead of 'hands' because it sounded cooler and allowed him to theoretically make them interchangeable with lobster claws, chainsaws, flame throwers, whirling Blades of Doom, etcetera. In this case, though, they looked just like three-fingered hands. Howard never had much use for his pinky finger and figured if Mickey Mouse can live without it, his robots could too.

more rakish angle. The robot planted the wooden table leg it had used to replace the perfectly good leg Howard had built for it atop the bedside table. A snippet of the soundtrack to *Star Wars* echoed from the speaker on its chest and Howard could tell the robot wanted him to envision the wind whipping through its hair.

It didn't have any hair, but a breeze from the open window did make the ratty feather stuck in the pirate hat bounce around a bit.[20]

"Get your stump off my table."

"I AM THE DREAD PIRATE ROBOT!"

"I didn't solder the connectors in your brain very well did I?"

"NO, YOU DID NOT DO A GOOD JOB THERE AT ALL." The robot limped across the room and sank into the desk chair with a clank. "AND THE AQUARIUM PUMP YOU USED FOR MY HEART KEEPS BLOWING BUBBLES."

"I probably need to bleed the lines."

"WELL IT FROZE UP MY LEFT ARM THE OTHER DAY WHILE I WAS JUMPING FOR A CHANDELIER. COMPLETELY RUINED MY EXIT FROM THE BANK."

"Bank?" Howard frowned at his creation. "What have you been up to since you ran off?"

"I AM A PIRATE." The robot shrugged and avoided its creator's eyes. "BUT IF A COUPLE OF GUYS IN BLACK SUITS ASK ABOUT ME, I'VE BEEN WITH YOU ALL WEEK."

"I'll try to keep that in mind."

"ALIENS!"

"The guys in black suits are aliens?"

"NO, I HAVE TO TAKE YOU TO SEE ALIENS!"

"I've seen it."

The robot stopped and Howard could hear its processors laboring as it chewed on that bit of data. The long processing

---

[20] Howard couldn't see the point of hair either. *His* hair just gave his mom something to complain about and in his experience, the stuff never did what you wanted it to do anyway. Much like his robots.

time gave him a chance to straighten his pajamas and find his glasses.

Now that he could see it clearly, it was apparent that his old robot had been living rough in the two years since its escape. Howard had fashioned it from spare parts and his mother's old vacuum cleaner with the thought that it would help him clean his room. He certainly did not design it to withstand a life of high seas adventure in a landlocked state. Missouri was about as far as you could get from a sea without leaving the planet. The metal man had gotten it in its head that Howard had illegally downloaded its operating system off the internet, and that made him and it a pirate.

"THAT IS IMPOSSIBLE." Then it added "THAT DOES NOT COMPUTE" because it seemed like the sort of thing a robot should say.

"I snuck downstairs one night after mom and dad went to bed and watched it on TV."

"BUT THAT IS NOT..." the processors whirred as the machine lost its logical grip again. Howard found his slippers and his bathrobe and tried to remember where he'd left his socket wrench. He and Gary had been working on their bikes earlier, so they were probably down in the garage. "...POSSIBLE."

"I think you're overdue for a tune-up, old friend."

"YOU WANT YOUR SNAZZY HELMET BACK, DON'T YOU?" The robot's interactors flew to its head. "YOU CAN'T HAVE IT! I NEED IT TO KEEP MY BRAINS IN!"

"It's actually the wastebasket from my dad's office and don't think I didn't catch hell about it when you bailed on me."

"YOU CANNOT HAVE IT BACK," the robot insisted.

"I don't want it back," Howard said. "But how would you like me to tighten those connections in your neural network? Maybe polish the old brain bucket while we're at it?"

"NO."

Howard stifled a yawn as he sized up the metal man. He knew how strong it was. If he tried to tackle it and turn it off, even with a faulty pump it wouldn't go well. He couldn't afford to wake up his parents. Since the lawn mower incident, he didn't need his dad thinking he was tinkering with robots again.

"Why don't you tell me about the men in suits."

"WHERE?" The robot leapt to its feet and scanned the room. "THEY KEEP COMING FOR ME, BUT THEY NEED TO... GO..."

Howard edged forward as the overtaxed processors whirred and somewhere in the robot's chest, a fan kicked on to dissipate the heat. If he could just reach the switch... the eyes flickered back to life and swiveled to gaze at him with a knowing glow.

"YOU CANNOT HAVE THE HELMET BACK"

"Wastebasket."

"WHATEVER."

Howard raised his hands and backed up until he was sitting on the bed again.

"Tell me about whatever it is you came here to tell me about."

"ALIENS."

"Fine. Tell me about aliens."

"THEY ARE COMING."

Howard waited, but apparently that was it. The robot tapped its peg and servos whirred as it tried to frown at him. The mouth wasn't built for it and it only managed a sort of half-hearted glower.

"Well, tell them to call first, mom hates surprise guests."

The robot made a frustrated noise.

"YOU ARE SUPPOSED TO BE AFRAID."

"Maybe later." Howard rubbed his eyes. As if he didn't already get too little sleep. "How do you know that the aliens are coming?"

"YOU WOKE THEM UP."

"You woke me up."

"WITH YOUR... WITH YOUR..." the robot gestured helplessly at the tools scattered across Howard's workbench.

"Experiments?"

"YES, EXPERIMENTS. YOUR EXPERIMENTS WOKE THEM UP."

"And how is that, exactly?"

"I DO NOT KNOW." The robot began to pace and Howard waited for his parents to wake up as his metal friend clomped back and forth across the floorboards over their heads. "THEY HUNT ME."

"The aliens?"

"THE MEN IN THE SUITS."

"Who are not aliens?"

"NO... AT LEAST I DO NOT THINK SO." The robot paused and looked troubled by that thought. "NO. NO, I DO NOT THINK THEY ARE."

"Well, I guess that's something at least."

"ARE YOU MOCKING ME?"

"Only a little," Howard shrugged. "In all fairness, you woke me up at three o'clock in the morning so you're lucky it's just mockery you're getting."

"YOU DO NOT BELIEVE ME."

"You haven't made a very good case."

The robot stared at him for a moment, whirring quietly. Finally, it reached up and undid the latches on its chest plate, pulling the doors aside to flood the room with greenish light. One interactor tapped the jam jar in its nest of wires next to the laboring aquarium pump that acted as its heart.

"THIS IS NOT SUPPOSED TO HAPPEN," it said. "THE MEN IN SUITS HUNT ME BECAUSE YOU WERE NOT SUPPOSED TO USE KOOL-AID FUSION TO BUILD A ROBOT TO CLEAN YOUR ROOM."

"Funtime Pops."

"WHATEVER."

"So someone's mad that I built a robot?"

"THEY ARE MAD BECAUSE IT IS IMPOSSIBLE TO CREATE FUSION WITH FROZEN FUNTIME POPS." The robot snapped his chest plate shut. "THEY WANT TO STOP YOU. THE DREAD PIRATE ROBOT MUST TURN YOU IN OR THE ALIENS WILL DESTROY THE EARTH."

***

Across town, the grasses of the playgrounds and ball fields

36

behind James K Polk Middle School danced and flattened in the downdraft from a helicopter that didn't make the satisfactory "Thwup Thwup Thwup" noise that other helicopters made. Their tennis shoes and leather wingtips worn by the team members made more noise than their aircraft.

WARD didn't like to make more noise than they had to.

Each tech was accompanied by a suit. Even with Deeds' paradox working against them, a five-foot lightning scar is difficult to miss. The needles danced as the teams gathered around the burn to stare down at the crunchy black grass.

The suits conferred while the techs gathered samples of everything in sight. Within minutes the helicopters lifted off again and only footprints remained to mark their presence.

A lot of what they found concerned them.

What they missed would have concerned them more if they had realized that they were being watched.

***

The man that students and staff knew as the science teacher "Victor Deeds" sat back from his computer monitor and chewed on his lower lip. The teams of men in their silent black helicopters would complicate his life, but he had been expecting them and knew how to evade them.

He stretched and rolled his neck. His vigil had been a long one and he would need to be up early to collect the tiny surveillance cameras he had hidden around the baseball diamond.

The finger froze a centimeter shy of the power button as a bare foot came into view.

That's odd.

The companion foot (also bare) followed its mate across the screen and Deeds switched to a camera with a wider view of the baseball diamond. He blinked at the screen as a small creature dressed in what looked like trash bags tottered across the field to stand in the center of the time machine's burn scar. It looked sort of like a pig walking on its hind legs.

The head tipped back, he presumed to follow the retreating helicopters across the night sky, and then rolled to stare directly at the camera. At which point its head was both backwards and upside down.

The figure winked and then was suddenly gone.

It took Deeds a full minute to stop shaking long enough to dial the phone.

Voicemail again.

"This is Deeds again. This is getting serious -- we need to meet."

5. Perfectly Normal Lives

The morning after his late night visitor, Howard sat yawning over his Cheerios and trying to concentrate on the novel propped against the cereal box. His brain was having trouble focusing on the antics of the kids in the story, imagining them scattering as men in dark suits descended on them.

In some households, reading at the table is strictly forbidden, or at least discouraged. The Carter table was arranged so as to catch the best light for everyone seated around it. In fact, the house itself had largely been chosen for the massive bay window in the kitchen that caught the morning light and made breakfast reading pleasant and warm most of the year. It was the only kitchen in the neighborhood with reading lamps.

For Howard's parents, words were just as important as food. As long as you were willing to look up and discuss what you were reading, it was not only acceptable, it was encouraged. The family's furniture had been chosen with reading comfort in mind rather than anything an interior decorator would recognize as *style* unless "library" was a style.

The house was comfortable, clean, cluttered and well lit.

"Are you feeling okay, Howard?" his mom asked. Howard smiled as she set aside her novel to lay a hand across his brow.

"Just tired."

His dad tapped the book that Howard had been failing to read and leaned close.

"Stayed up all night reading *The Mad Scientist Club*, didn't you?" His dad laughed. "Told you you'd like it -- I did the same thing when I was your age."

Howard smiled and eyed his dad's cup of coffee and wondered if he was too young to develop a coffee habit.

Probably. All the things adults liked most were things he was too young for.

His wandering gaze came to rest on the sign his mom tacked to the wall over the stove. It said: *"Many people have eaten here & gone on to live perfectly normal lives."*[21]

Howard thought of his new friends Ericka and Gary and wondered if they lived perfectly normal lives. Whatever perfectly normal might be, he was pretty sure that it didn't include being hunted by aliens. If nothing else, perfectly normal people probably got more sleep.

He couldn't decide how seriously to take the vague threat, but the robot had walked halfway across the country to give him the warning, which made it hard to ignore.

"If you're done, stop picking at it and go get ready for school." His mother had a knack for spotting day dreams just as they got started and heading them off before they could gain any real momentum[22]. For once Howard was thankful for that and he leapt to do as she ordered.

Howard disposed of his uneaten cereal and put his bowl in the dishwasher before hurrying upstairs. He checked the front door to make sure it was locked as he ran past and as he scrambled to get dressed and find his school books, he paused occasionally to glance out the window.

He was going to be spending the day watching for large men in dark suits or alien spacecraft hovering over the school.

It was going to be a long day.

***

---

[21] Howard was sent to his room when he wondered aloud who they were and how they'd managed it.

[22] Howard suspected that hidden somewhere among the thousands of books in the house was a manual of instruction that had taught his mother these little tricks. He was rarely left alone in the house, but on the rare occasion that he was, he always devoted at least part of the time to searching for this mysterious book. He harbored vague plans of publishing the thing on the internet and making millions charging other kids for access.

Deeds' plane landed in Massachusetts in the wee hours of the morning and the drive took until dawn. He reached the campus of Arkham Tech and dozed in the rental car until the offices opened.

"Victor Deeds to see the Professor." Deeds presented his credentials to the young woman behind the desk.

"I don't have an appointment for anyone of that name."

"I made the appointment last night."

"Not with that name..." She trailed off meaningfully and waited while he fumed. Finally he reached inside his jacket and pulled out a second set of credentials.

"Doctor Villainous Deeds, PhD." As he pronounced his real name, the lights dimmed and concealed speakers thundered a descending minor chord played on a pipe organ. "What the hell is that?"

"Like it? We just had it installed."

"So our secret headquarters plays ominous music every time one of our names is spoken?" Deeds growled. "And someone thinks this is a good idea?"

"An *evil* idea," she corrected. "She's with a student, have a seat."

Deeds returned his ID to his pocket and chose the least rickety-looking chair. His nerves were still jangling from the organ serenade so he spent his time watching the others waiting with him. He was sitting between two grad students who were making red marks on their own papers in hopes it would curtail the scorn of their notoriously-finicky advisor. A forgotten backpack lay under the chair closest to the desk, and in the chair across the way, a woman was engrossed in a pamphlet titled *"So You Think Your Child Is an Evil Genius."*

Deeds smiled to himself. His father had written that. He was especially proud of the bit about reprogramming his Teddy

Ruxpin to read only HP Lovecraft[23].

Deeds wondered if Howard Carter's parents could suggest some timely updates.

The door opened and a teenager came running out. The young man's face was pale and his eyes were red and puffy. To his credit, he managed not to break down into sobs until he reached the elevator.

She was in fine form today.

"Mr. Anderson," the secretary called. "Your turn."

Deeds could spot which one of the grad students was Anderson by the sudden loss of color in his face. Deeds didn't blame him. He glanced at his watch as the student gathered his things and walked slowly through the door into the office. He had some time to kill before his appointment, so he grabbed the abandoned backpack and headed for the stairs.

***

"You forgot this." Deeds dropped the backpack on the step next to the sobbing student. The young man looked up at the wild-haired figure above him and gave a shuddering nod of thanks. "You don't look like a chemistry student."

"Why not?"

"You still have your eyebrows," Deeds said. "Let me guess, Egregious Engineering?"

"English."

Deeds blinked at him.

"How did you end up with the Dean of Mad Science as your advisor?"

"I was thinking of making a change."

Deeds grunted and stared out across the manicured lawns of the college. On a distant hill, he could just make out the venerable old pile of stone that marked Arkham,

---

[23] He hadn't actually planned for the bear's eyes to glow red. That had happened on its own.

Massachusetts's *other* university, Arkham Tech's crosstown rival, Miskatonic U. Some of the happiest times of his life had been spent kicking a soccer ball at the head of a goalie wearing the Miskatonic jersey.

"Is your name really Villainous Deeds?"

Deeds blinked out of his memories to stare down at the student. Deeds ignored the question.

"What's your name, kid?"

"Kevin."

"I'm going to call you Igor."

"But my name's Kev..."

"Get used to being called Igor," Deeds interrupted. "My lab assistants don't last long enough for me to bother learning names."

"Lab assistant?" Kevin/Igor blinked up at the scientist standing over him. "I don't understand."

"Which is why you probably won't last very long, but you'll last longer as my assistant than you will around here." Deeds glanced at his watch and turned to go back into the building. "Be ready to leave in an hour."

"Is your name really Villainous Deeds?" his new assistant called after him. Deeds turned with his hand on the door.

"Names aren't important. Be ready to go in an hour, *Igor*."

***

In the breast pocket of the old suit that ran WARD was a document that was treated with greater care and secrecy than any other stored in the vaults, sub vaults, sub-sub vaults or mattresses and box springs of all the many WARD bunkers scattered around the United States.

At the top, printed in capital letters, were words that would drive a stake of fear into the hearts of any whose name might be listed below it. It said PEOPLE WHO REGULARLY ANNOY ME.

The list was not alphabetical; it was ranked.

At the top of the list were the technicians but he was smart enough to know he could not run the agency without them, so all of his contempt was saved up for those poor saps who were next: the scientists. Scientists were expendable -- there was always another brainiac in a lab coat looking for a government grant.

So when the list of vacant positions in the city government of Sedville, Missouri landed on his desk, he immediately ranked the open positions in order of what he considered tolerable. At the bottom of the list he found something that made him smile for the first time in days, an assignment that he viewed as marginally worse than a firing squad: substitute science teacher.

6. Accept no substitutes

Howard watched his mother speed away and merged into traffic to the tune of a dozen horns blaring. He loved her dearly, but she was a terrible driver.[24]

"Of all the alleys in all the world, why did you have to fall into ours?"

Howard turned to look at Gary.

"What?"

"Don't tell me that you've never seen *Howard the Duck*."

"Gary, I'm not sure anyone younger than my dad has seen that movie."

"Hey, it was better than *Radioland Murders*." Ericka said as she stepped up beside Gary. "He made me watch both back-to-back."

"The George Lucas Movies That Sucked double feature at the dollar movie theater," Gary said. "But I actually like *Radioland Murders*."

"Yeah, well, you also liked *Howard the Duck*," she sniffed.

"George and I are misunderstood outsiders who will only be appreciated in the centuries to come."

"I don't think you can call the guy that made Star Wars a misunderstood outsider," Howard said. "C'mon, I don't want to be late for science class."

"You didn't hear?" Gary said. "Deeds called in sick, there's going to be a substitute."

Howard was watching two men walking back and forth

---

[24] It's sad but true. One of Howard's first inventions was a better safety harness for his car seat when he was three.

across the baseball field with metal detectors. They were trying to make it look like the sort of thing that they did for fun.

They might as well have been carrying signs that said "Please Don't Notice Us".

"Substitute?"

"Yeah, the janitors say he was dropped off this morning by a black suburban." Gary's parents were both teachers at the high school, so they dropped their son off so early he sometimes got to watch the sunrise over the ball fields. Sometimes, the custodians let him wait in the boiler room, so he got to hear the school gossip first and sometimes smelled vaguely like the pink sand they used to soak up the puddle when someone got sick.

"He's wearing a bow tie..." Gary trailed off at the odd look on Howard's face.

"Howard?" Ericka poked him. "You're catching flies, Howard."

Howard closed his mouth and dragged his friends around the corner of the building. He had even less time than he'd thought.

***

Albert Einstein was fond of saying that you don't really understand something until you can explain it to your grandmother. One direct effect of this bit of advice was the creation of a secret society known as The Dozing Grannies, their only mission to overthrow the physics establishment and replace it with good little boys and girls who don't pester granny to read them *A Brief History of Time.*[25]

The other effect of Einstein's maxim was the misconception that being an expert in your field automatically qualified you to talk to children about it. Children who didn't have the luxury of

---

[25] Which would not have been so bad except that the little scamps insisted that they do the voices...

dozing off mid-lecture.[26]

The man sent to infiltrate the school disguised as a substitute teacher, was James Skillion, an expert in ornithology, among other things. He considered the assignment an opportunity to spread his love of birds to a new generation.

Deeds had not prepared his students for this brand of teaching. He is not a bird watching, lecturing from a book sort of science teacher. He regularly blows things up, sets things on fire, freezes things in liquid nitrogen and shows his class how to make stink bombs. His philosophy is that students learn something and gain a valuable skill that will serve them well in college.

If nothing else, his students stay awake because they aren't sure when they might be called upon to hide, run, grab a fire extinguisher, or applaud wildly.

Skillion began his lecture by telling the class how in 1735, a Swedish physician named Carl Linnaeus decided that while calling a flower a 'pretty pansy' was easy, it was also bad because what's known as a 'pretty pansy' in England was the 'rose pensée' in France. Someone needed to make sure that a pansy was a pansy no matter where you went, and Carl came up with a method of naming things 'scientifically'.

Then his followers spread across the earth looking for new things to name and telling bemused natives that the red-breasted bird that heralded the advent of spring would henceforth be called *turdus migratorius*...[27]

Gary's hand shot up.

Skillion frowned at the skinny boy in the third row. The students around him were already snickering, which even an

---

[26] The second most common misconception is that everyone will care as deeply as they do about the nesting habits and mating rituals of the American Robin or whatever and that anyone who finds it boring is stupid rather than the expert being a boring old fart who needs a more interesting hobby.

[27] That this sort of behavior didn't lead to the slaughter of scientific explorers is likely best attributed to the almost universal habit of treating people that you think might be crazy with care and maintaining your distance.

inexperienced teacher knew was a bad sign. Another misconception common among experts in any field is that they can answer any question a twelve year old can think of.

"Yes, what is it, Mr--" he consulted his seating chart -- "Mr Parker?"

"Did you just say that turds are migratory?"

Skillion blinked at him. "No... what?"

"Perhaps the robin carries it," Howard suggested.

"How would they carry it?" Ericka asked.

"Maybe two of them carry it on a vine."

"That is quite *enough*!" Skillion shouted. "*Turdus Migratorium* does not mean, migratory turd! It is the Latin name for the American Robin! Genus and species, a binomial naming system -- all birds and beasts are categorized by Kingdom, Phylum, Class, Order, Family, Genus, and Species, which you can remember by saying *Kangaroos Play Cellos, Orangutans Fiddle, Gorillas Sing.*"

Gary's hand shot up.

Skillion didn't have to check for a name this time.

"This had better not be scatological, Mr. Parker."

"I don't know what that means."

"It means *do you have a question, unrelated to turds?*"

"Yes."

"And what is it?"

"You got that backward," Gary said. "In *The Jungle Book*, it's the Orangutans that sing."

"What?"

"And I think the bears play bongo drums, but don't hold me to that."

"It's true," a girl at the front of the room agreed.

"No, it's just a mnemonic device," Skillion stressed. "It's a little ditty you memorize to help you remember something else. *"Kangaroos Play Cellos* stand in for *Kingdom, Phylum,* and *Class,* see?"

A girl piped up from the back. "I'm not sure my mom would approve of a science class that teaches us that the animals in

Australia are musical."

"Orangutans are from Africa, dummy," another girl scoffed.

"They're from Sumatra, actually," a boy from the front row countered.

"Stop. Just... stop!" Skillion sputtered.

But it was too late to stop; the center of gravity had shifted to the class and egged on quietly by Gary, Ericka, and Howard, other students joined in.

Howard was the only one who saw Skillion flee the room in tears.

***

"Your little town is at the center of quite the tempest just now, Doctor Deeds." The Professor spoke without turning around as Deeds walked into the office. He glanced past her out the window and across the quadrangle where a group of post-mortem biology undergrads were playing a pickup game of zombie soccer.

Neither team was winning. *Amateurs*.[28]

"So I hear."

"Certain government agencies seem to think there's a time traveler in your town." She turned to glare at him. "You wouldn't know anything about that, would you, Villy?"

"Why don't you ask me what you want to ask me, sis."

"Have you been playing with grandpa's time machine?"

Deeds sank into a chair and stared up at his twin sister. Finally he shook his head.

"No." He pulled the sample jars filled with scorched glass

---

[28] The rules are simple: whichever team's zombie is the first to cross the goal line with both the ball and their head intact wins. Contrary to what you see in movies, zombies can't run and can't really walk in a straight line either. Very rarely is more than one point scored in a game. Deeds still had the record for the highest score ever in the game, but he cheated by taking to the field himself disguised as a zombie. To be fair, in the mad science department of Arkham Tech, they kick you out if you *don't* cheat.

and dirt out of the pocket of his lab coat and set them on the coffee table. "No, this person's a rank amateur. Flashy. I think they might actually have a Tesla coil mounted to the top of the thing to create a light show as they show up."

"Grandpa would be mortified," she agreed, walking over to pick up one of the jars. "The agencies are noticing this person."

"I know."

"How could *you* know?"

Deeds smirked at his sister. She was jealous of anyone getting information faster than she, especially if it happened to be her brother. He let her stew for a moment before letting her off the hook.

"The black helicopters and men in suits wearing sunglasses after dark were my first clue."

The professor was silent for a while, staring out the window at the grad students chasing a zombie that had wandered off the playing field, trying to herd it back to the pitch. Finally, her shoulders raised and lowered in the sort of insolent shrug that would have earned one of his students detention.

"I think it's a kid."

"A *child* did this?"

"There were similar incidents recorded all over Ohio last year," he said. "And one of my students just transferred into my class from Dayton."

"Could be a coincidence."

"Yes."

"What is this child's name?"

"I'm not ready to say for certain," Deeds hedged. "The kid doesn't show any propensity for evil. He's weathered some bullying that most of the students here would have answered by bringing a robot to school to send the bullies packing. This kid just takes it -- he's practically a ghost."

"Any other reasons to suspect him?"

"I can't spend all of my time chasing phantoms -- I have classes to teach," Deeds growled. "Which means meeting the state's standardized testing minimums."

"Ah yes, one of our greatest and most subtle plans."[29]

"Being a teacher used to be so much fun," Deeds grumbled.

"Get him to take the entrance exam, and we'll know for sure."

"If you had answered my first call, maybe, but now the feds are in town and we don't have time to dilly dally," Deeds growled. "If they get too close, I might need to pull him out of there."

"Without knowing for sure where his allegiance lies?" She reared back as if he'd suggested she eat a plate of live leaches. "Or whether he's smart enough to enter the apprentice program?"

"If he fails the test, we can always throw him into the henchman class."

She stared out the window. She did the twisty thing with her hair and Deeds knew that his sister was mulling it over. Finally she made her decision and turned to glare at her brother.

"What do you need?"

"An assistant, for starters -- that kid that ran out of here crying earlier will do."

"You always did have a soft spot for the liberal arts majors."[30]

"They work cheap and they're always so appreciative to have a job that I can get them to do almost anything," he said. "Once I train them to stop quoting Shakespeare at me, they make ideal lab assistants."

"What happened to the last one?"

"He sleeps with the fishes."

"Oh, Villy," she tsked. "What have I told you about breaking your toys?"

---

[29] Don't believe me? You explain them then. Subtle evil is subtle.

[30] She never let him live down getting his MA in art history before finally returning to the family business.

"Honest, I tested the fishman serum on him and had to release him into the Mississippi. Fish food got too expensive."[31]

"Sure, Villy, whatever you say," she said. "Is there anything else?"

"Yes, get rid of the stupid pipe organ that plays every time my name is spoken."

"Not much chance of that."

"Stop calling me Villy?"

"Even less chance of that," she cackled. "Have a nice flight back to Kansas or whatever backwater state it is you live in."

He was on the plane home before he realized that he'd neglected to mention the strange creature he had spotted in his cameras.

***

"I don't see why you can't just go back in time and tell yourself not to invent the thing." Gary whispered.

"Because I can't travel farther back than the invention of my time machine -- it's a rule." Howard explained.

"I meant the robot," Gary muttered as Mr. Larky the baseball coach walked by.

After Skillion ran out, the class had been chaos for about ten minutes until the assistant principal arrived to restore order. The students were told to study quietly and Mr. Larky was asked to keep an eye on them while a search was underway to locate Dr. Skillion.

As soon as Larky was out of earshot, Gary twisted in his seat to face Howard. "I meant the robot," he repeated. "None of this happened until the robot attracted attention, so go back and stop yourself from building it."

"It's not the robot that's the problem, it's the reactor in the

---

[31] Thankfully, Deeds had planned far enough ahead that the serum was a species of catfish, ideal for the muddy waters of the Mississippi. Had he used clown fish the result would have not only looked silly, but also required a plane ticket to the tropics.

thing's chest."

"And you can't travel back in time far enough to stop yourself from inventing the reactor because you had to do that before you could build the time machine?" Ericka asked. Howard nodded. "OMG, Howard, how do you get yourself into these messes?"

"I come from a long line of troublemakers, I guess."

"Parker! Platt! And..." Larky snapped his fingers, unable to remember Howard's last name. "New kid! All of you shut up and get back to work!"

The class all glared at Gary, who they blamed for being forced to handwrite "I will not make the substitute teacher cry" over and over again for the rest of class.[32] Gary smirked, secretly loving the attention.

Howard wasn't writing sentences, he was one of the students making columns of words instead of sentences. It looked like he'd written "I will not make the substitute" two hundred times.

Which was odd, because he didn't know how to make people yet.[33]

He couldn't go back in time to stop himself from inventing the time machine. So maybe Gary was right, maybe if he just went far enough back to stop himself from building the robot it would be enough to escape notice from both the aliens and the men in suits.

It was the only plan any of them had come up with so far that made any kind of sense.

But it would take a lot of Funtime Pops to provide the kind of energy he would need to open a wormhole all the way to Ohio and that far into the past. Lots and lots and *lots*.

The bell rang and Howard joined the stream of students

---

[32] This time-honored punishment is the only holdout from the days of yore when principals were still allowed to chain kids to dungeon walls and make them sing for Pink Floyd concept albums. Ah, *those* were the days...

[33] When he asked for a cloning kit, his mom said no.

heading out the door, his head still buzzing with half-formed plans.

7. The Goonies Paradox

One cold winter's day back in the fourth grade, Howard stayed home sick from school and he and his dad had their first "Don't Tell Mom I Let You Watch This" movie marathon. That day they watched some of his dad's favorite movies from when *he* was a kid. *Stand by Me, Goonies* and *The Christmas Story* flickered on the screen one after the other as Howard's fever soared, his hallucinations joining the adventurous bands of misfits gathered to outsmart murderers and teachers and pirates and parents.[34]

In some ways, that day set the tone for their relationship as his dad began thrusting movies and books into his hands that inevitably featured clever kids besting spies and pirates and evil wizards mostly by breaking every rule and defying every adult they came across. Howard learned pretty quickly that adults loved those stories right up to the point where their kids began acting anything like the characters.

Howard thought of it as *The Goonies Paradox*: "This is awesome, but don't ever do anything like this."

The key difference between the world of movies like *Goonies* and the world Howard lived in was that parents were comically oblivious to the sort of things their kids got up to in those stories. In Howard's world, teachers and principals had the phone numbers of parents and regularly made use of them to inform parents that their little darlings did things like make a substitute teacher cry. Also, those kids always seem to manage to get around town without ever once getting into a car with an embarrassed and angry parent at the wheel.

---

[34] Not to mention Santa Claus.

Howard didn't even make it out of the parking lot.

"Do you know what it's like to be pulled out of an important business meeting to talk to a principal who wants to inform you that your son is a *thug*?"

"I don't have a son," Howard muttered[35]. The car lurched to a halt and his mother twisted completely around in her seat to glare at him, ignoring the horns from the cars behind her.

"Don't you smart off to me, young man!" she snapped. "Don't you do it!"

"Sorry."

"Are you? Because I don't think you are."

"Mom, everyone's honking!" Howard glanced around to see if anyone he knew was seeing him getting bawled out in the parking lot. The only real thug he knew, Billy Wexler, was sauntering toward them through the cars. The larger boy spotted them and headed closer, craning his neck to see and ignoring calls from his dad that their car was the other way.

"Can we *go*, please?"

"Oh, I'm sorry, Howard, am I *embarrassing* you?"

Howard knew better than to answer that one. Nothing he said was going to move the car forward.[36] Finally, his mom got tired of staring at him and turned to wave apologetically at the angry parents behind her as she lurched back into traffic. The rest of the drive home took place in complete silence, his mother seething and occasionally throwing him disappointed looks in the rearview mirror.

At the secret training camps where mothers were prepared for the antics of preteen sons, Howard was certain that there were lengthy training sessions devoted solely to the fabled

---

[35] In all fairness, Howard probably would've been in just as much trouble if he hadn't answered the question. Howard referred to this problem as *The Mom Paradox* but never out loud.

[36] If there was a time to tell his parents he was being chased by aliens and secret government agencies, he wasn't sure what it would look like, but he was pretty sure this wasn't it. Maybe a nice note sent via carrier pigeon from an undisclosed location high in the Alps...

Disappointed Stare. As far as Howard was concerned, it was as close to actual magic as anyone could get. He couldn't imagine that there was a natural explanation for why he could actually *feel* someone's gaze on his skin.

He shuddered to think what she had in store for him once he was a teenager.

His hand was on the door handle before they came to a complete stop, but the automatic locks clicked down before he could make his escape.

"Look around, Howard." He was startled to hear tears in her voice. "Tell me what you see."

Howard glanced around them, at the back seat of the car, from the scuffs on the back of her seat to the edge of a discarded gum wrapper sticking out from under the floor mat. He looked out the windows at the yards and houses of the cul-de-sac. Mr. Hatfield was mowing his lawn and across the road Ericka was dragging her feet up the front walk behind her dad who was obviously just as angry with her as his mom with him.

He imagined that Gary's lot was the worst of them all since his parents were both teachers.

"What am I supposed to see?" he asked.

"Life."

"Oh." He frowned out the window until his breath fogged the glass too much to see through. It was spring, but still cool in the evenings. "Why am I in trouble?"

"Because what happened today was all you, kiddo." She sounded far away. "It has all the earmarks of a plan hatched in the brain of Howard James Carter, criminal genius."

"I'm not a criminal genius."

"No, you get caught too much to qualify for that degree," she agreed. "For now at least, you're just a plain old ordinary run of the mill genius who's bored to tears by public school."

"Does it matter that the guy was out to get me?" She didn't answer. Without looking he could tell that she was staring at him in the mirror.

"You *wanted* to go to public school, Howard."

"I know."

"You begged us to let you go to school like a normal kid."

Howard didn't answer. He was tired of saying 'I know'. She turned around to look at him directly. "*Begged*, Howard"

"What do you want me to say?" he shouted.

She lapsed into hurt silence and Howard felt horrible for shouting. He just wanted to get out of the car, out of range of her stares and her anger at him, escape into books where clever kids who outsmarted adults were celebrated instead of persecuted.

"What happened today and what happened back in Dayton, can't keep happening, Howard."

"I know."

"I don't want to have to find a new job again, Howard."

"It wasn't my fault we left Dayton."

"No, of course not, nothing is ever your fault." She sighed. "And the lawnmower incident was all just a big misunderstanding."

He held his tongue and stared out the window, waiting for her to unlock the doors. Lawn mower robots were unpredictable beasts. Of course it had been a misunderstanding, but when he couldn't even convince his mother of that he knew better than to even suggest it to the county sheriff.

Howard didn't want to get run out of another town either. But if Skillion was any indication, he was beginning to wonder if when the time came, whether or not he'd have a choice.

Finally, his mom gave up and unlocked the car doors. Howard grabbed his backpack and bolted up the front steps and through the front door. He rounded the foot of the stairs by grabbing the newel post and rebounded off the wall, dropping his backpack and kicking off his shoes without stopping.

He got as far as the kitchen before he heard their voices and came to a sliding halt as the two adults at the table turned to look at him.

James Skillion wasn't crying anymore. The old man had taken off his ridiculous red bow tie and without it he looked less like a buffoon and more like a large and angry adult. Howard felt the familiar hand of doom stretching out to grab him. Howard opened his mouth to shout a warning to his father that the man was not to be trusted as Skillion opened his mouth to say... something. Howard never found out what because his mother walked in.

"Howard, you have a guest."

Howard, his father and Skillion all stood as his mother entered the kitchen. She was followed by a tall man with prematurely white hair standing in a shaggy halo around his pale face. Howard's heart leaped at the sight of his rightful science teacher. Deeds certainly looked like he'd been sick; his eyes were bloodshot he had dark circles under his eyes.

Deeds stepped forward to extend a hand to his startled substitute.

"Thank you, Skillion, but Howard is my student and I'll take it from here."

There was nothing left for the man from WARD to do but leave, conscious of the eyes on his back as he gathered his things and made his exit with as much dignity as possible.

***

Kevin wasn't technically breaking and entering. His new master had given him a key to the school building and the alarm codes. All the same, he was fairly sure that if Deeds was allowed to wander off with a student file in his briefcase he wouldn't need his new assistant to go in after dark and walk out with it tucked in his jacket.

Only one day into his new internship and he already had a felony. He couldn't wait to get home and write his mother to tell her all about it -- she was going to be so proud. He decided to sign it *Igor*, she'd like that.

8. Practically a Law of Nature

In 1891, a man calling himself by the improbable name Throckmorton Q. Calabash returned to America from what he claimed was an epic journey around the world. America was astonished by this because no one knew who he was or noticed that he'd left. The tales of his travels drowned out the cries of "Wait, who are you again?" and he lived for a short time in fame and glory, feted by the glitterati of the day.

Calabash told stories that would turn your hair white and it was said he asked the elders of each village he passed through to tell him the stories of their people. TQC (as he was called by his friends) eventually published a book in which he proposed a framework for using these cultural epics to create fiction. The writer who followed his simple principles could then sit back to "watch the fame come galumphing in to lavish fortune upon the writer like an exuberant golden retriever."

Essentially his advice could be boiled down to this: Think up some characters, give them something to do that seems impossible, make a series of interesting things happen and when they're done, write "The End".

In keeping with the mythological theme, he also advocated including a couple of talking animals to keep things interesting.

His research was dismissed and forgotten when it turned out he never took his round-the-world journey and most of it was cribbed from *How to Write a Bestselling Fiction Novel in One Week or Less*, by James McShane, which wouldn't be published until 2015.

Time travelers try this sort of nonsense all the time.[37]

I only mention it because rule number ten in the Calabash principles of storytelling diverged ever-so-slightly from the book that he plagiarized. McShane was content with subtle storytelling, but Calabash stated that a titanic struggle must *always* ensue when two archetypal opposites meet. Nature simply won't allow two opposites -- a boy genius and a mad scientist, for example -- to enter the same room without coming to blows.

Lightning strikes, explosions, arm wrestling... *something* has to happen.

It's practically a law of nature, said Calabash.

Howard's parents had never heard of Throckmorton Q. Calabash or James McShane[38] and didn't put much stock in arm wrestling[39]. They sent Howard to his room so they could talk to Mr. Deeds alone. Howard sat on his bed for an hour or so, listening to the distant murmur of their voices until sleep overtook him.

As he slept, as is so often the case, his fate was decided by the adults downstairs.

---

[37] Which goes to show how simultaneously subtle and yet short-sighted a time traveler can be. If he'd written about his actual adventures, he might have made more money and achieved real lasting fame. In the 1890's time travel stories were all the rage and he'd have scooped H.G. Wells by a good four years. It also just goes to show that people will go to any length to achieve even the smallest amount of fame.

[38] McShane would achieve fame a year or so later when he was at the center of an event known as "The Aardvark Incident" which captured headlines the world over and brought him a notoriety that publishers just can't help but throw book deals at. Unfortunately, the epic scale of the Aardvark Incident defies a mere footnote so you'll just have to wait and see. Oh. And wear galoshes that day. Just trust me on this one.

[39] Which is just as well, really. Howard's stature tends to the long and lanky and that does not an effective arm-wrestler make. His long fingers, however, make him an excellent thumb wrestler.

***

Deeds arrived home later than usual and at least three times as tired. There was only an hour difference between Arkham, Massachusetts and Sedville, Missouri, but his body felt like he'd swum the ocean. He released a sizeable yawn he had been saving for just such an occasion and watched it caper about as he dropped his keys in the misshapen ceramic dish on the table next to his front door.

The dish looked like the sort of thing a kid would bring home to a parent or uncle[40]. It gave yeoman service holding his keys and spare change, and gave the impression of a man with the sort of family ties expected of a teacher.

The modest house in the heart of Sedville was full of such nuances. A child's drawing adorned the fridge, signed to his attention by a loving nephew that didn't exist. The drawing and change dish alike had been snagged recently from the wastebasket at school to reinforce the image of a distant and loving family. A family of actors he had hired populated several framed photos on the walls and pictures in his wallet.

Even the studio photographers hadn't known they were part of an elaborate charade.

Deeds had repeated the stories so many times even he had almost forgotten that they were lies. A teacher never knew when a parent or colleague would drop by or if a secretive government agency might search their home in search of evidence of overlooked young geniuses.

He glanced around at the photos and furnishings with a casual eye, mentally checking off that everything was where he'd left it. Deeds detected four telltale signs that WARD agents had penetrated his home.

Skillion.

He'd suspected as much. Only a government agent would be that ham-handed with a bunch of kids.

---

[40] In a bygone era it would have been called an ashtray, but he had been informed in no uncertain terms that these days it was a "change dish".

Young Howard Carter had been wise to sink that sub before he had a chance to notice the budding super-genius sitting in his classroom. That he'd acted mostly by tricking his friends and classmates into leading the charge spoke well of his potential as a supervillain.

The yawn and its attendant weariness vanished as he fished his smartphone out of his pocket and scanned for listening devices. He had been correct: there were four. Lucky thing they hadn't installed cameras; he would have to be more careful.

Deeds spun at the rattle of a key in his front door and lunged to meet his new assistant with a hand over his mouth before he could speak.

"How was your day, *nephew*?"

He didn't remove his hand until the kid nodded that he understood.

"Just fine, Uncle Vill... er... Victor."

"Did you get that paperwork you need to be a substitute teacher?"

"The office was closed, I'll... I will go back tomorrow."

Deeds crooked a finger and walked to the framed portrait of an imaginary sister and her family grinning like idiots around a department store Santa and twisted the wall sconce hanging next to it. A click echoed from inside the wall and the picture swung forward.

Without looking back to see if his assistant was following, Deeds crawled through the waist-high hole in his wall and descended the ladder into the basement. Darkness enveloped him as Kevin closed the portrait above and followed him down the ladder.

As he stepped off the ladder, stiff cloth brushed his shirt sleeve and he paused to take the lab coat off the hook and slip his arms into the sleeves without bothering with the lights. He felt the mild-mannered science teacher fall away in the darkness as he buttoned the double-breasted lab coat and settled the goggles atop his head.

He felt like laughing maniacally, but suppressed the urge. His laugh had been known to send new assistants diving for the nearest window. He needed the kid to stick around.

"Lights!"

The underground laboratory was flooded with light on his command. The subterranean chamber was under the basement of his own house and extended beneath the houses on either side, unbeknownst to the owners of those homes[41].

Kevin whistled as he stepped off the ladder.

Deeds ignored his assistant as he plugged the phone into the terminal on his desk and powered up the system. Kevin whistled again at the sight of it and Deeds felt a flush of pride. He had cobbled together the super computer mainly from cellular phones and game systems he had confiscated from his students. By linking them together in series with a pile of second-hand computers and free software he'd found on the internet, he had a super computer that would put anything NASA was using to shame.

Deeds kicked the machine a few times to wake up the hamsters[42] and listened to their tiny wheels squeak and spin as the computer stuttered, sputtered and finally lit up.

As he waited for his rodents to get up to speed, Deeds turned to find his new assistant spreading the gains of his evening of burglary across the lab table.

There is a relatively short list of things that can evoke true terror in the heart of an American child: spiders or snakes maybe, if the kid's squeamish; kisses and cheek-pinches delivered by whiskery aunts; rides and candy offered by creepy strangers; bringing home failing grades to parents who've heard all the excuses... But the real terror lies in the hands of school secretaries in a document known only as *The Permanent Record*.

---

[41] The nice thing about building a secret lab is that you don't have to ask anyone's permission. The sticky points of building codes and permitting are the least of your concerns if your secret laboratory is discovered.

[42] Yes, hamsters. He used to use weasels out of an affection for the breed, but they got tangled in the wheels. Why hamsters? Because the energy drain of a computer like his would be noticed.

There's a segment of the population that put the permanent record up there with the likes of bigfoot, the chupacabra, and secret government agencies sucking tons of concrete into hidden underground bunkers[43]. The paperwork would be simply too great to keep an accurate tally of all the childhood foibles of the American youth that would follow them around for the rest of their lives.

These people underestimate the file-keeping ability of the average school secretary.

Deeds and his new assistant spent the rest of the night perusing the permanent record of Howard James Carter, boy genius. And quite a record it was. By the end of the night, Deeds was wondering why it took the government this long to start tracking the kid.

***

In large black vans positioned at key points throughout the city of Sedville, men in suits paced the cramped aisles behind the technicians keeping themselves busy monitoring the listening devices scattered throughout the town. Their screens displayed real-time imagery transmitted by the satellites that had moved into orbit overhead, alert for any signs of illegal robots or time travel.

Thousands of voices were fed into the computers and complex search algorithms mined the conversations for key words. They heard Deeds and the Carters discussing private tutoring for their son. They heard the parents of Howard's classmates bawling out their children for bringing a substitute teacher to tears. They heard Skillion weeping into his pillow (an alert tech filed that tape away for future blackmail and/or personal amusement). They heard everything and learned nothing.

In short, the agents from WARD monitored the city too

---

[43] Only one of these is actually mythical and it's the one that most people believe in. Yes, those free trip people have a lot of explaining to do.

closely to see anything.

Seriously. A refrigerator magnet or maybe a nice key chain with the Deeds Paradox written on it would have saved them a lot of frustration.

***

The alien watched television, its body mass shifting periodically as it spotted nuances of earthling anatomy that it hadn't picked up right away.

It had spent its day on a surveillance sweep of the city and came back with a good deal more than the agents of WARD could claim. The alien, for instance, knew exactly where to find The Dread Pirate Robot and all about the real identity of "Victor" Villainous Deeds and his new Igor. It knew about Deeds's secret lab and watched with interest as Kevin stole Howard Carter's file.

None of these things interested the visitor. There was plenty of time for it to achieve its goals and it had come a long way from a patient planet.

In the mean time, there were episodes of The Muppet Show to watch.

9. That Kind of Place

"So where are we?" Old Suit paced up and down at the front of the room, forcing his subordinate suits to follow him with their eyes. The techs didn't look up from the handheld game systems disguised as Blackberries. He couldn't tell whether they were playing games or looking at important global telemetry from the satellites and they knew it.

He tried to ignore them.

"There haven't been any new energy spikes since the first one," a young suit piped up. "We're monitoring all wavelengths of visible light and... um..." the suit ran out of memorized lines and had to check his notes. The techs all glanced at the suit and then exchanged smirks.

The suits were so cute when they tried to speak technobabble.[44] Old suit didn't wait for him to find his page.

"Nothing?" he growled. "You come to me with *nothing*?"

"We're monitoring the situation and have units in the field."

"You are *monitoring* the situation?" Old Suit glared the younger suit into silence. "How?"

"We've infiltrated the city of Sedville at every level, sir." Another suit spoke up. "We have agents in every role from the mayor's office to garbage collection."

"We have a list of all the registered engineers and scientists in the area..."

"And we're working on getting a new agent into the middle

---

[44] An enterprising young suit fresh from his Ivy-covered university had once tried to cobble together a technobabble phrasebook for his fellow suits, but gave it up after it became apparent that the techs had noticed and retrenched, making up whole new words and phrases daily until he gave up.

school..."

"We've bugged half the town..."

"Let me get this straight," Old Suit growled. "We have a rogue robot with an unknown power source running around loose; there's an unknown number of time travelers popping up in schoolyards; and my leading science advisor won't get out of bed because a bunch of sixth graders were mean to him?"

"They made fun of his birds," the first young suit muttered, seeing the chance to deflect the old man's derision toward the scientists. A dozen men and women in lab coats stood against the wall, stony faced as their leader was treated to a round of giggles, chuckles and snorts.

"So the best-funded and most elite secret organization in the entire federal government has been on the ground in Sedville for two days now and all we have to show for it is the disdain of a handful of eleven year olds and some promising new careers in garbage collection?"

A moment of stunned silence was followed by everyone attempting to make the last forty-eight hours look like something less than a complete waste of time and resources.

"Um..."

"Well..."

"Ah... the thing is..."

"You see..."

"What the heck was *that‽*"

All heads swiveled to look at the man who had dropped an interrobang into the discussion.[45] He didn't look around, dropping his Gameboy to run to a computer monitor on the wall.

Old Suit followed and the rest of the crowd fell in, gathering into a ragged semi-circle around a large computer display. A blue grid overlay displayed the location of units scattered across

---

[45] Unusual punctuation in the presence of Old Suit always required a proper explanation. A young suit once dropped a casual percontation point in front of the old man and found himself demoted to janitor before he could get his *Lexicon of Unusual Punctuation* back into his pocket.

the city of Sedville and the surrounding county.

Northeast of town, a faint green dot blinked steadily.

One of the suits reached out to tap the screen as if it would make the blinking dot either get bigger or fly away like he was trying to scare away a bug on the opposite side of a windowpane.[46]

"It's not a touchscreen."[47]

Conscious that everyone was staring at him, the suit withdrew his hand. The blinking dot grew strong for just a moment and then faded and didn't come back.

"Great, you broke it!" Old Suit cuffed the touchy suit on the back of the head. "What was it?"

"It had a signature close to the time machine, but not as strong." The young tech was so caught up in his work he forgot to bury his report in obscure language. His compatriots exchanged money.

Old Suit ignored all of them, his eyes locked on the spot where the green dot had vanished. The location was on a steep hillside overlooking a winding creek. Trails crisscrossed the area and the satellite image showed a spar of pale rock jutting out over the valley below.

He turned to his suits.

"That list of engineers and scientists." He held out a hand and someone filled it with a printed sheet of paper. Old Suit squinted at the list. "Anyone we know?"

"The science teacher Victor Deeds has popped up before for minor infractions: built a small robot when he was a kid and tried to strap a jet engine to his Chevy Nova when he was a

---

[46] They did this periodically not because it accomplished anything, but because the suits always seemed impressed when they did it.

[47] WARD used to have touch screen monitors all over their headquarters, actually -- in fact, they had them before anyone else -- but the suits always seemed to have sticky fingers and delight in leaving trails of fingerprints behind them as they walked from monitor to monitor, tapping them just to see them jump. After the great Whiteout incident of 1991, the techs quietly removed them.

teenager. Basic stuff. Since then, he's kept his nose clean." A young suit reported. "Other than that, there's just this person here: Carter."

"Carter?"

"Moved to Sedville from Dayton, Ohio shortly after the lawn mower incident."

"The lawn mower incident?"

"Robotic lawn mower got loose in suburban Dayton and mowed the first one hundred and fifty digits of *pi* into the ball field at a city park." The young suit paused to consult his notes. "And the phrase 'Go stick your head in a pig' over and over again before it ran off."

"And I suppose we never caught it?"

"No."

"Dispatch a helicopter to check out that spot." He reached out and tapped the screen, daring the techs to say anything. "And I want Deeds and Carter in a cell by sundown."

Techs, suits and scientists scattered to their appointed tasks or if they didn't have an assignment, tried to look like they were hurrying off somewhere important before backtracking to the base canteen.

It was Thursday. The headquarters chef always made blueberry pancakes on Thursdays.

***

The time traveler stepped out of the grove of fragrant cedar and looked around.

She was at the foot of an enormous outcropping of granite, sticking out of the hillside like an enormous thumb, as if this part of earth was trying to hitchhike to some place where local kids didn't feel it necessary to adorn her thumb with generation after generation of their names. Locals called it Sunshine Rock, but she thought of it as Graffiti Granite.

She laid a hand over the cool stone and moved along the face to the place where her own half-forgotten name should be etched. It wasn't there yet. She was early. That explained why she had stepped across the decades to find herself in the middle of a sticky, fragrant grove of red cedar bushes that weren't on her chart.

Shedding nostalgia and cedar needles, she began unpacking the instruments from her canvas satchel. In moments, a small box covered in blinking lights sat atop a tripod, aimed at the North Star. With the flip of a switch, the wondrous little box made millions of computations, calculating solar drift and universal expansion until it beeped.

She pushed a button and read the display.

A whole day early.

For the first time since she met him, Howard Carter had managed to get her someplace early. There truly was a first time for everything. She broke down the time-telemetry box and tripod and put them away.

The map refreshed memories long dormant. There were houses, a church and even a cave or two nearby. Plenty of places to hide until the time came.

For the time being, she would watch the sun rise. It had been a long time since she'd had a moment of silence to enjoy such a simple thing. She liked to think that Howard had intentionally sent her back early just to watch it.

He could be sweet in the strangest ways.

As the light of the rising sun began to creep across the forest floor below, Ericka Carter-Platt swore she could feel it touch the scar running across her cheekbone, a pale pink line across her warm dark skin. She had learned the hard way not to move when Howard said it was better to stay put.

Wait, he said. *And when you get the chance, stop me.*

She would swallow the impulse to find her eleven-year-old self and hide her someplace safe. She had to trust that her husband knew what he was talking about.

* * *

Ever since they had thrown the British army out of their country in the mid 18th century, the United States of America had cultivated an official story of "Sent them packing, never looked back." But in truth, most of the country had spent most of that time looking wistfully across the Atlantic, wishing they had a cool accent too. This was manifest in the number of American youths who could recite every word of *Monty Python and the Holy Grail* and the number of women who pined for Lord Darcy.[48]

America designed itself as a place where you can reinvent yourself and a place that took what they liked from every culture that they came across and built a holiday or theme restaurant around it.[49] Sometimes both.

When Omar Wertsel came to America, he did the most American thing he could think of, he bought the local German restaurant and shut it down. Missouri was a state settled mainly by German and French immigrants, which meant there was precious little demand for French or German food[50]. Wertsel nailed a lot of dark wood to the walls and hung up a glowing green shamrock. He named the place 'The Song Rider' and declared it an Irish place. Which is to say that there was a Guinness sign above the bar and especially generous drink specials on Saint Patrick's Day.

It was almost immediately adopted as a biker bar because it had the word 'Rider' in the name, which is like catnip to bikers.

---

[48] Also, films produced by Americans were overrun by English actors playing villains, but really that was really mostly out of annoyance that the British actors made fun of their fake accents.

[49] Some cultures view this attitude as predatory, but it's worth noting that even America itself isn't safe from this and the favorite target for this treatment by far is a sanitized version of the 1950's with plenty of bobby socks, saddle shoes and poodle skirts and precious few Joe McCarthy impersonators. (Which is a shame, really. The Joe McCarthy impersonators need the work and are probably tired of being mistaken for the Charlie McCarthy impersonators. Which is an easy mistake to make.)

[50] Their forefathers, after all, had come to America to get away from endless vistas of schnitzel and wursts.

Wertsel didn't care as long as everyone was Irish for the duration of their stay. Something about the big German in the green bowler hat trying to layer an Irish accent over his thick German was endearing.

The alien observed the denizens of The Song Rider for several hours before it decided to venture inside.

It has long been rumored that the first images of Earth that were broadcast strongly enough to aliens to see was the 1936 Olympics. This is not the case. Due to an anomaly in local space, the first visual record to reach alien eyes had actually been the February 26, 1977 broadcast of an early episode of The Muppet Show. The episode featured a creature called a "frog" dancing and singing the song *Lydia the Tattooed Lady* to a gyrating creature called a "pig". The aliens liked the pictures and the song and especially the pig covered in tiny drawings of significant historical events.

The drawings puzzled the creature until its observations of the patrons that frequented The Song Rider had led to the conclusion that humans had pickled their memories in thick black beer to the point where they had to draw pictures of loved ones and significant events on their skin in order to remember them. Several of the bikers apparently couldn't even remember their mothers without a little help from their biceps.

When the alien stepped into the bar looking remarkably like a pig covered in drawings, the owner had not panicked. The alien had thoughtfully procured a green bowler hat, just like Wertsel's. The bar owner launched a round of Finnegan's Wake and poured his new customer a pint of Guinness.

The other customers didn't even notice the felt pig in their midst.

It was that kind of place.

When it wasn't wandering the city pursuing its mission parameters (and staying alert for felt frogs, because it had the impression that they were in charge and really wanted to meet one) it staked out one end of the bar with a television tuned to a station that played a lot of Muppets and Sesame Street. Sometimes, this was interrupted by images of talking rabbits and violent clashes between cats and mice.

The Alien was beginning to like the earthlings.

They were silly.

It was too bad so many of them were going to die soon...

10. Hiding in Plain Sight

Gary and Ericka eyed Howard with something bordering on anger as he slammed the car door and watched his mom swerve her way into traffic to the usual cacophony of blaring horns and upraised fingers (mostly the middle ones).

Howard summoned all of his courage and turned to face his friends.

He caught the glares and gulped past a dry throat. He had been expecting this. It was hard enough to face his mother when she was still addressing him as "Mister" and speaking in clipped phrases. He had spent the morning in the frightening silence of her ire, pretending to read his book to avoid looking at his parents' disappointed faces.

His dad hadn't even asked him about what he was reading, which was always a bad sign.

Facing his friends after they had to weather the same from their own parents... Howard knew better than to expect open arms at the schoolhouse door. Gary seemed more receptive than Ericka -- at least *his* initial flash of annoyance faded quickly to a blank look as Howard came within earshot.

"I'm sorry."

"My dad says I'm not supposed to associate with troublemakers like you." Ericka allowed a single tear to escape and track across her cheek. If possible, it made Howard feel even worse and he cursed the interference of the goons in the suits and their pet science teacher. He could see that the initial faith he had inspired by showing them his time travel device had been burned away by the heat of parental wrath. Yesterday, they'd been willing to believe he was ducking some sort of government plot, today they looked like they were ready to hand him over to the first suit they met.

He opened his mouth to make excuses, but mercifully, the bell rang and his friends allowed the force of the crowd to carry them through the doors. The halls were far too noisy to allow proper conversation and there wasn't any room for him to grovel anyway.

As they passed the office, an arm snaked out and grabbed Howard by the back of his coat. Howard looked up in fright and alarm and realized that Morena Limbsley, the assistant principal had him.

Howard fought the urge to slip his arms out of his coat and run as she marched him through the front office and dropped him in a seat in front of her desk. *Now what did I do?* He thought.

"Did you think you were going to get away with it, Howard?"

"Get away with what?"

"Get away with..." She had a look on her face he was all too familiar with: she looked like she was fighting the urge to smack him. "Did you think we wouldn't notice that your permanent file was missing?"

"I don't..."

"Don't lie to me, Mister Carter."

"But..."

"Ms. Limbsley," a voice from the doorway interrupted, "I can assure you that young Howard is innocent." Howard looked up to find Mr. Deeds standing behind him.

"Mr. Deeds, I don't recall asking you to attend this conference."

"You were yelling; I could hear you from the copy room." Deeds brushed away the attempt to get him to leave as if he hadn't noticed. "Howard could not have stolen those records."

"And how do you figure?"

"Because I was at his home last night, meeting with his parents until quite late."

"Really?"

"I talked to the police detective this morning as he was leaving, we're old golfing buddies," Deeds lied smoothly. "The break-in occurred while I was present in the Carter home, arranging for him to get private tutoring with my nephew Kelvin," he glanced at the palm of his hand, "Kevin."

"Private tutoring?"

"Young Master Carter had a prolonged absence from school when his parents transferred here from Ohio and will need additional assistance catching up with his classmates." Deeds glanced down at Howard and quirked an eyebrow. "And since I understand my entire first period class is in detention all week, it's a perfect chance to begin."

"But his records..."

"I am certain they will turn up." Deeds toyed with something in his jacket pocket as he spoke and Howard noticed Ms. Limbsley go slightly limp, her eyes glazed over. "You should check with the school secretary, I am certain the break-in was just student hi-jinks and his records are around here somewhere."

"Yes..." she mumbled. "Yes, Doctor Deeds, I think you are right."

"Mister," he corrected hurriedly. "I'm just a humble science teacher."

"Just a humble science teacher, yes," she agreed. "You may go to class, Howard."

"Th- thank you."

Howard bolted from the room, certain of one thing more than any other: that Deeds was anything but a humble science teacher.

***

WARD had agents in all walks of life, feeding the illusion that the agency did not exist. Mostly, they did this by being as obvious as possible. Their deepest and most closely-held secret technologies were fed to Hollywood until they became the accepted fodder of science fiction movies and television shows to a point where people who spotted them went to sleep that night certain they had seen not a team of elite WARD agents in full kit, but a bunch of costumed fans headed for a science fiction convention.

As Old Suit leaned on the railing and watched his troops assembling on the flight deck below, even he had to remind himself that the troop of men and women assembling next to the parabolic shuttles were real. The mechanized armor was new, but the gaming and sci fi industry had taken it and run with it to a degree that surprised even him and now he couldn't look at his own troops without getting the sneaky suspicion that they'd been infiltrated by fans of one of the many space marine video games currently on the market. [51]

"Sir, the ballistic shuttle is ready." A man in armor addressed him from the floor. Old Suit grunted and made a shooing motion with both hands.

The armored soldiers stood at attention as a suit and a tech boarded the shuttle ahead of them to act as minders and chaperones. Servos whirred and helmets glistened in the artificial light of the hanger as the soldiers moved to grab their gear with maximum attention paid to catching the light just so.

Old Suit turned and left them to it.

But he was definitely going to order uglier armor next time.

***

"Howard, this is my nephew..." Deeds glanced at the palm of his hand. "...Kevin."

"Pleased to meet you, Howard, I've heard a lot about you."

"Um... Okay." Howard accepted the teenager's hand and tried to spot a family resemblance. There wasn't one. Kevin was

---

[51] Once, during a operation in San Diego, the suits running the op realized only on day three that the armored soldiers they thought were their backup troops were actually a bunch of college kids who thought the whole thing was some sort of live-action role playing game.

tall and handsome and well-kept, his skin was pink and his hair dark, unlike his uncle's pale face and disheveled white hair.

Maybe he was adopted.

Deeds clasped his hands behind his back and stalked back and forth in front of Howard and his alleged nephew. The science teacher seemed jittery and kept glancing out the door where across the hall, the assistant principal was minding his class through their detention. Deeds stopped pacing and stared at Howard.

"Did your parents tell you what we talked about last night, Howard?"

"They're still mad at me," Howard said. "Not a lot of discussion this morning."

"I see." Deeds clasped his hands behind his back and went up on his toes for a moment in much the same way Howard did when he was forced to explain himself.

"Your parents wouldn't be this disappointed in you if they didn't expect the best from you," the teenager piped up. Deeds's heels hit the tiles and he leveled a glare at his nephew.

"Sorry, that's not very comforting," Howard said.

"Yes, it seldom is," Deeds growled. "You only disappoint the ones you love, Howard."

"Great."

"Ms. Limbsley has detained your friends for detention every day after school for the rest of the month," Deeds continued. "You will serve your detention in private tutoring with my nephew."

"What kind of tutoring?"

"*Science* tutoring," Deeds purred. "You've arrived late in the year and we don't want you to fall behind your classmates."

"I'm not."

"Don't be silly, Howard, you had an extended absence from school between Ohio and here," Deeds scoffed. "Anyone would be lost jumping from one school to the other."

"Kelvin will be able to..."

"*Kevin.*" His assistant interrupted, earning a fresh glare from

Deeds. "My uncle would forget his head if it wasn't attached."

Deeds glared him into silence.

"As I said, *Kevin* will be able to get you up to speed in just a few short hours of tutoring."

"Great."

"What does your father do for a living Howard?"

"He's an artist, a painter mostly."

"And your mother?"

"She's a robotics engineer."

"I see." Deeds smiled and looked up at the ceiling for a moment to compose himself. "Do you know why I want you here, why I am taking such an interest in your schooling, Howard?"

"No, why?"

"Because you have potential Howard," Deeds purred. "More than anyone else in your class, you have the potential to do some genuinely crazy science."

"Crazy science?"

"Howard, I cannot stress enough how important it is that you excel in the sciences." Deeds leaned close until Howard could smell the mouthwash on the man's breath. "Do you lie awake at night and wonder why we aren't living in domed cities on Mars? Where are the jet packs and space cruisers, Howard?"

"Um..." Howard didn't know what to say. It was as if the man had read his journal, speaking the words aloud that Howard only ever whispered in private. "I don't know."

"They could exist, Howard." Deeds waved at the ceiling. "We could be out there, right now! Instead of mucking about with space shuttles and malfunctioning tin cans in low earth orbit, we could be out among the stars, claiming our place as a species!"

"Why aren't we?"

"Because there aren't enough people willing to devote the energy necessary to do the science," Deeds growled. "This is *our* world, we scientists. We know the rules of the natural world and how to break them, we make the technology that keeps us entertained and keeps us safe, and when the time comes it is our voices that will lead mankind into a golden age of flying cars and bases on the moon."

"Sign me up," Howard whispered. He stared up at the wild-haired man in the white coat, his doubts of the morning gone. He didn't care that the man had some strange power over the assistant principal or that he couldn't remember his nephew's name. If it led to a moon base and a decent flying car, Howard would follow this man anywhere.

"Excellent," Deeds whispered the word. He successfully fought the urge to laugh maniacally, but couldn't help but tap his fingertips together in the time-honored fashion. "Excellent, Howard, we have much to accomplish together. And if we have enough time, I've no doubt whatsoever that you and I will lay the cornerstone of the first domed city on Mars."

"Can I bring my friends?"

"Howard, my boy, you can bring anyone you want."

11. The Jig Is Up

Some mad scientists feed off chaotic surroundings. The volcanoes and islands of the so-called "Ring of Fire" that circle the Pacific Ocean provided secret headquarters for many of Deeds classmates. Undersea labs anchored over the Marianas Trench and subterranean fortresses beneath the volcanoes of Hawaii provide scenic vistas of strange undersea creatures and/ or seas of molten rock, but Deeds wasn't willing to pay for the view.

It was one reason Deeds was one of the few surviving members of his graduating class.

Deeds wasn't above creating an earthquake machine if he needed one, but he made it a life goal to live someplace he rarely had to wonder "Was that the planet or was that me?" So when the alembics and test tube racks began to shake and shatter, splashing toxic mixtures[52], he knew the jig was elevated.

Or was it up? He would have to look it up later if he found time.

Deeds just wasn't very good at idioms.

Overhead, he could hear his new assistant shout "Earthquake!"

Not an earthquake, an impact tremor.

"Igor, I need you in the lab," Deeds called.

"Really, Doctor Deeds, could you just call me Kev... *urk*!"

---

[52] Incidentally creating a new life form in the stew that would have - a millions generations in the future - found a new intergalactic empire... if it hadn't been for the fact that Deeds was bad at keeping his pets in their cages and the new thing was eaten by an escaped hamster.

Deeds watched his new intern writhe on the ground and marveled at the young man's self-control. When *he* walked into 50,000 volts of electricity, he wasn't nearly so circumspect in his choice of language.

The kid didn't even pee himself.

The kid might have The Stuff after all. It might even be worthwhile learning his name. Realizing that the gurgles had faded to inarticulate gasps and wheezes, Deeds released the Taser and removed the electrodes he'd shot into the lad's chest.

"Sorry, Kelvin, I can't have both of us getting captured." Deeds returned the Taser to his desk drawer and pocketed a ray gun and some traveling money. He stared down at his assistant for a moment. "Calvin? Nevermind. Igor, I need you to meet Howard Carter as scheduled and you can't do that if you are locked up with me in a prison cell."

Igor foamed at the mouth a little to show that he understood and then fainted.

The shaking stopped as Deeds crawled through the escape tunnel in complete darkness, whistling softly to himself and wishing he'd remembered to ask Igor to look up the whole 'Jig is up' thing.

***

Throughout history there have been places that seem to act like magnets, drawing together groups of people who will take everything that came before and change everything that comes after. Sometimes it's a nexus of knavery and sometimes it's an intersection of intellectuals. The greatest minds of a generation for good or ill are drawn to one another and in the rare cases when the greatest of the great and the worst of the worst are drawn to the same locale it's best to buy a ticket out of town.[53]

---

[53] When the attraction is great enough to draw mechanical intellects *and* time travelers such as the gathering under way in Sedville, Missouri, the minimum safe distance is generally agreed to be somewhere on the far side of the Pluto (even if it isn't a planet anymore).

In other parts of the galaxy, this phenomenon is known as Genius Geo-Location. On Earth it's known as *"Whoa, that was weird."* What is less understood even in the galaxy at large is how the tipping point is reached between gathering players and the onset of the game.

The scales are usually tipped not by an event, but by an unknown player entering the game. In our case, the scales tipped not by Old Suit issuing an arrest order, but by the arrival of the Carter family lawn mower.

Over the years, many cats and dogs that were either lost or left behind by a family moving across the vastness of the United States have turned up several months and a thousand miles later. Generally these animals don't like to comment on how they got from, say Ohio to Missouri, but it's an impressive feat for a small quadruped that doesn't know how to read a map or compass.[54]

For a robot, it's a fairly simple exercise of elementary mathematics.

$$Time = \frac{Distance}{Rate\ of\ Travel}$$

The lawn mower had been slowed somewhat by it's habit of stopping to mow cryptic and vaguely insulting messages into the lawns and meadows it passed along the way.

The lawnmower didn't know about WARD and wouldn't have known what to do with the information if it had. Its creator had only gifted it with as much intelligence as necessary to mow lawns, which meant it had an intellect vaguely equivalent to that of a well-trained golden retriever or perhaps a drunken poet.

---

[54] It has been postulated that there is a secret society of pet travel agents moving in the background of these events, but any effort to publish a paper on the subject has been suppressed by parties unknown.

Golden retrievers and drunken poets are many things, but they are not sneaky. Even the Deeds Paradox wouldn't help conceal a walking lawn mower tromping along a railroad siding as the tracks passed close to a raucous Irish biker bar on the outskirts of Sedville.

It was early morning, but the sounds of karaoke and harsh laughter still echoed from inside the ramshackle establishment. They were singing *It's Not Easy Being Green,* but the robot did not know that.

"Hello, robot."

The green robot clanked to a halt and swiveled it headlights to focus on the fuzzy pink piglike creature addressing it. The headlights blinked and it cocked its head at the strange creature. It did not fit within the parameters it had been given for PEOPLE.

The alien glanced at the black van trying to hide among the motorcycles in the parking lot. It didn't have a lot of time. The agents inside the van would eventually notice the strange metal creature in their midst.

"Can you take me to the person who built you?"

The robot took a step back and glanced around and a laser range-finder shot out of its head in every direction, mapping the location of the objects around it and charting several avenues of escape.

"You cannot speak can you?"

The robot shook its blocky head. The alien frowned at the metal creature. It had been studying human interactions on the television and wasn't certain whether it was supposed to break a lamp or coo comfortingly at the robot. Since it didn't have a lamp handy, it opted for cooing.

"Oh, you poor little thing," it said in what it hoped came across as a soothing tone. "I am not familiar enough with your manner of construction to repair you."

The robot took a step in the direction of one of its escape routes but paused when the alien did not make any motion to follow. Then something stepped into its laser map and it didn't need to run anymore.

"LEAVE THAT ROBOT ALONE, VARLET!"

Alien and robot turned as one to a strange figure standing atop the biker bar. A tiny triangular plastic hat was perched atop its dented copper head and half of it was alight with glittering twinkle lights.

"You are the Dread Pirate Robot."

"YOU HAVE HEARD OF ME?"

"Who has not?"

"I..." The metal man didn't know quite what to say. No one had ever heard of it before. It jumped to the ground to stand with its back to the blinking green shamrock and get a good look at the strange creature addressing it. "WHAT MANNER OF CREATURE ARE YOU?"

"I am a human being, of course."

"NO," the robot said. "YOU ARE A..." The robot was at a loss. It had never seen the Muppet Show and Howard was a bit old for Sesame Street, so he settled on "FUZZY. HUMANS ARE SQUISHY, YOU ARE FUZZY. WERE YOUR TATTOOS DRAWN WITH MAGIC MARKERS?"

The alien frowned down at the pictures on its arms. It did not know what a magic marker was but its arms looked like the ones it had seen on the television. None of its fellow patrons at the Song Rider had minded the cartoonish drawings, but they were mostly inebriated. It had noted that inebriated humans seemed more accepting of everything.

It had a working theory that this might be how the green frog creatures maintained control of the populace. The robot misinterpreted the strange pig creature's silence for anger.

"SOME OF MY DECORATIONS WERE ADDED WITH A PAINT PEN." It held up one interactor to catch the emerald glow. "IF YOU LOOK ON MY ARM, YOU CAN SEE THAT MY CREATOR MISSPELLED 'INTERACTOR' AT LEAST TWICE BEFORE HE GOT IT RIGHT. AT ONE POINT, I THINK HE WAS JUST DOODLING BECAUSE I HAVE NO IDEA WHAT THIS IS SUPPOSED TO SAY."

Together they frowned at the ornate pictograms running between the burnt-out bulbs on the robot's arm. The alien blinked and turned to glance at the silent lawn mower and then back to the Dread Pirate Robot. It ran through a mental list of responses it had learned from its study of American television. It settled on a response that had always garnered maximum praise on the shows it had enjoyed most.

"Eleven!" The alien said. It said it decisively. The two robots glanced at one another and back to the alien.

"BEG PARDON?"

"A. Apple. Aardvark. Appendectomy."

"ASININE," the robot muttered. "WHAT ARE YOU TALKING ABOUT?"

The alien tried again. There was more to this human language than it had initially thought. It had seen several movies where humans used mathematics as a language of peace. It dredged up the number that the humans spoke with the greatest portent and majesty.

"Forty-two!"

"L. LOONY BIN." The robot held its thumb and finger in an L-shape and held it to its forehead in the international gesture favored by those dealing with politicians and mad people. "I DO NOT KNOW WHAT SPACE SHIP LANDED YOU HERE, PIG MAN, BUT..."

"Yes! Space ship!" The alien shouted and hopped up and down, suddenly excited. "You got it! A space ship."

The men from WARD stumbled out of their van and blinked at the strange threesome in the middle of the parking lot. When they arrived, Wertsel had spotted them right off and sent out his prettiest waitress, Hilda, with some spiked drinks. If there's one thing Wertsal understood it was business and his business sense told him that you couldn't run a successful biker bar with a federal surveillance van posted in the parking lot.[55] They had spent most of the night dozing fitfully atop their keyboards, dreaming of a world untroubled by robots.

As a rule, shouting, bouncing pig creatures trump even a round of spiced rum and chloral hydrate.

The strange creature turned to face them and the four men were suddenly quite sober and wished they weren't. The two wearing blue jeans and tee shirts dove under the van while the two in suits fumbled pistols out of their shoulder holsters and tried to decide what to point them at. They settled briefly on pointing them at the techs who had been annoying them all night with their incessant snoring and then recalled themselves and pointed them at the two robots and the largish pig creature that looked like it might have been constructed of foam and felt.

The pig creature shifted and changed and was suddenly pointing rather a lot of gleaming silvery objects back at them while the two robots fled down the road at a dead run. Neither of the metal men looked back at the flashing lights and loud booms that followed them down the road.

***

Howard awoke in the cold and bleary light of morning, wondering what it was that had dragged him out of his ice cream dreams. He lay in the darkness, listening to his stomach rumble and wondered if his parents would ground him an extra day if they caught him raiding the fridge.

The whole house shook and Howard knew what had awakened him.

Somewhere deep in the core of his being, he knew that it wasn't an earthquake. Not James Skillion in his ridiculous red

---

[55] His best customers weren't *actually* criminals; they were mostly orthodontists and lawyers. You could buy a small house in the suburbs for what some of the bikes lined up in front of The Song Rider cost and they were the only ones who could afford to blow that much cash on a scooter. They liked to pretend they were on the lam and Wertsel did his best to support them. Like I said, he was a sharp business man.

bowtie, but large dour men in sunglasses and suits. He was in trouble and he was out of time.

Howard jumped out of bed and dug around in the darkness under the box spring before he came up with a shiny chrome ray gun. It was one of the first things he'd ever built, long before he'd ever envisioned pirate robots or time machines. It never occurred to him that he'd have to use it for more than plinking soup cans off a fence.[56] Considering what the fence usually looked like afterwards, he wasn't sure he *could* use it even if he needed to.

The house shook again and Howard heard a shout from his parents' room.

The tremor was followed by a pounding on the front door and the doorbell ringing over and over again. Howard grabbed his helmet and pushed his arms into his coat as another tremor threatened to knock him to the floor as he looked for his sneakers.

Howard ran to the landing over the front door and peeked out through the curtain. The nearest street light shone on the dull green surface of a bulbous metal... thing with glowing yellow eyes. Stubby wings protruded from it at odd angles and all around it, a spiderweb of cracks went out in every direction. It was a dropship. He'd seen them in enough video games to spot one.

It looked like the Space Marines from any video game or movie you cared to pick had just landed on their cul de sac. Large men -- at least he hoped they were men -- in dark armor and insectoid helmets were pouring out of one end of the thing. As he watched, one of them pointed at the streetlamp and with a flash, it went dark.

Howard reeled back from the window. He had never given much thought to the expression 'His heart was in his throat' but sure enough, he was having trouble breathing and he'd swear it was his heart trying to escape through his mouth that was

---

[56] And vaporizing the fence along with it. As it turns out, there's a knack to aiming ray guns and Howard didn't have it.

causing the problem. He crawled to the railing overlooking the front entry and gripped the stiles with both hands like a prisoner in his cell.

The door below shook again and Howard mouthed silent warnings as he watched his dad and mom shouldering into their bathrobes and shuffling into their slippers and reaching toward the door.

"No, don't!" Howard got the words out too late.

"What is the meaning of this?" Howard's dad demanded as he flung the door open. "What kind of prank are you pulling here? Decent people are asleep at this hour!"

No one could shout like Howard's father. He glared down at the man in the suit and around at the enormous men in their fancy armor and every one of them took an involuntary step backwards. The man in the suit looked abashed for a moment and even glanced at the fancy chronograph imbedded in the back of the nearest gauntlet rather than meet Mr. Carter's eye.

Watching and listening from the landing above, Howard felt pride and joy for the first time ever at the tone of his dad's voice. He almost felt sorry for the space marines and their handler.

One of the armored soldiers prodded him forward with the tip of his weapon and he gathered himself, straightening his tie.

"Is... Is this the Carter residence?" A manicured finger flipped a page in his notepad. "Home of Jonathan, Deloris, and Howard Carter, late of Ohio?"

"What of it?" Howard's father demanded. The man arched one eyebrow in a practiced manner obviously meant to quell the Carters's rebellious spirit, but it just made Howard's dad angry. "Is there something amusing to you about waking me up at all hours, son?"

"Um... no sir, I..." He stammered until he realized that the shaking shoulders of the armored men around him wasn't fear, but mirth. The soldiers were *laughing* at him. He squared his shoulders and shot his cuffs[57]. "I have an arrest warrant here."

"For who, there are no criminals here!"

"Whom. And perhaps you are right, but nonetheless, there is someone here with some robots to explain." He pushed Mr. Carter back to see the person behind him. "Mrs. Carter, I'm afraid you need to come with us."

"What?" Howard's parents spoke in one voice as the armored soldiers ducked through the door and reached out to grab her. Howard panicked. They were going to arrest his mom! He couldn't risk firing his ray gun in the tight confines of the foyer. He might hit his mom and dad. His mind raced, fighting for purchase in this strange reality where space marines showed up to arrest his parents in the dead of night.

"Mom!" Howard cried as he flung himself out into space and landed on the hard shoulder of one of the soldiers. The man staggered a little as his suit fought to compensate for the sudden boy on his shoulder. Howard pounded on the helmet with the butt of his ray gun, screaming inarticulately.

The soldier chuckled as he plucked the struggling boy from his shoulder and held him at arm's length by the scruff of his neck. Howard struggled and scratched at the armored gauntlet, but he might as well have been caught in the hand of a statue for all the good it did him.

"Well, look what I have here, Commander Keyes." The soldier shook Howard until the ray gun fell from his nerveless fingers.

"Quite the scrapper," another soldier chuckled, leaning in close. "You going to zap us with your little laser gun, kid?"

"That's a good way to get shot, kid," one of them muttered, a female.

"This isn't Star Wars, boy," the soldier holding him muttered, looking to the suit as Howard went limp. "What do you want me to do with the kid?"

---

[57] Which, incidentally, is a phrase that always troubled Deeds as well. He tried it once and almost lost a hand.

"Let him go," the suit ordered.

Howard landed on his feet and balled up both fists, ready to attack the man in the suit. No armor there... Howard's dad stopped him with a firm hand on the back of his neck.

"Relax, kid, we just have some questions for your mom," the man in the suit said. "We'll bring her back and no harm done."

"It's okay, Howard," his mom said. "I'll be back before you know it."

"If you would get dressed, Mrs. Carter, we can be on our way."

***

Deeds came out of the bushes and took a long look around. Several dropships had smashed cars and hedges in the neighborhood around his house, disgorging the most ludicrous assortment of mechanized infantry he'd seen since his last bit of channel surfing ended him on the Science Fiction Network.

Leave it to WARD to go to the trouble and expense of maintaining fleets of silent helicopters while next door, their engineers were cranking up the parabolic catapults to throw titanium dropships halfway across the continent.

Deeds snorted and turned the other direction. Let them search his home, they would find nothing. His Igor could continue the tutelage of Howard Carter as he waited in the wings for his plans to come full circle.

He was just at the distance where he felt safe with a good solid maniacal cackle that had been building all day when he almost ran into the soft and fuzzy chest of a strange pig-snouted creature with an impressive array of variable-phase disintegrator pistols aimed at him.

Deeds raised his hands and took a long step back, glancing around. There was never a marine in silly armor around when you needed one.

"Hello, earth scientist," the creature spoke. "I believe your jig might well be up."

"So I have come to suspect."

12. What Would Howard Do?

The sound of the ships crashing into her cul de sac brought young Ericka Platt out of a dead sleep. At first she wasn't sure she'd woken up at all. The silence in the wake of the crash was almost thick enough to touch as the back ends of the ships opened to allow small groups of large men to emerge. At first her sleep-addled mind thought she was witnessing an alien invasion, but then the first suit appeared.

The men in suits of armor spread out through her neighborhood without a word, the only sound she could hear as she raised the sash was the distant whirr of servos from their mechanized joints.

All she could think was *Howard was right*. Not that it did him a lot of good. She watched the suit gather up a few of the armored troopers and head toward her friends' front door, her mind racing for a plan. *What would Howard Do?*

Travel back in time, probably.

She was tempted to lie back down and pretend none of it ever happened. No space marines tromping around her neighborhood in impossibly cool suits of powered armor, no bulbous dropships embedded in the concrete in front of her house and no time-traveling troublemakers getting her detention.

Ericka rubbed at her eyes and face and slapped herself. The slap hurt. The space marines were still there. She could see Howard's parents standing in the rectangle of light that shone through their front door, talking to the man in the suit.

The large men surrounding Howard's door took a step back in the face of his dad's shout. Nothing compared to how angry her dad was going to be if she got herself involved.

She walked to her backpack and emptied it on her bed. At the bottom she found a wrinkled envelope. Howard's careful, blocky handwriting crossed the front of it: **OPEN ONLY IN CASE OF MEN IN SUITS!!!**

Howard had slipped it to her on in the hall and asked her to hold it for him, just in case. She fingered the envelope and glanced out the window at the scene below. Even watching him enter a time machine and disappear hadn't been enough to convince her he was for real or that someone was really after him. She had no idea why she'd gone along with the plot against Mr. Skillion; Howard was hard to say no to.

She'd shoved the envelope in her backpack and thought nothing more about it. As she ripped the envelope open, she discovered that all of her anger at him had evaporated.

Two twenty dollar bills and an index card fell out on the bed. Money and instructions.

Ericka felt one last twinge of temptation to just shove everything back into her backpack and get back into bed. Instead she dug out the for-emergencies-only cell phone her mom had given her and dialed Gary.

Her mom would be mad, but if this wasn't an emergency, she didn't know what qualified.

**

"Telephone for you sir."

Old Suit looked up from the report on his desk and glared at the young suit standing over him. The man paled and held out a cellular telephone.

"That is not a telephone, it's a..." he trailed off, unable to think of a description scathing enough to be appropriate for the office. Old Suit hated cellular phones. They were too light, too small and too prone to dial when his cheekbone hit the screen or keypad. [58] He preferred rotary dial phones, but most of the young bucks who worked for him had never seen one outside of their boss's office.

He took the thing between two fingers and held it up to his ear.

"Yes, what is it?"

"We are under attack!" Old Suit jerked the phone away from his ear and glared at it as an excited voice continued to babble from the tiny earhole.

"Shut up!" Old Suit barked into the phone and the excited babble fell silent. "Explain yourself!"

"Our van was destroyed and four men are dead, vaporized into nothing!" the voice sounded almost giddy. Was the man drunk? "It was an alien, sir! It was fuzzy and its skin was covered in strange runes and sigils and it vaporized the van! Woosh! Gone!"

Old Suit almost dropped the phone. He placed a gnarled hand flat on the desk and pressed the phone to his ear. He had been waiting his entire life for this call. *A real live alien?* He had to be careful. It might be a trick.

"Where are you?"

"A biker bar on the outskirts of Sedville."

"Secure the scene," he ordered. "Lock down the entire town! We have troops already on-site interviewing engineers and scientists. Make damn sure this isn't some trick being played by the person that built that robot of yours."

"It was with the robot! And another robot too!" the young suit chortled. "They were together when we found them!"

"Did you capture it?"

---

[58] In a cruel trick of nature, his cheekbone structure was, in fact, perfectly aligned to accidentally call a number in Brussels, Belgium that provided the sort of over-the-phone services that never failed to raise eyebrows when the phone bill arrived. Abraham Lincoln had the same problem but since he was born before the invention of the cellular telephone, was spared having to explain to Mary Todd why he was calling someone named 'Trixie' in the middle of the night on a weekday.

"It blew up the van and ran off!"

Old Suit growled and turned off the cell phone. He'd had enough exclamation points for one conversation anyway.

"Warm up the catapults -- we need more boots on the ground in Missouri," he ordered. "And get my plane ready, I'm going out there."

"Yes sir!" The young suit caught the phone as it hit him in the chest. "May I enquire as to what it happening?"

"No, but you can call the Security Council, the Home Secretary and the White House and tell them to crack the seal on their Magenta Books."

The young suit was silent as the old man stalked past him. The Magenta Book! If King Arthur himself rose from the grave and shook the young man's hand, he couldn't have been more surprised. He used his elbow to break the glass over a switch on the wall and yanked hard on the handle.

The switch had never been pulled before, but technicians oiled it daily so it didn't resist. It almost felt eager to be flipped at long last. For a moment, nothing happened as computers and secret satellites in orbit around the planet awoke and ran through their start-up routines. It took a full two minutes and twenty-seven seconds before the alarm klaxons began to wail in secret bases scattered around the globe.

***

"Did I make you?" Deeds took a step back from the strange creature and held up both hands.

"Did you make me do what?" The creature tried to frown, but it hadn't the knack for it yet.

"Did I create you in my lab? There have been so many abominations over the years I forget sometimes..." Deeds shrugged. "Because I don't have time for vengeance fights with past monsters right now -- if you want to schedule one, my social secretary is currently drooling on my basement floor. You'll have to go wake him up and buy him a cup of coffee. I think next Thursday is free..."

"No. I do not..." The alien stomped its foot and fought the urge to vaporize the earthling. This language they were speaking was not at all straight forward; everything seemed to mean more than one thing. It sighed and resorted to the old standby[59]. "I come in peace."

Deeds was silent for a moment as that sank in.

"I can't believe you just said that."

"Neither can I."

"You are an alien?" Deeds waited for the strange pig creature to nod. "Do all aliens look like rejects from the Muppet Show or just you?"

"It seemed like a good idea at the time."

Deeds glanced behind him. The last thing he needed right now was for the government to catch him mid-escape debating 70's television with an illegal alien.

"Well, it was nice to meet you, sorry about that whole 'demoting Pluto' thing, and I hope to see you again sometime." He smiled in what he hoped was a winning manner and tried to step around the creature, but the alien moved to cut off his escape. Deeds dropped the smile. "Seriously, Pluto was not my fault. If you want to discuss it with Neil Degrasse-Tyson, I'd happily give you his home address."

"I do not know what you are talking about."

"Then what do you want?"

"Howard Carter."

Deeds froze. He blinked. The creature was still there.

"Say again?"

"Howard Carter."

---

[59] Yes, cliché's are truly universal and universally avoided. Most space traveler's guidebooks stipulate that if one wants to avoid misrepresenting their culture it is best to learn the local clichés and avoid them at all cost. The same goes for local fast food restaurants, which has the additional benefit of ensuring one is not served spiced Garlackian Harnog disguised as Martian Sandbeetle. This is how interstellar wars are avoided.

"That's what I thought you said." Deeds reached oh-so-casually into his pocket and wrapped his hand around the handle of his variable-phase laser pistol. He wasn't sure what a laser would do to a creature of foam and felt, but he was ready to find out.

"Is this a time for hamburger?"

Deeds blinked again. It was like having an argument with his sister -- just as he began to get a handle of what they were arguing about the alien changed the subject.

"I just want to be clear before I accidentally try to vaporize you," Deeds pulled the pistol out of his pocket and pointed it at the pig creature in as non-threatening a manner as possible. "Are you suggesting that I might like to *become* a hamburger, or are you proposing that we go someplace with a more favorable ratio of mad scientists to space marines and get a couple of them to eat?"

The alien grimaced at the laser pistol and thought about it longer than Deeds was comfortable with. Finally, it spoke.

"The second one, I think."

"Excellent." Deeds pocketed the weapon and glanced back the way he'd come as he took the alien by the elbow and pulled it along down the sidewalk. "May I suggest a truckstop down by the highway? They're open late and they've probably seen stranger things than you anyway..."

***

The store clerk frowned at the two kids on the other side of the counter.

"Shouldn't you be at home in bed?"

"Our parents sent us out for supplies," Gary answered. "Didn't you feel the earthquake?"

"But... Funtime Pops?"

"Forty dollars worth, please," Ericka said. She laid the two twenties on the counter and waited for the man to do as she'd asked, fighting the urge to grab him and shake him. "And can you make it snappy? We're in a hurry."

13. Magenta Alert

Sitting on a shelf in an office in the deepest depths of the United Nations building in New York City, is an unregarded report bound in a leather that speaks simultaneously of its age and the poor taste of the binder. The leather is dyed the sort of violent magenta that puts one in mind of youthful experiments in how many pink pixie sticks and strawberry sodas ones stomach could hold.

Staffers whisper that the mysterious contents were so banal, so utterly obscured by the dense language of legalese and international diplomacy to a point that barely a glimpse of the unbound leaves drove the bookbinder and his apprentices mad.[60]

The report is an exact copy of one that resides on a utilitarian metal shelf in the Pentagon in Washington DC and another that sits on an ornate and priceless shelf in a vault deep underneath the Palace of Westminster[61]. Bootlegs and partial copies reside elsewhere, but only those three have the iconic cover.

This curious document is titled *Possible Scenarios for*

---

[60] In reality, it was only the calligrapher who wrote the report who went mad, mostly because his beautiful work was bound in the ugliest manner imaginable. It's said that his mad scrawling on the walls of his cell at the Bellevue Asylum in New York was so beautiful and eloquent that his cell became highly sought-after accommodations by the insane glitterati of the day until the building was burned to the ground by an inmate attempting to make a custard tart in their room.

[61] In an office used by Her Majesty's Secret Service, which was once used by a fellow named Guy Fawkes to store some spare gunpowder he had lying around. Of course, when parliament found out that he was using their storeroom rent-free, they had a hissy and his effigy is burned in public gatherings to this day... or something like that.

External Events of Planetary Concern. When this report was written by the still newly-formed Wartime Advanced Research Directorate for President Zachary Taylor, that was considered very clear and concise language.[62]

Unfortunately, President Taylor died of gastroenteritis before he could read the report, which gave it the air of a curse about it, lending to its mystique. At the time, relatively few people knew of the report's existence and among those who still do, very few know that it actually contains the contingency plans for an alien invasion.

It contains myriad other items of note to President Taylor as well, most of them ignored. For instance, on page thirty-seven, there is also the oldest known recipe for instant pistachio pudding, but rather like the stories on page two the day Japan bombed Pearl Harbor, President Taylor's dessert preferences get overshadowed by the alien stuff.

Of those who *do* know the contents of the report, few are willing to admit to it. The main reason for this is that despite the assurances of scientists, mathematicians and astronomers that extra-terrestrial life was not only likely but a mathematical certainty, the general public tends to view people who actually *believe* in aliens as tinfoil hat wearing wackos of the first order.

WARD worked hard to achieve that result.[63] Old Suit was occasionally miffed that his office was not blessed with a copy of *Possible Scenarios.* Not because he needed one, but because he liked ugly things. He knew the report's contents by heart. Every director since the report was bound had been required to memorize the report, especially page twelve, subsection

---

[62] In the modern parlance it might be titled *In Case of Alien Invasion, Break Glass.* In fact, it was once put forth that the thing should be put behind glass with just such a sign. Preferably tinted glass. Maybe a brick wall, actually, with a jackhammer kept handy just in case. But when consulted, scientists suggested that a book that color should not be trusted alone in the dark.

[63] Their most successful funding stream to date has been selling ad space in their many websites and magazines dedicated to "Unexplained Phenomena" and UFO's. And you would not believe how much they make on those tinfoil hats.

nineteen, paragraph two. *The onus of planetary defense falls to the stalwart men and true of the Wartime Advanced Research Directorate.*

He had looked up the word "Onus" on his first day. It meant 'An irritating responsibility'. He thought the writer was too pessimistic by far, but then in 1850, control of planetary defense might not have sounded as fun as it did in the 21st century.

The ache of arthritis slipped from him as he watched the tractors pull the dropships into launch position at the base of the ramp. The ground under his feet vibrated with the machinery preparing to fire the bulbous ships into the stratosphere on a carefully-calculated trajectory to land them in a small city half a continent away.

The parabolic catapult was by far his favorite secret invention in the WARD arsenal.

Old suit had just gotten off the phone with the president, who had not known that WARD even existed until the alarms had wailed and the magenta report had landed on his desk. It had been a satisfying phone call on a good, solid, plastic handset tethered to a base with a cord like a telephone was supposed to be. He was in charge. The planet was depending on him. Move forward carefully and keep the White House apprised at every turn.

Fat chance of that.

An executive order to that extent was making its way through the bureaucracy already, but he didn't wait. This moment had been long-prepared for and he wasn't about to let a mere elected official slow him down now.

The tech at the controls turned to look at him. It was time.

"Launch."

***

Howard pounded on the door and rang the bell, his head swiveling to and fro, half expecting to feel the armored hand of a soldier on his shoulder at any moment. The cracked and pockmarked pavement of the street in front of Mr. Deeds's house told him that the dropships and space marines had visited Deeds too.

He and his father had spent a tense and silent morning waiting for the phone to ring, for some word of where his mom had been taken or what they wanted from her. Howard sat with his hands wrapped around a warm mug of hot cocoa his father kept refilling every time he got up to make more coffee.

Guilt had kept him silent and drinking cocoa and he tried to figure out what to do. He had the time machine hidden in a safe place and if all went according to plan and his friends hadn't given up on him after their trip to detention, he'd have fuel rods waiting for him when he got there.

But it was no good traveling in time if he didn't know what to do when he got there. And for that, he needed to know what was happening and what exactly had drawn the attention of the men in the sunglasses and suits.

If it was just the robot, he could go back and stop himself from building it and all would be well. He would return to a timeline set to rights. But he had a feeling it was more than just an errant robot, and he had a sneaking suspicion that Deeds (or whatever his real name was) knew more than he was letting on.

Howard pounded on the door again, hard enough to rattle the whole house.

He looked around and wondered how hard it would be to break into the house.

A noise from inside stopped his pounding and the door popped open with a jerk. His erstwhile science tutor peered at him through the screen. The teenager leaned heavily on the doorframe and rubbed at his stubbly cheek.

"Howard?" Kevin blinked red eyes and stared at his watch for a moment as if he was trying to remember how to tell time. "It's really early, Howard, did we have a tutoring session this morning?"

"No." Howard jerked the door open and bulled past the teen, glancing around the room. He wasn't sure what he'd been expecting, but the worn rug and comfortable furniture wasn't it.

Bubbling alembics, bottles of mysterious fluids, jars holding unknown life forms floating in formaldehyde... not pictures of Deeds posing uncomfortably alongside grinning relatives.

He picked up a misshapen change dish from the table next to the door and upended it. It had Gary Parker's name scratched into the bottom. His handwriting hadn't gotten any neater in the years since he'd scrawled his name in the wet clay before it went into the kiln.

Suddenly the whole place began to look like a theater set.

"What's this?" He held up the dish.

"You're making a mess," Kevin bent down to pick up the fallen change and pocket lint. "His nephew made it... um... my cousin, Gary."

"And where does Gary live?"

"Cincinnati."

"No, my *friend* Gary made it in school," Howard pushed the bottom of the dish toward the older boy's face and pointed to the class number and date. " See here? That's Mr Mahaffey's third period art class. At *my* school. And I've been to Cincinnati, so don't try to lie to me."

"What do you want?"

"The truth."

"There's no such thing."

"Start with your name."

"Kevin Sorenson," the older teen mumbled. "The truth is that my master's so absentminded that he can't even remember my name. The truth is that there were soldiers here last night trying to arrest Doctor Deeds, soldiers that arrived in a frigging space ship! And the truth is that my master tazed me to keep me from escaping with him."

"They weren't space ships," Howard put the dish back on the table and walked into the living room, peering at the photos. "They were drop ships. Their only engines are the thrusters that slow them down enough to allow them to land; didn't you see the flat bed trailers that they had to bring in to get them out of here?"

"I don't know, I was probably being questioned at the time."

"What kind of questions did they ask?"

"Robots and strange energy signatures that they detected from whatever space station they call home. They kept asking about a time machine." Kevin glanced at the ceiling as if he could feel them watching him. "This is *so* not what I signed up for."

"What *did* you sign up for?"

"*Igor* work," Kevin threw his hands in the air. "Sweeping the lab, digging up specimens from the graves of newly-buried felons, kidnapping fair damsels. All I've done since I got here was clean the catbox and stalk you."

"You've been stalking me?"

"Deeds told me to."

"And who is Deeds?"

Kevin shut his mouth and shook his head. However dissatisfied he was with his job, he wasn't about to betray the man he called master. Howard growled in frustration and rubbed at his face with both hands. He was getting nowhere.

Then he spotted the picture.

All of the smaller pictures were ruler-straight, but the big one was crooked. He would've expected them all to be knocked cockeyed by the tremors caused by the dropships crashing into the planet, but they were all level except the big one.

"No, *wait*!" Howard grabbed the big portrait and yanked it off the wall before Kevin could stop him. There was an open panel behind it and a ladder descending into moist darkness.

"Bingo."

14. Signal-to-Noise Ratio

The trouble with television and radio signals is that they are -- for want of a better word -- noisy. Until very recently, television broadcasts went out in every direction at once trying to hit as many antennae and receiver dishes as possible. The stronger the signal, the further it goes and the longer it remains coherent along the way. Too far away and you get interference and the signal begins to degrade, torn apart by other signals, some of which are caused naturally by radioactive decay and some of which are the result of things that happened millions of years ago, many light years away from earth.

The technology required to send a carrier wave into space is so simple that humans were doing it accidentally for decades before it occurred to anyone that Someone Might Hear[64] at which point we began to do it on purpose. Sometimes we just did it because we could, or to demonstrate to the people who paid for a gigantic radio telescope that they got their money's worth, but most of the time we're just hoping there's someone out there somewhere, watching our stuff.

The human race is, overall, a race of exhibitionists.

Most of the time, we don't think about how our television

---

[64] Not that knowing has slowed us down any. Imagine walking up to the head of a large media conglomerate and asking them to stop sending signals out into space because there are bug-eyed monsters out there who might be listening in. You would get laughed out of the room. At best, they would instruct their ad people to start adding 50 billion bug-eyed monsters to their ratings number. And you don't want to see the advertising that would produce. Just don't go there.

shows present us as a species.[65] For instance, we do not live in a place where talking animals, monsters and other strange creatures walk among us unremarked, teaching our children important lessons about counting and eating tasty words that begin with "C". In point of fact, when monsters, talking animals and strange creatures from other planets try to teach our children valuable lessons, we have a tendency to scream, run and even (especially in the United States) *shoot* at the strange tattooed creature asking our kids about these "cookies" they've heard so much about.

It had been a vexing week for the alien visitor sitting across from Deeds at the truck stop.

"Do they have cookies here?"

"Probably, but you should try the pie,"[66] Deeds said. "Is that your natural form?"

"No." The alien plucked at the nubbly felt of its forearm and wrinkled its piggy nose. "We no longer come here in our natural form."

Deeds made a mental note of the hinted return engagement and filed it away too ask about later. There was something he wanted to know...

"Why a puppet?"

The creature stared at Deeds for a time and then looked away. Deeds had a feeling that if its felt cheeks could blush

---

[65] If all you knew about the human race was what you saw from our television broadcasts, your view of us would be dim indeed, or at least very very skewed. For instance, we are not -- as a rule -- as pretty as the people we allow to appear on our televisions, nor do we kill one another quite as often as our television counterparts. There are at least four or five people in the United States who haven't killed anyone and then gotten amnesia and relentlessly sought the mysterious killer.

[66] Having watched a lot of educational television preparing for this trip, the alien was familiar with the concept of mankind's grasp of the mathematical constant *pi*, but this reference to eating the ratio of a circle's circumference to its diameter was puzzling. The alien didn't say anything because it couldn't think of a joke that was funny enough not to wander into the realm of cliché. And besides, it was no crazier than anything else that humanity did.

properly, they would be rosy red right about then.

"Can you change into something less conspicuous?"

"I would need to expend an enormous amount of energy to do so, and at this point, I am not certain that it would do any good." The alien shrugged, the one human emotional cue it had mastered.[67] "I am already exposed to these men who are chasing you."

"The cat has escaped the sack?" Deeds frowned and thought about it. That wasn't quite right. "The cat's out of the bag? Yes, that's it."

"Why do I get the feeling you are as much an alien to your species as I am?"

"I don't know what you mean." Deeds shifted uncomfortably. "Hey, at least I use contractions."

"I do not..." The alien gave up and changed the subject. "I need to get to Howard Carter."

"Why?"

"Because he is your only hope."

"Our only hope of what?"

"Survival."

***

"You build robots for a living, Mrs. Carter?"

"No." Howard's mom grabbed her glass of water as the room shook again. Ever since they entered the weird space ship thing, it had been periodically tilting and shaking. She assumed that they were in flight, but to where, God only knew.

"It says here that you do." The man opposite her ignored the rumbles and shakes as he paged through a folder she couldn't see, presumably her dossier. "Works for Wellthorp Industries, robotics engineer."

---

[67] That and wiggling its ears, which it had discovered to have a delightful pacifying effect on crying children for the moment or two before their parents began shooting...

"Robotics engineers don't build robots, they design them," she snapped. "I haven't built a robot myself since I was in grad school. We have machinists and technicians doing that."

"I see." The man pulled a photograph out of the folder and slapped it on the table. "Tell me about this robot."

She set the glass down and leaned forward to look. It showed a strange figure that had been photographed walking across the street near a familiar corner of Dayton, Ohio. She peered at the thing's torso, which was apparently fashioned from an old-school industrial vacuum sweeper. She used to have a vacuum cleaner just like that one; it was a beastly, heavy old thing that she had lugged around until it finally gave up the ghost. And then, like all the household appliances that went south in her home, she had given the carcass to her son the tinkerer.

Howard. Oh God, they were after Howard!

Deloris Carter was an accomplished stoic. She had years of practice from forcing herself not to laugh even when something her precocious offspring had done was so wrong it had circled around to being hilarious again. It was her job to be outraged at such antics, even when she wanted to laugh and applaud his ingenuity...she was, in short, a mom. This practice served her well now as she froze her face before the man could pick up on any sign that she recognized the strange robot.

"What about it?"

"Do you recognize it?"

She glanced down at the photo. She recognized the old copper wastebasket that had gone missing from her husband's den. She recognized the battered old vacuum sweeper and even the assorted bits of brass lamps and washing machine parts that formed its arms and legs. If it was walking around, her son was even smarter than she'd thought, and that was saying something. *Oh Howard.*

She looked back up, her face bland.

"Nope."

"Then why did it follow you to Missouri all the way from Ohio?"

***

108

Howard stepped off the last rung of the ladder with Kevin's howl of protest still hanging in the air high above. He fumbled around in the darkness for a light switch and finally found one. With a buzz, the vast underground room flooded with light as rows of fluorescents flickered to life.

Other things were apparently keyed to the same switch. Across the room, sparkers ignited blue jets of flame under the copper base of a massive boiler. As he stood and watched, gauges and little pinwheel mechanisms sprang to life. Needles bounced from black to red and before he knew it the first chug of a piston moved a massive gear meshed with other, larger gears and ran noisily for a few moments before a whistle rattled the test tube racks and the whole massive contraption shut down. A little door under the gauges popped open.

Howard leaned down and saw a mug that looked like it was filled with foam.

"It's a cappuccino machine!" Howard laughed, enchanted by the tiny cup of coffee produced by the enormous machine. "He really is a mad scientist!"

"I prefer *mildly irked* scientist, actually."

Howard spun around, scanning the room for the source of the voice. Deeds was here?

"Doctor Deeds?" Howard called.

"Pay no attention to the man behind the curtain," said the voice. "Look in the corner."

Howard spotted the curtained alcove across the room at the end of one of the lab tables. A bright blue light was shining from underneath the curtain's hem as he approached. He took a deep breath and whipped the curtain back.

He was hit with a burst of warm air and the smell of hot plastic. The alcove was completely filled by a steel rack filled with every imaginable video game console, including some Howard had never heard of. Cell phones, laptops and computer towers were also embedded in the nest of wires and Howard could see Deeds' face on all of the screens.

"Where are you?"

"The main terminal is to your left." The voice emanated from all the many speakers at once, slightly out of sync. It was a strange effect and made Deeds sound like a robot. Howard turned and stepped deeper into the alcove to an old-fashioned cathode ray tube monitor. The old screen gave the doctor a greenish cast and Howard could see his parents' kitchen over a shoulder as well as some sort of large stuffed animal.

"Why are you at my house?"

"Same reason you are at mine, I suspect." Deeds looked annoyed. "Didn't my worthless assistant put up at least a little fight before allowing you into my secret lab?"

"He said 'No, wait, don't' or something, but I didn't listen." Howard shrugged. "Who are you?"

"I am Doctor Villainous Deeds, PhD." Deeds bowed, taking him momentarily out of frame. Howard could swear the stuffed animal sitting in the chair next to him blinked and moved, but Deeds was back before he could be sure. "I am, as you say, what is generally known as a mad scientist, though I generally prefer Doctor of the Apocryphal Sciences."

"Your mother named you 'Villainous'?"

"She never forgave me for ruining her figure."

"And what are the apocryphal sciences?"

"It means they originate from questionable sources -- you know, post-mortem biochemistry, mega robot engineering, that sort of thing," Deeds shrugged. "The mad sciences, if you want."

"How do I know you're for real?" Howard asked. "It takes more than a whiny lab assistant and a spiffy cappuccino machine to make a mad scientist."

"I have certificates from Arkham Tech, or you could just ask Igor to show you my flying cats on your way out," Deeds growled. "But we don't have time for my resume Howard, your mother has been arrested."

"I know that, I was there."

"Howard, we can get her back and then get you hidden if you come to me right now."

"No thank you, I have a plan."

"You can't time travel your way out of every problem, kid." Howard blinked. *How could Deeds know about the time machine?* Deeds held up a piece of paper. "Do you know what this is, Howard?"

"No."

"It's the test that feckless assistant of mine gave you that first day," he said. "You didn't just pass it, Howard, you scored higher than anyone ever has, including me."

"So what?"

"So, my people will hide you, heck, they'll fight for the privilege."

The mad scientist was so close to the camera that Howard took a long step backward as if Deeds was in the room, breathing in his face. He shook his head, the speech Deeds had given him about cities on mars echoing in his head.

"I don't want to be a villain," Howard turned and walked away, ignoring the calls and curses that the scientist shouted after him. He glanced at the clock on the wall. Out in the real world, the sun was rising over a world that had no idea that there was a struggle going on behind the scenes, between secret government armies and mad scientists.

He was done here. Deeds might know about the time machine, but if he thought it was still in the Carter's garage, he was sorely mistaken. Ericka would have been awakened by the crash of the drop ship in the cul de sac outside her window same as he had been. If she opened his envelope and did as he'd asked, he would have his mother and his world restored before dinner time.

It was time to find out who his friends were.

15. As Sparks Fly Up

Deeds dropped the Smartphone on the kitchen table and hung his head, still muttering curses. The boy's father and the alien visitor watched him, watched each other, and held their silences. The clock ticked and the mad scientist fumed, wracking his considerable brain for a plan. Any plan at all.

Finally it was the alien that spoke.

"If the boy goes back in time and changes things sufficiently to escape this fight, your species will not survive this solar cycle."

"Year," Deeds muttered. "We won't survive the year."

"Can you really help my wife?" This from Howard's father. "Can you get her back?" He wasn't worried about the boy, Deeds noted. The boy had demonstrated that he could take care of himself. *How chivalrous.*

The tear-streaked and pale face of Howard's father was resolute, the energy behind the eyes the product of caffeine and fear. So much had happened in the past twenty-four hours that when his son's science teacher had appeared on his doorstep with a giant puppet that he introduced as an alien, the man hadn't blinked. He'd offered them some of his cold coffee. Both of them passed.[68]

"Without the kid, my people won't help either one of you," he said. "And according to our friendly neighborhood alien

---

[68] The alien visitor was intrigued by the strange solution of brittle alkyds suspended in tepid water. Their rejuvenating effect on the human was obviously waning, but the creature suspected that if served hot, they would be just the thing to compliment a Plutonian scone it had saved from its last pit stop at a way station in the Kuiper Belt.

puppet here, we can't save our planet without him."

"What are you going to do?"

"Do you know where he went?"

Mr. Carter looked down at his cold cup of black sludge for a moment before he answered.

"He asked me to take something out to a church on the edge of town," he finally said. "It was something he said was a prop for a Sunday school skit that one of his friends asked him to help build."

"Was it a prop?"

"Howard builds things all the time, sometimes he does it for his friends ," Mr. Carter muttered. "When he has any, that is."

"What was it, Mr. Carter?"

"He doesn't think we pay attention to what he's up to, but we do." The man was no longer paying attention to Deeds; he almost seemed to be thinking aloud to himself. "I saw it during the move -- it was something he built, but not for Sunday school."

"Where is this church?" Deeds demanded. Something in his tone seemed to snap Howard's father back from whatever inner dimension he was exploring in the absence of his wife and child. He scowled at Deeds.

"Howard doesn't trust you, why should I?"

The alien sensed that the mad scientist was at the end of his rope and spoke before Deeds could lash out at the man out of frustration.

"Father Carter, your offspring will either save the world or he will not"

"He's just a little kid."

"He's just a kid who builds time machines in the garage after school!" Deeds snorted. The alien threw him an inscrutable look.

"In some cultures, he is both a man and a warrior."

"This is *not* one of those cultures!" Mr. Carter pounded his fist on the table, making the condiments jump.

Deeds stopped pacing and stared at the sign on the wall.

"Many people have eaten here & gone on to live perfectly normal lives."

"This sign was wishful thinking, wasn't it?" He pulled the sign down and tossed it on the table in front of the shell-shocked father. "Your lives have never been normal. I have Howard's records from school, I know that the sheriff suggested you leave town after one of his robots carved up every front lawn in town."

"So what?"

"So, if Howard *is* just a little boy in over his head, let me help him."

"Help him or take advantage of his genius for your own ends?"

Deeds grimaced. He was no good at these parent-teacher conferences. "At the moment, Mr. Carter, our ends are the same: keeping your family alive and Howard safe so that he can do whatever it is he needs to in order to fend off the attack of the fuzzy puppet people."

Mr. Carter's gaze was piercing for just a moment and then subsided back into sleep-deprived shock.

"I don't remember the name of the church, but it's south of town along M Highway," he said. "I'll write some directions for you."

"Big, old fashioned place with a steeple backed up against the woods with all the trails and things?" Deeds waited for Mr. Carter to nod. "I know the place." He clapped the man on the back and motioned for his felted friend to follow. On their way out the door, Deeds stopped and looked back at the man hunched alone over his cold coffee.

"If it's any consolation, I've never found normal to be all that perfect anyway."

***

When young Howard Carter identified the deployment vehicles that dropped WARD troops into his town as "drop

114

ships", he was in error.[69] Generally speaking, a drop ship is a re-entry vehicle that comes down from either a ship or space station. The vehicle Howard saw and the one in which his mother was being interviewed is a *jump*ship. Rather than descending from a fixed position in space, they are fired up a ramp that is of a length, angle and distance (with a little assistance from the rocket-propelled catapult) necessary to hurtle off the end and enter into a parabolic trajectory which has been calculated to send them into Low Earth Orbit and land them somewhere near their target.

Think of it as putting a brick on a skateboard and then sending it hurtling off the end of your nearest skate ramp. The skateboard would fall away and -- at least for a short period -- the brick would continue under its own momentum before crashing into the ground.

The brick analogy was used early on to describe the trip to the first troopers assigned to climb into one of them. They now refer to the jumpships as "Riding the Brick". As a result of that first flight[70] small retro rockets and minimal control surfaces were added. Which meant that unlike a brick, the jumpships could slow themselves down. A little. And they had some maneuverability. But not much. As the engineers at WARD explained it, if you load a bunch of people into a catapult and toss them in the general direction of Missouri, you're at the mercy of physics and should consider yourself lucky if what arrives does not resemble butterscotch pudding more than a battalion of space marines.

In short: they're great for getting a large number of troops into an area quickly and in a manner all but guaranteed to make

---

[69] You might want to cut him some slack, he was under a lot of stress and I doubt anyone could do much better under the circumstances.

[70] Plummet might be a better word. But only because English lacks a word for "Thrown screaming into orbit and then brought back to earth by gravity in what at the time resembled a poorly-shielded garbage scow." That's known as a 'lexical gap' but quite frankly, there's just only so much a language can do to keep up with the times.

anyone seeing it pee themselves.[71] They are not, however, quite so good at getting home quickly under their own power. The lurching that Mrs. Carter had been thinking were characteristics of flight in the strange craft was actually the jumpship being lifted onto a flatbed truck and driven down the highway under a tarpaulin marked with the logo of a famous circus company.

Howard was passed by the convoy of slow-moving trucks on his way out to the church on the outskirts of town. He had to get off his bike and wait for the circus to pass rather than get knocked off his bike by the wind of their passing.

He had no idea that his mother was inside one of the odd shapes beneath the canvas and no way of finding out. He barely glanced at them.

***

"Hey, look at this!" Gary stopped to look at the sign on the edge of the parking lot. Ericka braked and came to a halt next to him. They were both winded and huffing from the long bike ride out into the country. The Bible verse was from the book of Job.

"Yet man is born unto trouble, as surely as the sparks fly upward."

"Ain't that the truth?" Ericka said.

"Nerdfighters for the win," Gary wheezed. "Where do we find the machine?"

"The map says that there's a shed out back." She pulled the envelope out of her pocket and unfolded it to show Gary the map drawn on the inside of the envelope. "The time machine is buried under a pile of junk behind it."

"Then what?"

"Then we take it into the woods so we won't be disturbed and wait for Howard."

---

[71] Inside and outside the ship, actually. After some early electrical issues caused by this phenomenon, the space armor was equipped with moisture management systems.

"We seem to be doing a lot of that," Gary mumbled. Ericka nodded and didn't say anything. As bad as she'd gotten it for allowing Howard to draw her into his schemes, Gary had gotten it ten times worse. His parents were teachers in the same school system and they were mortified when they found out their kid had been involved in driving a substitute teacher into a nervous fit. It had taken a lot to draw Gary out of his house once he learned that it was to help Howard.

"Come on." She got off her bike and pushed it around the side of the small church. The gravel parking lot expanded into the trees quite a ways and at the back of the lot she could see the opening of the nature trail. Howard hadn't mentioned all of the "No Trespassing" signs posted everywhere.

They were going to get in trouble again, she just knew it. Gary echoed her concerns.

"I did not strap ten pounds of Funtime Pops to my bike and pedal all the way out here just to get arrested for trespassing."

"We're not trespassing," Ericka muttered. "At least not yet."

"Will these things even work if they aren't frozen?"

"I have no idea." Ericka dropped her kickstand and got off her bike to stretch. Everything was sore. Howard was going to have a lot to answer for when he showed up.

With Gary still muttering and complaining, they found the shed around back and the junk pile hiding a time machine behind. At the sight of the gleaming brass and snaking cables, Gary's complaints seemed to melt away. Whatever whim drove Howard to create the thing, it had been an artistic impulse that moved his hand in the design.[72]

They pushed the time machine along the edge of the forest toward the trailhead. When they got there, they found the Funtime Pops already piled against a tree and Howard waiting for them.

Seeing the storm building on Gary's face and the guarded

---

[72] If his mom hadn't already been in federal custody over her son's unlicensed use of the contraption, she would have been so very proud.

look in Ericka's eyes, he didn't give them a chance to speak.

"I'm sorry," he said. "I'm sorry for the detentions and the trouble and everything. I don't know if it makes anything better, but I'm sorry and I'm about to go back in time and do something that will keep any of it from happening."

"What about those?" Gary pointed at the No Trespassing sign just over Howard's shoulder. Howard barely glanced at it.

"Those are hopefully going to guarantee that some random civilian won't stumble upon us before we can calibrate the machine," Howard said. Ericka and Gary both frowned and nodded reluctantly.

"It didn't take very long last time," Ericka said.

"I'm going back a lot farther than I did last time," Howard explained. "And I'm taking you with me if you want to go."

16. This Must Be the Place

"I can't eat that." Howard's mother pushed the sack of hamburgers away with the tip of a finger. The cramped space smelled strongly of beef and ketchup as the soldiers, now shed of their armor, swapped sandwiches and stole one another's French fries.

The young suit glared at Howard's mom until he remembered that she had more practice at the Withering Stare than he did. His features spasmed for a moment searching for an appropriate Man From the Government look before they eventually gave up and settled for bland disinterest.

"What's wrong with it?"

"I'm vegan."

"So eat the cheese."

"Vegans don't eat cheese, you idiot," she said. "And everything in that bag is soaked in fat."

"So what are you going to eat then?"

"I'm your prisoner, so I would say that's your problem." She crossed her arms and leaned back. She wasn't a vegan or even a vegetarian, but she wanted to see how far his orders went to keep her happy and quiet. Even more she wanted to know if *he* was entirely certain how far they went.

The young suit fumed and fretted for a few minutes while the craft tilted and rumbled and his hamburger grew cold. Finally, he walked to the bulkhead and keyed the intercom.

"We need to make another stop."

"Where to?"

"A grocery store -- our guest is vegan."

"Where's she from?"

"She's vegan, she can't eat hamburgers."

"You gotta be..." the rest was thankfully lost in a burst of static as the suit took his finger off the button. He tried not to notice that across the compartment, his men were snickering at him. He stood over his cold hamburger and eyed the woman, trying to find something, anything, that would allow him to get the better of her.

He swept the cold burger and fries back into the sack and tossed both into the bin. They were terrible once they grew cold and he wasn't about to suffer through the indignity of cold French fries in front of his prisoner.

"So, you're going to land your space ship in front of a Kroger and go in to buy me a salad?" she asked. "That's subtle."

He pretended she hadn't said anything.

"Tell me about the robots you build."

"Design," she corrected.

"Fine, tell me about the robots that you *design*."

"They bend sheet metal to make tool boxes."

"How are they powered?"

"We plug them into a wall like a washing machine or a television set," she said. "Some of them use compressed air."

"They don't look like other industrial robots I've seen." He held up a photo of one of her machines. "They look like something out of Jules Verne."

"I believe that we've lost some important aspects of our culture in our race to make everything look the same as everything else," she said. "I wrote my master's thesis on the subject."[73]

"It says here that your thesis was considered controversial."

"If your thesis isn't controversial, you might as well not be

---

[73] Originally titled "Why Do Our Industrial Machines Have To Look Like They Were Designed By Aesthetically-Challenged Children & What We Should Do About It" but they asked her to change it to "Problems In Industrial Robot Design". Thesis advisors have no sense for the dramatic.

there." She glanced up at his hairline. "After all, what's the point if you can't flip some toupees? The stodgy old coots that run the planet need a bit of shaking up now and then."

He realized his hand was going to his scalp and dropped it. That jerk at the store had promised him no one would notice.

"Some of your robots look like they'd get up and walk around."

"Engineering and architecture students come in from all over to view my machines."

"Can they walk around?"

"Engineering students?" She arched an eyebrow. "Most of them, but there are a few who you have to wonder how they even get out of the dorm some days..."

"The robots."

"Of course not."

"And yet here's this robot that showed up in Ohio while you lived there and again in Sedville after you moved." He slapped the photo down on the table. She didn't even glance at it. "A robot that uses a very unusual power source; a robot that has been designed and decorated very similarly to the ones you use to build tool boxes."

"So?"

"So, I think you built it."

"Oh please," she scoffed, pushing the photo away. "That thing looks like it was built by an eight year old."

Mistake.

She froze her expression, praying that he had missed the cue. Slowly she turned to meet his gaze and her spirits sank at the smile creeping across his face as he flipped through the file and stopped. She could see Howard's school photo paperclipped to the corner of a page and her heart felt like it slipped into her stomach.

"You have a son, don't you, Mrs. Carter?" He leaned back and folded his hands across his stomach. "I seem to recall him biting one of my marines."[74]

"Howard."

"And how smart is Howard, Mrs. Carter?"

She was silent for a moment as her mind raced. The young suit closed the file and walked to the intercom on the bulkhead. "Turn around. We need to go back for the kid."

"What kid?"

"The one that built the robot."

He turned and found Mrs. Carter inches from him. She grabbed his tie in her fist and yanked him down to her level, drawing the knot so close to his throat that he could no longer breathe, just listen as she leaned in so close that all her could hear was her whisper.

"If you touch one hair on my son's head, I *will* build an army of those things," she hissed, "and by God I *will* come and get him." [75]

***

"This must be the place," Gary sighed. He dropped his box of Funtime Pops on the ground on the trail next to an enormous rock under the trees beside the trail. His face was red as he sank down to sit on his box. This day was offering up more exercise than he usually got in a week, but he looked like he was having the time of his life.

"I think Sunshine Rock's bigger than that," Howard

---

[74] In point of fact, he did *not* try to bite the marine. That was beneath his dignity. He tried to zap him with a ray gun that failed to fire and left a bite-like mark on the man's arm instead. Turned out later that Howard had forgotten to recharge it the night before, which just goes to show that genius has its limits.

[75] In situations like this, people tend to say things like "Hell hath no fury like a mother bear whose cub is threatened." Extending that metaphor, Deloris Carter was a mother bear with a slide rule and a master's degree in using it to build giant machines capable of folding Sherman Tanks into handy storage containers. Now if *that* image doesn't keep you up nights, nothing will...

chuckled. "And probably sunnier."

"So, how did you find out about this place?" Ericka huffed as she pushed the heavy time machine over another tree root. "Didn't you just move to town?"

Howard shifted his box of pops to the other shoulder and reached out to steady the contraption with his free hand.

"I overheard some of the older kids talking about it," he said. "I think they come out here to neck in the woods."

Ericka snatched her hand back from where it had just brushed his. They both found other things to look at. Their fingers had grown cold in the late autumn air and dry from handling the mostly brass machine and the two large cardboard boxes they had been maneuvering through the woods.

"Why do we have to come this far out into the boonies to do this?" Gary complained for the thirtieth time that hour.

"It will take time for the machine to reach operational temperature," Howard explained again. "Also, the math for what we're about to do is tricky, I'll need time to work it out or we could be up to a year off either way."

"I can't believe you do math for fun," huffed Gary as he got up and lifted his box again.

"I can't believe you don't," Howard shot back.

"Weirdo."

"Stick figure."

They walked as they bantered, moving forward by will alone as the machine hung up on every branch, stone and tree root.[76] When the older kids had talked about Sunshine Rock, it hadn't sounded so far from the parking lot to the rock itself. His plan hinged on using the rock as a landmark, since it wasn't likely to

---

[76] It hadn't been designed for off-roading, which Howard made note of for future redesigns. Forget building a time machine into a sports car, by the second mile of trail, Howard was ready to build his next one into a monster truck.

change no matter how far he traveled in time.[77]

They arrived suddenly. One moment they were deep in the trees, sweating and grunting under the weight of their burdens and the next moment, they were out of the forest and looking out along a trail that hugged the face of a steep bluff toward an enormous pale outcropping of stone jutting out over the shifting waters of the creek below.[78] The sun had broken through the clouds and the white limestone seemed to shine with its own light to the point that they had to squint to look at it.

"Wow." None of them was sure who said it; maybe they all did. It was Howard that found his voice first, echoing all of their thoughts.

"Sunshine Rock is well named," Howard whispered. Ericka and Gary nodded. "C'mon, guys, one last push and we're there."

***

The alien disengaged its safety harness and stepped out of the vehicle to look around. A small white building of obvious religious significance to the locals was centered in a large field of tiny white stones. It was very pretty. A sign nearby advised humans that their race was prone to trouble. The alien thought it uncommonly good advice.

It turned to find the scientist leaning against his vehicle,

---

[77] What Howard had failed to mention to his friends is that one of the many problems with a machine that travels in both space and time is finding fixed points of navigation for its instruments to key off of. Major geological formations work best because they change very little even over the course of thousands of years -- assuming your time machine was stout enough to make such a trip, which his machine was not. Of course, time is fickle and nothing's really permanent in the face of a construction crew's determination to light a stick of dynamite...

[78] Funny thing about the people of Missouri... The state is split in two by the broad expanse of the Missouri River and bordered on the east by the Mississippi and the two massive rivers converge near Saint Louis. Which means that the 'creek' that Howard and his friends are looking down upon would be a river in Colorado but only just qualified as a creek for the jaded river folk of the Show Me State. Anything less than half mile across is just a drainage ditch.

staring into the bottom of a small and apparently empty plastic container. It had a label, but the alien couldn't read it from where it stood.

"Is there a problem, Doctor Deeds?"

"It's just..." The mad scientist trailed off and shook his head. He capped the bottle and tossed it back into the vehicle. "Just remind me to stop at the pharmacy later."

"I do not know that word."

"It's a place where we sell chemicals," Deeds said. The scientist's face had a strange cast, and his eyes seemed a bit unfocused as he walked past the alien, barely glancing at the salubrious advice featured on the sign. The alien frowned at his back for a moment before it followed him up the steps of the church and into the cool darkness of the sanctuary.

A man looked up from polishing a wooden pew as they walked in. He frowned past Deeds at the strange figure following him and seemed to decide to ignore the strange tattooed creature.

"May I help you... um... gentlemen?"

"I'm looking for a couple of kids that were last seen headed this way."

"There aren't any kids here, but there are some trails out back." The man hooked a thumb over his shoulder. "We put up signs, but it never seems to stop them."

"Where do the trails go?" Deeds asked.

"Sunshine Rock. It's beautiful, but it's very steep and we just can't afford to be sued if some kid falls and hurts themselves," he explained. "I swear, kids get up to all sorts of nonsense out there."

Deeds frowned and tried to picture the bookish Howard Carter and his friends on a trail that's described as 'steep'. Could the boy's time machine be light enough to carry all that way? He shook his head to clear the fog.

"We must go," the alien whispered in his ear. "The boy must not be allowed to escape into another era." Deeds spun around and was surprised to discover the felt puppet figure was still back by the door. He could have sworn... He blinked and made another mental note to fill his prescription *before* the end of the world next time.

"Thanks," Deeds mumbled and turned to go. He grabbed the alien by the shoulder before it could say anything and frogmarched it back down the aisle.[79]

***

There is a myth -- reinforced by centuries of books, movies and internet rumors -- that the sciences and the arts exist in separate and distinct camps and that anyone who does both is a rare bird indeed. Never mind that music is a mathematical expression, sculpture is practically an engineering discipline and both painting and ceramics are more than half chemistry (or physics, depending on how you apply your paint).

This perception can be both a blessing and a curse. It's a curse when an artist is trying to get the respect of the scientific community or a scientist the art community, but a blessing when space marines land in your front yard to arrest your wife and overlook you because you are 'just a painter'.

Howard Carter's father sat in silence for a long time after Deeds and his alien counterpart left, staring into the depths of his coffee mug. The mug had long grown cold before his curious visitors had arrived, but what the mad scientist had taken for shock was actually contemplation. If Deeds had taken a moment to look at the paintings on the wall, he might have realized they were in fact painted by one of the world's leading mathematical minds. Inspired by the fractal studies of Benoit Mandelbrot, Carter had pursued the infinite geometric possibilities down the rabbit hole and almost accidentally carved out a niche for himself as a professional artist.

It was often said that staring at an original Carter oil painting could give the viewer a sense of vertigo, as if they were

---

[79] "Frogmarch" is a strange term to be sure and yet more evidence for the alien that secretly, the frogs were in charge of the place. And for all I know, he may be right...

teetering on the edge of eternity, staring into the infinite reaches of the multiverse. Which they were, in a mathematical sense.

Mr. Carter walked into his study and removed an armload of books and awards from the shelf to reveal the keypad of a safe missed by the soldiers in their cursory search of the premises. The ten-digit code returned a pile of papers and something that looked like a cordless telephone handset . He carried his treasures over to lay them on the desk between his sketchbooks and his Fields medal. Carter glanced down at the stainless steel waste basket next to the desk.

The words he'd spoken to the mad scientist echoed back to him. Howard always assumed his parents didn't know what he was up to.

Silly boy.

Once upon a time, he'd had a copper wastebasket where the stainless steel one now stood. His son had swiped it back in Ohio and worked into one of his projects. Carter suspected that he knew what that project was and thought it was high time he got it back.

Or at least got reimbursed.

He sat for a moment, picturing the algorithms in his head and made a few last-minute adjustments before he began punching numbers into the keypad. His mind formulated contingencies as he listened patiently to the rings until a voice answered. Carter continued pushing buttons at random until the robotic voice was replaced by a testy human one that asked what he wanted.

"Operator, I need your assistance to place a person-to-person call to a robot's brain."[80]

---

[80] You only think it's impossible because you've never tried it.

17. Time & Space

They set up the machine in a small depression in the shadow of the huge rock outcropping. Out of the sun, the time machine looked more like an enormous brass picture frame mounted on a rolling base and festooned with wires and knobs.

"Will this even work with melted pops?" Gary asked. He and Ericka had stacked rocks under the base and pulled out the last of the stops to open the fuel chamber, revealing the gleaming rows of glass tubes where they'd inserted the frozen Funtime Pops last time they'd helped Howard travel in time. "What do we do, pour them down the tube?"

"No, they have to be frozen or it'll overheat," Howard said. They turned to find him rummaging through his backpack. "You might want to stand back."

Ericka and Gary backpedaled out of the way as Howard stood up with what looked like a red plastic squirtgun with copper tubing coiled around the barrel.

"Please tell me that's a freeze ray," Gary whispered. Howard nodded and flashed a toothy grin. "Can I do it?"

Ericka and Howard moved well back as Gary took hold of the freeze ray. The red plastic pistol looked innocent enough in his hands, but the tip began to glow a cold blue as he aimed it at the stacked boxes of melted ice pops.

"Just be careful," Howard called. "A short burst should do it, about thirty seconds."

"Okay." Gary breathed out and pulled the trigger. A strong scent of ammonia filled the little dell as the pistol grew cold in Gary's hand. It smelled like someone was cleaning windows, but nothing else happened. "Um, I don't think it..."

"Just give it a sec," Howard said. Sure enough, a few moments after he pulled the trigger, the barrel frosted over and a stream of blue fluid shot out of the barrel and hit the top box, pouring down over the one below in a cascade of ammonia-scented ice. The temperature in the near vicinity quickly dropped several degrees as the mysterious blue fluid seemed to suck the heat out of the air.

"That should do it," Howard finally said and Gary released the trigger and returned the pistol to his friend.

"That was epic!" Gary sounded like he was barely restraining the urge to howl and dance around the frozen boxes. "Oh my God, that was so cool!"

"Yeah, literally," Ericka snorted. Gary scowled at her for raining on his cliché as Howard used a rock to knock the icicles off the boxes. When he finally pulled back the flaps, it revealed stacks of perfectly-frozen Funtime Pops.

"Remind me to call you for our family's next cookout!" Gary enthused. "Dad's always complaining about the cost of buying ice."

"Help me break them up and get them into the machine, it's almost noon." Gary and Ericka didn't ask Howard why he cared what time it was if he was going back in time anyway. It was too late to turn back; they had to trust him to know what he was doing.

***

Howard's mother sat in sullen silence in the corner of the jump ship, mentally designing a machine that would get her out of the handcuffs and help her overcome a troop of burly space marines and their twiggy chaperone. She didn't have any of the tools or parts she'd need to build the machine she envisioned, but that was a worry for later.

One thing at a time.

First I design, then I build, then I escape and rescue Howard.

Assuming he even needed her help.

Mrs. Carter had no illusions about her son. At the age of six, he had designed his first computer program utilizing a predictive algorithm to find a hidden cookie jar. It didn't take a genius (or even two of them) to realize that this would be a child in need of a special parenting plan.

It did, however, require an excellent dental plan -- the boy loved his sweets.[81]

Howard's parents hadn't put much stock in parenting advice or guidebooks even before Howard was born. Once Howard came along and began to display his gifts, advice and opinions began raining down upon them from all quarters. Everyone had thoughts to share and felt almost driven to share them.

Opinions, Mr. Carter had become fond of saying, *are like underwear: you should have a complete set, keep them clean and in good order, and for heaven's sake never show them anyone.*

As a result, they shielded him from the advice of those who thought they knew how best to "maximize his potential" and allowed him to find his own way... more or less.[82] This sort of thing didn't work with some children, but Howard wasn't a normal kid. His gifts and natural bent turned out to be a reflection of both his parents and neither of them, which nicely rounded out the family, she thought.

What on earth had the boy been thinking?

She would bet her eye teeth that the robot had been intended to help him clean his room.

Mrs. Carter looked up at the approach of the young suit, who stopped well clear of her reach. He looked smug, despite the red skin she could see peeking up around his collar where she'd tried to throttle him. He adjusted his toupee and squared his shoulders before he spoke.

---

[81] When he was eight, his father made him swear to use his brainpower only for good and never for evil. The young Howard hesitated and made his oath contingent upon snickerdoodles not being evil.

[82] There's only so much of that sort of thing a mother's nerves could take.

"We've received orders to participate in the capture of your son and the mad scientist."

"What mad scientist?"

"A guy named Deeds," he said.

"That figures."

"We'll be turning around at the next exit, so you might want to hang onto something."

"Exit?" She played back the brief glimpse she'd had of the craft from the outside as she was trooped across the front yard surrounded by a cordon of armored space marines. Barring some advance in engine design and aeronautical engineering that she was unaware of, the thing could never fly. Which meant they weren't in the air, they were on the highway.

Of course.

She could eliminate building a parachute or hang glider from her escape plan.

"I still haven't eaten anything," she said. "Do you at least have a candy bar or something?"

"You can eat a candy bar but not a hamburger?"

"Unless your candy bars come with meat in them I can." She smiled as he went to find her a candy bar.

Idiot. He's never going to see this one coming...

***

The Dread Pirate Robot fretted and shifted its weight from one interactor to the other and back. It wasn't entirely sure what it was doing, clinging to the suspension cables of a bridge as traffic rumbled past far below. His laser rangefinder told him he was twenty-seven feet over the asphalt, which was as close as the robots could get to the traffic without getting knocked into by one of the tractor trailers whizzing past.

It was not accustomed to getting orders any more than it was accustomed to following them, so when a dormant part of its brain began ringing it hadn't thought twice about picking up. The peevish voice of an operator and the unmistakable whistle and click of a new subroutine downloading over the line followed and before they knew it, both of them were dangling from a bridge. They were watching over a cellular connection to the internet as the traffic cameras leading up to the bridge went dark one by one, heralding the approach of the convoy.

No one took a picture of a WARD convoy. They were the only government agency in history whose photo didn't eventually end up on the internet unless they darn well wanted it to.[83]

No sooner did the camera overlooking the last exit ramp before the bridge blink out than the robots saw the trucks rounding the bend and heading toward them.

The Dread Pirate Robot sternly told its fingers not to let go. It didn't have time for a daring rescue; they had an important appointment in Denver and were going to be late. Places to go... Doctor... Dentist... Coupon for a free oil change...

Its hands, head and feet politely refused his orders and the robot watched helplessly as the giant trucks with the circus logos and fluttering flags roared toward them. A bell rang in the wastebasket dome of its head and the lawnmower next to it let go.

The Dread Pirate Robot resisted the impulse for all of three-tenths of a second.

Small victory, it thought as it began to plummet toward the tarpaulin stretched over the back of the speeding truck.

***

"Status updates?" Old Suit barked as he stepped off the plane at the small airport outside of Sedville. The techs and suits

---

[83] As strategies go, blacking out the cameras ahead of your secret convoy was a clever ploy if what you were worried about someone snapping a picture. But even with decoy convoys going by alternate routes, it made it easy for Howard's father to pinpoint their location as well as direction and rate of travel so that he could maneuver his agents into place ahead of them. That the computer program he used for this was originally designed to find cookie jars just made it all the more delicious.

surrounding him consulted notes, cell phones and an astrology chart before answering.

"We're up," said one.

"Your chopper is standing by at the terminal," said another.

"It's a good day for Cancers and Libras, Gemini is having a bad one and Leos should just stay in bed," reported another.

"Someone smack him in the head."

"Ow!"

Old Suit let them chatter, his mind elsewhere as they crossed the airfield toward the small building which could only charitably be referred to as an airport terminal. He stole a cup of coffee from a pot meant for pilots, silently daring anyone to say anything, and passed through to the other side where three black helicopters sat warming up.

"Do you have the target pinpointed?" he asked. "I don't want any mistakes this time."

"The energy signature has moved twenty yards to the southeast and is holding steady at that position," a female tech reported. "With the winds out of the North, we should be able to make good time."

"Excellent!" Old Suit stepped up into the back of the helicopter and was about to signal for the pilot to take off when the door of the terminal burst open and another tech came running toward them.

"Sir!" the tech stopped and wheezed, his hands on his knees as he fought for breath. "The... the convoy called... Agent Aldritch was... questioning the woman and it turns out it's not her... it's not her, it's her kid."

"Kid?" Old suit grabbed the tech and hauled him upright. "*What* kid?"

Skillion leaned out of the helicopter and smiled. "I told you about that kid."

Old Suit glared around at all of them, but saved his steeliest look for the scientist. He was in no mood to tolerate a round of smug scientific I Told You So's.

"Get me to Sunshine Rock!"

***

"Howard!" Deeds shouted as he stepped into the clearing. "Howard, stop this before it's too late!"

The three friends spun around to face the mad scientist and the giant pig thing coming toward them out of the forest. Howard raised the squirt gun freeze ray and backed up a step, glancing at the gauges on the control panel of the time machine out of the corner of his eye.

Still climbing.

"Howard, if you do this, you'll destroy everything!" Deeds called.

"Don't listen to him," Howard shouted over the growing roar of the time vortex. "He's a mad scientist."

"A mad scientist?" Gary's voice sounded like he was fighting the urge to follow that with 'Cool!' "How do you know?"

"He made a bunch of winged cats, his assistant showed me," Howard took aim with the pistol and wondered if he'd have the will to use it. He had no idea what it would do to a person and didn't' want to find out.

"Hey, those cats *wanted* wings," Deeds said. "Have you ever tried to catch a bird? I did them a favor."

"Don't listen!" Howard repeated. "I've been in his lab, he's evil."

"Whoa, now, let's be careful how that word gets thrown around." Deeds stopped and held up his hands as the kids backed away from him toward the spinning time device. "I always recycle, I drive an electric car and I only buy mermaid-free tuna, how could I possibly be evil?"

The kids were silent for a long moment.

"There's no such thing as mermaids," Ericka finally said.

"Sure there are, they get caught in the tuna nets all the time."

"You mean dolphins." Ericka crossed her arms.

"Fine, don't believe me," Deeds dropped his hands. "But when the zombie mermaid apocalypse wipes out you and all your tuna-salad munching kin, don't come crying to me."[84]

"Just when you thought it was safe to go back in the water," Gary muttered. "Sheeze, he *is* mad."

"As a whole tea party full of hatters," agreed the alien. Deeds spun to stick his finger in the felt pig's nose.

"Don't *you* go mastering idioms, puppet, *I* have to live here!" He seemed to realize what he'd just said and slowly retracted his finger. He clenched both hands into fists and turned back to the kids. "I'm telling you, kid, if you go back in time, humankind is doomed!"

"We're going." Howard gestured with the freeze ray. "Don't try to follow us."

"Howard! If you get in that time machine, we're all dead!" Deeds shouted, eyeing the pistol. "Your mom, your dad, the winged cats, this weird puppet thing, all your friends, we're all goners!"

"You're the mad scientist, do something about it."

"That's not my job, kid, it's yours."

"Howard Carter, you must listen to your science instructor," the alien said. "He may be crazy, but he is correct. There are aliens coming, *other* aliens who do not appreciate the subtleties of earth culture, aliens who will destroy your world."

"I don't even know who or what you are, but if you come one step closer, I will shoot," Howard warned, trying to keep his hand steady. "I *will*!" He glanced at the gauges out of the corner of his eye.

Almost there.

"Do not do this -- do not doom your world."

"What if he's telling the truth, Howard?" Ericka whispered.

"He's not."

"But what if he is?" Gary asked. "What if traveling back to fix whatever it is really will kill everyone?"

"They have my mom," Howard said. "I'm going, with or

---

[84] They'll never see *that* one coming.

without you."

"Don't make me stop you kid," Deeds growled. "You tumble with a mad scientist you could wake up with a bad case of Igors."[85]

"He just wants the time machine!" Howard shouted. "Don't listen to him!"

Deeds howled as their end of the wormhole snapped into place in the fourth dimension of the frame, displaying the whirling eddies of space and time snaking away into the past. Howard and his friends donned their bike helmets and safety goggles and ran for the time machine with the mad scientist and the alien hard on their heels.

They didn't see the tall, stately woman with the scar across her cheek step out of the forest and aim her rifle in their direction.

---

[85] Proving that Deeds does have a grasp of the idioms of his own people, if not the more familiar phrases of the common folk.

18. Mandatory Safety Equipment

Howard's mother knew something about candy bars and nutrition that the men who had captured her did not. It is, in fact, something the rest of western civilization seems largely unaware of -- that the caloric value of food is not meant to express how fat it's going to make you. It is an indication of how much potential energy is locked in a foodstuff's cellular structure, which your body will slowly release or store as your activity level and metabolism sees fit.

Calories don't make you fat, what you do (or don't do) with them makes you fat. If you release them quickly, they're as dangerous as any explosive.

What did you think she was planning to do with that candy bar, eat it?

Perish the thought.

A calorie is the amount of energy necessary to raise the temperature of one gram of water by one degree Celsius. With the thousands of calories pent up in the cellular structure of a candy bar you could theoretically heat up a great deal of water. But hot water wouldn't get you out of hot water, unless you can release all that energy at once, preferably in a helpful direction.[86]

Shortly after the men gave Mrs. Carter the candy bar, she asked, oh so very politely, if she could get up and walk around to "stretch her legs". Confident that she could not escape from a

---

[86] Assuming you can do so without blowing yourself up during the conversion process from a concoction of chocolate, nuts and nougat to rocket fuel, that is. Though it must be said that it made Mrs. Carter a bit nervous since she had no idea what nougat is, nor had she ever met anyone who could tell her with any certainty.

locked space capsule strapped to the back of a speeding truck and that they could overpower her if she tried, they let her.

The jump ship, she discovered to her delight, was equipped with a full surgical suite in a compartment at the back. When you don't have a chemistry lab handy, a surgical suite is the next best thing.

With the help of some necessary ingredients pilfered from the surgeon's kit[87], Mrs. Carter had the candy bar mostly broken-down into its volatile base components when there was a thud on the roof, followed quickly by another.

Everyone looked up, as if they could see through the metal hull.

"Did we hit something?" a marine whispered as if whatever it was might hear him. The suit dove for the intercom so fast that he almost left his hair behind.

"Driver, what's going on?"

"Something fell off of the...urk!" The return transmission dissolved into a burst of static and entire room lurched suddenly to one side as the driver lost consciousness and control of his truck. The suit and his soldiers lunged for the grab handles strung along the ceiling as the truck hauling them began to swerve wildly.

Mrs. Carter clung to the surgical table (which was thankfully bolted to the deck) and balled up the viscous grey goo in a discarded hamburger wrapper. It no longer even remotely resembled a candy bar, but looked like what it was: an unstable and highly-combustible ball of tinfoil.

"LADIES AND GENTLEMEN, THIS IS YOUR ROBOT HIJACKER SPEAKING, YOU MIGHT BE EXPERIENCING SOME TURBULENCE FOR THE NEXT FEW MILES." The voice was jovial and electronic. *"IT WOULD BE HELPFUL IF YOU WOULD RETURN TO YOUR SEATS, STRAP YOURSELVES IN AND SELF-ADMINISTER A TRANQUILIZER AS IT WOULD EASE YOUR MINDS AND MAKE THIS HAIR-BRAINED RESCUE ATTEMPT EASIER."*

---

[87] No, I'm not going to tell you how to do it. The last thing the world needs is yet another reason not to eat a candy bar.

"What does he think he's doing?" the suit shouted as the truck lurched again. He grabbed a marine by the shoulder and shoved him aft. "Get up there and regain control of this vehicle! That's an order!"

The large young man barely felt the shove, but moved obediently toward the locker at the back of the ship that held their space armor. He came to a halt when he came nose-to-crumpled ball of foil with Mrs. Carter.

His eyes crossed as he tried to get a good look at the item in her hands.

"One false move and we all go up in smoke," she said.

"That's a hamburger wrapper," the marine said.

"It's what's inside the wrapper that you have to worry about, sweetie."

The young space marine glanced at the suit and then to his senior officers for instructions. They were all frowning at the ball of foil, as if trying to decide if or how she could have put anything more dangerous than a bit of candy bar or leftover hamburger inside.

The intercom came back to life with a pop of static and the hijacker's voice filled the room.

"JUST TO CLARIFY, WHEN I SAID 'ROBOT HIJACKER' JUST NOW, I MEANT A HIJACKER WHO HAPPENED TO BE A ROBOT, NOT A PERSON THAT HIJACKS ROBOTS," the voice announced. "THAT WOULD JUST BE WRONG. I MEAN SERIOUSLY, PEOPLE."

The marines moved forward and Howard's mother felt the cold burst of air and smelt the perfume of diesel exhaust moments before the steel fingers wrapped themselves in her jacket and hauled her upward through the open hatch and out into the cold air.

She hadn't seen the lawnmower since it ran off, but it looked wonderful for the moment she hung suspended from its claw. It dropped her on a pile of canvas that it had ripped up trying to locate the hatch in the top of the ship. The robot didn't say a word as it took the foil ball from her numb fingers and tossed it back down the hole. It stomped at the fingers of the men trying to climb out and slammed the hatch.

The lawnmower turned to regard her with glowing eyes and cocked its head as the *whump* of the candy bar igniting rocked the truck. It reached down and grabbed her ankle, latching the other hand around the handle of the hatch as the truck lurched again, this time because the driver was careening wildly through traffic. She briefly became weightless, anchored only by the hand on her ankle as the truck skidded sideways.

Cars and trucks around them blared their horns and tires screamed against pavement as drivers swerved to avoid the out of control tractor trailer. The truck jerked as its tires dug into the soft gravel shoulder and went into the ditch. Dirt and sod showered them as the nose of the truck plowed into the soft earth.

Mrs. Howard's weight returned all at once and she came down hard. Over her pounding heart, the sounds of angry traffic built behind them as somewhere in the distance, a siren began to wail. She rolled over to stare up at her rescuer. She had forgotten how dangerous the thing looked with its blades and hedge-trimmer attachments spinning.

"Thanks," she croaked. "I think."

The lawnmower didn't respond. It lifted her in its arms and jumped down to set her on the grass. They were met by the robot she'd been shown in the picture, which had now added a black plastic pirate hat that had been meant for a child's Halloween costume. It looked gloriously ridiculous and at the sight of its battered copper wastebasket head, she had no more doubts in her mind that it was Howard's creation.

And to think she had thought to rescue him.

When she caught up with her son, she was going to hug him and then ground him for life.

***

While time may not normally exist in any real, tangible, sense, there are times when we force it to coalesce into something we can interact with. In those times, what some people refer to as the fabric of the universe acts a lot like a river

-- there are backwaters and eddies and if you're unlucky, you encounter whirlpools and cataracts from which you will never return.

It takes something extraordinary to make this happen.

Shooting a functioning time machine with a high-powered rifle would do it.

Howard and his friends barely heard the shot, but they saw the results as the spinning brass frame of the time machine cracked and began to wobble. Howard screamed and lunged for his friends as positrons discharged into the open air, leaking through the suddenly unstable wormhole, causing a cascade of small implosions as matter met antimatter.

He wrapped Gary and Ericka in his arms and they all went down in a heap as the time machine was hit again and again by bullets seemingly from nowhere.

Deeds hauled the kids to their feet by the scruffs of their collective neck and hurled them back down the trail. "Run!"

The gunfire had stopped, but the time machine was cracking and the river of time was in full flood. Eddies and cataracts swirled across the clearing, turning saplings into oaks and oaks into saplings in the blink of an eye. Roots dug into solid stone and retracted from the paths they'd already dug as the erosion of hundreds of years took place in an instant. Stone flowed like water and where it was still solid the hillside began to buckle as parts of it reverted to different periods of its creation.

The ground rumbled and lightning arced around them, the death throes of the time machine hammering the trees and hillside around them as they fled.

Behind them, Sunshine Rock held its ground as names and dates appeared and disappeared from the graffiti smeared across the stone until it was pristine once more. The bare stone was beautiful and unblemished for the ten full seconds it took for the section below it to revert to a time when it hadn't been compacted and buttressed by the slow pressure of the rock's weight. One last surge of antimatter fireworks caressed the hillside and several thousand tons of limestone surrendered to gravity and began to surge down the hill.

The three friends were thrown to the ground as the ball of green anti-fire that now obscured Howard's time machine was carried down into the valley and disappeared under tons of limestone and granite.

In the wake of the time machine's demise, things fell silent once more.

They all lay on the ground in the haze of dust, their hair standing straight up, alive with the electrostatic echo of the lost device. Howard shocked himself as he loosened his helmet and let it fall away. Dust and ash fell from his hair as he ran his fingers through it.

So *this* was why his mother insisted on the helmets.

He wondered what he looked like. Before this was over, his hair would look like Deeds' and he might even be almost as crazy.

A tall figure walked through the clouds of swirling dust toward him. Howard had glimpsed her in the heart of the chaos, standing firm and firing shot after shot into the frame and reactor of his beautiful machine.

She looked like she had stepped out of a television program about beautiful warriors from some dark future time where everyone had a bottomless charge account at a black leather retailer. She even had a light scar crossing her cheekbone, a line of pale pink on her dark skin. Despite the scar, he thought she looked regal, like a queen or general, someone used to her every order being obeyed.

Tears of rage and frustration cut channels through the dust coating his cheeks as he opened his mouth to demand that she explain herself.

At least he tried to; his mouth moved, but no sound came out.

Howard tried again and still no sound issued from his lips. He was talking, but he couldn't hear himself. The regal face lowered into a frown for a moment. Confusion creased the skin between her brows. Then the dawning realization and fear swept away the uncertainty and she dropped into a crouch, unslinging her rifle once more and staring upward through the haze.

It took Howard a second to realize what had frightened her.

The dust should have settled long ago, but it was still swirling around them and in fact seemed to be increasing. As if a helicopter was hovering overhead, unheard and unseen in the haze and silence. He screamed silently.

Two more figures emerged from the dust, their faces buried in the crooks of their elbows. Gary and Ericka's goggle-protected eyes stared at Howard over the forearms they had thrown over their mouths. Ericka dropped her arm to ask Howard a question and something electrical happened that Howard couldn't attribute to the static aftereffects of the time-space dilation and he suddenly *knew*.

They were both Ericka.

She had come back from the future to stop him.

Deeds and the puppet creature came running toward them out of the murk and, startled, the woman cold-cocked the mad scientist with the butt of her rifle, sending him to the ground. She aimed at the large felt alien thing and took a step backward, her eyes wide and fearful.

Her mouth moved, but still no sound came.

Howard would have given good money to know what she'd said. He had a feeling Ericka's mom would wash her mouth out with soap if she'd spoken those words with her eleven-year-old-mouth. He would give even more to hear her explanation: for the scar on her cheek, for her Matrix wardrobe, for the destruction of his time machine.

He felt something hit the ground next to him and turned to see a coil of rope in the gravel behind him, trailing upward, strung up into the sky like something from Aladdin.

What the?

The woman... *Ericka,* Ericka the Elder, spotted more coils of rope dropping all around them and mouthed *Run!* She dropped her rifle and grabbed her younger self, tucking the startled girl under her arm and bolting into the dust.[88]

Howard didn't need any more reason to run. If the impressive warrior was scared of whatever was coming down that rope, he wanted nothing to do with it either. Howard grabbed Gary's arm and they followed her into the woods.

***

It's a curious phenomenon of quantum mechanics that quantum particles separated by any distance, even light years, once paired will mirror the actions of each other exactly. This bears the delightful title of "Spooky action at a distance" and is much remarked upon, but very little in the way of successful science has come out of the knowledge.

Well, nothing of the "World of Tomorrow" definition of successful anyway.[89]

Some early studies *have* been undertaken in quantum teleportation, but to the disappointment of most of their backers, the largest thing they've managed to move across a distance is a muon. And who wants to invest heavily in a muon transporter?[90]

Most people don't even know what a muon *is*.

---

[88] Meeting yourself in another time is embarrassing enough. If something happens to startle you both, the human instinct for self-preservation can really complicate things as your urge to protect yourself wars with your desire to protect yourself. If there are three of you... well, it's best not to go there.

[89] Scientists of all varieties hate the "World of Tomorrow" metric of success. They complain that they could pioneer a way to re-grow a missing limb and nine of every ten people they show it to will say "That's neat, but when am I getting my flying car?" It gets to a point where you almost have to wonder if they aren't refusing to explore proper flying car technology purely out of spite.

[90] Well, lots of people, as it turns out mostly communications companies, but not in the manner in which the public wants to see teleportation. Face it, sending a subatomic particle across a lab isn't very Star Trek. (See previous point about the World of Tomorrow metric.)

If you've ever taken apart something and once you've put it back together discovered that you'd mysteriously acquired a plethora of extra bits and bobs, you have an inkling of why it's so hard to disassemble someone in one place and then reassemble them correctly in another.

No one can get it right, at least no one you've ever heard of.

To his great frustration, *Doctor Villainous Deeds, PhD* is a name very few people have heard of. And of those who have, most of them are the sort of scientist you wouldn't want to have over for dinner. Deeds couldn't build a proper human-sized teleporter either[91] so he did the next best thing -- he built a quantum bungee cord.

Which is why, soon after the woman cold-cocked him with the rifle butt, he vanished from the spot where he fell. He wasn't teleported. A strand of invisible particles across the galaxy contracted automatically, dragging with them their twinned particles and the man they were part of. Deeds experienced this as a tug somewhere around his solar plexus and a terrible pain, as if he was being turned inside-out on a molecular level.

But don't worry, that's only because he was.

They call it "mad" science for a reason.

---

[91] At least not one that worked properly, in case you were wondering what the real story was about his last assistant turning into a fish. Don't tell anyone, ok? It was terribly embarrassing for everyone involved, not least of all the poor Igor who got turned into a catfish. Sort of hard to explain that one to your family at holidays.

19. One Bad Idea After Another

Most young people are so busy running from childhood pell-mell into adulthood that they rarely take time to glance over their shoulders, and most people simply haven't been alive long enough to have a "Good Old Days" to look back upon.

At least one should hope not.

Gary Parker, however, grew up in front of a television. His parents had plopped their son down in front of an educational TV show and for the ensuing years the characters of public television were his siblings and companions. So when Deeds walked out of the woods with what appeared to be a giant misshapen puppet at his shoulder, he had been dumbstruck by the first wave of nostalgia he'd ever experienced.

If Howard hadn't been pulling him forward, he might've stopped to stare at the living incarnation of his early childhood.

Might have. Huge soldiers in space suits dropping from the sky all around you tends to inspire running even as you're fighting off a wave of déjà vu. In those cases, running is the only impulse your body has room for.

Howard kept hold of his friend's arm and ran, other than a sudden wave of sympathy for every character they had ever played in a video game, his only thought was catching up to the Erickas. Huge men encased in armored suits came at them from every direction. Enormous hands swept at them, passing so close that they ruffled their hair as they ducked and wove through their legs, trying to keep the slim form of the running woman in sight.

The air crackled and suddenly they could hear birds and the distant rumble of traffic on the highway. They were clear of the cone of silence but now they could hear the ominous crunch of armored feet running behind them as the soldiers closed-in.

A blast of hot air hit them and both Gary and Howard were blown backward. Howard lay stunned for a moment as cedar needles and dead leaves and dirt rained down on them.

A concussion grenade, Howard diagnosed. Against a bunch of kids.

Who do these guys think we are?

An armored hand grabbed him by the front of his coat and hauled him up to helmet-height. Howard could see the man through the thick glass of his helmet.

He couldn't resist.

He reached up and smeared a muddy hand across the man's windshield.

The man's mouth moved, and Howard was glad that he couldn't hear what he was saying.[92] He wondered where Gary was and then thought *"Oh"* as he felt something get pulled out of his hand and the stench of ammonia ripped through his sinuses.

***

As Howard's mother and his robots ran back along the line of stopped traffic they scanned the cars they passed until she reached a truck that had been left with the doors open and keys in the ignition while the driver wandered up the line to either help or satisfy his curiosity.

He must have been pretty far away, because she didn't see anyone running after her waving their arms as she whipped the truck around and drove the wrong way down the highway shoulder back towards Sedville.

Howard's mother wasn't terribly good about following traffic laws at the best of times.

The robot who insisted upon being addressed as the Dread Pirate something-or-other expressed admiration for her

---

[92] Which is really for the best for one and all since Howard's mother was angry enough already.

technique and kept whooping and hollering each time she cut across oncoming traffic. She blew across the bridge and through a stand of stalled cars before bouncing across the grassy median to the side of the highway where the traffic was actually moving in the same direction she wanted to go.

Mrs. Carter reached over and knocked on the copper dome of the piratical robot.

"Where's my son?"

"I DO NOT..." the robot began, but he was cut off by a ringing sound echoing through his copper cranium. "OH, FOR HAL'S SAKE, I AM NOT A SWITCHBOARD," it grumbled before her husband's voice took over.

"Are you safe?"

"Yes! Where's Howard?" she shouted. "What's happening?"

"Deeds is out looking for him..." her husband hesitated for a moment. "He's been building robots again."

"ACTUALLY HE BUILT ME FIRST," muttered the robot, but the humans ignored him.

"Deeds?" she growled. "That quack's going to get him killed!"

"He has a companion that claims to be an alien with him."

"Claims?"

"It looked like something that escaped from Sesame Street," Mr. Carter responded. "It doesn't matter, whatever the thing is it's smarter than the scientist. How soon can you meet us at the Flat Creek bridge?"

"Us?"

"I'll explain when you get here. Take M Highway -- I'll download the coordinates to your friend here."

The lights in the eyes dimmed as her husband dumped a data parcel into the mechanical man's brain. The robot jittered for a moment and then slumped against the window. Mrs. Carter hoped it was just sulking rather than actually damaged and pushed the accelerator the rest of the way to the floor.

He left our son with nothing but a daffy science teacher for protection, she thought, but don't worry, he has an alien with *him.*

She willed the stolen pickup to go faster...

***

Gary depressed the trigger and spun in a circle with the modified water pistol leveled at their captor's knees. The ammonia-scented solution splashed and fell everywhere. The men yowled and cursed and even Howard yelped as a drop hit his dangling hand.

"Got 'em! Run!" Gary grabbed him by one dangling foot and yanked down. Howard let his arms go limp and slipped out of the jacket, leaving it hanging in the hand of the armored soldier as they dodged around the frozen circle of marines, slipping and sliding on the blue ice coating the ground. Armored hands reached for them, but they were too slow and their feet and knees frozen.

Howard looked ahead, the female warrior and her younger self had vanished. He chose a direction at random and headed that way.

"Howard!"

Howard turned to see his father beckoning from the crest of the next hill. He blinked and rubbed at his eyes, but the man was still there, standing among the maples and waving his son to run faster.

***

When Deeds reappeared nanoseconds later in an unused lab in the basement of Arkham Tech, he was the first man in history to travel by quantum bungee cord. As he lay on the floor of his old lab, twitching and drooling, he had a hard time feeling particularly triumphant about his world record.

He opened his eyes and found himself staring down the barrel of a gauss gun, held in the mitts of a startled-looking man in space armor. For a moment, he thought he hadn't gone anywhere, but the hairy soldier was most certainly *not* the

149

beautiful woman who had cold-cocked him.

He blinked and wondered if maybe his eyes were just the last part to materialize. Some giddy portion of his brain postulated that they might still be in Missouri, floating in the air and waiting for his body to come back and get them.

That would be a story to tell at the next faculty mixer.

Deeds blinked again, but the space marine was quite stubbornly still there. Worse yet, the gun was still there too.

"Didn't I just leave this party?" He climbed to his feet and rather unsteadily delivered his best professorial frown. "What are you doing in my lab?" he demanded. "Are you a new student?"

He was answered by an extended burst of static.

"*Kssssssshhhhhhhttt!*"

"Yes, well, your argument is persuasive, young sir, but I'm afraid we have a rule about allowing secret government agencies to wander around on campus." He waggled a finger at the third soldier from the left. "You'll need to check in at the main office and obtain a pass."

"*Kssssssssshhhhhhhttt!!!*" the trooper repeated.

"I am forced to admit that your logic is irrefutable." Deeds took another unsteady step toward the door. "No doubt you are the pride of the Philosophy department. I shall cede the point and allow you the use of this room for no less than thirty-eight minutes, which I shall need to get a suitable head start on my getaway."

He bumped into someone and spun around.

His head was spinning and the room seemed to tilt as his vision filled with soldiers. He worried that with these side-effects, quantum bungee jumping was never going to catch on... though he knew a few grad students who liked doing things that made one's eyesight fuzzy and made them see spacemen. The endless commercial applications of his invention blossomed before him and he fell to his knees and threw up on the nearest trooper's boots.

"Oh, Villy, you are something else." She tsked and helped

her brother to stand. "A quantum bungee cord? I didn't think even you were that crazy."

"Sis?" he said. He blinked at his twin. "What is going on here? What are you doing?"

"You got in the way, silly Villy."

"I got in the way of what?"

She didn't answer, but he supposed the handcuffs she locked around his wrists were supposed to be his answer. She smiled at him and then stepped out of the way as the space marines moved forward to take him into custody.

***

"Hello, Howard," the old man boomed as Howard and Gary skid to a stop at his feet. Howard looked around, but it was only a wrinkled old man in a rumpled grey suit at the crest of the rise.

"Who are you?" Howard wondered if he'd gone crazy. He would've sworn that he'd seen his dad. "Where's my dad?"

"I work for the president," Old Suit said. "I wanted a chance to chat with you, man to man."

Howard was immediately on his guard. He had data that indicated that any conversation that begins with an adult wanting to speak to him "man-to-man" was 99.8% less likely to end with a free trip to Disney World than a conversation which begins with any other cliché.[93]

I told you that there was good reason to be wary of those things.

"Well, there's an army of moon men chasing me just now, so if it can wait, I'd appreciate it." Howard began to back away, looking around for any sign of his father. "I'm looking for my

---

[93] And 96.2% less likely to end up in Disneyland. Though the odds of a shoddy carnival set up overnight in a parking lot somewhere hover in the mid fifties for some reason. Howard was hoping that this was a statistical aberration because the guy in the rumpled suit looked like the shoddy carnival type.

dad."

"Your father is up by the highway, no doubt planning elaborate rescue scenarios with your mother." The old man sounded tired. "Considering the manner in which both you and your mother have already escaped from us once, I've no doubt that it will be spectacular."

"All of this is *your* doing?" Gary asked.

Old Suit frowned at the boy and then back at Howard.

"Technically, this is all Howard's doing," he said. "Come with me." He walked along the ridgeline toward a stand of trees. Howard and Gary glanced at one another and then back in the direction the old suit had indicated Howard's parents waited.

The man stopped at the tree line and stood staring out over the smoking ruins of the valley, seemingly ignoring the two kids watching him.

"Don't go over there," Gary whispered. "This is a trap."

"No, the thing at the rock was a trap, this guy's being reasonable."

"Because we escaped his traps!" Gary insisted. "God, Howard, don't you ever watch *any* movies?"

"You should go home, Gary." Howard moved to follow the old man, but Gary grabbed his arm and stopped him.

"At least take the freeze ray."

Howard looked down at the plastic pistol that Gary had used to save him from the soldiers. The tip was still frosted and Gary had to hold it with his sleeve pulled over his hand because he'd lost his glove at some point. The modified toy looked pathetic in light of the spaceman armor and silent helicopters.

He waved it away.

"You keep it."

"This is a bad idea."

"My whole life has been one bad idea after another," Howard said. "And apparently that continues for years to come, since Ericka came back to stop me from getting into the time machine."

"Is that what happened?" Gary huffed. "I was wondering where Ericka's mom got the sniper rifle."

"That was Ericka." Howard paused and thought about it for a moment and then discarded the idea.[94] "Don't you see? I was about to make another colossal mistake!"

"That doesn't make following this old fart a good idea."

"I've been doing whatever I want to do all my life and this is where it's gotten us." Howard waved at distant helicopters and the dust-filled valley below. "This time I'm going to do what I don't want to do and see what happens."

"That is stupid."

"Yeah, well, being smart's not all it's cracked up to be."[95]

Gary stood watching as Howard walked away, waiting for his friend to change his mind, to come back and do the sensible thing, to slip the noose and laugh in their faces and join Gary in a good solid sprint for the highway.

Howard didn't even glance over his shoulder before he disappeared into the trees.

---

[94] He couldn't imagine anyone's mother wearing a leather outfit like that. And truth be told, he didn't really want to.

[95] That's an unfortunate truth, just watch television and count all the smart people who have the cops constantly bugging them, demanding that they help solve all the grisly murders that seem to happen when they're around.

20. Inlaws & Outlaws

Gary heard the patrol coming toward him through the brush long before they got to him and ducked into the hollow center of a large cedar bush. The two Erickas were already there, fingers laid across their lips as if he needed to be reminded that there were soldiers out there looking for them.

Pursuit had begun again almost immediately after Howard had wandered off to meet with the old guy. He'd hoped that once they had the boy genius, they would leave his sidekicks alone.

No such luck.

Gary took the opportunity to study the two iterations of his friend close-up.

At first glance, he had seen a leaner, meaner version of Ericka's mother -- perhaps an aunt or close cousin with a military background and an affection for dressing like one of the X-men. On closer examination, though, he knew Howard was right -- there was no mistaking the woman as anyone but an older, harder version of the girl he'd been friends with since kindergarten.

Only after the patrol had walked out of earshot did Gary dare ask the question that had been weighing on him.

"How come you don't implode in orange gooey weirdness when you two touch one another?" He sounded vaguely disappointed. Both Ericka's frowned at him. "I mean, matter can't occupy the same place at the same time and all that."

"What are you talking about?" the Erickas asked as one.[96]

"*Timecop*," Gary answered. "It's a movie."

"You never change," the older Ericka muttered.

"Nice to know," Gary said. "What are you doing here?"

The time-displaced woman ignored the question. "I need to find Howard's parents before they can do anything stupid."

"Stupid?"

"His parents are as gifted at doing the wrong dumb thing as he is," she chuckled. "Surely you've noticed by now."

Howard and young Ericka exchanged looks.

"We haven't met his parents yet," Gary said.

"His mom cut mine off in traffic once," young Ericka offered. "What are you afraid they're going to do?"

"Knowing those two, anything is possible."

***

The old man was waiting for him as Howard stepped through the opening that had been cut in the barbed wire fence that stretched along the far side of the trees. A line of identical vans and black Suburbans with tinted windows lined the gravel road on the far side of the fenceline. Howard had been seeing the vans tooling around town all week and suspected that they were allied with Skillion and his minders.

As if summoned by the thought of his name, Skillion emerged from the largest of the vans and scowled at Howard as he passed. Howard watched the man walk along the line and duck into an SUV.

"Pay him no mind," the old man rumbled as he opened the door of the large van. "He's just a scientist."

"But I *like* scientists..."

---

[96] This sort of "group think" is a curious side effect of having more than one of the same person in the same place. Even over vast spans of our lives, our responses to our friends asking dumb questions tends to be remarkably consistent. Get enough temporal clones in one place at one time and ask them a dumb question and you've got yourself one heck of a Greek chorus.

155

"You'll get over it once you've been around them long enough."

Howard followed the man up the steps into the big van. The inside was the size of a large mobile home and the walls lined with computers, maps and monitors. Old Suit harrumphed loudly and the technicians took the hint. Howard stood aside as they trouped past and out into the cold, leaving him alone in the command vehicle with their boss.

The old man reached out and turned a master volume control and the chatter from the field was silenced, leaving them with only the sporadic beeps from the radar. The look he finally turned toward Howard was grim.

"So you're the one that built the robots?"

Howard nodded, too busy rubbernecking at all the cool gadgets to give the man his full attention. Half of the machines were of a sort he'd never seen before, though after his experience in Deeds's lab, he suspected at least some of them were devoted to the production of coffee.

"You're a mite too industrious for my taste, kid."

"I do what I can."

"But not what you should," the old man said. "And that's when we have a problem."

"So I built a couple of robots," Howard said. "Who cares?"

"Do you know who I am?"

"You work for the president and the guys in the armor work for you."

"I'm the guy whose job is to deal with people like you."

Howard laughed. "And *this* was your plan?" Howard waved his arms to take in the entirety of the WARD operation. "You kidnap my mom and then drop an army of super soldiers into my town to mess things up until I come to you?"

"Honestly if we knew you were a kid, we'd have done all of this differently."

Howard rolled his eyes and turned to leave.

"Where do you think you're going to go, kid?"

"A better question is how do you think you're going to stop

156

me?" Howard countered. "Nothing you've done so far has resulted in much more than a lot of smoke and damaged equipment."

"You think you and your little band can run forever?"

"Mister, from what I've seen so far, I'm not so sure we even need to run."

***

Mr. Carter didn't stop when he hit the traffic backed up from M Highway, but pulled over to drive up the shoulder. Off to the right, he could see what looked like smoke rising from where the little map on his GPS told him Sunshine Rock was located.

Ignoring the annoyed shouts of his fellow motorists, Carter got as close to the roadblock as he dared before stopping his car. He had been right -- they had set up the blockades at the Flat Creek Bridge, a natural choke-point in the road.

He got out of the car and walked around to rummage through the trunk. He took out the net gun he had found duct taped to the underside of his son's workbench. Near as he could tell, the compressed air cylinder would fire a fishing net with weights fixed along the perimeter and snare anyone in front of the barrel.

Why Howard thought he needed one was anyone's guess, but the batteries had been low on the ray gun.[97] He didn't want to kill anyone anyway and thought it likely he might need to net his wife to keep her from killing someone if Howard looked even the slightest bit rumpled with they found him.

He glanced up and down the road to see if anyone other than the angry drivers had noticed him getting out of his car. If the officers at the blockade had noticed, they were doing a good job of hiding it as Mr. Carter shouldered his net gun and aimed his Howard Detector down the hill.

---

[97] At low power, at best the ray gun would give someone the equivalent of a nasty rug burn. Considering the armor on the men who had arrested his wife, he was understandably skeptical that a rug burn would slow them down much.

"Howard's less than a mile away..." he trailed off when he realized that his companion wasn't standing beside him. He turned and found Kevin still in the car, his fingers gripping the dashboard so hard his fingernails were turning white. "Hey kid, you coming or not?"

"Just... just give me a second." Deeds's lab assistant pried his fingers out of the dents he'd pressed in the vinyl and unbuckled his seatbelt. He'd stopped screaming once it became clear that his protests were having no effect on Mr. Carter's driving. In fact, he suspected that it might have egged the man on.

"You okay, Calvin?" Howard's dad asked.

"Kevin," he shouted. *"Kevin!* How hard is that? And I'll be fine once the vertigo stops."

A stolen pickup skidded to a halt just shy of where they were standing and Kevin squealed and fainted dead away. Mrs. Carter and the two robots piled out of the truck, leaving it more or less how they found it: doors open, keys in the ignition, engine running, and a mere seventy miles south of its original location.

"Who is this?"

"He's Howard's science teacher's nephew or lab assistant or something," Mr. Carter said and he reached out and flicked the dented copper wastebasket under the Dread Pirate Robot's hat. "I've been looking for that."

"YOU CAN'T HAVE IT!" the robot shrieked. "EVEN IF YOU GET IN MY HEAD AGAIN, I WON'T GIVE IT TO YOU! IT'S MINE, I TELL YOU!"

"Tell you what," Mr. Carter said, "Help us get Howard out of this mess and you can keep it."

"I WAS GOING TO HELP YOU ANYWAY," the robot muttered. "HUMANS! I ASK YOU, WHERE'S THE TRUST?"

The lawn mower said nothing, just cocked its head and hoisted the unconscious lab assistant up onto its shoulder.

Mrs. Carter stared out over the fields at the distant plume of smoke rising out of the trees. She knew as only a mother can that her son had somehow caused it.

Howard was in rare form today.

Without a word, she snatched the net gun and leapt down the embankment. The others had no choice but to follow. By the time they reached the treeline, she was thoroughly annoyed with everyone and even the Dread Pirate Robot knew better than to complain about the big scratch the barbed wire had carved across its posterior.

"Stop!"

They turned on the edge of the woods to see an African-American woman in leather running toward them across the field. She had two kids that the Carters recognized from the neighborhood on her heels, struggling to keep up to her long-legged strides.

Mrs. Carter would've netted first and asked questions later if not for the kids she had with her. She couldn't figure the space marines for having eleven-year-old agents, but she kept the net gun handy, just in case. The woman drew up just short of them.

"What do you want?"

"Whatever it is you're planning to do, don't do it," the woman said. "Howard has to handle this himself."

"Who are *you* to tell me what Howard needs?" Mrs. Carter snapped. The beautiful woman's demeanor annoyed her, her leather outfit *really* annoyed her, and if her husband didn't stop looking at her that way, she was going to get really *really* annoyed, at which point all bets were off.

The woman glanced at her two young companions uneasily and then squared her shoulders and turned to face Howard's mother.

"I'm the queen of earth," the woman proclaimed. "And I am also Howard's wife."

***

Old Suit didn't answer Howard's challenge right away. He turned his gaze to the blips on the nearest screen that told him where his troopers were as they scoured the valley and surrounding farms searching for the kid standing in front of him.

"You ever been to New Mexico, kid?"

"If you're going to give me the Space Invaders storyline, you can skip it," Howard said. "My robot gave me your song and dance already."

"Back in the 1950's, an alien scout ship was shot down near Roswell, New Mexico."

"I've seen the movies."

"Have you? Then you also know that the boys in the labcoats were able to download some information from that ship's computers." Old Suit had just about had enough of the smartmouth kid. "And you already know that those aliens were the advance scouts for a race of scavengers working their way across the galaxy, stripping the minerals from the planets they invade and enslaving any inhabitants."

Howard had to take a moment to catch his breath before he found his courage again. *The man is lying,* he reminded himself. But that was beginning to sound thin even to him.

"And what do my robots have to do with any of this?"

"Robots are a dime a dozen." Old Suit snapped his fingers. "But unshielded fusion reactors the size of a jelly jar are another story entirely."

"So?"

"So, the first atomic bombs we set off at the end of World War Two are what got their attention in the first place," Old Suit said. "What do you think cold fusion would do if we let it walk around? With technology like that, they have to hit us soon or they never will."

Howard didn't have an answer to that. The old man walked to one of the monitors and hit a button that a tech had marked for him earlier. The screen on the attached computer went black and then green.

A gnarled finger tapped the largest, roundest green splotch on the screen.

"This is one of the fifty alien ships that were scanned as they passed the Voyager space probe on their way into our solar system -- they're headed our way and they're early." The old man folded his arms and regarded Howard under shaggy eyebrows. "You've got their attention, Mister Carter, now what are you planning to do with it?"

"They're coming for *me*?"

"They're coming for all of us," he growled. "And it's your fault."

***

If you have never been married, I should point out that meeting your in-laws for the first time can be a stressful event even in the best of circumstances. A parent must come to the point of accepting that their child is an adult gradually, and that they're ready to take the very adult step of beginning their own family is the greatest single leap in the parent-child relationship.

It's dangerous to generalize, but history teaches that any small thing, no matter how unintentional or innocent it seems at the time, can come back to haunt you in the strangest ways. It's the sort of meeting that even diplomats who are willing to sit between sworn nuclear-armed enemies and hammer out elaborate peace treaties will make excuses to avoid.

Sorry, can't make it. Orthodontist's appointment. Need to clean my keyboard. Rotate the air in my tires. Polish my ethics. Pick up my brain at the dry cleaners...

So imagine, if you will, that you're meeting your in-laws after traveling back in time to a point in history when your future spouse is still only eleven years old.

Awkward doesn't begin to cover it.

Mrs. Carter blinked at the tall woman for a full count of ten. She took in the strange outfit, the scar on her cheek, her obvious bravery, intelligence, grace, beauty and bearing... She was a catch by any measure. Any mother would be proud to have her as a daughter-in-law.

Mrs. Carter immediately decided that she did not like her one bit.

Not even a little.

She opened her mouth to tell her so, but the troop of soldiers that picked that moment to drop out of the sky and land in a circle around them with guns pointed at them forced Mrs. Carter to save the strange woman's comeuppance for later.

"Freeze!" one of them shouted through a loudspeaker mounted on his armor.

Gary was universally regarded as a Good Kid by teachers and family. Obedient to a fault. He tried to obey but the blue stream of freezing liquid that came from his squirt gun fell well short of the man he'd aimed at and then the gun sputtered and fell silent.

Well, that figures. Gary thought.

"Are you nuts, kid?" one of the soldiers asked as he walked up and took the red plastic pistol out of Gary's hand. Gary didn't fight him - there was no point. "Shooting a water pistol at a soldier like that is dangerous!"

"Which one of you is Howard Carter?" the first soldier asked.

"I am!"

Everyone turned to stare at the younger Ericka. She had been silent since her future self had announced that she was destined to marry Howard.[98] The soldiers glanced at one another. *A girl named Howard?*

"No, I am!" Gary shouted, stepping between young Ericka and the soldier.

"I AM HOWARD CARTER!" the Dread Pirate Robot proclaimed. It struck what it considered a Howard-like pose and played a snippet of the Darth Vader theme from Star Wars for emphasis.[99] "AND SO IS MY FRIEND." He clapped the lawn mower on the shoulder that didn't have a mad scientist's

---

[98] Yeah. Awkward doesn't even begin to cover that either.

[99] In case you haven't already noticed already, the Dread Pirate Robot had a bit of trouble discerning between good guys and bad guys. Howard had it on his list of *Things I'm Working On*, but it was pretty far down the list...

unconscious lab assistant slung over it. The lawn mower looked uncertainly at the soldiers and sidestepped a bit further away from the pirate.

"And I suppose you're Howard Carter too?" the lead soldier asked Howard's father.

"Yes, and so is my wife," Mr. Carter drawled, brandishing the net gun. The soldier blinked at him and glanced at Howard's mom, who was still glowering at Ericka the Elder.

"Great, they're all Spartacus," the lead soldier muttered. "Arrest everybody! We'll sort it out when we get back to base." The soldier listened briefly to a voice chattering in his earpiece before continuing. "And whatever you do, don't give them any candy bars."

As the soldiers closed in, Howard's mom leaned close to her husband and whispered.

"When does your plan start?"

"It already has," Mr. Carter whispered back.

***

Howard's vision became fuzzy around the edges and his face felt hot as he stared at the fuzzy image of the disk-shaped spacecraft headed their way.

All he could think was: *A flying saucer... really?*[100]

"I know you think we're the villains here, Howard," the old man mused. "And if we'd realized earlier that you were just a kid, we'd have handled things differently, but we're all that stands between *this* and your town."

"I just wanted a little help cleaning my room," Howard muttered. "And mowing my lawn, maybe walking the dog if we

---

[100] Howard knew that flying saucers, though popular in movies of the 1950's, are not the most efficient shape for flying through a planet's atmosphere and in space it didn't matter what shape your spacecraft took. If asked to describe what he thought an alien spacecraft would look like, Howard would have described something less streamlined in its geometry, more akin to a floating New York City.

ever get one, doing my English homework..."

"Well, I'm sure if you tell them that, they'll turn right around and go away," Old Suit drawled. "Oh, and you forgot the time machine."

"That was homework related too at first," Howard said. "What can I do?"

"You can come back with us and help us prepare for the invasion."

"And what if I say no?" Howard asked. "What if I walk out that door?"

"You won't."

"And why wouldn't I?"

The old suit didn't answer, just pointed at something on the wall. Howard turned and momentarily lost the ability to breathe as he watched on the monitors as the soldiers closed in on his parents and friends.

His mom shot the soldier that came for him with his net gun. The other soldiers laughed uproariously as their comrade thrashed on the ground and rolled about.[101]

The Dread Pirate Robot turned and ran for it. A soldier raised his weapon, but the lawn mower dropped someone it had slung over its shoulder and tackled him. The scuffle didn't last long, lawnmowers simply aren't built them to resist that kind of fire power.

Howard didn't see what happened to the Dread Pirate Robot, but at the end of the fight, they had to use a dustpan to load the lawnmower into a van. He felt sick to his stomach as the van doors slammed shut with his family and friends inside.

He turned to face the old man's steely gaze.

"I'm just a kid."

"And we're just trying to defend the planet," Old Suit growled. "You're under arrest."

---

[101] For the record, Howard had never intended for it to fend off a battalion of space marines or he would've given it a bigger net and maybe electrified it, or maybe mounted it on a tank.

Howard didn't resist as the old man put handcuffs around his wrists and led him out of the van.

***

END OF PART ONE

Part II
The Impossible Boy

21. Play Dumb

When last we left Fermi's paradox, it was being ushered into the wings to give center stage to the less prestigious paradox penned by Doctor Villainous Deeds. That was then, this is now. And since Doctor Deeds is in chains and under heavy sedation in a secret underground bunker anyway, there's no better time for us to return to this cameo by a real superstar: Enrico Fermi. Fermi, you may recall, was the person who said *"We know someone's out there, so where is everybody?"*

Assuming that cultures Out There follow the same essential patterns of rise and fall as we've seen here on earth (which is a pretty big assumption) then those civilizations should be sending out ripples into the vast ocean of space. What's more is we should be able to detect them.

But we don't.

We know that aliens are out there, and we scan the skies with our most powerful radio telescopes listening for a hint of alien traffic reports or snippets of extraterrestrial sitcoms about the wacky hijinks of the bug-eyed monster next door, all we hear is a great deal of nothing. We've been listening for decades and we still haven't seen a single episode "Gliese 581g's Got Talent."

Which is unfair, because those people can *sing*.

We know they're out there because they have to be, but no one's answering the doorbell or answering our phone calls. It's almost as though the rest of the universe is hiding behind the sofa hoping we'll just go away.[102]

It's enough to give a species an inferiority complex.

If Deeds wasn't currently off his meds and in double-secret lockdown, or if you had the temerity to bring the subject up in one of his lucid moments, he would tell you that the real question we should be asking is *"How do you treat the neighbor we most remind you of?"*

It's worth wondering whether or not it's such a good thing that we're making enough noise to be heard in the next solar system over. And have you *seen* the state of our front lawn? Never mind the state of the planet itself, there's so much space junk in orbit around the earth that tracking it requires the full time attention of an entire agency to keep it from crippling our own communication satellites.

Let's not even dwell on the actual *content* of what we're broadcasting willy-nilly out into space. It's no wonder the interstellar welcome wagon doesn't come calling. Honestly, we're lucky no one's called the sheriff yet.

One of the reasons most often posited for why we haven't seen aliens before this is that it's just too far to travel on a whim. The vastness of the interstellar void cannot be overstated and assuming that you cannot travel faster than the speed of light (which our current understanding of physics says is impossible) the amount of resources necessary to travel that distance is so great that you would have to have a darned good reason to make the trip.

So far, we've only encountered the one alien in this story and that one has spent an enormous amount of time and effort trying to make contact with an earthling that is -- by the standards of our culture at least -- a child.

If you were to make a list of the top twenty reasons to expend the enormous amount of time and resources necessary

---

[102] "Oh no! It's the humans again! Everybody hide!" Paranoid? Sure, but just because you're paranoid doesn't mean that everyone's not really out to get you... or in this case, ignore you.

to visit earth, would you put "visit some kid in Missouri" on the list? I'd lay even money that you wouldn't even put "visit Missouri" on the list. Sure, the barbecue is top-notch, but it's not exactly the Grand Canyon is it?

Put it this way: would you spend the equivalent of the Gross National Product of the United States and Europe combined plus untold years in a suspended animation chamber to visit *any* of the places on your list?

Just for some kid who had likely only just been born when you left your home planet?

Though calling Howard "just some kid" is much the same as calling Leonardo DaVinci "just a painter". Being a kid was just something Howard did in addition to doing everything else. Being a kid wasn't even the thing he was best at. So, any other reasons for undertaking such a journey aside, we're left with this: Howard's was the sort of mind that an alien would travel light years and don a ridiculous puppet disguise just to touch.

So you can imagine how it played out when Howard's mom leaned in and whispered in his ear as they were led away: "Play dumb."

Howard loved his mother. He wanted to make her happy. A lot of what had happened had been because he'd wanted her safe. Even so, at a conservative estimate, "Playing dumb" was destined to last about twenty seconds.

***

Howard stood in his bath robe staring around at the blank white walls of his cell and feeling very small and alone. Also naked. He had on a terry cloth robe, and while that was nice and all, he really wanted to put some clothes on. When he'd come out of the shower, his old ones were gone from the corner where he'd flung them on his way to the shower.

Why the government would want to seize his dirty underwear wasn't something he cared to dwell upon. As long as they didn't replace them with a suit and tie.[103]

The echoes of the old man's shouting still rang in his ears as he toweled himself dry. Gone had been the affable old codger who talked him out of making his final stand against the space marines and their handlers atop the smoking rubble of Sunshine Rock.

Yet another mistake for his tally.

His last words to Gary haunted him, his own voice echoing back to mock him. Whether he chose what he *wanted* to do or what he thought he *should* do, it seemed inevitable that he was going to end up doing what someone else wanted him to. He felt small and lonely and scared in the glaring light of the single bulb lighting his stark cell.

He wondered what happened to Gary and the Erickas and deep in his heart, he truly ached for his mother to tell him it was all going to be okay. To tell him that she knew he hadn't meant to cause a fleet of alien warships to come sweeping out of space to bomb earth back to the Flintstones.

The moment she'd asked him to play dumb loomed large in his mind, but they had been together for only a few seconds to calm everyone down, to prove to Howard that they were alive and well before he was arrested and led away.

He pinched the bridge of his nose and wondered if secret government agencies had a school nurse, because he was feeling sick. Maybe she would write him a note.

Dear Stuffy Old Dork-in-a-Suit; Please excuse Howard from today's alien invasion. He's not feeling well and his mom will be picking him up as soon as she can get away from work...

The door tweedled and Howard palmed the tears from his eyes before swatting the release panel. The doors hissed open and he found himself face-to-face with the supposed nephew of Doctor Deeds. Gone was the oversized lab coat and pocket

---

[103] He'd give his favorite set of screw drivers for a suit of Space Marine armor, but that was probably wishful thinking. Granting prisoners access to advanced power armor wasn't a recipe for keeping them around for long.

protector, replaced with the jeans, snarky tee-shirt[104] and headphones that marked him as one of the technicians that seemed to run the place.

"K-Kevin?" Howard took a step back. "What are you doing here?"

"You okay, kid?"

"I'm fine," Howard lied. "What are you doing here?"

"My job."

Howard blinked. He'd underestimated how far the agency had been willing to go to catch him. Kevin held out a bag that had been dangling from his hand.

"You really got the old guy going," Kevin chuckled. "I don't think I've ever seen him change that color before." Howard accepted the bag and peeked inside. It seemed to contain jeans and tee-shirts. He hoped there was underwear as well, but he wasn't about to go digging for it with Kevin watching. On top of the clothes was a thick white envelope.

"I've been in trouble before."

"I think you might be grounded for life."

"What's this?" Howard pulled the envelope out and opened it. It was stuffed full of cash.

"You won the pot."

"I what?" Howard eyed the bulging envelope suspiciously.[105]

"Your dad gave me a couple of bucks back on the transport and asked me to take care of you while you're here," Kevin said. "Five bucks was the buy-in and I figured you had a good chance of doubling your money."

"I don't..." Howard fumbled the money. "My dad?"

"We have a standing bet on who can make Old Suit melt down," the tech explained. "The pot goes to the person who

---

[104] This one said "Mad Science: See the world, meet interesting people, and extract their brains for your questionable research."

[105] Howard's mother had told him what to do if someone ever offered him pot, but this wasn't how he'd pictured it happening.

gets him to say *techno-babble* the most in a single breath. You set a new record -- I thought we were going to have to give him oxygen."

Howard fished a handful of money out of the envelope, all five dollar bills. There must've been a hundred of them. He'd never handled that much money at one time in his life. It was just his luck that it came at a time when he couldn't go shopping.

"If I knew that ticking off old men could be this profitable," Howard muttered, "I'd have tried it a long time ago."

"Empires have been built on less, kid." Kevin laughed. "After you sank Skillion like that, we should've known you were a ringer."

"I'm sure Deeds would say the same about you," Howard said. Kevin's smile slipped, but Howard didn't get an explanation.

"Don't spend it all in one place."

Howard looked up at Kevin's back as he turned to go. He had never bribed anyone before, but he had the general idea of things from television.

"Can you help me get out of here?" Howard's held out the wad of cash. "I - I'll make it worth your while."

Kevin didn't even look at the money.

"We need you, Howard," he said. "I'm sorry, but like it or not, you're here for the duration."

"The duration of what?" Howard asked.

Kevin didn't answer.

Howard sat staring at the useless handful of money after the technician had left. It had never occurred to him before that there would be a time when a fistful of money wasn't enough, or that adults could be as lost and confused as he was. The look in Kevin's eyes had been hauntingly familiar -- he hadn't answered because he didn't know the answer.

Howard wondered if anyone did.

***

Several floors deeper into the earth, separated from Howard by several tons of earth and concrete and several layers of government-issue paint, Dr. Villainous Deeds paced his cell and sang softly to himself, keeping time with his footsteps.

Deeds had a lovely baritone singing voice that rolled out of his cavernous chest in a manner that most people found startling, if not downright unsettling.[106] He flashed back to one of the Christmas carols his father had taught him.

He sees you when you're sleeping,
He knows when you're awake,
He knows if you've been an evil jerk,
So build a cloaking device for goodness' sake![107]

One guard offered him a cookie to knock it off. Deeds ignored the offer and kept pacing, though the mention of the cookie did force him to wonder where his puppety friend had wandered off to. Without his medicine, he could not entirely be certain that the puppet had been real, or the boy and his gadgets. He wasn't even entirely sure about the cave he was trapped in.[108]

Deeds knew he was slipping and did the only thing he could think of, the one thing that inevitably calmed him down, the only problem he'd never solved...

He asked for a piece of chalk so that he could calculate his

---

[106] Deeds never told anyone, but he'd stolen his singing voice while visiting a karaoke bar as a young college student in Massachusetts. Deeds happened to have a vocal trap in his pocket that he'd swiped from his father's study and he had been just dying to try out. The guy wasn't really using his voice anyway... at least not well. It was Deeds's first standing ovation.

[107] It's an important lesson for a budding evil genius to know first and foremost that they are under constant surveillance. For a budding young supervillain hoping to find a chemistry set or maybe a 'Build Your Own Death Ray' kit under the tree, Santa Claus was the first nemesis that had to be overcome.

[108] He sort of hoped the cave was real, because it would take forever to dig his way out of the earth if it turned out not to be.

birthday.

The singing slipped to a bare whisper as he happily drew diagrams and crafted careful equations on the bare concrete walls, pouring all his concentration into the math.

***

Ericka Carter-Platt sat on her bunk in complete darkness and listened to the distant scritch of chalk on stone and the muttering of the mad scientist. She was happy for the solitude and didn't much mind the whispering and singing.

Where she came from there was a lot of that.

The darkness was a blessing, hiding her from the inquisitive stare of the guards walking by and making her a dim shadow in one corner of the camera that was monitoring her from across the corridor.

It would have been perfect if a strange stuffed animal sitting in the far corner of her cell wasn't glowing ever so slightly as it watched her with glassy button eyes. It wasn't hers, but it had appeared in her backpack at some point during her run through the forest with her younger self tucked under her arm.

The suits from WARD had let most of the others go, but she didn't have any ID and possessed a few worrisome gadgets that she didn't feel like trying to explain. They had tossed the small stuffed animal in her cell to keep her company.

They thought it was funny.

She did too, but only because she knew what it was even if they did not. She had only to wait for it to speak. It took longer than she'd expected for the alien's curiosity to overcome its caution.

"Greetings, Queen of Earth," it whispered. "What are you doing here?"

22. Someone else's trousers.

The psychology of a buffet line isn't a subtle one. Nowhere else do most people find themselves faced with the choices of sausage, bacon, meatloaf, ham, roast beef, smoked pork shoulder, roasted chicken, fried chicken, or spaghetti & meatballs. And on the occasion of being faced with this choice, nowhere else do diners feel compelled to eat all of them in one meal.

Especially for breakfast.

Howard didn't count the potatoes, rice, peas and scrambled eggs piled on the trays around him. As far as he could tell, these things mainly served to keep the marinara sauce separated from the maple syrup.[109]

The pancakes were apparently a signal to the denizens of this windowless world that this was a *morning* meal. Howard would have to take their word for it; he hadn't seen the sun since his surrender. His transfer to the secret base had been a series of trips in SUVs with blacked-out windows and small private jets with similar window treatments.

His study of the trays around him distracted him for a few blissful moments from the bandage on his hand where the instafreeze solution had splashed him and the oversized tech's tee shirt with the caffeine molecule mapped on the chest that he wore. At least his jeans (laundered and mended during the night) were still his.

---

[109] In case you're keeping track at home, and perhaps planning your future education, sauce segregation is a field of civil engineering that is woefully under-appreciated. If you're interested, inquire at Arkham Tech's Edible Engineering department. Ask for Professor Brown and bring lots of salt.

No one wants to face their fate wearing someone else's trousers.

It was all Howard could do to keep the realization from crashing down on him that the people around him weren't just another crowd of restaurant patrons. They were his captors. The technicians, engineers, scientists and soldiers were the residents of the secret government base where he, his parents and friends were being held prisoner.

He played mental games with their trays of food because if he thought about it too much he was afraid of what he might do, and his fellow diners were apparently earth's only defenders. The rest of the planet wouldn't thank him if he did anything that kept them from their task.

Assuming indigestion didn't do the job for him.

"Where are the others?" Howard asked.

"What others?" Kevin looked up from his burgeoning tray and shook his head to show his confusion.

"My family and friends -- where are they eating this morning?"

"There's another cafeteria in the detention wing." He frowned at the bowl of cold cereal that sat alone on Howard's tray. "Don't you at least want some bacon?"

"My mother doesn't let us eat bacon."

"She's not here, live a little." Kevin tossed a few pieces of bacon onto Howard's tray. "I'm not kidding Howard, you need to load up. You have a full day ahead and you're going to need them."

Howard didn't throw the bacon back, but he didn't eat it either. He used to fantasize about the way he would feast if his mother wasn't looking over his shoulder all the time. Now that she wasn't there, he didn't feel up to it.

"Why am I eating here if they're in the detention wing?"

"Because you surrendered and they had to be captured," Kevin said. "It's regulations."

"Regulations."

"Yes, the old suit is a stickler for the regs." Kevin rolled his eyes. "Besides, your mom blew up a troop of marines with a candy bar, so they're being careful about her food supply."

Howard followed Kevin out into the sea of tables that crowded the underground room. He looked around, but among the curious glances thrown his way weren't any faces he knew. He wondered which table was the cool kids' table.

He was willing to bet that it probably was not the one that Kevin was leading him toward.

The tech plopped down at a table against the far wall beneath an enormous poster with a robot wearing handcuffs, above big block letters that said "If we don't enforce the laws of physics, who will?" Kevin noticed his gaze and looked up at the poster.

"You like it?" he asked. "I designed it for last year's competition."

"Sure, I guess." The hangdog pose of the shackled robot made him sad, so he arranged his chair so he wouldn't have to look at it as Kevin prattled on about his ideas for this year's poster contest.

The meal passed slowly and mostly consisted of Howard not looking at the poster and trying to calculate the number of ways he could use the calories on Kevin's tray to escape the underground base. Finally, Kevin glanced at the time on his phone and pushed away his half-eaten meal.

"Time to go."

"Where?"

"To see a man about a robot."

***

Kevin led Howard down several levels until they were walking through concrete corridors painted with yellow lines on the floor. Each floor was apparently color-coded rather than numbered and they were on yellow level. Which was fine with him, except that it reminded Howard that he should have stopped to use the restroom before they left the cafeteria up on blue.

Howard's discomfort was momentarily forgotten as they walked out into a room so vast that Howard could not see the ceiling. Jumpships were arranged in rows along one wall, even the damaged one that his mother had apparently blown-up with a candy bar. Some of the soldiers and one of the suits had bandages and gave Howard's mother a wide berth.

His mother was watching the technicians and engineers trying to undo her handiwork and looked as though the manacles on her wrist were an accessory to her wardrobe. The others were with her, wearing borrowed clothing as befit their stature. Even Doctor Deeds was there, though he was wearing a straitjacket and stared through everyone as if they were made of glass.

Howard ran to his mother and father and the three of them hugged as best they could wearing handcuffs. Gary and Ericka were only slightly less enthusiastic in their greeting but no less glad to see Howard alive and well. If they were mad that he'd gotten them in trouble again, they'd tabled it for later. The older Ericka stood off to the side. Howard wondered what she had seen in the future that made their surroundings so unimpressive and everything his imagination suggested sent cold shivers running up his spine.

He broke away from the hug and stepped over to look up into the woman's scarred face. She met his gaze and nodded slightly. Howard had a million questions to ask the time traveler, but he was afraid of what the agents might do if they realized she was a time traveler.

"Why did you stop me?"

"You asked me to," she asked. "And I never could say no to you."

Before Howard could think of anything else to ask that would sound innocuous to the guards, Old Suit emerged from the damaged ship and walked toward them. As the gnomish figure approached, all eyes were on him.

The soldiers were their guards, but this was their captor.

He came to a stop in front of them and folded his hands behind him. For a moment, he said nothing, just walked up and down the line, meeting the eyes of each in turn. They tried to meet his cold gaze, but none could withstand his scrutiny for long except Deeds.[110] Whatever Old Suit saw in the mad scientist's eyes, he didn't like at all and moved on quickly.

Finally, he spoke.

"Welcome to a base that does not exist, headquarters of a government agency that also does not exist," Old suit growled. "The reason that we do not exist is so that we can prepare to defend our planet against threats that also do not, officially, exist."

"I don't understand," Gary said.

"You aren't supposed to understand, kid." Old Suit leaned in until he was nose-to-nose with his young prisoner. "Some of the best money that money can buy has been spent to see to it that you will not understand or believe anything that I am about to tell you."

Old Suit turned and waved for them to follow, which they did, strung out in an uneven line, rubbernecking like tourists. They crossed the expanse of concrete for what felt like miles until they came to the opposite wall and an enormous door, labeled Hanger 18.

Their guide turned and waited for them to catch up.

"Our planet is at war, and for the first time in our history, it is not with each other but with an outside threat. This war began in 1947 when a spaceship was shot down over New Mexico and we discovered that it was an advance scout for a full-scale invasion." He paused to let that sink in. "Using some readings that we took from the instruments aboard that spacecraft, plus input from a number of scientists including Albert Einstein, we discovered that the invasion fleet was due to arrive sometime in Summer of the year 2060 and a plan was formulated and a secret alliance was formed under the leadership of the United

---

[110] Actually, Deeds managed to stare him down, though in fairness to Old Suit, the mad scientist thought he was having a staring contest with a giant goldfish and was a bit disappointed that he didn't get three wishes when he so obviously won the contest...

States, specifically me.

"So why are we here?" Ericka the Younger asked. "What does this have to do with us?"

"Because you live here," the old man said. "You're a partisan in this fight, you volunteered simply by being born on this rock. And because our calculations were wrong -- the invasion fleet crossed the outer marker last Friday at 1900 hours, Earth time."

"They're early," Mr. Carter whispered. "Where is your outer marker?"

"The Kuiper Belt, on a planetoid out beyond Pluto," Old Suit answered. "We think they have other scout ships that noticed young Master Howard's experiments and they sped up their timetable to keep us from getting so advanced that we might fend them off."

"Or maybe your assumptions about faster-than-light travel are simply wrong," Mrs Carter said. "Maybe they were just faster than your calculations predicted, did you think of that?"

"You can argue with the physicists if you'd like." Old Suit shrugged. "Nothing would give me greater pleasure than those guys being wrong, but it doesn't matter. Whatever the case, we're not ready to face them."

"And that's where I come in?" Howard said.

"Follow me and I will show you where you come in."

Old Suit slapped the large red button on the wall next to him and machinery began to churn inside the wall. After a moment, the massive hanger door began to move with what Howard and his friends couldn't help but characterize as an ominous hiss.

23. The Dream Factory

On Howard's first day at his new school, he wore his favorite tee-shirt with the photograph of Albert Einstein sticking his tongue out and the quote "Imagination is more important than knowledge." Deeds had spotted the shirt and made fun of him, saying "Only if you don't want to actually *do* any of the things you're imagining."

When the hanger door opened, Howard wondered if Deeds could appreciate how much the knowledge of what lay beyond outstripped his wildest imaginings.

Howard had toured some of the factories where his mom had designed elegant machines to bend and weld steel into cars or toolboxes or any of the other millions of uses that steel origami could be put to.[111] But even in his secret dreams, he never thought a factory could look like this one. He felt like Charlie seeing Willie Wonka's Chocolate Factory for the first time. If instead of finding the golden ticket Charlie had been arrested and hauled across the country in a blacked-out airplane to a secret underground bunker built and funded by a government entity that does not exist.

Otherwise, it was exactly like that.

Hanger 18 had a lower ceiling than the room where they stood (if only insomuch as you could see it without binoculars) crisscrossed by a network of rails for the cranes and hoists needed to build the robots.

---

[111] Once upon a time, she had actually designed a machine that made steel origami cranes and flowers. It didn't have any practical applications to speak of and she hadn't been hired to do it. Like most things that are truly awesome, she had done it just to see if she could.

Robots. The word didn't seem large enough for the machines being built in front of him. Just inside the door, a robot head the size of an SUV sat waiting to be lifted into place. The sparks showering from the welders high above reflected in the gleaming steel skin and lifeless glass eyes. Beyond the enormous head, row upon row of gargantuan machines stood in various stages of completion almost hidden by the scaffolding and gantries that allowed their builders access to their creations.

They covered their ears as a crane roared along the ceiling tracks with a giant gear hanging from its hook. That one gear was probably the size of his house. These weren't the industrial robots his mother designed. Everything about them from the empty gun mounts to the angular armored plating screamed that these were soldiers for a new kind of warfare.

The aliens may be coming, but Earth would not go silently.

Howard approached the enormous steel head and laid a hand against the cold steel of the cheek. He couldn't reach the bottom of the eye. Three stories above him, the workers were bolting the giant gear onto the chassis. It took Howard a moment to realize they were assembling a hip-joint. Which meant that the scaffolding next to it held the other leg and the finished robot would be taller than a six-story building.

He stopped thinking about his family and friends and started wondering if anyone had ever died from an overdose of awesome.[112]

Someone calling his name forced Howard to tear his eyes away from the hanger's mechanical wonder. When he turned his head to find everyone watching him, he wondered how many times his name had been called before he heard it above the

---

[112] Thankfully, a steady diet of awesome has built up a resistance to this sort of thing and fatality rates from over-exposure to awesome have fallen steadily since the invention of the Atari 2600. Very few people outside of WARD know it, but video games were actually invented to boost the awesome immunity in the general population. (It's worked a little too well, actually. These days a simple sunset isn't enough unless there's a car chase taking place in the foreground with gangsters leaning out the windows firing laser pistols and flinging lightsabers at one another.)

glorious sound of gears clanking in his head. Old Suit gestured further into the room.

"This way, young man."

Howard didn't need a second invitation. He walked with his head tilted back, craning his neck to see the towering creations coming together in the heart of each scaffold.

"Geez, mom, did you ever imagine a factory like..." Howard suddenly realized that he talking to himself. "...this?"

He turned back to see his parents and friends standing behind a line of soldiers that had materialized between them. His father's face was red and his fists were clenched and Howard's mom had gone squinty-eyed like she was wondering how far she'd have to walk to find a box of candy bars.

"What's going on?" Howard demanded. "Why can't they come with me?"

"What they've heard already, plus what they've seen from that door is more than even the President of the United States knows," Old Suit said. "Though in his case, it's because he just hasn't asked. Don't worry, Howard, they'll be here when you get back."

He placed a hand on Howard's shoulder and steered his young charge along the wall to a metal humanoid figure that was seated on the floor, slumped against a wall, as if too tired to stand upright. It was the only completed robot in the room, though it was barely tall enough to reach the knee of the behemoth Howard had been watching the technicians assemble.

"What is it?"

"It's our first robot." The old man's raspy voice held a note of affection Howard hadn't heard before. "It was cobbled together back in the 1950's mostly out of old tractor parts just to prove that it would work."

"It looks pretty beat-up." Howard stepped closer. Even though he wasn't a farm kid, Howard had lived his entire life in the parts of the country that grew food and he could pick out the different bits and pieces of old tractors that had gone into building it. "What happened to it?"

"It's a battle robot," the old man growled. "It got in a fight and lost."

"Poor thing," Howard muttered. "What beat it up?"

"The next model, which was demolished by the one after that and the one after that." The old man sounded annoyed by the question. "It's how we tested designs until we found one we liked."

Howard looked up at the cold glass eyes shadowed by a jutting chrome brow cut from what looked like the front bumper of a delivery truck. He couldn't imagine building a robot this big-- if it was standing, it would easily be twenty feet tall.[113]

"How are they powered?" he asked. "Assuming you overcame the balance and torque issues of moving something that big on only two feet, how could you generate that much power?"

"We can't," the old man answered. "Once we get much bigger than this, the weight of the power plants and pneumatics and whatnot gets to be more than the steel can support, collapsing the whole thing. If we beef up the thickness of the steel to compensate, it's too heavy and we have to go with a larger power plant and then the thing collapses again."

"So you either need a breakthrough in metallurgy, or..."

"Or a lighter power source," Old Suit finished his sentence for him. "We've tested every power plant we know of and nothing we have works on a robot much larger than this one."

"You don't have an engine that will run it, but you're building them anyway?"

"We were running out of time." The old man gazed up at the robots being constructed above them. "Our scientists told us it

---

[113] His dad had nixed his Christmas request for a crane a few years past or The Dread Pirate Robot might not have been small enough to sneak through his window. Though that would've complicated the room-cleaning aspect of its room-cleaning duties. Howard envisioned a removable roof on his room secured with Velcro or maybe giant Lego blocks...

was more likely we would find a new power source before we found a metal strong enough to run with the ones we have, so we moved forward with production in hopes that something or someone would come along powerful enough to make this happen."

"Why not build something more practical?" Howard asked. "Something smaller?"

"The declaration of war reads like a challenge to a duel, only instead of pistols or sabers, we were to field an army of robots," Old Suit answered. "Our instructions were quite specific -- if we do not meet the alien forces on the battlefield with robots like these, at the appointed time and place, they'll nuke us from orbit."

"So if we have robots..."

"We have a fighting chance."

Howard frowned and scratched his head and looked up and around at the towering rows of giant robots and their builders. There were a number of things wrong with what the old man was telling him. None of it made a whole lot of sense, but the idea of talking his way out of a front row seat for a showdown between two armies of giant robots was unthinkable.

Old Suit thought he knew what the kid was thinking. He usually played a game with himself in these situations trying to guess which of the questions he'd already heard a hundred times the senators or scientists in front of him would ask: Why would they surrender such an obvious advantage to fight it out in the mud? Why would they do such an insane thing? Why give us a fighting chance at all? How do we know they're not just trying to distract us from spending money on defending ourselves from the more logical bombardment from space?

He needn't have worried. As a red-blooded eleven-year-old boy, the idea of sending an army of giant robots to repel an invading army of giant *alien* robots was far too cool to risk not getting to see it happen.

It was almost enough to make Old Suit wish he had more eleven-year-old boys to talk to.

"That explains why you want my fusion reactor."

"No more of your nonsense about feeding it popsicles," Old Suit growled, remembering his first failed attempt at getting the kid to cough up the design. "The fate of the world hangs on this."

"What's its name?"

"What?"

Howard reached out and laid a hand on the fallen robot's enormous thumb. The green enamel paint was flaking off, leaving flakes on his hand.

"What was its name?"

"It was a machine, not a pet," the old man growled. "We called it BB Mark 1"

"Bee Bee's a good name," Howard patted the robot's thumb. "I would've called you Crash or Clank or something, though."

"It's time to decide kid -- are you going to help us or not?"

"I can only help you if you're willing to accept that my reactor uses Frozen Funtime Pops." Howard turned his gaze to the rows of metal giants and shook his head. "Though I think you might need to buy your own ice cream truck to house your supplies... or maybe a fleet of them."

The old man stared at the kid and then glanced at the robots and back at the kid.

Old Suit had given up cussing when he'd been recruited to the agency in 1944, fresh from the Marine Corps (it was forbidden on page two of the handbook). Nevertheless, the first twenty or thirty responses that flashed through his brain would not have gone over well within hearing of the boy's mother.

He curled and uncurled his fists and glanced back at the kid's parents, distant figures behind the line of troops keeping them out of the room. He could just make out the Howard's mother and it occurred to him that maybe a Funtime Pop reactor shouldn't surprise him from a kid whose mom could blow up a shuttle with a candy bar.

He unclenched his fist and held out an open hand toward Howard.

"If all you need to get us up and running is a Good Humor

truck, then I think we can do business." He squeezed Howard's hand and released it. He glanced over his shoulder for a moment and then added, "But you get to tell your mother."

24. Hardly Mad At All

Saying goodbye to your family for the first time is a momentous occasion, at least it's supposed to be. It should be a greeting card commercial, swelling music and tears and lingering hugs and a train departing into the mist while you hang out the window waving to those you left behind on the platform. But the reality is that everyone usually gets so wrapped up in all of the details that they forget to have that train platform greeting card moment.

Howard didn't have a train platform for his family to stand on or a train to wave from.[114] He said goodbye to his parents and friends under the watchful eyes of Old Suit and a detachment of WARD soldiers wearing what Howard still couldn't help but think of as space marine armor. He reluctantly suffered a goodbye kiss and bone-cracking hug from his mother and his father's firm handshake.

Truth is he was in a hurry to go and play with his new army of giant robots. He had seen to it that their release was a condition of his help and stuck to his guns until WARD gave in.

What should have been a prolonged moment actually took all of eight minutes. His family and friends were marched off toward a waiting airplane and Howard was taken by golf cart to the lab that was being prepared for him deep in the heart of WARD headquarters.

If Deeds had been there, he might have warned Howard not to be so trusting, but Deeds wasn't there and Howard hadn't

---

[114] Anyway on modern trains, I don't think they allow that sort of thing. Like most of the fun things that Hollywood likes to tell us we should be doing, leaning out the window of trains is far too dangerous to be allowed.

seen his old science teacher since that morning. The man was obviously deranged and he hadn't made Deeds's release part of his negotiations.

As soon as Howard was out of sight, men in lab coats administered injections to each of the prisoners. Once they had collapsed into the arms of the waiting soldiers, half were loaded on the planes and the rest were taken elsewhere.

Howard was too busy and too far away to see it, but the following morning, an article ran in the local Sedville newspaper:

THREE MISSING HIKERS RESCUED FROM SUNSHINE ROCK SLIDE
by N.L. Embry

SEDVILLE - Two children and one adult were rescued last night from a small cave where they apparently sought refuge from the landslide that destroyed local landmark, Sunshine Rock.

Members of the Missouri National Guard working with the US Army Corps of Engineers to secure the hillside reported hearing faint cries from the debris field as the sun was setting. Crews labored well into the night to reach the cave where the two children and their apparent chaperone were sheltered from the slide.

The three told rescuers that they were out on a nature walk on Thursday when they heard a rumble and felt the ground shift. "It felt like an earthquake," said Gary Parker, 11, of Sedville. "The ground just jumped and bounced around like in that great Charlton Heston movie they made back in the 1970's." The children went on to say that as the ground began to move underfoot, their chaperone for the hike, Mr. John Carter, a local artist and father of one of their classmates, pulled them into the shallow cave where they remained for three days, subsisting on rainwater and energy bars.

Mr. Carter was unconscious at the time of rescue and has not regained consciousness.

The trio were evacuated to Goodwill Chapel and taken by National Guard helicopter to Bozwell Hospital, where Mr. Carter remains in a comatose, but stable condition. The children were treated for minor bumps and bruises and were released into their parents' custody.

Carter's son, Howard, and wife, Deloris, are still missing.

Popular local science teacher, Victor Deeds was also reported missing after failing to show up for work at James K. Polk elementary where he teaches. All three children are in his first period earth science class, though it is not known if he was with them on the trail that day. His car was found near the trailhead and he was last seen by a chapel caretaker in the company of an unknown man, who may also be missing. Authorities did not say whether the children mentioned their science teacher when they were interviewed.

Though it is a popular local destination, Sunshine Rock is on private property owned by a local church and the trailhead is marked with "No Trespassing" signs. The county attorney reports that the congregation's governing board has decided not to pursue trespassing charges against the hikers and is praying for the safe return of the missing.

Despite reports of an earthquake, the seismology lab at the University of Missouri reported no seismic activity the day of the slide. The cause of the rockslide remains unknown as of press time. Authorities have dismissed rumors of military activities as well as local reports of strange lights in the sky near the time the rock fell.

A candlelight vigil for the three hikers who remain missing is planned at the Goodwill Chapel beginning at 8:00 pm tonight.

If Howard had been there, or been paying attention, he might have wondered what happened to his mother and Ericka the Elder and Deeds. He might have turned on Old Suit and demanded an explanation, might have looked past how cool it would be to see the army of robots battling the army of aliens and asked the questions he should have asked to begin with.

Howard didn't see the article. Old Suit had been playing this game longer than Howard had been alive and was smart enough to keep the kid too busy to allow him time to think.

So it's for the best that like so many inventors before him, Howard built a machine to do his thinking for him. And like every hero before him, Howard had friends who would see to it that it did.

* * *

The Dread Pirate Robot sat alone atop its rubbish heap, listening to the bubbly fluids whoosh through its aquarium pump and staring dolefully out across the wreckage of appliances and rusting cars.

It was a bit worse for the wear since last it had stood atop the same heap in the same junkyard watching a flying saucer land in the field beyond. It was banged-up and had lost a hand in the scuffle with the space marines. The aquarium pump was bubbling worse than ever and it had a deep scratch across its backside from a close encounter with a barbed wire fence.

At least this time it knew where its hat was.[115]

But even a cool hat couldn't make the mechanical man feel particularly piratical. (Though it *did* feel dreadful and that was something at least.)

Back then, the robot had thought it wanted to be alone. But that was before it reconnected with its brother lawnmower and the kid who had created them; before it had encountered the men in suits; and before meeting the strange puppet creature outside the biker bar.

Now it was lonely and somehow even playing chess with bored library computers in the dead of night didn't count any more.

All of the humans that the robot considered friends or at least friendly rivals had been captured by the armored men, packed up and carted away in a caravan of armored Winnebagos. The robot had tracked the caravan as far as the airport without ever seeing an opportunity to rescue them and had to stand helplessly by as they were trooped onto separate airplanes and flown to some unknown destination.

Not even the control tower computers knew where they were headed. That the computer had felt particularly bad about this didn't help, though the two of them now had a standing chess date once the crisis had passed.[116]

The robot's spirits had sunk so low that it was almost wishing for one of Mr. Carter's phone calls to rattle its copper cranium. But the newspaper he had found in the trash that morning said Mr. Carter was in a coma and his creator was missing.

---

[115] Never one to repeat mistakes, the robot had taken the precaution of securing the hat to its head (at a suitably rakish angle) with a hot glue gun stolen from Howard's room. If the hat wanted to go on any more adventures, it would have to take the robot along.

[116] The Dread Pirate Robot might not be particularly good at being a pirate, but it was good at making friends. Legacy of being based on a model railroad, he supposed. Unlike his creator, almost everyone he met was immediately predisposed to want to play with him.

You might recall that Howard had built the robot's eyes with photo-receptors embedded in Play-do, which didn't allow for crying. But the robot was reasonably certain that if he could, he would be.

A rattle and crash caused the robot to sit up and pivot around to discover that two young humans were sneaking up on it. Once they realized they'd been spotted, the female child dragged the male out into the open and they walked toward the beat-up metal man with an air of purpose.

The robot recognized them as Howard's friends. It didn't know their names, but it had the strange feeling that it was about to get a new mission.

At least this time its head wasn't ringing...

25. Frozen Funtime

The science and history books used in every school in the world are in many ways a long and glorious list of things once thought impossible that were accomplished anyway by someone determined enough to keep going in the face of popular opinion. Though this sort of thing happens less often in modern times, modern science was in many ways created by these rogues.

So when Dr. Skillion and his peers in the WARD science labs reeled back from the flare of light in the glass jar where Howard had just inserted a normal everyday Funtime Pop and declared it impossible, they were paying their young guest a compliment.

"That is impossible," Skillion repeated for good measure and the others nodded agreement.

It's easy to see anyone in a single bad moment of their life think that you know all you need to know about that person. Having a classroom full of jeering fifth-graders drive you to tears, for instance. While I will grant you that Old Suit didn't like him and neither did Howard, that doesn't make Dr Skillion a bad person or even a bad scientist. Being not particularly gifted at teaching and having no talent with children doesn't make you bad, or even all that uncommon.

Even if you are a teacher.

Nevertheless, he was a gifted scientist[117] who had earned his lofty position in the WARD hierarchy by working his way up

---

[117] As well as an ardent birdwatcher, as we have already seen.

the ranks the old fashioned way.[118] So when he declared something impossible, you could generally take it to the bank.

When that impossible thing was sitting on the lab table it posed a particular problem to a man like James Skillion. He did not watch television, read books or enjoy art (at least not any of a sort that were unrelated to science or birdwatching). He was not the sort of man who could suspend his disbelief long enough to enjoy such entertainments.[119]

His disbelief was generally impervious to suspension.

He raised his goggles and rubbed at his eyes, but the Funtime reactor stubbornly refused to not exist. He thought this rather cheeky and suspected a trick. He and his colleagues had been watching the boy every step of the way, but he had once seen a musician pull a coin out of his son's ear. (Actually, it might have been a magician; he wasn't sure, but refused to listen to music just in case. No sense cluttering your mind with the work of charlatans.)

"If it's impossible, how do you explain those readings?" Old Suit jabbed a finger at the gauges, all of them with needles firmly pointing to either green or red areas of the dial. He didn't know what any of the gauges meant, but he was certain that it was good for him and bad for the scientist and that made him feel like clicking his heels together and perhaps uttering "Yippee". Not that he would be caught dead doing either thing in public.

The manual expressly forbade it.

"Can we hook it up to Bee Bee now?" Howard asked. The scientists and suits started as if they'd forgotten the kid was

---

[118] Age and treachery. But you have to hand it to him, he never got caught, which means he's smart. Almost incidentally, he's also a competent scientist, unlike his predecessor in the position who is doing quite well, I hear, and learning to cope with that extra arm he grew after Skillion slipped him the mutagenic compounds in his morning tea.

[119] As a child his parents took him to see Mary Poppins at the theater and he spent so much time decrying the impossibilities of what was happening on the screen that they left before the opening credits were finished.

even in the room.

"What are you talking about, boy?" Skillion barked. "Hook it to what?"

"Bee Bee Oh-One," Howard pointed toward the hanger. "Your test robot."

"Oh." One of the scientists grunted. "Oh no, we don't use that clanky old thing anymore. We have a test subject much closer to our final designs."

"Hook it up," Old Suit ordered. "It's time to see if this was worth all of the effort."

***

Deeds spent the first few days of sanity just exploring the well-lit portions of his mind. He left the dim and dusty corners for later, it was a delight to have any portion of his cognition back under control and he concentrated fiercely upon the equations that he had scrawled on the walls of his cell. They weren't why he'd regained his faculties. The robot army gathered in that hanger had shocked him back from his internal wandering.

But the calculations anchored him in the rational, even though the lion's share of the numbers were irrational and many of them simply nonsensical. Just as you cannot divide by zero, you cannot divide by infinity. Yet there it was in the lower left hand corner of the far wall.

His birth date.

It's amazing how important it is to human beings to know our own birth date. And how lightly we hold our existence when we do not know the simple fact of our own age. How many years have we existed? How many years do we have before death? When are we legally allowed to vote, to drive, or any of the other things that are age-dependant: like drinking a beer or buying a lottery ticket or getting a senior-citizen discount at a restaurant or voting Republican.

Time. The thing we measure obsessively even though it only exists as a firm belief in how far along we are on the road between birth and death. Deeds knew his place on that road for the first time in a long time.

He knew what today was.

It was at one of the most important junctures in modern history.

It was the moment when everything changed.

Today was his birthday.

***

"We have movement at the edge of the lake." The techs glanced at one another and then over at the gaggle of suits in the corner watching the experiments with Howard's reactor going on in the lab via the security monitors. The suits ignored them and Kevin slid his chair over to look at the monitor.

"Sirs! We have a perimeter alert!"

The suits heard him this time and did a quick round of ro-sham-bo and the one who lost detached himself from the group to come see what the technicians wanted.

"What is it?"

"There's an unusual pattern of heat signatures over the lake," the first technician reported. "Small animals are gathering."

"So what?" The suit sounded annoyed. "There's a national forest up there."

"These animals are gathered several feet above the surface of the lake." The technician tapped the bar on the monitor telling the altitude of the contact, but the suit wasn't paying attention.

"Birds," the suit muttered. "The turning point in all this agency's research and you're bugging me about a bunch of birds."

"Sir..."

"Send some soldiers to check it out," the suit interrupted. "Have them file a report."

"But sir!" But the suit was already walking away. Soon he was indistinguishable from the rest of the blue pinstriped woolen herd. Kevin shrugged and pushed himself back to his station.

Suits will be suits.

As soon as he was sure that no one was looking, he brought the live feed up on his monitor and watched the familiar shapes circle over the lake in mesmerizing loops and spirals.

"Happy birthday, Doc."

***

"Did this guy really graft wings onto a bunch of cats?" The guard hooked a thumb over his shoulder at Deeds, who was lagging behind again, fascinated by his reflection in the highly-polished tile floor.

"How should I know?" Howard's mother asked.

"Yes, he did," Ericka the Elder answered for her. "But he had his reasons, I'm sure."

"I like cats," the soldier growled, casting a hateful look at the mad scientist. Deeds looked up and met the man's gaze for the first time since he'd arrived. The guard took an involuntary step backwards.

"I like cats too," Deeds said.

"Then why did you experiment on them, you sick freak?"

"It wasn't an experiment." Deeds shook his head. "Oh, no, an experiment is a test for an hypothesis, usually something you're not sure will work."

"And I suppose you knew this would work, did you?"

Deeds smiled and shook his head again. "The cats did."

"Ask yourself, sergeant, if you want to chase him down that rabbit hole," the elder Ericka cautioned, but the soldier ignored her, stepping right up to Deeds's bars until the scientist couldn't see anything except his vast expanse of uniformed chest.

"Are you telling me that the cats *wanted* you to do this to them?"

"Have you ever tried to catch a bird?" Deeds asked. "Without using any tools or gadgets or guns?"

"No."

"Neither have I, so I had to trust them, didn't I?"

The large man growled and reached through the bars, knocking Deeds backward onto the floor. The mad scientist didn't protest his treatment, just fell on his butt with a sort of deflating noise. The others drew back from their cell doors as two guards pulled the sergeant back from pummeling Deeds with many a "Cool it" and "He's not worth it, man".

Finally, the large man pulled himself free and stepped back, seemingly under control again.

"Oh, my head," Deeds groaned. The soldiers cursed and Deeds lay on his back and refused to move until the guards decided that he'd been hurt when the sergeant knocked him down. A brief argument over whose fault it was ended with the determination that they'd better take him to see a medic or face the wrath of Old Suit for damaging a prisoner.

Two soldiers stood in the doorway covering their sergeant with Tasers while the sergeant went in to shackle Deeds for transport to the infirmary. Deeds hung limp and one of the soldiers holstered his Taser to help drag him out to the guard post where a gurney waited.

As they dragged the scientist past the cell of Ericka the Elder, a voice called from her cell. "Tell the nice men what the cats gave you in return."

"Litter boxes in the rafters, mostly." Deeds smiled up at the guards, who promptly dropped him "Oh, and this handcuff key." He produced the key with a flourish as he stood up and displayed his bare wrists.

The guards lunged for him as a winged black cat seemed to materialize out of the shadows to land atop a soldier's head. The cat latched hold with its claws as the man shrieked and Deeds grabbed the sergeant by the nose.

"Honk!" Deeds squeezed the nose hard enough to make the man's eyes water, but only long enough to distract the guard from the pinch of the needle piercing his skin. "And did I mention this hypodermic needle full of a highly-experimental sedative?"

As the sergeant pushed him away and fell back, Deeds pulled the stun gun out of the man's belt and shot the third soldier in the center of his chest as he was trying to fumble his out of his belt. All of the soldier's muscles seized and the taser pins ricocheted off the concrete to lie useless in the open door of Deeds's cell.

The winged cat sprang free as Deeds shot the second man, sending him to the floor next to his compatriot.

"Thank you puss-puss." Deeds picked up a fresh stun gun and hoisted the big cat up onto his shoulder. "Time to leave, puppet!" he called into Ericka the Elder's cell. He had recognized the odd voice as belonging to the alien visitor. Which was a relief since he hadn't been entirely certain that he didn't hallucinate that whole thing.

He reeled back as Ericka the Elder stepped forward with the alien -- now in the guise of a strange rodent similar to a chinchilla -- on her shoulder. Deeds blinked at her and somewhere in the depths of the still-shadowy portions of his brain, a long-dormant memory flashed brightly and then vanished.

"You don't belong here," he whispered.

"Neither do you."

26. King for a Day

There's a theory that the sound of an alarm klaxon was chosen because it triggered a deeply-buried instinctual response in the human psyche because it hits the same sound profile as the cry of a sabertoothed tiger. Somewhere in our primitive core, there's a caveman who reaches for his club and turns to fight every time he hears it.

This is nonsense, of course; the sound was chosen simply because it was the most annoying sound that mankind was capable of making at the time. When WARD commissioned the building of a new and unique alarm system for their headquarters, they recruited the world's top creators of annoying sounds. Little brothers, chalkboard manufacturers, and other makers of the world's most annoying sounds were recruited from across the globe to come and create the most annoying alarm system ever devised by mankind.

It was the biggest payday a professional bagpiper ever claimed in the history of the instrument.

It had only been tested once and the witnesses had required substantial psychotherapy to stop them from awakening in the dead of night in cold terror and weeping.[120] To ensure that the people hearing it would react to the emergency rather than devolve into crying and maniacal giggling, the final product had to be tuned a notch lower on the Albrecht Annoyance Scale.[121]

It is impossible to describe so I won't even try.

---

[120] Except Old Suit, but there is a persistent rumor that he'd been an oboist in high school.

[121] Most eponymous scales used by scientists are named after the person who came up with them: The Beufort Scale, the Richter Scale, etcetera. The Albrecht Annoyance Scale was created by Greta Fuchs of Innsbruck, Austria and named after her little brother, Albrecht. It's said to be the most accurate scale of annoying sounds ever devised.

Suffice to say that when it went off, Howard clapped his hands over his ears and stared up and around, expecting to see alien soldiers closing in from all sides with disintegrator rays aimed at the assemblage of WARD scientists.

Because nothing on earth could possibly make such a horrible noise.

Old Suit's ruddy face turned white as he stared up at the wailing trumpets bolted to the ceiling high above them. The sirens that split the usual silence of the underground base when he'd ordered the magenta alert were of the normal sort that had been warning cities of the approach of tornadoes and enemy bombers since the creation of recorded sound. The Annoyance Alarm (as it was known) was reserved for those special moments when WARD's carefully-laid plans were gone seriously awry. Such as when the young genius helping you defend the planet is in danger of discovering that you'd reneged on your promise to release his entire family from your secret prison.

Howard stood watching as the men and women around him shook off their initial shock at the terrible sound and sprang into action. The test reactor was wrenched out of his hands and handed to someone else as he was carried out of the room and hustled down corridors full of soldiers who were moving in tight formations, looking grim and determined as they buckled their space armor in place.

He watched the action with a mix of fascination and alarm until he was pushed through a door into an empty room at the end of a long hallway with ISOLATION ONE stenciled on the door in red block letters.

As the door sealed, he glimpsed a woman standing amid the chaos of soldiers and running technicians who was watching him with an unsettling gaze. She bore a striking resemblance to his old science teacher.

He felt a moment of relief as the thick steel door hissed to a close between them.

***

When the Annoyance Alarm sounded, Deeds was assisting Mrs. Carter down from a vent high in the wall of an unused laboratory. To his credit, he didn't drop her. The three escapees cowered against the wall with their hands over their ears until the wailing finally stopped.

"What was that?" Mrs. Carter whispered.

"Mad science of the highest order." Deeds sounded impressed. "At a guess, I would say it's a combination of bagpipes, an off-kilter oboe played by a drunken German, and at least a hundred babies shrieking on an airplane at 30,000 feet."

"That's not what I meant," Mrs. Carter muttered.

She didn't like Deeds and she didn't like her future daughter-in-law and was trying to think of a good way to escape the base and them at the same time. For her part, Ericka didn't seem to care much what Mrs. Carter thought of her, busying herself with tinkering with the Taser she'd taken from one of the guards.

"It was an alarm," Ericka the Elder answered, ignoring her mother-in-law's glare. "Probably triggered by our escape."

"I was getting to that," Deeds said.

The mad scientist wasn't paying much attention to his companions, busying himself with the contents of the laboratory shelves. The lab obviously wasn't used often, or at least not for anything particularly interesting or useful to their predicament. He turned to inform the women of this fact when he found his nose pinched between the fingers of Howard's mother. The irony of getting what he gave the sergeant not ten minutes earlier was not lost on him. He yelped, but the jab from the hypodermic did not follow.

He opened one watering eye to find Howard's mother staring down at him with a look that would have inspired a charging rhino with a sudden desire for a nice cappuccino at a lovely café it had heard about in another zip code.

"You know who I am, Doctor Deeds?"

"Not a clue," Deeds lied. He tried to rise, but his vision dimmed and he shrieked as she did something horrible to his favorite nose. The mad scientist collapsed to the floor held up only by the woman's grip on his nose. "You're Howard's mother!"

"And who is she?" Howard's mother hooked a thumb over her shoulder at the other woman. Deeds peered at the statuesque woman across the room out of the corner of his eye.

"She is Ericka Carter-Watt and someday she will be the queen of Earth," Deeds hissed.

"That doesn't make sense!"

"He's telling the truth," Ericka the Elder placed the Taser on the table and sank into a chair. "Sometime next week, there will be a battle between alien forces and those robots you saw in the hanger. As a result, the Wartime Advanced Research Directorate will gain alien technologies that will make them unstoppable and by the end of the year, the earth will be united under a tyrant named Cat Deeds."

"United?" Mrs. Carter whispered. "You mean conquered."

"Really?" Deeds honked. "Mom always said she would be the one that amounted to something... Ow!"

"And what happens to Howard?" Mrs. Carter asked.

Ericka the Elder took a deep breath and glanced at the scientist on the floor.

"In my timeline, Howard escaped capture by traveling back in time," she said. "WARD found the time machine that he left behind and was able to reverse-engineer the reactor design and install it in their robot army anyway."

"And how does that make you the Queen of the Earth?"

"Eventually, your son -- my husband -- rises up to oppose Deeds's sister and defeats her, making him de facto king of the planet."

"Then why did you stop him?" Deeds squeaked from the end of Mrs. Carter's arm. "You shot the time machine."

"Because Howard told me to," she whispered. "He spent years tracing back the causal connections between actions and events and it all pointed to that one event -- his escape, which left WARD in control of his time machine. He sent me back to prevent it."

"And now what?" Mrs. Carter asked. "Now that we're in the grip of these tyrants, what happens?"

"I don't know," Ericka admitted. "This is a fresh timeline full of potential and peril -- a whole new sequence of causality began the moment I destroyed the time machine."

Mrs. Carter nodded slowly, her eyes fixed on the younger woman's.

Most mothers would be ecstatic to learn that their sons were destined to become kings. Under other circumstances, Mrs. Carter suspected that she would be too. She almost felt guilty, as if she was supposed to feel that way, to be doing everything in her power to make that future come to pass.

King!

But not like that. Something she saw in the younger woman's eyes reminded her of what her father looked like when he came back from the war. A distant look, the faint lines left by squinting to block out the horrors. There was a tension in the shoulders that no amount of massaging would ever dissipate.

What must her Howard look like in this strange future the woman was describing?

The women's eyes dropped and fell heavily on the mad scientist still in the grip of Mrs. Carter's thumb and forefinger. He tried to grin winningly, but that's not easy when someone has your nose in a death-grip.

"What about him?" Mrs. Carter hoisted him to his feet. "Is he hero or villain?"

"The Deeds I met was a villain," Ericka answered, turning to address the scientist. "Well, Deeds, what about it, are you a villain?"

"Well, I certainly try, Your Majesty," he said. Mrs. Howard squeezed and he shrieked. "Ahhhhhhh! But people can change!"

"People never change," Mrs. Carter growled. "That's a lie we

207

tell ourselves when we're allowing bad people to keep doing bad things."

"Of course they change," Deeds objected, "why I once changed a man into a nine-foot-tall green lemur."

"Tie him up and leave him for the guards," Ericka advised.

"Does it matter that it was a nine-foot-tall *glowing* green lemur?"

"No, it does not," Mrs. Carter turned him so that he could see the once and future queen of the earth. "But you can redeem yourself here and now."

"H-how?"

"By telling me why you knew she was Howard's queen before she told you."

"The alien told me."

"What Alien?"

***

He heaved a massive breath of recycled air and went to sit on the only chair in the room. His mind whirled with possible reasons for the alarms. Alien invasions topped his list. The words *"they're here"* and *"they're unfashionably early"* kept echoing in his head.

His feet barely touched the ground as he spun in a slow circle, matching movement to his inner turmoil as he surveyed his new cell. The only gaps in the walls were tiny air vents up next to the ceiling, each barely larger than his arm and the only furniture was the chair and a cushion laid in a nook that he supposed was intended to serve for a bed.

He noticed that there was a bed but no toilet and worried about how long the weird alarm meant he'd be kept locked up.

A faint scrabbling noise like claws came from behind him and he turned to find himself being watched from one of the tiny air holes by a small rodent-like creature. As it pulled itself into the room, the form resolved into a sort of chinchilla. If chinchilla's were made of felt.

The creature blinked and pulled itself falling into the room, dropping to the floor and lying there for a moment as if stunned by the fall. When it didn't move right away, Howard rose slowly and reached out a hand to touch the felt skin, but snatched his hand back as the creature hopped up onto its back feet.

He continued backing up until he was sitting on the floor in the far corner, watching the felted creature unfold its tiny form into a much larger creature. Dark plastic eyes turned to regard him from much higher than any chinchilla could stand.

A sibilant voice whispered "I have been looking for you, Your Majesty."

27. The First Casualty of War

Women's hosiery has long been remarked-upon for its ability to warp the fabric of space. Not only in its effect upon males of the species, but the ability to fold into a form the size of a duck egg and then expand to the size of a fully-fledged human leg. If you had a fabric with those same qualities that was also shot through with nano-circuits and electrical pathways aligned in a pattern bearing a remarkable similarity to the human brain, you would be able to build the creature that was bowing to Howard Carter and calling him king.

On any other day, this might have frightened Howard, but after his recent experiences, all he could think was: *Oh. This must be the alien everyone was talking about.*

To be fair, at his age, Howard had precious little knowledge or curiosity about women's stockings and since he still wasn't entirely certain at that point that girls weren't in fact an alien species, it would be difficult to separate the two blind spots in his otherwise exceptionally perceptive mind.[122]

One moment there was a small rodent and the next he was being addressed as *your majesty* and bowed to by a largish piglike creature that was covered in childish drawings. And in between there had been a good deal of unfolding and stretching

---

[122] To his credit, he would figure out that they were indeed human by the time he was 21. For most adult male humans, it takes until they are 43 to be entirely certain of it. Howard was a prodigy in many ways. Incidentally, what brought the comparison to mind were the plastic hosiery eggs that his mother periodically purchased from the parts of Macy's that made him discover that the ceiling and carpets were suddenly worthy of his in-depth study. He had a monograph on the ideal texture and weave of department store carpets on his computer at home, but couldn't find a journal that would publish it.

of the strange feltlike fabric that made up its skin. He couldn't tell if there was anything inside the creature, but couldn't imagine anything that infinitely compressible.

Howard recognized the pig creature he'd last seen with his old science teacher shortly before Ericka the Elder blew up his time machine. At the time, the puppet disguise had hidden the fact that the thing was a robot.

Sort of.

At the very least, it was an artificial life form.

He tried not to stare. He wasn't sure what the politics of contact with alien races might be, but he was pretty sure that staring would be considered rude. No wonder the alien was particularly enamored of Jim Henson's puppets, for puppet it was and an alien puppet at that.

"Why do you call me that?"

"Call you what?" One magic marker eyebrow raised querulously. "I do not understand."

"Why do you call me Your Majesty?"

"Out of the utmost respect, I assure you," the creature said. "I was sent to find you."

"By who?"

"I come as emissary of those souls aboard the fleet of ships that are drawing near this planet as we speak."

Howard would have moved farther back from the creature if it had been possible without a tunneling machine.[123] He half expected the creature to attack him at that point, but it just stood there, staring at him with its black plastic eyes.

"What do you want with me?"

"I want you to play a game."

Howard waited but that was apparently it. He watched his reflection in the dark button eyes blink several times and shift

---

[123] As it was, several designs he'd been noodling with in the back of his head for a journey to the center of the earth flashed through his head. It occurred to him -- and not for the first time -- that he really needed to start traveling with a box of Popsicles and a bin full of spare parts. He just needed a way to fit it all in his pockets...

from foot to foot. Finally he sighed and nodded.

It was official.

Every robot he knew was crazy.

***

Mrs. Carter kept a close eye on Deeds as he led them out of the laboratory and into a long dark corridor. They were obviously in a portion of the base that was not used very often, but they imagined the distant tread of soldier's boots and the hiss and whir of space armor approaching around every turn. It made them jumpy as they crept down long corridors lit only by every fifth light fixture.

The heavy vault doors they passed were marked 'Evidence Room' and a number. Each door boasted one of the hand outlines that they assumed meant a palm-print ID lock or they might have tried a few in hopes of finding something that would help complete their escape. After all, Deeds reasoned, what kind of evidence did WARD collect if not strange artifacts capable of who knew what feats?

As they turned a corner, a loud clang sent Deeds sprawling on the floor and scrambling to get out of the way as the women spun and trained their Tasers in the direction of the sound.

Nothing was there to shoot.

The corridor remained dark and silent for a moment and then the clang was repeated, louder this time and from around the corner. The three crept back toward the corridor from whence they came and peered around the corner. Past the closed door of the lab where they'd interrogated Deeds, another door was open and light was drawing a door-shaped beam on the concrete floor.

Someone had apparently been behind them and failed to spot them.

Ericka signaled for silence and they moved toward the sound, stun guns raised and at the ready. As they drew near, they heard a man muttering to himself in a language that neither of the women recognized.

But Deeds knew those words, that accent, that voice. This strange language had been spoken in the kitchen of the Deeds home while English ruled the parlor, as his mother used to say. As far as he knew it hadn't even been spoken on earth.

At least not in *this* timeline.

Ericka made a grab for the tail of his lab coat as he bolted past her and skidded to a halt once he was bathed in the beam of light coming out of the evidence room. The women caught up with him just as the figure in the room turned and spotted Deeds.

The figure was a stooped and gnomish old man swathed in unseemly amounts of tweed. He had wild white hair that stuck out at every angle and a three-day scruff of stiff white bristles on his wizened cheeks. The old man pushed a hank of his mane out of his eyes to turn and regarded Deeds with shock that faded rapidly to disgust.

"Crap," the old man growled in heavily-accented English. "I should have known you would show up."

The women turned to look at Deeds for an explanation, but the mad scientist looked like he'd seen a ghost. Finally he spoke, not to them, but to the gnomish figure who seemed so put out by his appearance.

"Grandpa?"

***

The hardwood floors creaked underfoot as the Dread Pirate Robot limped back and forth along the wall of photos. In each of them, Deeds stood cheesing with his imaginary family. Setting aside for a moment that they were fake, there was something odd about the photos -- something odd about Deeds himself.

The robot was certain that the answer was right in front of

him, if only it could lay its hook on it.[124] It had run all of the possible answers through its data processors and gone back to start in on the impossible answers.

Still nothing.

At least the cats were gone now. One would think that a bunch of cats with wings wouldn't be underfoot all the time, but even the addition of wings cannot rob a cat of its innate desire to trip people.

The kids had brought the robot to the mad scientist's lair at its insistence and it was loathe to tell them that it didn't know why. Its metal brain had sussed-out the entrance to the basement laboratory immediately, but the lab held very little of interest to the two kids or their mechanical companion.

Except the cats, of course.

Even the robot had been enchanted by the flying cats. And they were a work of art, a pure act of mad genius. You can't just graft a bird's wing onto the back of a cat and expect it to be able to fly. Flight is about more than just having wings; a bird's entire body is devoted to attaining and maintaining flight. Bones and sinew, the bird is a creature of the air and the cat a creature of the draperies. To make a winged cat had been a hand-crafted act of sculpture undertaken at a genetic level.

In the lab journal they found, Deeds actually referred to them as genetic sculptures[125] and his sculptures lost no time

---

[124] Neither Gary nor Ericka were up to building it a new hand, but truth be told, the mechanical man was secretly quite happy with the hook it had fashioned to replace it using a coat hanger and some duct tape. Between the hook and the stump of table leg where its foot should be, the robot was feeling happily piratical for the first time in weeks. Sadly, Deed's bungalow was short on chandeliers or rigging to swing from, but there was hope that the alien attack might include some appropriate plank-walking or other assorted derring do.

[125] Though he maintained a policy of calling them 'Genetic Sculptures' in his notes, Deeds really called them: Whisper, Fussbudget, Ripley, Dustbunny, Gandalf, Oscar, Figaro, Cleo, Bradbury, Zorro, and Tinker. Deeds knew that no journal would accept a paper with notations about how Tinker and Dustbunny didn't get along. Even the *Proceedings and Review of the Mad Sciences* had certain standards.

escaping as soon as they discovered that these new humans and their metal friend didn't come bearing tasty treats.

That was three days ago and they didn't come back, much to their disappointment.[126]

"IS IT ODD THAT THE MAN HAS NO REAL FAMILY PHOTOS OF HIMSELF?"

"He's a supervillain." Gary didn't even look up from the television. It was his turn to robot sit and he was finding himself wondering why they didn't just leave the metal man moping in the landfill. "I don't really picture the Evil League of Evil decorating their lair with family photos."

He was saved from further robotic questioning when the door opened and Ericka[127] walked in with an armload of Funtime Pops for the freezer. She surveyed the litter of potato chip bags, half-eaten sandwiches and Popsicle wrappers with an air of disgust.

"This is someone's home, Gary, not a clubhouse."

"It's the lair of a man named Villainous Deeds," Gary shot back. "I kid you not, that's his real name -- I found his birth certificate."

"What was his father's name?"

"It didn't say, but he has a twin sister named -- get this -- *Catastrophic* Deeds." Gary cackled and propped his feet up on the coffee table. "This whole family's crackers -- I wouldn't want pictures of them around ei... what?"

Gary had noticed that the robot had stopped stomping back and forth in its habitually annoying manner and turned to stare at him. The lights of its eyes flickered slightly as they tended to do when it was lost in thought.

---

[126] Ericka especially harbored a secret hope for tiny winged kittens to take home with her and if he was honest, so did Gary. Deep inside the robot it was still a vacuum cleaner and the thought of cleaning up after a flock of fluttering kittens was appalling.

[127] The younger one, naturally. The elder Ericka was still at WARD headquarters and if another version had appeared I'd have told you about it, I assure you.

"WHERE DID YOU FIND THE BIRTH CERTIFICATE?"

"In the desk drawer." Ericka and Gary followed the robot as it clomped out of the room and down the hall.

In the spare bedroom they had found a large desk with an old-fashioned desk set and blotter and a stack of personalized stationery featuring the motto 'Live Long & Laugh Maniacally'. They had been searching for a computer, so they left the desk alone but Gary had returned to ransack the drawers after Ericka left to get more fuel for the robot.

The top drawer held a handful of grainy black and white photos. The photos were old and yellowed and would have felt delicate if the hand holding them had been capable of registering such telemetry.

Deep inside its mechanized innards, a search algorithm turned up a quote from Sherlock Holmes. "ONCE YOU ELIMINATE THE IMPOSSIBLE, WHATEVER IS LEFT, NO MATTER HOW IMPROBABLE, MUST BE THE TRUTH."

Holmes had never met Doctor Villainous Deeds.

Gary found his voice first. "But that's Howard."

28. Family Reunions

Plays often introduce a character for a scene or two, and then chase them off stage once they've done their bit. However, because it's also common for small theater companies to have too few actors, somone has to play more than one role in the same play. An audience who is accustomed to this sort of thing will gamely go along with it and ignore the déjà vu. It's just part of the quirky experience of live theater.

When this happens in real life it's a bit harder to ignore.

One would think that with several billion people on the planet, there would be enough actors to go around, but time travel makes for a fickle playwright.

If you chose two random names out of the billions on earth, the odds of those two people meeting is pretty remote.[128] But if you travel to a point on the timeline when you are alive, the odds of running into yourself are astoundingly high. The reason for this is simple: you are still essentially the same person. You have the same habits and like the same sorts of thing as your double.

It can lead to awkward conversations as your older, presumably wiser, self tries to persuade you to avoid donuts. Which is bad enough, but as we've seen, it gets even worse when you run into family members. Family reunions are difficult enough without multiple versions of everyone telling

---

[128] Though the odds of them knowing one another through fewer than six intermediaries is fairly common considering the size of the numbers involved. That is called the Everyone Knows Kevin Bacon phenomenon and it's another thing entirely. Not to mention the fact that it lost any trace of being legitimately interesting back in the mid 1990's.

embarrassing stories about you that haven't even happened yet.

It's enough to make anyone crazy.

The gnomish old man bent over the fallen robot that took up most of the storage room looked familiar to Howard's mother. With his ragged white hair, he looked a lot like the mad scientist standing next to her, but she didn't just recognize him, she *knew* him.

She knew him as well as you can possibly know your own father-in-law.

Then Deeds called the man 'Grandpa'. Except that her husband didn't have any siblings, which could only mean that Deeds...

"Howard?"

To her credit, Ericka didn't let her mother-in-law hit the floor when she fainted.

The old man frowned watched her fall and then turned back to his grandson.

"Who the hell is Howard?"

***

The Professor leaned against the railing and looked out over the factory floor where the robots were being assembled. She smiled at the sight of it. So much potential for mayhem if they could just get them powered.

Her name was Catastrophic Deeds. Her brother called her "Cat" and everyone else called her The Professor. She liked that -- it had the right air of menace about it to anyone who had attended a real school. Not one of those places where students called their professors by their first names, but a proper university where the approach of someone in tweed brough an appropriate sense of terror.

She turned to face the old man in the wrinkled flannel suit slumped in the chair behind her.

"Did the kid's reactor work?"

"I don't know," Old Suit rumbled. "The alarms sounded before the reactor could be hooked up to the robot."

"But it does work, yes?"

"Skillion seemed troubled by it, said it shouldn't exist."

"As long as it works, who cares if it exists?"

Cat Deeds stretched languidly as Old Suit resumed his pacing back and forth behind her. Aside from being a Professor of Impossible Physics and Dean of Mad Science at Arkham Tech, world domination was her only vice.[129]

Old Suit frowned at the woman.

There were things she wasn't telling him. She knew far too much about this impossible boy and his impossible toys, but he couldn't put his finger on what or why. Much as he didn't like Skillion, the degree to which the boy's Popsicle-powered reactor unnerved him was only funny for a moment or two -- then it dawned on him how many unsettling things he'd seen Skillion take in stride over the decades.

Old Suit hadn't been a habitual pacer until he'd met Professor Deeds and found himself enmeshed in her schemes -- since then, the groove in the tile had worn completely through to the concrete in some places.

He kept telling himself that it was for the good of the country -- for the good of all mankind.

They just had to get through the next few weeks and it would all pay off. Then he could retire happy to a nice square state where there were no mad scientists to disturb his calm. He would buy a ranch so far from everyone else that if he wanted to wear a cowboy hat, there would be no one around to make fun of him.

"Sir!"

And no technicians either. If there were any there when he arrived, he would call an exterminator and have them removed. Old Suit glared at the female technician standing in the doorway, waiting to be acknowledged with that aggravating air

---

[129] If Deeds wasn't distracted by his bruised nose, he would have happily pointed out that while he was mostly content to sit home and build winged cats from scratch and occasionally turn his lab assistants into fish, his sister wanted to conquer the planet, and possibly the galaxy if she could find the time.

of insouciance that he couldn't seem to drum out of them.

"Have you come to tell me the escaped prisoners have been captured?"

The woman shook her head. "Commander Keyes is conducting a floor-by-floor sweep and reports that they haven't turned up anything." The technician consulted the screen of her smartphone, not because she needed to consult her notes, but because she knew it would irk the old man. "The first ten sublevels are clear, and they're pushing into the deeper areas."

"Let the soldiers deal with the mother and the mad scientist," Old Suit growled. "Bring the boy and the test robot to the hanger -- it's time to see if this has all been for nothing."

The technician nodded and ran off. Old Suit turned to find her watching him.

"Do not underestimate my brother."

"He's doubled." Old Suit waved her concerns away. "He'll be out of his mind for the rest of forever -- it's the mother that bothers me."

"Because she blew up your tank with a candy bar?" she scoffed. "My freshman chemistry students could do as well or better -- it's the kid you need to watch out for."

"He's just a kid."

"If he finds out you're lying to him, neither of us will be able to stop what happens next."

"Would you rather we let your brother go?"

"No, but there was no reason to keep the others."

"His mom and your brother and that woman, whoever she is, are contained in the basement and the kid is stuck in isolation where they couldn't reach him if they tried." He tried to sound soothing, but his voice wasn't geared for that sort of thing. "Anyway, we have his reactor and once we get it hooked up to our robots, his part is complete and you can chuck him into a black hole if you want to."

He turned to leave, in no mood for her mad scientist rants.

"This had better work, old man," she said. "If these robots

aren't ready when those ships make orbit, you're going to be out there facing those aliens instead of the robots."

"They'll be ready."

He didn't turn around as the chair she'd been leaning against smashed into the door behind him. As he walked toward the hanger, he kept his scientist-free ranch firmly in his mind's eye.

***

Howard's step was less jaunty as he stepped onto the floor of the robot factory a second time.

For one thing, this time, he wasn't alone. He gripped the stuffed animal tucked under his arm so tightly that the disguised alien made a little strangling noise. Thankfully, the hanger was too noisy for the rest of those gathered around him to hear and despite his fears to the contrary, no one pointed at the cloth creature under his arm and asked why they hadn't seen him carrying it before.

He was a kid and no one paid any attention to kids.

As they walked through the scaffolding, the steel giants seemed to loom overhead with something less than their previous awesome majesty. The metal creations carried a menace that he hadn't noticed the first time. In every angle and gunmount, every dangling cable and hiss of a welding torch, these were the mechanical manifestations of war.

When he first contemplated the idea of combat robots, the idea had seemed cool. Giant robots duking it out with aliens... what more could a boy ask for? He'd let the idea overpower his better, wiser half. The half that wanted to know why the aliens would bother to land and fight when they could subdue earthly resistance from orbit and never have to touch the ground.

They stopped in front of a smaller robot, only fifteen feet or so tall.

"Howard, this is War Bot One." Old Suit's gravelly voice interrupted his train of thought. "We wanted you to be here to see the first test of your new reactor." He banged a fist on the metal as far up as he could reach, where the designation WB01 was stenciled just below the white blotch of Antarctica on the cartoon world adorning the metal abdomen.

The adults pulled Howard out of the way as technicians wheeled a hydraulic lift into place in front of the robot. One of the technicians rode up to the robot's chest and opened it with a wrench.

There was a void where the leads from all of the wiring in the robot ended in three large plugs and the two technicians hefted the glowing reactor out of its crate. Since he'd built it, the test reactor had been fitted into a housing with connectors that matched the ones already in place.

"The robots had to be finished," the professor explained. "I had to trust that we would come up with your reactor in time and had my people build it to accept as much current as would be needed to power the units."

Before she finished talking, the technicians had completed the connections and were bolting the carriage into the war bot's chassis. The eyes had already taken on the familiar green glow and Howard backed up as he watched the fingers begin to twitch and flex.

Howard wondered what they'd used to make its brain. He was willing to bet that it hadn't been intended for model trains.

The technicians wheeled their lift out of the way and the robot stepped out of the gantry hooks that had been keeping it from falling over. The enormous metal man teetered a bit and held its arms out to catch its balance as everyone scampered clear in case it fell.

But it didn't fall. Like a young animal finding its feet for the first time, it wobbled for a bit and then stood upright and looked around with glowing eyes. Cat Deeds cackled maniacally and hit a large red button on the console next to her and the robot staggered again as the body plating slid and spun and suddenly the metal man was bristling with rockets and guns.

Howard yelped as the robot's eyes swiveled and fell on him, the Gatling cannons whirring and the rocket launchers spinning. The professor and the old man laughed at him as he backed into them.

"Don't worry, kid, it's not armed yet," she said. "That will wait until we get it to the field."

He heard the creature under his arm squeak.

Howard scanned the room and did a quick mental tally. Fifty giants were under construction in the main hanger and along a far wall stood two ranks of eleven smaller, shinier robots with a cartoon representation of the planet earth painted on their chests as though they were wearing sports jerseys.

Go Earth.

The alien had been right.

Why had his future self sent Ericka back to force him into this? How could this be better than whatever would have happened if he'd escaped? Unless escape had meant this happened anyway and he wasn't around to stop it...

The adults were too transfixed by the capering robot to notice as he put the alien down and bolted into the scaffolding nearby. By the time they turned and pushed his doppelganger unceremoniously into the care of one of the soldiers, he had found what he was looking for.

29. Doubled and Troubled

Of course, it is impossible for Howard's dead grandfather to be in the basement of the WARD headquarters, vexing Howard's mother to the point where her brain couldn't handle anymore and she fainted. It doesn't make her weak; it means that she had been asked to accept one too many impossible things in one day.

You really ought to space these things out a bit if you can.

It is also impossible for Howard Carter and Doctor Deeds to be the same person. And it fits most definitions of impossible to achieve cold fusion using Funtime Pops. If you're going to follow time travelers around, I would suggest that "Impossible" is a concept that you let go of.

Younger brains are thankfully more resistant to these kinds of stresses.

Since a few minutes after Gary found the thirty year-old photo of his friend Howard in his science teacher's desk Gary walked into the room, that was a good thing. It was a Gary gone prematurely grey and with deep lines in the corners of his eyes, but it was still Gary's wit and fey humor that danced in his eyes.

When he said "Howard sent me to get you," they weren't even surprised. Though Ericka was glad she wasn't the only member of their little group to get to experience the little frisson of seeing their future face. Gary was just glad that he hadn't opted for leather for *his* trip through time, his double was wearing a plain black jumpsuit like he was about to jump into or out of an airplane at any moment.

Old Gary wouldn't answer any questions as he led the two kids and their robot out of the house and into a sedan that they recognized as belonging to Howard's parents. They each pulled their seatbelts tight as he tore through the empty streets of Sedville.

Gary was still "out sick" after his purported ordeal in the caves, but Ericka had returned to school and the classrooms were so empty they called it at a half day. Since drop ships and space marines crashed the suburbs and then Sunshine Rock was turned to gravel amid rumors of strange lights and soldiers manning roadblocks, almost the entire city had seemingly found a reason to be elsewhere.

Sedville was practically a ghost town.

Gary pulled into the parking lot of the hospital and parked across two parking spaces. He killed the engine and hopped out.

Ericka and Gary tumbled out of the car and followed in his wake. As they entered the hospital, they expected to be stopped, but halls and waiting rooms were empty. Old Gary took them up three floors and into the extended care unit where a man wearing a natty grey suit and a brown trench coat looked up from examining Howard's father.

At first, they thought it was Deeds, but then they realized the significance of the picture in Deeds' desk. Howard had his white hair cropped close to his head and wore a beard, but it was the face of their old science teacher who greeted them over the comatose form of Howard's dad.

"It's nice to see you again looking so young and hopeful," Howard said. "I can see that you're starting to figure things out. I'll do my best to explain the rest without driving you insane."

"What's wrong with Mr. Car... er... your dad?"

"He's been doubled, which means we're all in a good deal of trouble." Howard frowned grimly and they were taken by the depths of the worry lines on his face. "I threw myself to the lions and now I've come personally to see to it that I make the correct decision at the correct time."

"And what exactly does that mean?" Ericka asked. She felt her temperature rise inexplicably as her future husband cocked an eyebrow at her. She had never considered Howard handsome, but he was certainly going to age well. "Sh-she... I mean I did what you asked, why are we still in trouble?"

"Because even though you saw to it that my escape was thwarted, the timelines are still in flux and this," he lay a hand on his sleeping father's chest, "means that the man who put them in flux is here and working against me."

"What does Howard have to do?" Gary asked.[130]

"He has to do what I could not do when I stood in his place," Old Howard said. "He has to accept responsibility for saving the world, knowing that he could destroy it in the process."

***

Mrs. Carter couldn't hide her disappointment when she awoke to find her future daughter-in-law leaning over her. She had hoped the whole thing was a dream. Behind the queen's head was a concrete ceiling lit by flickering fluorescents and somewhere nearby, two male voices were arguing.

"You could have warned me that you had someone with you who didn't know what was happening," a raspy voice grumbled. "How was I supposed to know she'd faint?"

"Never mind her," Deeds shouted. "How can *you* be here?"

"By the simple device of being here, of course -- you really are a bit daft, aren't you?" the other growled. "And there's no need to shout."

"Dad took you to the seventeenth century and left you there!" Deeds kept shouting. "You couldn't get your hands on so much as a stray microprocessor, how the heck did you build a time machine?"

"Did you know you can laminate microchips between flakes of mica?"

---

[130] Gary refused to play temporal games with their doppelgangers. As far as he was concerned, they were guests in *his* time stream, so his Howard was his Howard, he was Gary and Ericka was Ericka. The rest could call themselves whatever they wanted and he was not about to get into pronoun wrestling.

"I..." Deeds couldn't think of anything to say. Bereft of silica and any convenience of modern engineering, the old man had built one of the most complex computing engines imaginable and then the machine to put it into.

"I have to admit I am impressed."

"And I'll admit that maybe you're not so daft after all." His grandfather chortled. "I was there when Charles Babbage built the Difference Engine, boy, do you really think the idiot that dreamed up all this nonsense could stop me if I wanted to leave?" He waved to the walls around them.

"Dad wasn't an idiot," Deeds muttered.

"He trusted these idiots – so he's an idiot by proxy," the old man said. "Tell me, Villy, why did you kidnap the queen?"

"She came here on her own."

"Why?"

"I think her husband asked her to."

The old man glanced from Ericka to Deeds and back again and latched hold of his grandson's lapel, dragging him down until the white bristles pricked his grandson's ear.

"Stupid boy," the old man growled. "If they stop us, we'll never fix the timeline."

"The timeline can't be fixed." Deeds wrenched free of the old man's grip.

"What's wrong with the timeline?" Mrs. Carter asked.

"It's all wrong!" the old scientist roared. "Can't you feel how wrong it all is?"

"I don't understand."

"Villainous, who *is* this woman?"

"The royal mother-in-law." Deeds's tone was deadpan. "Mrs. Deloris Carter."

The old man dropped his arms to his side and stared at Mrs. Carter as all color drained from his face. She felt a certain satisfaction seeing that he was as shocked to see her as she to see him, even if she didn't know why.

The old man stared down at the broken robot at his feet and didn't seem to know what to do with his hands. Mrs. Carter glanced down and thought she recognized the remains of her old lawn mower among the jumbled bits of robot.

When he finally spoke, it was with a soft voice, almost a child's.

"If you could look outside this dank basement, you wouldn't see any domed cities or flying cars," the old man said. "No one has a rocket belt or commutes to the moon."

"Of course not."

"Like I said," the old man shouted. "Wrong! It's all gone wrong!"

"Don't let him talk to you like that," Deeds interrupted. "Especially since it's all his fault."

"What is?" Ericka asked.

"Do you know what a difference engine is?" Deeds asked.

"It was a primitive computer," Mrs. Carter, the engineer, said. "It was the first computer, but no one ever built one."

"Not for want of trying," the older Deeds muttered, but his grandson ignored him.

"Grandpa Not, my father, my mother, my sister and I were all in a time machine one day when grandpa decided to make an investment in copper," Deeds said. "Only he wanted to make his investment in 1820 to capture a surge in the price when the American Civil War breaks out. The investment upset the copper market and made it impossible for the inventor of the difference engine, a man named Charles Babbage, to build it just a few years later."

"So?"

There was a tense silence as the two Deeds men waited each other out, trying to out glare each other. Finally, the old man relented.

"So, in the timeline I come from, the difference engine ushered in the age of computers almost a century earlier than in the timeline you remember." The old man sounded wistful. "Domed cities on the moon, rocket belts, flying cars, trade with alien species... it was all an honest-to-God reality by the 21st Century."

"And you messed it up by making an investment in copper?" Howard's mother asked.

"It's the small things that get you," the old man admitted. "I've been trying to put it right ever since."

"His first attempt to put things right is commonly known as World War One," Deeds growled. "That's when my father marooned him in the 17th Century."

"I can still fix it," the old man insisted. "I just need the boy."

"You've tried to fix it, Gramps." Deeds shook his head. "Over and over and over again, you've tried and failed."

"Look at this robot, Villy, really *look* at it!" the old man said. "This is a sucrose reactor. That boy has tapped into your memories. *Look!*"

Deeds did look. He looked and what he saw made him queasy because it was impossible. Utterly, completely, and inalterably impossible.

The mad scientist stood up and faced his grandfather with hope buoying his heart. So much hope that he shot the old man with the Taser his cat had swiped from Ericka when she wasn't looking. While the women were recoiling from the winged cats that were hissing at them and too startled to stop him, he shocked them too.

As he calculated the correct dosage for the same sedative that he'd jabbed the guard with, he whistled a jaunty tune. Hope is a dangerous thing. Hope in the impossible will make you *do* dangerous things.

See what I meant about giving up on the concept of impossible?

It just causes trouble.

30. Casus belli

Very few things that we know on earth are truly what you would call 'universal concepts'. So far, we've noted that waving, hitchhiking and duplicity are pretty much going to exist no matter where you roam. Two more related concepts that are nearly universal are the insult and the duel.

One person insults another by declaring their homeworld a 'dwarf planet', or waggling their eyebrows at the other's sister, or stepping on their tentacle, or calling them a feckless goolflazzle[131] and before you know it, you're standing back-to-back holding phase disruptors. It's all fun and games until someone loses a tentacle.

Howard knew this with the innate sense of anyone subjected to elementary school playground politics. As he stalked the corridors of the sub-basement for longer than he knew, his mind gnawed on the question of why the aliens would land and fight a duel with mankind and if they did, why they would get to chose the weapons. Everyone knew that the challenger didn't pick the weapon.

He couldn't picture humankind choosing "Giant Robots" as their weapon of choice.

So it logically followed that mankind was the challenger, but he couldn't wrap his mind around a sequence of events that would end with earth dropping the gauntlet against a

---

[131] Trust me, you don't want to know. And anyway, I'm not sure a correct anatomical analog is possible in earthling physiology. The most famous instance of its use was the *Plutonian Goolflazzle Proclamation*, which was issued by the government of Pluto when word reached them that earth had unilaterally decided that they were not a planet. It ended "...and so's your maternal unit."

technologically superior alien force.

Howard was so deep in thought that he was almost even with the open door before he noticed it. The scuffed toes of his sneakers were already in the beam of light streaming through the open door. He took a startled hop backward, his soles squeaking on the tile floor as he landed. His heart pounded in his ears as he glanced up and down the hall.

All the doors he'd passed had been marked 'Evidence' and locked tight with palm-print scanners like he'd seen on TV. Except on TV, he'd have a photocopy of an unconscious guard's hand to slap on the scanner or something. He'd started out wondering what they held evidence of, but got bored with the unrelenting rows of locked doors and turned his mind to interstellar dueling.

He craned his neck to see inside the open room and his breath caught at the sight of the metal figure lying on the floor in pieces. The lawnmower. Rage coursed through him and he had to blink rapidly to fight back the tears. And to think he'd imagined for a moment that these people were cool!

"Are you going to hang around out here all day, or are you going to come in and help me with this?" a familiar voice called from inside the room. The white coat was a bit more wrinkled than when last he saw it, and there was more stubble on his cheeks, but the ragged white mane of hair stood undaunted and caught the light as his science teacher stepped into the light.

"I should have guessed that they wouldn't let you go," Howard said. "What are you doing down here?"

"Not sure." Deeds shrugged. "In my day, we locked the crazy relatives in the attic."

Howard pushed past the mad scientist to kneel beside his broken robot. The head was separated from the body and one of the arms was off. He would need tools and parts to repair it.

He wiped furiously at his eyes and stood up to look around.

"What is this place?"

"It's an evidence room." Deeds tapped the large block letters painted on the wall. "My sister has been collecting genius from all over the world and squirreling them away in the basement."

"Including you."

"Apparently."

Howard walked up and down the shelves, opening boxes and reading tags. WARD had been seizing technological advancements to fuel their own effort to build the ultimate army. He found broken rockets and half-melted laser pistols stripped of their components. Each bore a tag detailing the origin and date of seizure.

It was the most intriguing collection of junk he'd ever seen, but it was junk. Under other circumstances, he would have been enthralled, but he only had a short window before someone took a close look at their prisoner and noticed that the boy in their isolation cell was made of felt.

"What are you hoping to find?" Deeds called from the door.

"I need a socket wrench and a soldering iron," Howard said. "How did you open this door? Can you open any others?"

"Can I borrow your robot's arm?"

Howard nodded and followed the mad scientist out into the corridor. Deeds walked twenty paces down to the next door, marked EVIDENCE 030 and stared thoughtfully at the palm reader as he scratched his head with the robot's limp fingers. He glanced at Howard.

"How long do you need to do what you're planning?"

Howard frowned at him. "I don't understand."

"If I crack this door open, I can't say for certain how long it will take for this hallway to fill with guns and armor and the soldiers necessary to use them," Deeds mused. "If you need more than ten minutes, you should think of an alternate plan."

"You opened the other one without that happening."

"I got lucky."

Howard thought it over and stared at his hands for a few minutes, running complex mental calculations faster than you or I could calculate whether or not we had time to make it to the market before they closed. Finally, he looked up and nodded.

Deeds used the robot's arm to smash the palm reader off the wall, reached in and grabbed hold of a handful of wires. He twisted them into the broken wires hanging from the robot's shattered shoulder joint and let it hang for a count of ten.

Then he shook hands with the robot arm and the door opened.

"That was..." Howard didn't like to use the word 'impossible' because it was used so often against him. "...wild."

"You obviously haven't met my sister yet."

"Wild-eyed woman with black hair?" Howard asked. Deeds nodded. "I understand completely."

"You have ten minutes," Deeds said. As they crossed the threshold the lights came up and the alarms sounded. "Possibly less!" Deeds shouted over the din.

Luck was with them and the room was used to disable new inventory. On a bench was an assortment tools and the gadgets that were in the middle of being stripped.

Howard recognized some of the bits and spun to survey the shelves.

Deeds watched him go to the shelves and start flipping tags. He finally came to the box he was looking for and let out a low whistle that was lost in the alarm's wail. Deeds shouted something that he couldn't hear, but it didn't matter what the man was saying. He had the beginnings of a plan.

He grabbed a box off the shelf, shoved a wrench in his belt like a sword and bolted for the first room. His heart was pounding as he opened the lawnmower's chest plate and laid a hand flat over the cool glass jelly jar of the dormant reactor.

It was still cold.

He looked up into the eyes of his science teacher and recognized himself in the mad delight that he saw reflected there. He was surprised to find that he wasn't surprised. He'd been called a mad scientist by too many people too many times to be surprised to find that he'd become one.

A long time ago, he'd promised his mother that he'd never use his peculiar gifts to retaliate against the bullies that pestered him at every school he went to. The words of the promise echoed in his head one last time and then fell silent.

For the first time in his life, Howard Carter was going to

fight.

***

"What is that?" a suit demanded as the control boards lit up and beeped urgently.

Kevin wheeled his chair over to a new monitor and brought up a schematic of the base. Only authorized personnel and his master's winged cats registered on the levels outfitted with heat sensors, but they only went down to sublevel nine. He could see the guards fanned out throughout the base, chasing the cats into and through the ducting.

Giant armored soldiers chasing lithe, winged felines through a maze of narrow ductwork. Needless to say, they hadn't caught any of them yet, though they had provided something new for the technicians to bet on. The current line on a soldier catching one was paying five-to-one against.[132]

"One of the evidence rooms on sublevel ten was opened without using a valid handprint," a tech from across the room reported. "I can't control it from here, they must have busted the door controls in the process."

Kevin felt a cold tingle run up his spine and turned to find The Professor watching him from across the room. She frowned and walked over to his workstation.

"What are you waiting for?" She demanded. "Gas the lower levels!"

The techs blinked at one another and then looked to the suits. Finally, they all looked to Kevin, wordlessly designating him as their emissary to the mad science lady. Kevin cleared his throat.

"I'm sorry, what?"

"Flood the lower levels with nerve gas!" she ordered. "Do it now!"

"We... we can't do that," Kevin said. "Why would we even

---

[132] Deeds didn't skimp -- when he built a flying cat, he didn't build dumb ones. In fact, Kevin couldn't be certain the mad scientist hadn't boosted their native intelligence.

have that capability?"

"What kind of secret underground lair are you running here?"

"The kind that doesn't have the ability to pipe neurotoxins into the living spaces," Kevin muttered. "What if there was a computer error or something malfunctioned?"

"Then vent the oxygen out of the rooms and suffocate them!"

"Can't do that either."

"Explosives?"

"Um... no." Kevin looked around, but all of the techs and even the suits were avoiding his gaze. "I can, um... I can lock the doors?"

"I think we already did that," whispered one of the techs nearby.

"What's going on here?" Old Suit entered the room and immediately all eyes except the mad scientist's went to him. He strode up to Kevin's workstation and only halted when the mad scientist spun around to jab him with a finger.

"They're breaking into the evidence rooms!" she shouted. "I told you not to underestimate my brother -- God knows what they'll find in there!"

"The lower levels are already sealed off, we..."

"That isn't good enough," she hissed. "Kill the boy. *Now*."

Old Suit was silent for long enough to take a deep breath before he shook his head.

"We're not assassinating a child on my watch," he growled. "And I think we've had just about enough of you."

"*What* did you say?"

"Arrest this woman." Old Suit pointed a knobby finger at the Professor. Several suits reached inside their coats before they realized they weren't allowed to carry weapons in the base. They glanced around, but none of the soldiers was present. "I said, arrest her!"

"Igor," Cat Deeds hissed, "Give the order."

The female technician to Kevin's left planted a foot against his chair and pushed him out of the way. She leaned in close to the microphone and spoke calmly.

"Troopers three and four, eliminate the prisoner."

Old Suit's face went gray as the technicians reached under their consoles and came up holding disruptor rifles, which they used to herd the suits into the corner. Cat Deeds stood in the center of the room, watching her revolution unfold around her and enjoying the clenched fists of Old Suit.

"Really, James, did you think it would be that easy to stop me?" she cooed. "With the boy gone, I will rule this planet for a hundred years..."

"Professor?" Kevin interrupted. Cat Deeds pulled out a small handheld disruptor and aimed it at the fool who interrupted her moment of triumph. But she didn't fire, her gaze fixed on the bright red flare on the screen outside the isolation chamber where Howard Carter was being held pending his execution.

"What... is... that?"

***

"Troopers three and four, eliminate the prisoner."

The alien visitor heard the orders at the same time as the troopers they were aimed at. It cocked its Howard head and watched the two men exchange uncertain glances. It sensed their uncertainty and their desire to disobey the order.

But they had been trained to act for the greater good and that the voice on the radio was the voice that guided them in that direction. And still they doubted because at their heart, they were good men.

The alien got tired of waiting.

By the time they turned to suss out the source of the strange noises their prisoner was making, it was no longer a child that faced them, but a ten-foot-tall pig thing, festooned with shiny and dangerous-looking bits.

They no longer hesitated to fire, but it was far too late.

31. Keep Calm and Release the Giant Robots

There's nothing certain in revolution. History has shown us that most revolutions are poorly planned and ultimately only succeed in throwing things into chaos for a time. Most of them only hurt those they were meant to help, but the memories of the few that worked out well keeps hope alive in the hearts of both the scheming and the oppressed.

Yes, the schemers plot revolutions too.

As Howard climbed down from the air vent and caught the robot head that Deeds dropped down to him, he noticed that the workers on the scaffolding were in an uproar. Bands of technicians and machinists were gathered to shout slogans at one another and there was no sign of the soldiers he'd feared when he first set out on this mad plan.

He waited for Deeds to hit the floor before they tucked their robot bits under their arms and bolted across the open spaces, sticking as much as possible to the shadows underneath the scaffolding.

The chaos above allowed him to get all the way to the far wall where the large and shiny steel warbot stood silent and dark over the fallen BB-01. Howard reached out and touched the foot of the large warrior, but it did not react.

Maybe they had pulled the power supply after the test, maybe they had just shut it down to keep it from larking about, Howard couldn't say. He was just relieved to find that it wasn't going to stomp on him as he went about his business.

***

"You will never get away with this," Old Suit fumed.

"I already have, you old fool," she muttered.

Old Suit smirked at the bald-faced lie -- she had not solidified her hold over the base or over his men. The soldiers at least were well-versed in the appropriate chain of command as well as military laws regarding mutinies. So far as he could tell, her command only extended to the technicians and some of the scientists and lab assistants.

He was almost curious what she planned to do next.

Other than wear his pacing rut deeper than it already was.

He kept his hands folded to hide the handcuffs on his wrists, pretending he was watching the technicians arguing out on the floor of the robot factory, but he was really watching her pace back and forth in the reflection of the room. His calm was a thin layer over his boiling anger.

An alien fleet is days away and she pulls this stunt now?

A flash of movement at the feet of the incomplete giants caught his attention and he shifted forward. He spotted him again, darting across an aisle toward the back of the hanger with something tucked under his arm. A technician with white hair followed him... Deeds. Of course.

He wasn't sure why it surprised him, the kid didn't know how to die. Old Suit swallowed the urge to shout a warning and settled in to watch what happened next. It wasn't like the kid could escape or do any real damage, but the chance to watch Catastrophic Deeds deal with him was too good to pass up.

He was willing to bet that she was about to live up to her name.

You would think that by now, he'd have learned not to underestimate Howard like that. You should give him the benefit of the doubt and just assume he was too distracted to think straight.

***

Howard felt the metal begin to rumble under his hand even before he'd finished bolting the chest plate back into place. The

238

cry went up as he rose to his feet. They'd been spotted by someone up high and momentarily at least the shouting had shifted to include alarms.

"Welcome to the ranks of the supervillains," Deeds said as he cracked his knuckles and braced to meet the crowd coming at them.

"I'm not a bad guy," Howard muttered as the crowd broke to allow a troupe of five guards to run through. Deeds wasn't listening; he was chanting.

"Remember, remember, the fifth of November, the giant robot treason and plot," Deeds shouted as they stood and turned to face the soldiers racing toward them. He threw both hands toward the men and the room seemed to erupt into flames. "I know of no reason why gunpowder season should ever be forgot."

Howard and the rest of the crowd went down on a knee and covered their ears as the pyrotechnics shook the base. When the smoke cleared and the bright spots were blinked away, the armored soldiers skidded to a halt, encased in frozen glaze ice.

Deeds cackled and shouted more meaningless poetry as the techs fell back to avoid the fate of the soldiers. Silence reigned for a moment as everyone cast nervous glances around at the blue ice coating the floor and part of the nearby scaffolding. If you thought a freeze ray was awesome, you've never seen a freeze ray landmine go off.

"You aren't going anywhere, young man," a woman's voice snarled from the back of the crowd.

The technicians and scientists got out of the way as Cat Deeds led the old man in the suit forward to confront Howard across his newly-formed skating rink. As she stared around with undisguised hatred and fury at the frozen soldiers and damaged scaffold, Howard noticed the old suit was in handcuffs, but looked faintly amused.

"Lady, the only reason I'm here is because I let you catch me." Howard pulled out an old pair of brass goggles he'd found in the box in the Evidence Room. "But it's time for me to go." Beside him, he could see Deeds already lowering the matching pair into place over his eyes as they opened their jackets to reveal the rocket belts that had been stored alongside.

"Are you nuts?" the old man shouted.

"You're not going anywhere!" Cat Deeds shouted. "War Bot One! Seize the prisoners and kill them!"

The floor shuddered again, this time under the tread of War Bot One's iron foot as it stepped down from the gantry and stepped over the crowd arrayed against Howard and his science teacher. The spiked cleats made short work of the ice and in two strides it was standing over the escapees.

Howard stared up at the giant battle robot bristling with guns and rocket launchers. The weapons were just for show, the old man had told him they weren't armed yet. The robot's only weapons were its hands and feet.

Which made it a fair fight.

Howard smiled up into the face of the giant and stood aside to allow his champion to rise to its feet. Grinding gears and the whine of pneumatic cylinders filled the sudden silence and the watching crowd caught their breath. Even War Bot One took a cautious step backward as the tatterdemalion giant woven of broken tractors rose to its feet.

Bee Bee towered a good ten feet over its newer, shinier replacement. The rusty old robot stood in silent contemplation, looking down at Howard before slowly rotating its head to fix its eye on the upstart War Bot. Flakes of red and green paint rained to the ground around them as one rusty hand raised toward the shiny new war bot and poked the globe painted on its chest somewhere in the vicinity of Paris.

War Bot One staggered at the blow and raised both arms to aim all of its weapons systems at the old robot. Bee Bee cocked its head as the smaller robot's weapons twirled and clacked impotently. The robot tried again and again as Bee Bee stood, waiting for something to happen. The younger robot stared down at its shiny hands in disbelief as the original battle bot rolled a steel hand the size of a Mini Cooper into a fist and cocked back a tremendous arm.

The smaller robot dodged, but it wasn't fast enough. The fist grazed its shoulder and sent it reeling into the legs of its massive and unfinished big brothers. The crowd scattered as the scaffolding broke at the frozen joints and a giant leg tumbled to the ground.

Old Suit stopped being amused. A fight of this magnitude in the manufacturing bay could be catastrophic. He grabbed a tool out of the pocket of a nearby technician and relieved himself of his handcuffs.

He shouted orders, but it was too late.

He watched helplessly as the massive scarecrow form of Bee Bee followed the dodging war bot through the jungle of incomplete robots. The larger robot was unrelenting, a red laser painting the landscape and plotting its next move with the same manic precision it once gave to carving rude sayings into unsuspecting lawns.

War Bot One fought with the heart of a warrior, but Bee Bee was a toy fighting to defend its child. Outflung arms and scything kicks and flying bits knocked off the war bot flew up into the scaffolding. Technicians and scientists jumped for their lives as the structures began to shake and collapse as the two robots locked onto one another and rolled through the factory.

Cat Deeds and Old Suit screamed conflicting orders at their troops, but their voices couldn't be heard as crane sections and bits of their robot army thundered to the floor in the wake of the two battling prototypes.

The masterminds of WARD's conquest of the planet could only stand back and watch helplessly as their army of half-built torsos fell like dominos.

Howard and Deeds didn't wait around to see who won the fight, but as they soared aloft on a cloud of billowing white smoke, up into the darkness of the tunnel out of the underground base, they couldn't help but glance back.

Through the smoke and heat haze of their rocket belts, they witnessed the destruction of WARD's robot army. Bee Bee may have been past its prime, but the brain he'd inserted in the rusty cranium had always had a bent toward the destructive.

The secret robot army was no more -- WARD would never

conquer the planet.

But as they lost sight of the chaos, Howard felt a new weight descend on him. The planet was undefended and there was no turning back. If the world was going to be saved, it would be up to him.

Thankfully, he had a plan.

It wasn't much of a plan, but he'd rather stand alone and naked in front of the alien horde than allow Cat Deeds and her minions to do it. Thankfully, that wouldn't be called for.

At least he hoped not.

***

"Master?" Kevin called into the darkness. He knew should have brought a flashlight. "I brought the vitamin B you asked for..." he froze as one of the cats materialized out of the shadows and meowed at him. The sound ended on a chirpy high-note and the beauty of the master's creation made his heart leap.

"Hullo, puss puss." He reached out a hand, but the cat disdained it, so he shoved it in his pocket. Of course, the master had given them a mission. This was no time for ear-skritches. "Take me to him?"

The cat fluttered a few feet into the darkness and landed again to look back. He followed the glimmer of its eyes and the bobbing white dots of its tiny white paws as it bobbed along the hallway.

He came on them so suddenly that he almost tripped over the tall black woman lying sprawled against the base of the wall. In his texted orders, the master had called her the queen of earth and Kevin tried to keep this in mind as he helped her sit up and apologized profusely as he rolled up her sleeve to jab her in the arm with the vitamins the master ordered to assist her recovery.

There were two others in the darkness beyond, a woman and an old withered figure who was snoring so loudly, he doubted that he'd have really even needed the cats to locate them. All family members. Royalty to be protected as the master's plan unfolded in the floors above...

He felt a thrill of fear shudder through his limbs as more of the cats materialized out of the darkness to sit near him and stare with him up at the ceiling, from whence came the rumble of distant thunder.

***

The alien visitor crawled the last few feet out into the open air and collapsed in an unseemly pile on the edge of the lake.

It was night time and the memory-felt robot had expended the last of its energies scrabbling out of the ruins of the WARD base just to see the strange skies and dream of home as its processors shut down one by one.

As it lay there, its photo receptors took in the white contrail left by the escape of Howard and one of his other selves. They were free. The mighty army of the conqueror was a pile of rubble.

Mission accomplished.

Howard would be king.

As its perceptions faded, its focus widened to take in the narrow swarm of white stars stretched across the night.

A strange sensation, it thought, *this shutting down. Like the kneading of tiny feet on its felted skin...* The curious felted creature from another planet drifted off into strange dreams as the winged cats gathered around to guard its sleep.

As they settled in atop the blanket, the cats thought it not at all strange to find this battered and twitching old electric blanket atop a dormant volcano in Oregon.

They just assumed it had been put there for them.

Cats are like that.

End of Part II

PART III
KING OF THE WORLD

32. The Least Chosen One

Howard Carter had never been chosen first for a team in his life. If you wanted to win the game, you wouldn't chose him first either. Usually, he was picked in the last handful of kids and assigned to play a position that had the least opportunity to impact the game. He couldn't kick, catch or hit a ball with any degree of assuredness that it would go where he wanted it to go.

If you were going to choose someone to represent the earth in the first interstellar Olympics, Howard would not be the first person to come to mind. It was an honor that he would have gladly passed along to someone else except that he didn't really know how to pass either.

Earth's chosen one was the one chosen last.

This thought was foremost in Howard's mind as he paced back and forth in the hay of a large barn near Gresham, Oregon. The barn had been the closest building to where their rocket belts had run out of fuel and shelter from the rain falling on them as they dropped below the clouds.

He still felt a small thrill at the base of his neck as he remembered soaring up through the smoke and fume and out into the fresh air. The thrill was dampened, however, by the knowledge that an alien fleet was arriving shortly and he and his mad science teacher were all that stood between humanity and annihilation. He wasn't sure what the aliens would do when they arrived and found that the Earthlings hadn't mustered a force of robots to stand across the field from them.

It would be an insult.

Humanity had shot down their ship and then as a gesture or peace or apology, extended an open hand across the void, only to close it again moments before they arrived. Whatever happened next, he suspected that death rays would play a large part in the festivities.

WARD had fifty years to create their team of robots and then subvert them into machines of conquest. And now someone too young to drive a car would have to stand in their place. His only consolation was that the game still had to be played by robots, so at most he would be their head coach. Except that he didn't have any robots to coach.

"Now what?" Deeds asked for the fortieth time since they'd arrived. The mad scientist had grown bored with watching his former student pace and had started poking around in the old barn. Then he'd gotten bored with that too and returned to pestering Howard.

Howard shook his head and kept pacing. He knew what he needed to do, but had no idea how to start. He suspected that Deeds could help him, but didn't know how and wished that the man would leave him alone long enough to figure it out.

"I wish we'd been able to save Bee Bee."

"Bee Bee?" Deeds looked confused.

"Battle Bot Oh-One," Howard answered. "It's what *they* called the robot that got the lawnmower transplant."

"Oh, the one they built from old tractor parts."

"Yes."

"Parts like the ones over there."

Howard stopped pacing and stared at Deeds, then followed his arm to where he was pointing. The back of the barn was cluttered with old tractors and the parts to repair them.

For a kid who had turned his family lawn mower into a robot in his garage, it was an embarrassment of riches. Except that these parts were enormous. Tractors weigh a ton. Literally.

There was no way he could lift pieces that big into place. He was going to need help. He turned to Deeds and stared past his old teacher at the distant farmhouse, just visible across the rainswept fields. He wondered if they had a computer...

"Did you see any stores as we flew over the town?"

"There's several, why?"

"I need a box of Funtime Pops and a vacuum cleaner."

***

Old Howard stopped at the top of the stairs to take off his hat and catch his breath before opening the door to step out onto the roof. The sun warmed the top of his head as he stepped out into the open air and he noticed the kids' eyes going up to the copper crown that he wore.

"It's a tripler," he said. "There are three versions of me in this time line and without this, all but the native version would go mad."

"You would get mad?" Gary frowned up at the adult version of his friend. "Why?"

"No, I would *go* mad, as in crazy."

"Why?" Gary repeated. He glanced at his older doppelganger, but couldn't see any copper glinting through the mass of graying curls. "And why doesn't he need one?"

Howard exchanged a wry glance with Old Gary.

"It took me forever to figure it out -- certainly longer than it should have." Howard dropped to a seat atop a boxy bit of air conditioner unit. "Even I couldn't help but notice that I looked an awful lot like Villainous Deeds as I got older. At first I thought maybe he was my real father or something, but eventually the obvious answer occurred to me... that he was me."

"Obvious?"

"To me, yes. Time itself is broken, probably for good, and Deeds' grandfather was responsible for the breaking." Howard stared out over the rooftops of Sedville for a moment before continuing. "I went looking for him and found him wandering around in the 17th century pretending to be a magician. Deeds' father stranded him there to keep him from doing any more damage trying to repair his mistakes. When I recognized him as my grandfather, it all began to fall into place."

"If Deeds is you, why is he older than you?"

"The Deeds I know is obsessed with a math problem, an insanely complex and unsolvable math problem with an unsupportable number of variables," Howard said. "Once, during the insurrection against his sister, we were allied for a short time and he told me that it was to figure out his birthday -- Deeds was born on a time machine while it was in transit between two points on the timeline."

"But you weren't," Ericka said.

"No, I was born in a hospital in Cincinnati like a normal person," he chuckled. "But his presence here and his madness explains one important thing that's always puzzled me."

"Why you do science like it's a magic trick," the younger Gary guessed. Howard's eyebrows raised and he nodded approvingly.

"Very astute," Howard said. "For whatever reason, being doubled-up in this time line gave me access to parts of Deeds' memories and intellect that were cut off from him. His madness was my magic trick."

***

"WE WILL BE TAKING ALL OF YOUR FUNTIME POPS."

The clerk looked up from his comic book to the metal man across the counter. He blinked at the odd sight as if hoping it would go away. *Was that an upended trash can talking to him?*

"Sorry, what?"

"RESISTANCE IS FU… WELL, ACTUALLY I SUPPOSE IT'S NOT FUTILE, BUT IT IS HIGHLY UNADVISED," the upended trashcan advised.

"Really?"

"WELL, TO BE HONEST, WE'RE NOT ALLOWED TO HURT YOU -- ASIMOV'S LAWS OF ROBOTICS AND ALL THAT -- BUT I CAN MAKE YOUR LIFE PRETTY DARNED INCONVENIENT." It pointed a finger at him in what he supposed was intended to be a threatening manner. "I WAS BUILT FROM AN OLD PRINTER, SO I AM PARTICULARLY ADEPT AT ANNOYING HUMANS."

Behind the metal man, a group of small round robots scampered through the doors and loaded the freezer case on their backs and carried it away. The freezer was being stolen by a herd of robotic vacuum cleaners?

As the automatic doors closed behind them, the robot hit a button on its chest. A slip of paper shot out of a slot and it handed the slip to the clerk.

"WE APOLOGIZE FOR THE INCONVENIENCE, BUT IT'S A MATTER OF PLANETARY SECURITY."

The robot reached up as if it wanted to tip a hat to him, but, of course, it wasn't wearing one, turning the gesture into a sort of bizarre salute. The clerk nodded wordlessly and watched the robot turn on its heel and march back out the door.

Once it was gone, he looked down at the slip of paper it had handed him.

It was a receipt signed by someone named *Ward*.

***

The trouble with robots is that they are neither easy nor quick in their journey from the scribbled idea on a napkin to a walking, fighting metal giant. Usually, years of research and development and armies of failed prototypes litter the ground behind one successful machine.

Sometimes it took decades.

Howard didn't have decades. He didn't even have weeks to get his robots from idea to reality.

And tractors, it must be noted, are very heavy.

A fact that shortly became all too clear for Howard as he and his erstwhile mentor tried to position the tractor axle intended to form the shoulder of what he intended to call Bee Bee Two. They collapsed as it slid the final three inches and came to rest in approximately the spot Howard had marked. Deeds and Howard let go of the rope to fall flat on their backs in the hay, wheezing and wondering when the muscles of their backs and shoulders would stop twitching and jumping.

"I have travelled the multiverse and visited myself in many time streams," Deeds wheezed. "In none of them was I a tractor mechanic or a body builder."

"That reminds me," Howard wheezed back. "If you're me and I'm you, why do you have a twin sister and I don't?"

"There's a one-in-sixty chance of twins in every pregnancy," Deeds answered. "Play that out across the multiverse."

"Ah."

"You aren't missing anything."

"At least my evil twin turned out to be a boy."

"Yeah, but you cheated and got one from another universe."

"At least mine would look alright in a goatee."

Howard and his old teacher laughed the tired, raucous laughter of those too tired to finish thoughts too ridiculous to dwell on. Howard levered himself up on his elbows and gazed through the tears at the pitiful assortment of parts that they'd managed to drag into the places he'd chalked onto the dirty floor. The chalk outline was roughly human-shaped, but obviously too large to be human, like the chalked outline of the victim in a vicious robot murder scene…

"This is taking too long."

"Maybe you should start smaller and get the smaller robots to help out," Deeds rose stiffly to his feet and glanced meaningfully at the printer robot.

Howard glanced toward the dejected robot standing amid the debris, staring dolefully at its feet.

At least the worker drones were working properly and out scavenging more parts from the local junk heaps. The robot meant to lead them was even more of a problem than his lawn mower with the artistic temperament or his rebellious Dread Pirate. It malfunctioned constantly for no reason and wasted all of its ink printing test page after test page.

As he watched, another test page erupted from the robot's chest and joined the others on the floor. The robot looked embarrassed and shifted its stare to the ceiling as its innards whirred and clicked ominously. Howard felt sorry for it and angry at the same time.[133]

"Would you *please* stop doing that?"

"I CAN'T HELP IT."

"I think you can," Howard growled.

"When my printer's malfunctioning, I usually whack it with a hammer," Deeds muttered. "It doesn't help, but it makes me

---

[133]It is my firm belief that printers were designed specifically to evoke that sensation and are part of a long-term study of human stress factors by parties unknown. For the moment, they remain the height of human optimism as to date, more homework has been eaten by printers than family dogs and yet each time we hit the print button we persist in our hope that *this* time, it will be different.

feel better."[134]

The robot glanced worriedly at the mad scientist and started to tremble and spew more test pages. Howard got up and went to lay a comforting hand on the shoulder joint.

"Don't worry, I'm not going to hit you," Howard soothed. "I'm sorry I snapped at you."

"THANK YOU, SIR. I WILL TRY HARDER SIR."

"This is never going to work, Howard," Deeds said. "You can build these things pretty quickly up to a certain size, I'll grant you, but WARD had twenty built for their team. You're going to need that many plus sentry bots just to secure the field and keep the government at bay long enough to play the game."

"I know."

"What are you going to do?"

"I don't know." Howard caught the next test page and stuffed it in his pocket. The printer robot looked like it wanted to cry and he almost wished he'd given the poor thing tear ducts.

A good cry was starting to sound like a better idea all the time.

"You know what your problem is kid?"

"Shut up and let me think, would you?"

"Your problem is that you're still trying to be a good guy." Deeds swung down from the loft to stand next to the trembling robot. "You're so caught up in this whole hero and villain schtick that you're not seeing that the only solution is to steal what you need and apologize later."

"I *won't* steal," Howard growled.

"Stealing is the lesser of the evils before you, kid."

"I don't believe in choosing lesser evils."

"Why choose the lesser evil anyway, when the greater evil is

---

[134] Actually, there's a school of thought that it really does help. It's called "Whomping Theory", which states that whacking something with a hammer has a near infinite ability to fix whatever's wrong with a malfunctioning system of any complexity. It simply requires the knowledge of where to apply the whomping and with which whomping tool. It is such a specialized discipline that whomping engineers can name their price anywhere in the land.

usually higher quality and will last longer before it breaks?" Deeds cackled. "Your prank with the receipt billed to WARD for the reactor fuel was funny, but you need to think in economies of scale."

"Why? Why is that anyway?" Howard demanded as one rebellious tear jumped the wall and fled down his cheek. "Why is it up to me? I'm just a kid!"

"You are the native version of *us* -- you have access to parts of my memories and the intellects of who knows how many other Howard clones that are running around." Deeds shook his head. "This is your time line. This is your world. It's time to save it."

"And if I can't?"

"Then we'll wish that we'd just stood back and allowed my sister to seize control."

"I can't assemble an army of giant robots with robotic vacu..." Howard trailed off as the ground shook and dust and cobwebs rained down from the rafters. Mad scientist and boy stared around and waited and it happened again.

And again.

And again.

Giant footsteps.

Drawing closer.

And it was too late to run.

Howard's mind immediately filled in the silences between the footsteps with mental images of an approaching army cobbled together from WARD's surviving robots. By the time the gravel in the lane outside was being crunched into dust, Howard and Deeds had drawn back against the far wall. They held their wrenches like swords in front of them.

As if they would do any good at all...

There was a pause that seemed to take centuries before the doors slid back. Two massive forms towered above them, one holding the other by the neck. They scrambled back as Warbot One collapsed at their feet. Howard and Deeds scrambled out of the way and peered up into the light streaming through the opening at the hulking form of Bee Bee. The huge robot clanked as it cocked its head at its small creator as he capered and danced with the strange white-haired man in the falling cloud of dust.

***

"Curse your sudden and inevitable betrayal!" Old Suit roared as he paced. "I knew you would turn on us eventually, because you're an evil, conniving witch, but how could you imagine you would get away with this even for a moment?"

Cat Deeds didn't answer. She hung limp between two hulking marines as the man she'd betrayed roared impotently as each successive wave of news reached him from the manufacturing floor.

None of the news was good. How could it be? Their vaunted robot army was so much scrap metal. The highest engineering aspirations of a species, the height of human achievement had come to nothing, destroyed in a single moment by the tantrum of a child who couldn't see the bigger picture.

Through the years, WARD had absconded with many a genius and their hairbrained inventions. For decades, they had been taking the greatest and most dangerous inventors and mad geniuses into custody and through a careful mix of bribery and coercion getting them to contribute to the project.

And a kid -- a mere boy -- had wrecked it all in less than a week!

"Sir?"

Old Suit stopped pacing and turned to glare at one of the unfortunate suits he had detailed to figure out how the base's systems worked since they couldn't trust any of the technicians. He had known they would turn on him eventually. Just like the mad scientist and her brother, it had just been a matter of time before they realized that they had the real power and didn't need the suits to write the checks and sign the forms.

"Sir!"

"What is it?" Everyone in the room blanched. They had never seen him mad enough to employ complex punctuation. "Someone give me some good news, dammit!"

"Crop circles, sir."

"Crop circles." It wasn't a question and the suit was smart enough not to say anything, just point at his screen. "Young man, we haven't done that schtick in twenty years! Not since people started mimicking us and we didn't have to make them anymore."

"I-I know sir," the suit stammered. "But these aren't normal crop circles, they're... gaskets."

"Gaskets?"

"Yes sir." The suit gulped. "Apollonian Gaskets to be exact."

"And what, is an Apollonian gasket?" Old suit asked. He sized up the young suit and took careful note of the younger man's thin build and thick glasses. A spy? "And bear in mind that you are five seconds from being arrested as a technician double agent."

"It's a fractal, sir," the young suit explained in a rush. "I-I was recruited to head up the video games unit and the techs talked about them all the time[135]. It's a geometric expression of mathema... um... just look at the screen!"

He jabbed a shaking finger at the screen of a computer that was showing a satellite view of the national park above the WARD headquarters. Enormous shapes were carved into the corn and soybeans, each filled with smaller and smaller circles. Where there weren't crops, there were stones lined up to form the images. Each was followed by another more intricate than the last as they progressed eastward across the states.

Old Suit was so stunned he asked the question he would never have uttered to an actual technician. "What does it mean?"

"The boy's lawn mower robot did this kind of thing on people's lawns all across the Midwest, it's how we tracked it." The young suit gulped. "The storage room that was broken into was the one that held the pieces of that robot."

---

[135] Our young suit is lying, of course. The poor chap actually minored in mathematics at Yale and studied under the father of modern fractal geometry, the late Benoit Mandelbrot. But he couldn't admit that sort of thing in mixed company or he'd lose his job. People who actually know how to do things aren't allowed to advance far in organizations like WARD.

"Shortly before the BB-01 went nuts," Old Suit finished for him. The younger man flushed at the knotty old hand clapped him on the shoulder. "I want that boy in custody before he does any more damage! Launch drop ships!"

"Sir?"

"What is it?"

"The President's on the phone." A suit held out the red cell phone with a shaking hand. "He wants to know how you plan to pay for all these tractors."

***

The dealership was closed, but that didn't matter to the swarm of tiny robots as they swarmed across the lot and round the tires of the parked farm equipment.

Their tiny tools made short work of the locks on the main building and the repair bay as well. Sparks and strange lights and noises might've alerted the authorities if the place hadn't been situated so far out on the edge of town for the convenience of the farmers who were their customers.

A giant hulk of a robot stood sentry as they worked through the night, idly drawing designs in the fields nearby as it walked its station.

By morning, the lot was empty.

The doors were re-locked and the mechanic's tools had been returned to where they'd been left the evening before. A note was left taped to the door to be found by the angry and dumbfounded owners the following morning. Sincerest apologies and an IOU signed simply "JK WARD" and bearing the address of the Federal Reserve offices in Washington DC.

The police found massive indentations in the ground that led away across the fields as far as they cared to follow them. One of the deputies commented that it was almost as if an enormous army had marched across the landscape and carried off the tractors.

He was laughed into silence by the others.

What a preposterous idea.

Then the call came in from another dealership. And a local

quarry. And a Funtime Pops factory. Then grocers and farmers across the county and then the state added their voices to the complaints.

Someone was stealing icy treats and farm equipment in unbelievable quantities and leaving notes and IOUs with a government return address.

No one mentioned the crop circles.

No one wanted to think about them.

By noon the next day there was an all points bulletin issued on state and federal channels across the Midwestern United States. A tractor and Popsicle thief named JK WARD and his accomplices were wanted for questioning.

Word began to spread and soon the thefts crossed into another state and it became a federal matter. The name "WARD" was poison on every lip and not even WARD's vast network of agents and dupes could stop it.

No matter what else happened, Howard meant to be sure that in the future WARD would not be able to rise up and subjugate the planet with whatever technology remained in their arsenal.

Hell hath no fury like an eleven year old super genius scorned.

***

Howard's mother wondered if the US Government would consider the Lear jet they had taken from the airfield stolen if they didn't know that it existed. She suspected that they would. Governments were like that.

As the sleek jet arced across the night sky, the old man muttered and paced the aisle and her grim-faced future daughter-in-law sat at the controls, deftly maneuvering the complex aircraft as if she did it every day. For all Howard's mother knew, maybe she did. She ached to ask the enigmatic woman the thousands of questions about her son and a future so dark he had broken the laws of physics to avert it.

But she didn't ask those questions or any of the others that occurred to her on that dark flight.

She was smarter than that.

Some things it's better for a mother not to know.

33. Natural Nurture

Everyone is the sum of their parents and their experiences, nature and nurture thrown into the whirling blades of a blender until the two ingredients can no longer be discerned one from the other. Time and experience go into the blender and before you know it, you are a person that your younger version would not recognize, a person you could not have imagined becoming.

To meet yourself, displaced in time, is to find a stranger with a familiar face.

When Howard's mother stepped down from the plane, the man who greeted her was unknown to her. Even though she could instantly put a name to him, she did not know him. He had her father's eyes and her husband's chin, hidden though it was by the close-cropped white beard, when she looked at the man in front of her, she could not find her child.

He was Howard, but not.

It wasn't until that moment that she accepted the things she had been told were true -- this stranger was her son's future.

Neither of them blinked for a long, quiet moment before Ericka the elder grew impatient and pushed past her to embrace her husband. Howard's mother dropped her eyes out of respect for the couple and turned to greet the man accompanying her future son.

"You are the spitting image of your father," she said as Old Gary took her hand and led her toward the two children waiting by the car.

She knelt to embrace the kids each in turn, feeling a bond to them even though she had only met them in passing as Howard's friends. After seeing the stranger with Howard's face, any reminder that her son was still a boy with a future unwritten was a godsend.

"Is he going to put a stop to this?" she asked. Old Gary frowned and shook his head, glancing back to the couple, who had parted and seemed to be having a heated discussion with the old time traveler.

"He can't," Gary whispered. "He can intervene sometimes and he can even offer advice, but only your Howard can do what needs doing -- we can't do it for him."

He was prevented from explaining further by the arrival of the others. Howard looked angry and his queen looked tense as they herded everyone into the car. Gary and Howard took the front seats and the kids had to sit on laps for everyone else to fit. It was terribly unsafe, but the roads were empty as they headed into town.

"While you were in the air, Howard has been busy," Gary said as everyone settled in. "All across the country, there are reports coming in of massive thefts of farming equipment and sightings of large robots on the march, heading this way."

"They're coming here?" Howard's mother inhaled sharply. "Why here?"

"Because Sedville is where the first battle of the invasion occurs," the older Howard said. "This is the front lines."

"And they are coming here to play a game?"

"That's why they were invited." Howard nodded. "But why they are coming is anyone's guess."

"Is it possible that at the end of this we might wish we'd just gotten out of the way and allowed that horrible woman to take over?"

Howard glanced at his mother in the mirror and averted his eyes to the dark and abandoned neighborhoods of his hometown. He didn't answer.

***

"Get the Leer jet warmed up and ready," Old Suit ordered. "We're headed to Missouri!"

He moved at the front of a herd of suits, dragging his prisoner down the long corridor toward the exit, pursued by the harsh trill of ringing telephones. The first calls had been from their liaisons to the other agencies, requesting instructions, then politicians who knew that WARD existed. Then, because politicians couldn't keep secrets if their lives depended on it, news and rumor caught up with each other and the first reporters began to call.

Who is WARD?

Why does WARD need ten thousand tractors?

How are they going to pay for them?

It was only a matter of time before a different sort of call was made and men in suits belonging to a different agency were dispatched with a warrant for his arrest. He could almost feel the ranch of his dreams slipping through his fingers. He was looking at prison or worse.[136]

This had been planned to be his agency's coming out party, the culmination of decades of groundwork that had been meant to prepare the populace for the reality of space marines battling alien invasions.

That was all a pipe dream now -- his only hope was to regain control of the kid and through him the mechanical army that was even now marching across the American heartland. He had to make this look like it was all going according to plan.

There was no retirement plan for the heads of secret agencies that unveiled their secrets before the appointed hour.

"The Leer jet is missing, sir."

"Stolen."

"The techs?"

"Can techs fly airplanes?"

"No, only pilots can fly airplanes."

"Aren't pilots just another kind of technician?"

"No, pilots have those cool leather jackets, when was the last time you saw a tech in a cool leather jacket?"

"That's a good point."

---

[136] In this case, "worse" for Old Suit would be retiring in disgrace and being forced to work in a place where he couldn't keep technicians and scientists under his thumb, or worse yet, to accept a teaching position that required him to deal with anyone younger than forty and/or people who didn't understand the need for neckties and strictly regimented hygiene standards.

"Shut up!" Old Suit roared. The gaggle of suits behind him dropped their voices, but continued at a low mutter. They no longer respected him -- he was teetering and one of them might get to replace him.

Old Suit pushed through the doors and shoved his prisoner into the first available elevator to the surface. He almost wished Cat Deeds would say something. He needed a little of her brand of crazy right now to balance out the chaos around him.

He stiff-armed the first suit who looked like he might follow, knocking him back into the arms of his fellows. Old Suit glared them all into silence.

"Stay here and secure the base," he ordered. "Get the marines in the air and the techs working on any robots that look like they might be serviceable and get them to the drop zone."

"Where are you going?" one of them asked.

"Missouri."

***

"If you're here, Howard can't die, right?" Howard's mother asked as they walked up the steps of the hospital. "*My* Howard, I mean. If you're here, he's going to be fine."

The older Howard drew to a halt next to her and waved for the others to go on ahead. He closed his eyes and took a deep breath before opening them again to meet the tearful gaze of his mother.

"My existence is no guarantee that your Howard will survive this, no."

"How is that..." Mrs. Carter couldn't finish the question. He reached for her, but she drew back from his hand and he dropped it to hang limp at his side.

"Howard is forging a new future for this world, a new timeline that is already quite a bit different from mine," he explained. "When he faces the aliens on the field, I have no way of knowing what will happen because it hasn't ever happened before."

"You're throwing my son to the wolves!" she shouted.

"I'm gambling with the only life that is mine to give."

"No!" she punched him in the chest and he grunted from the blow. "He is *not* you -- he's just a little boy."

"He is me, and I have no choice."

"You're evil."

Howard didn't respond right away. His hand massaged the area where her punch had landed and he searched her eyes for a long time before dropping his to stare at his shoes.

"You never asked how many subjects."

"How many what?"

"You know I'm the king of earth, but you never asked how many subjects my kingdom commands." His voice was barely above a whisper. "You never asked why I'm so bent on never having to wear this crown."

She tried to swallow, but there was no moisture in her mouth. She shook her head, refusing to accept the truth she saw on his face.

"Your son will never be king," he whispered. "He'll never have to raise an army of mechanized death to defeat a human army or sit in counsel to decide what part of the planet will get to eat this winter -- I'll storm the gates of hell to prevent it."

He turned and followed the others up the hospital steps, leaving her standing numb.

"My son doesn't want to be king!" she called after him.

He paused and turned halfway to give her a look that she finally recognized as Howard's -- the look that her son bore upon waking from a nightmare.

"That was my main qualification for the job."

Without another word, he turned and entered the hospital, leaving her no choice but to follow as overhead, warning sirens began to wail.

***

The pile of winged cats stirred as their chosen bed grew warm and began to shift. The sharp scent of ozone and ammonia filled the air and the cats jumped clear as the pile of alien fabric began to knit back together in the places where it had raveled and burned.

263

Unheard by the ears and listening devices of either human or catkind, the telemetry signals of the approaching alien fleet spread across the surface of the planet, mapping the geography and culture of the land.

They noted the curious sculpting of plant life that had been sown in neat rows, irrigated in perfect circles and then mown in intricate geometries. They noted the mechanical creatures that were mowing the patterns into the landscape and they watched as these creatures built more of themselves to join the march.

Their destination seemed to be a small farm near the center of the landmass.

The course was mapped and matched as alien voices uttered strange orders and their fleet of saucer-shaped vessels wheeled around the small blue planet's only moon to hover just beyond the artificial satellites and other space debris that hovered in low orbit. They hung there at the edge of the atmosphere, watching and listening as the communications of the planet below lit up in terror as the primitive planet-dwellers began to notice that company had arrived.

34. An Open Letter To the Skies

In a time before recorded history, primitive tribes of men drew together in a dimly-remembered attempt to communicate with whatever might live out beyond the stars. Without radio or other long-distance communication device, they created a message for the skies, an open letter to the powers that be.

We are here.

We are cold and alone.

Help us.

Humans are communal creatures and before they created sufficient numbers of their own genotype to feel cozy with the notion of being All There Was, they looked to the stars for succor. Even then, humanity knew instinctively that it would be an awful waste for whomever or whatever breathed life into their universe to have made a dwelling so large if it was only going to hold a bunch of hairy hominids and scary cats with enormous teeth.

In what we now know as England, they drew the famous Uffington Horse, as well as others, dotted across the English countryside, massive white equine figures. In ancient Peru, the Nazca people covered the landscape with massive spiders, human figures, and geometric shapes, like a bored schoolboy doodling on a massive scale.

Contrary to popular belief, humankind started shouting at the sky long before the invention of radio.

Howard Carter had done a report about it for his old history teacher back in Ohio when his life was somewhat normal. He had been reading about this when he built the lawn mower robot that now inhabited Bee Bee, and when the unfortunate android began carving glyphs and numbers in the lawns of Cincinnati, he wondered if he'd accidentally uploaded his homework assignment along with the operating system.

So, when it came time to communicate with the approaching alien fleet, he was ready to pen his own open letter to the skies. He didn't have a radio or any sort of transmitter, and though he could have put one together, he hadn't the faintest idea where to point it or what to say, or even that his message would be understood.

He did know that the only truly Universal language was mathematics, and he didn't need a radio to speak that language, just a large flat bit of land. There aren't many larger, flatter bits of land than the Great Plains of the American west.

As they descended from the Rocky Mountains and crossed into Kansas, his scavengers were ahead of him, turning every large bit of machinery they encountered into a recruit for his army. He sent out his mechanical minions to cut fractals into the cornfields as they marched across the plains, and as they accumulated more earth movers and bulldozers from their raids on local tractor retailers, they progressed to proper geoglyphs, massive geometries carved into the alluvial soil of the plains.

The message was kept simple and visible only from the skies: Meet us in Missouri.

***

Howard stood on the hood of his mother's car and peered across the stubbled cornfields with the binoculars she'd loaned him. She hadn't had the energy left to protest his dirty shoes on the hood of her car. Since their argument outside the hospital where her husband lay in a mysterious coma, she had largely ignored him, only speaking to him to answer a question.

He felt like her attitude shouldn't bother him, but it did.

Even in his forties, it mattered what his mother thought of him.

"What are they?" Gary called from below. "Is it Little Howard?" Without the benefit of binoculars, he was reduced to shading his eyes and squinting.

"It's his vanguard," Howard said. "They appear to be making crop circles."

266

"Seriously?"

"How else is he supposed to communicate with the alien fleet?" Howard asked. "It's brilliant."

"If you do say so yourself," muttered Ericka the elder. Gary chuckled.

Howard shrugged and returned his focus to the distant aspect of the massive metal figures walking in a circle in the distant field. Their large feet were crushing the wheat into the shape of a massive arrow-shaped Apollonian Gasket, the point of which was aimed to the East.

The kid wasn't just moving the goal posts, he was moving the entire field of contest. All the aliens had to do was recognize the arrows for what they were and follow them to Howard's chosen spot.

Then they would land and everything would change. Earth would never be the same after.

He wondered what the robots would do if he approached them. Would they recognize him as the older version of their master? Would they even notice him? Or would they stomp on him like a bug?

If they were anything like the robots he'd used to overthrow the Deeds Dictatorship, the last one was the more likely scenario. He decided to keep his distance. It was the kid's battle to fight.

"If you're not going to go talk to the kid, why are we even here?" Gary asked. "You can't interfere more than we already have, so what's keeping us?"

"We're waiting," Ericka answered.

"For what?"

"Him." Howard raised an arm and aimed a finger down the dirty track. Even Howard's mother climbed out of the car to peer at the distant figure walking toward them along the road, dirty white lab coat and tangled mane of white hair flapping in the breeze off the fields.

"Deeds?" Howard's mother asked.

"How the heck did you know he was going to be here?" Gary marveled. Even after all these years, his old friend continued to amaze him. Then he noticed that Howard had removed the copper circlet from his brow and he understood. "I thought you told the kids that if you took that off you would go mad."

"I took a calculated risk." Howard jumped down and set out toward the approaching figure on foot. "Stay here!" As he walked away, they saw him fish something out of one of his pockets and raise it to his ear like a phone.

***

"*WHEN IN DISGRACE WITH FORTUNE AND MEN'S EYES, I ALL ALONE BEWEEP MY OUTCAST STATE*," the robot muttered as it shuffled aimlessly around the living room of Deeds's bungalow. "*AND TROUBLE DEAF HEAVEN WITH MY BOOTLESS CRIES, AND LOOK UPON MYSELF AND CURSE MY FATE…*"

The robot trailed off into meaningless electronic noises. The boy who built him had uploaded a bunch of homework files and MP-3's along with the model train operating system. Why, the robot could only guess, but he suspected that along with room cleaning, his adolescent creator had envisioned his mechanical creation doing his homework as well.

Which meant he had a nasty tendency to spew Shakespeare in moments of duress.

"*WISHING ME LIKE TO ONE MORE RICH IN HOPE, FEATURED LIKE HIM, LIKE HIM WITH FRIENDS POSSESSED*," it muttered, "*DESIRING THIS MAN'S ART, AND THAT MAN'S SCOPE, WITH WHAT I MOST ENJOY CONTENTED LEAST…*" It clamped a hand over the voice port and willed itself to stop. The problem with Shakespeare was that no matter what was happening, there was a sonnet or snippet of a play that applied. So even though there was quite a bit of Wordsworth, Tennyson, and Frost stored on its central drive, it was inevitably Shakespeare that found its way from processors to voice box.

Maybe he should rename himself The Dread, Shakespeare-Quoting, Melancholic, Bored-to-Tears Pirate Robot. Somehow it didn't have the same ring to it.

To pass the time, it took apart Deeds' television and put it back together again. Then did the same with the antique stereo.

268

Now that it only had one arm, the process of destruction and reassembly took a bit longer than it used to. Ten minutes well-spent and then it was bored again.

Then the front door opened and a disheveled youth walked in. The figure looked so small and bedraggled, the robot almost didn't recognize him at first.

"Hello robot."

"MASTER HOWIE?"

"I'm sorry, robot, but I need to borrow your head for awhile."

"THAT'S OKAY, MASTER HOWIE, I'M NOT USING IT RIGHT NOW."

35. Howard the Pirate King

There are many reasons why a person might slip into a comatose state. Some of them are understood by medical science, but most are only understood by mad science. Howard's father was experiencing the latter sort and it troubled the old man greatly that he couldn't pin down why.

Noteworthy Deeds licked the electrodes and stuck them to the comatose man's temples, plastering them in place with bits of old chewing gum. The sleeping man jumped and twitched as electricity coursed through his body from temples to toe-tips, but even that did not awaken him. The eyes stayed stubbornly closed, and once the machines monitoring his lifesigns had time to recover, they persisted in their readings of an inert state.

"No matter what time line I find you in, you're always a lazy fool," the old man muttered. "Get up, darn you."

"What are you doing?"

The old man tried to snatch the electrodes away and hide them, but strings of sticky chewing gum betrayed him, stretching from Mr. Howard's temples to the old man's pockets. Gary had to help him extricate himself from the mess as Mrs. Howard saw to her husband.

"Honestly, I was only trying to help." The old man sulked as batteries and cables were removed from his pockets along with all his other toys and summarily dumped in the trash can at the nurse's station.

It took a lot of mother spit on a napkin to get the sticky residue off of the comatose man's skin.

When Mrs. Carter finally looked up, the Gary who wasn't Gary had the man who looked like her father-in-law tied to a chair. Gary who wasn't Gary was, of course, acting under orders of the Howard who wasn't Howard who had run off with another Howard who also wasn't Howard to do God only knew what.

Off to meet yet another Howard who wasn't Howard, for all she knew.

Her hands began to shake as her brain struggled to keep track of the bifurcating timelines and people who looked like people she knew. It was too much for one brain to take, but as Howard's mother, her brain was more accustomed to taking in the impossible than most.

Gary looked up and saw her face go pale as she glanced past him at a noise from the door. He spun around as two men in power armor wedged themselves through the door and pointed rifles at them.

Howard's mother began to shake.

Now *this* really was too much.

A man who looked far too much like her husband stepped through the door just in time to catch Howard's mother before she hit the floor. As her vision faded, she stared up into the face of her husband... but not her husband.

"Oh, not you too."

***

Gary and Ericka ran along familiar trails as the ground shook underfoot and the trees swayed above them. All around them, the bright white streamers of condensation were dissipating in the breeze like the feathers of an arrow pointing to where the WARD drop ships had slammed into the planet.

It all felt very familiar.

Up ahead, the tremors were sending the last bits of Sunshine Rock tumbling down the hill in sheets of gravel and dirt. Their minds painted the landscape around them with memories of their last flight down the trail, Gary being pulled along by Howard and Ericka borne on the shoulder of her older time clone.

Trees and smoke and men in armor pursuing them...

There had been a more recent trek down this path, strapped to stretchers, each carried by two members of the local search and rescue team, too stunned to protest, or struggle. One moment they had been standing in the hanger, listening to Howard bargain for their freedom and the next they were being pulled out of a dark hole, covered in stone dust and being told that they'd been on a school outing that never actually happened.

As they reached the sight of the rockslide, they had to duck under yards of caution tape and climb over fallen trees that bore the burn scars of the lightning storm that had followed the broken time machine down the hill.

They found Howard waiting for them at the top of the slide.

The proper Howard.

Their Howard.

Ericka was so happy to see her lost friend that she forgot her embarrassment at finding that she was supposed to marry him someday and grabbed him in a massive hug. Gary stood back, smiling and trying to hide his fright as more WARD drop ships arced across the pale blue sky.

Finally, Howard politely but firmly pulled away from the hug.

"Did you bring it?" he asked.

"Y-yes." Ericka pulled off her backpack and handed it to him. "But I don't understand why you needed it."

"I'm going to be representing the planet," he said. "The least I can do is put on a tie."

"The least you could do is take a shower," Gary snorted. "You're a mess."

"This will have to do -- I'm running out of time." Howard glanced down the slope toward the distant fields where his troops were putting the last touches on the final crop circles that would hopefully indicate where the aliens should land. "You can watch from here, if you like."

"We are not hanging back here while you go off and fight the bad guys!" Ericka snapped.

"I don't know that they're bad guys," Howard said. "It may turn out that this is all a game after all."

"If that's the case, those WARD guys aren't playing by the rules," Gary muttered. "Besides, do you actually know how to play any team sports?"

"Not really."

"Then you need me." Gary crossed his arms and frowned at his friend. "My dad is a sports nut -- I grew up steeped in the rules of everything from hockey to jai alai."

Howard chuckled.

"I don't even know what jai alai is."

"Then you need us," Ericka said. "Even your future self brought us with him."

"Did I?" he mused. "And where are they?"

"At the hospital with your dad, last I checked."

Howard nodded. That explained where Deeds had hared off to.

Without another word, he turned to descend the hill where Sunshine Rock used to be. Ten feet down the trail, he glanced back, just to be sure his friends were with him.

***

If you were interviewing for the job of Defender of Earth, there are a few things you might be looking for. Surely some sort of military experience would be at the top of that list.

Howard's only exposure to masses of people moving with military precision was watching a marching band in a parade. His family didn't watch football, so he didn't even have much exposure to half-time shows. The football problem bothered him almost as much as the military problems -- he didn't know how to play very many games.

An alien fleet was traveling God knew how many lightyears to play in an interstellar Goodwill Games and if they wanted to play anything more complicated than red rover, earth was in trouble.

As he stood in the doorway of Bob Engels' barn watching the robots muster on the plain, he felt like the most unqualified general in history. The tremors had stopped and the contrails of WARD's parabolic shuttles had dissipated, which meant his enemies were assembling somewhere nearby. What ends they were seeking at this point, he hadn't a clue.

273

The space marines were coming and he would soon be fighting on one front and playing a game on the other as he held his own government at bay long enough to engage the aliens in whatever game they wanted to play.

Maybe he could interest everyone in a nice game of Scrabble.

"Howard!" Gary called from inside the barn. "I think it's about ready."

Howard turned to glance into the dusty darkness of the barn where his friends had been watching the builderbots constructing their final robot, the largest one yet. He felt something bump against his foot and looked down as one of his swarm of robotic vacuum cleaners twittered up at him.

They were ready.

Howard picked up the tarnished copper wastebasket sitting next to his foot and handed it to the little robot. The vacuum sweeper twittered its thanks and bore the head of the Dread Pirate Robot into the darkness ahead of its master.

Howard joined Gary and Ericka and together they watched the copper helmet being handed up robot to robot, up and up and up until it reached the builderbots doing the final wiring of the giant's head. He held his breath as they carefully removed the old wastebasket to expose the rats nest of wiring that held the mind of his first and most troublesome robot and didn't breathe again until they'd embedded it in the center of the new robot's head.

As they bolted the new faceplate into place, the eyes were already alight and the enormous green hands already beginning to twitch. The tiny robots scattered and fell away as their creation rose to its feet, the wooden beams that had held it upright falling away.

Gary and Ericka backpeddled as it loomed above them, its head brushing the corrugated metal ceiling. Howard stood his ground, peering up into the gloom at his newest creation. He felt an overwhelming urge to cackle and shout "It's alive!" but managed to quash the urge.

The green giant bent and picked up the fallen copper waste basket that had once held its head and stared down at it and then turned to regard Howard.

The eyes flared with anger.

"I AM THE DREAD PIRATE ROBOT!" it boomed. "WHAT HAVE YOU DONE, HUMAN?"

"Not this time -- this time you are my general," Howard answered. "Your operating system was designed as a control system for trains -- today it will control an army of robots just like you in the last defense of earth."

"WHERE DID YOU GET THIS NEW BODY, BOY?"

"I stole it."

"I SEE..." The robot rolled its shoulders and tested its limbs and then looked down at its master once more. "THIS TIME, YOU ARE THE PIRATE."

Howard caught the copper waste basket as the robot dropped it.

"Yes, I guess I am."

36. Full Circle

Howard's history teacher back in Ohio had once told him that there were two kinds of pirates. There were the *real* pirates -- the kind in the movies -- who were just in it for themselves, and there were pirates who were commissioned by a country to do pirate type stuff against the ships of an enemy country. They were known as "privateers" and often the only difference between the two was a piece of paper called a letter of marque.

The difference between a pirate and a privateer was indeed paper-thin.

Howard hadn't laughed at that joke either and he wasn't laughing now. He didn't want to be either kind of pirate. He didn't want to be a general either, but he hadn't been given a choice. And since he didn't have a letter of marque (nor any idea where to get one[137]) he decided to do the next best thing... ask permission.

He approached the farmhouse where the Engels family sat yawning over their breakfast with leaden footsteps, his mind awhirl with what his options would be if the farmer said "No. Get your grimy mitts off my tractors!" Howard would have to argue his case and he'd never been very good at that sort of thing.

One of the benefits of being a pirate, he supposed.

He rang the doorbell.

After a moment's silence, he heard distant voices and then silence again. Howard glanced at his watch and rang the bell

---

[137] Since Howard was operating in the United States, the US Constitution gives the honor of issuing letters of marque and reprisal to the Senate, though it's a bit sketchy on the process for applying for one. Doctor Deeds had sent in a request for clarification back in 1973 and was still waiting hopefully for a reply.

again. After another bout of commotion half-heard through the thick door panels, the door popped open and an older boy stared down at Howard with a look of surprise.

"Hello, my name is Howard Carter, is your dad home?"

"Um… yeah," the older boy said. "Why?"

"Because I need to borrow his tractors," Howard answered. "All of them."

Zeke Engels looked down at Howard and then glanced over his shoulder and then back to Howard. Finally, he shrugged as if the boy begging tractors on his doorstep hadn't been the strangest thing that had happened that morning and stood aside to allow Howard to enter.

Howard allowed Zeke to lead him into the kitchen where a man and woman were staring out the window at the parade of giant robots lumbering through their yard. The man turned to peer at Howard.

"Who is this?"

"I'm Howard Carter, sir." He was acutely away that the fingernails of the hand he offered in greeting were dirty and he tried not to blush. *Be a general. You're too busy to clean under your fingernails, darn it!*

The man glared angrily at him and opened his mouth (Howard assumed to shout at him) but whatever he'd intended to say was drowned out as the flying saucer clipped the chimney. The family hit the floor around him as the glass shattered in the front window, but Howard stared up at the shaking ceiling and hoped that his heart would eventually stop pounding.

"What was…" the second flying saucer drowned out the rest of the farmer's question.

"I'm sorry about your tractors," Howard said. "I'll try to get them back to you in one piece, I promise."

He turned and the Engel family fell in behind him as he walked out through kitchen and garage to the driveway. The sky was above them was alight with a sickly green glow and everyone's faces looked yellow in the eerie light.

The General was waiting there, tapping its massive foot in the gravel. The family flinched as more flying saucers screamed through the air over their heads.

"When the government gets here, tell them I went on ahead," Howard Carter shouted over the cry of the alien fleet. Bob Engels nodded dumbly. What could he say to this odd boy and his robot army?

"What is this?" the farmer shouted. "What are you going to do?"

Howard glanced up at the gleaming silver discs circling the farm and back at the farmer. Howard glanced back at them and abandoned any hope of shedding the mantle of pirate. There was something in the man's eyes. A strange trust that Howard had never seen directed his way before.

He had seen it on the faces of the young suits looking at Old Suit and on the faces of his elders as they gathered to listen to the president speak. Not trust. At least not entirely. But they were nonetheless relying on him to know what was going on and to know what to do about it.

So this is what it feels like to be a king.

"I'm going to save the world," he promised.

The General bent down and picked him up to sit on its massive shoulder like a pirate's parrot. As they walked away across the fields, Howard glanced back to see the Engels family waving as he took the most expensive and important piece of farming equipment they owned and rode it off to war.

He couldn't suppress a strange thrill as the ranks of giant robots formed up and fell in behind them. Such a glorious thing to be a pirate king.

***

Everyone threw themselves to the ground as the alien ships passing overhead shook the hospital. Even the soldiers who had accompanied Graham Deeds into the room looked at the passing formations of flying saucers with pale faces.

"They're here." Deeds moaned from the floor.

"Villy?"

"Hi dad."

Graham Deeds picked Howard's unconscious mother up off

the floor and laid her on the empty bed next to her husband before he turned to give his son a hand up off the floor. They sized one another up for a moment before embracing. To an outside observer, they appeared to be the same age, but such is the fate of time travelers and time travelers' children.

Graham Deeds turned to greet King Howard and his queen and their companion, Gary. Howard grimaced at the older man as he accepted his too-firm handshake.

"Greetings, your majesty," Graham Deeds bowed. "I didn't expect to see you here."

"I came to stop this from happening."

Graham Deeds raised his head and narrowed his eyes, shooting a look toward his elderly father, still picking himself up out of a pile of fallen ceiling tiles. He made no move to assist his father.

"I see," he said. "You realize that I can't allow that."

Howard cocked an eyebrow and Gary and Ericka backed up a wary step. When Howard spoke again, all traces of affability were gone.

"You think you can stop me?"

"I think I've worked too long for this to allow you to muck it up now."

"I am King Howard the First, defender and protector of the earth," Howard hissed. "I have lived my entire life with the results of your grand plan, and if you think I will allow you to complete it and reduce the population of this planet by half, you are sadly and deeply mistaken."

"You…" whatever response Graham Deeds intended was halted by a sudden flash of light and sound that poured through the broken windows.

"Attention assorted Howards and other time-displaced members of my extended family." The thunderous voice was that of a young boy, but magnified a hundredfold until it was all they could hear. "You have all interfered as much as I am willing to allow."

"Howard?" Mrs. Carter rolled over and squinted into the light. "Is that my Howard?"

"I don't care who you were wherever you came from -- this

is my world to protect, and I'm starting to realize that this means my first duty is to protect it from your meddling," the voice continued. "The only Howard that belongs here is me, and in the end, there can be only one."

Gary muffled a cheer as his king and the Deeds family rushed to the window and looked down at the parking lot where a line of small robots stood in a silent circle. Each metal soldier protected a machine the size of an air conditioner unit that was pinning down one portion of the dome of blinding light that covered the hospital.

"This building is locked-down," young Howard intoned. "If you attempt to leave by any means, you will be stopped either by my force field or by my robots. Either way, your interference ends now."

***

Old Suit grabbed the edge of a computer bank as the van rocked violently in the wake of the passing alien fleet. Cat Deeds cackled madly with each screaming pass from the gleaming silver discs and the old man regretted bringing her with him.

"They're here! They're here!" the young suit manning the radar shrieked. Old Suit stuck a protective finger in the ear facing the young man as he repeated himself, louder this time. He almost missed the professional technicians who were so invested in appearing unimpressed by even the most bizarre occurrence their computers presented them.

"Shut up!" Old Suit barked. "For God's sake, we can all see them out the window, you twit."

"We have to stop this before that kid kills us all," Skillion growled.

"And how do you propose to do that, exactly?" Old Suit asked. "Really, Doctor, how do you propose that we stop him? He did in one week what you failed to accomplish in fifty years, so if you have any ideas, it's past time to share them!"

"I..." Skillion frowned, but didn't have anything to follow that up with.

"I didn't think so." Old Suit threw him a glare that would have wilted a lesser man, but the scientist was engrossed in the surveillance photos of the giant robots. "We have weapons that would take down one or two of these things, but he's built thousands of them in only a few days!"

"Self-replicating machines," Skillion moaned. "Even if the aliens give up and go home, we're going to be overrun by robots!"

"Any sign of the kid?" Old Suit ignored the scientist, who had been repeating the same mantra since they'd received first report of the tractor thefts.

"We have hundreds of large electronic signatures closing in on the fields below Sunshine Rock," a young suit reported in a calmer tone. "Or where it used to be anyway. Along with easily a thousand smaller ones, but there's no way to tell if any of them are carrying Carter."

Old Suit growled and fumed and paced along the row of computers set up in the airplane parked on a deserted runway near the Engels farm where what remained of WARD was assembling for battle.

He wheeled to face the drawn face of Skillion, and poked the scientist in the middle of his chest. "You're our expert, what happens if the aliens land and they're met by a kid?"

"They will most likely be insulted," Skillion answered. "What they'll do about it is anyone's guess."

"This kid thinks this is a playground game."

"You brought him into this," Skillion muttered.

The old man growled but didn't answer the challenge. He was losing ground with his own staff. The only thing that had kept the president from ordering him arrested for the debacle unfolding around them was that he was the only person in the country who had full knowledge of the situation.

Old Suit had made sure of that.

The van lurched to a stop.

"Why are we stopping?" he shouted.

"They're here," a voice from the driver's seat answered.

"We know that, you stu…" Old Suit trailed off as he stooped down to look past the driver at the enormous green tractor standing astride the road, glaring down at them. It was wearing one of the WARD drop ships as a hat.

The driver's knuckles whitened as a beat up old farm truck stepped around its giant compatriot to tap lightly on the window.

The driver gulped and rolled it down.

"WE'RE SORRY SIR, THIS AREA IS CLOSED TO TRAFFIC," the truck rumbled. "ALIEN INVASION AND ALL THAT."

37. The Conscience of a King…

Robots of every size marched, scuttled and rolled through the holes and gates in the perimeter fences that surrounded the field. Old rusted hulks of indeterminate origin stood shoulder-to-shoulder with glistening new combine harvesters and smaller robots built from trucks of every age, make and model scampered past at knee height.

Keeping in mind that 'knee height' was still twenty feet high, it was simultaneously the most ridiculous and the most awesome sight Howard had ever seen.

The robots moved in perfectly straight lines, interweaving at times with perfect spacing and precision like two thousand giant toy trains. They formed ranks and arranged themselves by size and specialties, small in front of tall and those equipped for throwing paired with dump trucks and boulders that they had liberated from the nearby quarries.

Howard had chosen his general well.

Several robots marching ahead of where Howard rode on the shoulder of the General unfurled great flapping banners that caught the downdrafts coming off the circling space ships as yet more robots of the vanguard produced massive purple gorillas they had taken from every car dealership they came across[138]. He'd wondered why the general wanted them until he noticed the large brass pipes sticking out of them. A thunderous hum cut through even the roar and scream of the invasion as the robots put metal lips to their bagpipes and sent their haunting

---

[138] Howard had expended a day or two wondering what giant purple gorillas had to do with buying a car but eventually gave it up as one of those things his parents refused to tell him about until he was older. A list that included confusing aspects of rated R movies and the philosophy of voting for lesser evils.

melodies screeching across the valley.

Howard peered at the odd instruments and turned to his General.

"Did those pipes come from an organ?"

"You told me to be creative."

"Do I want to know where you found it?"

"You would be amazed at what farmers keep in their barns." The General carefully avoided Howard's gaze. "I needed something to carry messages across the field if our WiFi signals are jammed by either the aliens or the men in suits."

"I think you have a bit too much Dread Pirate Robot left in you," Howard mumbled. "How are they blowing those things, anyhow?"

"Blacksmith's bellows."

Howard pondered his prospects of going to hell.

"If I find out those came from a church, I'm going to spray paint you magenta before they haul me off to jail." Howard could barely wrap his mind around the number of tractors his scavengers had absconded with, but at least he could explain those.

If they'd liberated an organ from a choir loft...

He was almost relieved when a skirmish broke out on the edge of the line and an extra rank of robots had to be sent to reinforce the line. WARD was testing his resolve, probably trying to provoke him to see whether he had directed his soldiers to ignore Asimov's laws.

Truth was, at this point, Howard no longer knew which or whether the robots would obey him. He had directed his builders to bring him soldiers. If the WARD troops pushed too hard, the robot warriors *would* push back.

Howard's throat was too dry to swallow, but he felt the need anyway.

He wouldn't bet his college fund that no one would get hurt today.

To his right and left Gary and Ericka rode the shoulders of two of the other commanders of his forces. He wished with all his might that he'd been able to isolate them in a force field as he had his parents and time clones.

They had only just found one another. He couldn't contemplate losing either one of them now.

Suddenly it got dark and all thoughts of his friends fled his mind. He craned his neck and watched as a massive ship the size of the entire field moved slowly overhead, scattering its smaller brethren. The craft was a ring instead of a saucer, the center annulus large enough to enclose the entire field.

If the aliens really had come to play a game, they had brought the stadium with them.

***

If shown two objects traveling the same speed, you will swear that the larger is moving slower. Scientists who study this phenomenon refer to it as "speed discrimination" and it gets worse the larger the object is and the more foreshortened your view.

If you are standing beneath a building that's flying overhead, the veridical perception will be that it's taking forever.[139]

Howard's parents stood on the hospital lawn with the mad scientists and their time-displaced sons, watching the mother ship pass over the city of Sedville. The massive gleaming ring filled the sky, several stories high and hundreds of meters across. Even when the sun peeked through the center, its light was weak and apologetic, as if Earth's star was in a hurry to find somewhere else to be.

Even Howard's robot sentries craned their necks to watch the alien ship pass overhead.

It seemed to take hours, though it was really just a few minutes before the sky was clear and the massive ship was out over the rolling fields west of town, following 50 Highway

---

[139] Though, to be fair, part of that is the innate fear that it's going to fall on you. Imagine the Washington Monument or Arc de'Triomphe hovering overhead and tell me your first thought wouldn't be to wonder how much time you had left to call your mother and apologize for spilling soda on the car seat that day when you were twelve.

toward the distant farm where Howard had chosen to make his stand.

Not a word was spoken as they contemplated the full weight that had fallen on the bony shoulders of their favorite twelve-year-old. Howard's mother wanted to scream. To slap the haughty look off her future son's face, to demand that he stop putting himself in danger at any age. But she saw something there she couldn't identify -- a tension that came from bone-deep weariness and the echoes of past horrors.

"What is it?" she whispered. "Why did you come all this way?"

Howard didn't answer. His face was ashen, even as the sun returned with an enthusiasm that seemed meant to apologize for its earlier cowardice.

It was Gary who finally spoke.

"We have to get out of here before this starts all over again."

***

Skillion stood beside Old Suit on the roof of the RV and watched the alien ship come to a halt over the field below with its center over the small troupe of robots with the banners and bagpipes. At least the arrival of the mothership had silenced the screech and wail of the pipes.

"Bagpipes?" Old Suit muttered. "That kid's *trying* to get us all killed."

"Maybe they'll like them." Skillion shrugged.

"Nobody's that daft."

"Didn't you tell me your family was Scottish?"

"Yes, but we had the good sense to leave the pipes behind when we emigrated."

Skillion grunted and turned back to watch the swarm of landing ships begin to descend from the inside edge of the hovering ring. He sighed. He'd always expected that he would be present at the end of the world, he just hadn't expected to be a spectator.

"I like bagpipes," he whispered.

"You would."

286

***

Howard stood at the feet of his general and shifted his weight uneasily from foot to foot as they waited. In his mind, he heard his mother's church whisper telling him to hold still.

Be patient.

Stop fidgeting.

For heaven's sake, Howard, can't you sit still for ten minutes?

Apparently not even a force-ten energy shield could stop a mother's nagging.[140]

He had expected the aliens to look like the felt robot that had helped him escape from WARD, an artificial life form created by a distant race so that they didn't have to endure the rigors of interstellar travel themselves.

He was not disappointed.

When the ring had slowed to a halt with its center over the field, landing craft had descended, the first wave of visitors had been massive felt puppets. Sadly, these had not been inspired by the works of Jim Henson, but had taken on amorphous forms and multiple limbs. Forms he assumed were more suitable to tasks associated with space travel.

He hadn't expected to meet an *actual* living, breathing alien.

As the Dread Pirate General lowered him to the trampled soybeans, he found himself looking up into the large black eyes of a genuine alien. It was taller than he'd expected, with long limbs and an enormous head dominated by its two enormous eyes. Part of his brain took note of the frost still clinging to its shoulders and the musty smell he associated with the chest freezer his parents kept in the garage.

He nodded to himself -- it had been frozen while its artificial counterparts took care of the ships.

Ericka and Gary stepped up on either side of him and each

---

[140] Howard had always suspected as much, but had never had the guts to try it. Besides, they frown on that sort of thing in most churches and he didn't like to cause a scene.

laid a trembling hand on one of his shoulders as they stood looking up at the creature.

The alien shifted its weight from foot to foot in an odd little dance. Howard wondered if he was expected to do the dance too. He wasn't very good at dancing.

The alien swayed a bit and then they heard its voice in their heads.

"I don't suppose you could point me to the nearest restroom."

"I'm sorry... what?"

"A lavatory," the voice in his head repeated. *"Please, I haven't peed since Alpha Centauri."*

***

Howard didn't know much about interstellar diplomacy, but he was pretty sure that telling the visiting team to go pee behind a tree was bad form. The WARD vans held the nearest restroom facilities.

Now Howard paced back and forth in front of the RV door waiting for the alien to emerge, acutely aware that Old Suit and Skillion were watching him from behind the line of robots that had forced them to the periphery.

He wondered if he should send a note to his parents to let them know he was okay.

Armageddon had been delayed by a potty break.

Finally, the door swung open and the alien stepped down into the road and looked around at the string of black vans and the massive robots holding back the grim-looking men and women in power armor and power ties. It tilted its head and looked down at the young boy in its shadow.

The voice in his head was louder this time and less stressed by the pressure in its otherworldly bladder. It spoke -- if that's the right word -- in accentless English, as if it had learned from a news anchor[141].

"*This is most impressive, young Howard,*" the alien nodded. "*There was some debate among our people whether or not you could pull it off. I think our technical staff even had a pool going.*"

"I get by with a little help from my clones."

"*Oh, not really.*" The alien shook its enormous head. "*That sort of thing is not allowed.*"

"Tell them that," Howard said. "I corralled some of them in town, but at this point I wouldn't be surprised if there were three or four more of me running around."

"*We are aware of your doppelgangers, Howard. I meant that their interference was not allowed to prejudice the experiment.*" The alien looked proud of itself. "*Our agent saw to it that Doctor Deeds solved his math problem in time for his birthday and your future self has been wearing a limiter circlet on his head for most of his time here to keep you out of his head.*"

"But all these robots…"

"*Came from your head, not theirs.*"

Howard stood quietly for so long that the alien grew bored and opened one of the compartments on the side of the RV and poked through its contents. It didn't find anything interesting and went back to watching Howard mull over what it had told him.

"But why got to all this trouble for a game?"

"*This was the game, youngling,*" the alien chuckled. "*The game wasn't with us -- we needed Earth's best and brightest to contest for the prize and you won.*"

"And what did he win?" Ericka asked.

Howard knew. Suddenly, he knew why his doppelganger

---

[141] Only because it had. Sports broadcasts had been among the first radio signals that had been beamed into space by unwitting humans at the dawn of the electronic age. Actually, he was lucky it hadn't arrived expecting to converse in German since -- as others have noted before me -- the first broadcasts of that kind sent out with enough power to reach deep space were the Berlin Olympics of 1936. Thankfully, signal degradation kept that from being our first intergalactic "Howdy".

was willing to fling himself and all his loved ones through time to put a stop to all of this and why the mad family Deeds had strived for so long and at such great cost to make it happen.

Gary figured it out before Howard could find his voice.

"You want to make him king," Gary said. "This is how it happened... happens... isn't it?"

"*You have shown yourself to be resourceful, ruthless, and intelligent enough to be worthy of being our representative here on Earth.*" The alien smiled, baring a row of needle-sharp teeth. "*This planet is now subject to the Empire of Nicton and half its population will be taken in tribute to the emperor while you remain here to rule the rest in his name. Congratulations, King Howard the First.*"

Howard glanced from the alien to the cordon of robots and space marines surrounding them, staring at him with faces pale and eyes wide. Even Old Suit's tunnel-dweller's pallor had grown another shade whiter. He watched the faces of his friends change, their eyes grow wide and afraid.

No one spoke.

No one knew what to say.

No one except Howard.

He turned to the alien and nodded.

"I accept."

38. King Howard the Truant

The alien was pleased beyond the ability of earthly languages to fully express his joy. Usually, when the fleet sent out challenges to prospective members of the empire, they were answered by adults. The empire was swamped with generals and petty tyrants eager for alien allies to help take over their world. But even the most hardened and callous usually balked when they learned that half their planet's population was forfeit.

Howard Carter hadn't even blinked.

Kids!

This could revolutionize the empire-expanding business.

"Will this take long?" Howard asked. "I have to get home to dinner."

"Does he get a cool alien scepter that shoots death rays or something?" Gary asked. "Oh! And a cape!"

"A *red* cape," Ericka agreed. "And you gotta have a crown too."

"One that lets me read people's minds and stuff, right?" Howard enthused. "Do I get a crown?"

The alien frowned down at the gabbling kids in front of him.

"*Are you sure you built all these robots?*" It frowned suspiciously at Howard's upturned grin. "*Well, there will be no death scepters or mindreading crowns. The very idea! Kneel.*"

Howard did as he was told and watched as it waved an appendage at one of the felt-forms nearby. The kids watched, wide-eyed as the creature reached into its mouth and pulled out a slimy circlet of copper wire, braided and twisted into a crownlike shape.

As the felt creature handed it over, thick globules of green goop dripped into the dirt.

Howard winced as the alien stepped forward and settled the

slimy crown in his unruly thatch of hair. He no longer wondered why his future selves had shock white hair -- after this, he was going to have to send his out to be bleached.

The alien spoke quickly, eager to get it over with. *"By the powers vested in me as Viceroy at Large, plenipotentiary for the Emperor of Nictos, etcetera, etcetera, I declare you King Howard the First, vassal of the empire and ruler in stead of the planet called Earth."*

As the alien stepped back, Howard rose to his feet and looked around at his new kingdom.

For the first time in his young life, he felt a surge of affection for his homeland... his home *planet*. Before, it had been rocks and dirt and water, slime molds and towering trees, animals that will bite you and animals that will befriend you and a whole mess of quarreling, confounding humans that kept the place interesting.

He was Howard the Impossible, that annoying kid at the back of the class who knew all the answers and did things with frozen kids treats that defied the laws of physics. Now, there was something new in his eyes and a different set to his shoulders[142]. He was Howard the First, king of earth.

This was his world and these were his people.

He caught the eye of every robot in turn and then his friends before he turned to face the aliens once more. He wanted to swallow his fear, but there wasn't any more room for it in his stomach -- he was full up.

He looked down and was surprised to find that Ericka's hand was wrapped around his. *So that's how it happens,* he thought. With her hand in his, he came back to himself and turned to face their conqueror.

"Tag or kickball?" he asked.

"I... I don't understand."

"You came all this way for a game and those are the only

---

[142] Howard was later forced to admit that the change in posture was actually the result of the slime that was beginning to drip off the crown and run down the back of his neck. The difference between noble bearing and arching your back because something icky is happening is surprisingly small.

two I really know."

"We didn't come here to play games." The alien smoothed its glimmering robe, looking agitated. *"I told you, that was a trick. I have your treaty already drawn up, so if you will come back to my ship we will get this over with."*

"I won't be signing anything," Howard continued. "It's time for you to leave."

The alien was silent for a moment, but Howard could feel it seething with barely-constrained fury. *"You seem to be under the mistaken impression that I am giving you a choice."*

"Kickball it is then." Howard dove out of the way as the robot's foot swept past them. The alien screeched and curled up inside the glowing green orb that popped into existence around it moments before the iron foot hit.

"You agreed to our terms, traitorous child!" the alien howled as it sailed out over the field and disappeared over the wall.

"That's *king* traitorous child to you." Gary shouted.

***

The Carter and Deeds families looked up at the sound of the screech. It had been a long, tense hour since the massive ring settled over a field on the edge of town and they sat on benches at the edge of Howard's force field. Even from atop the hospital, the highest point in Sedville, the battlefield was lost to sight, which left them straining their ears for the sounds of battle.

There had been strange, unearthly music at first, wailing pipes and drums, but that had faded as the mother ship landed and now only the constant hum of the force bubble and an occasional axle squeak from their ring of robot guardians disturbed the silence.

The silence was broken by an unearthly cry that grew louder as a glowing green orb appeared over the edge of the distant ship and grew louder as it flew toward them.

They dove for cover as the orb bounced off the force field and ricocheted off to slam into a nearby hotel. Over the sound of collapsing masonry, the sound of metal clashing against metal echoed across the land like a thousand car wrecks happening at once and the air was heavy with the whine and scream of alien engines.

The battle for Earth had begun.

***

Old Suit had watched the coronation of Howard the First with a mix of admiration for the kid's moxie and the sick surety that the planet was doomed. When the kid accepted the crown and then turned on his alien captor, he even felt a twinge of sympathy for the alien.

Howard Carter was not a kid to be taken lightly.

Then the robots attacked, the men from WARD watching, dumbfounded, as the kid's forces swept the field, pressing their attack with telephone poles and rocks, leaping up and smashing alien craft out of the air with gleeful abandon.

The kid was defending the planet with… sticks and stones.

"What the hell is he thinking?"

"James," Skillion hissed in his ear. "If you don't get off your butt and order our people to back that poor kid up, I will!"

Old Suit was startled. He hadn't heard his real name in decades. He hadn't even been aware Skillion knew it. He stared at the scientist for a long count of ten before he did something he had never done in his life: he took Skillion's advice.

"Commander, engage the aliens on all fronts." He dropped the radio and turned to his science advisor. "And just what do your people intend to do?"

"Have you ever read the Magenta Book? I mean the whole Magenta Book?"

"No, why?"

"Get headquarters on the horn and I'll show you."

***

Howard and his friends clambered up onto the shoulders of their respective robots as the alien forces began to return fire. Green energy beams cut through the air and the stench of burning oil and hot metal clogged their noses as their command team retreated and larger robots moved in to take their places.

This was the crucial moment in Howard's gamble -- they just had to hold the field long enough for the last phase of his plan to be ready.

The robots took the field with pure brute force. Harvesters reached up with massive iron paws to snatch flying saucers out of the air, flipping them into their fellows or flinging them like Frisbees into the towering walls of the stadium ship.

Lines of yellow robots built from the enormous machines that had been formerly tasked with ripping quarries into the earth's crust moved forward to support their smaller brethren with a steady barrage of boulders the size of buildings.

The boulders bounced off in a shower of sparks before they could reach the walls of the stadium ship like gravel thrown against the armored sides of a tank, but the constant barrage had changed the color of the field from a crystalline green to an angry, milky red. They could see felt-forms swarming toward the turrets and soon a steady stream of green light beams were cutting deep into the ranks of earth's mechanical defenders.

Robots fell and other rose to replace them as Howard's builderbots swept across the field, hurriedly building new robots from the fragments of the old.

Gary watched the battle unfold from the shoulders of Bee Bee. They didn't have enough robots to keep this up forever. Not even Howard could build robots from the molten slag that rained down wherever the green rays touched an iron chassis. If they ran out of spare parts, it was all over.

Luckily, Howard wasn't the only one with a plan, Ericka had added a few details of her own.

She had jumped onto the shoulders of another smaller robot they had dubbed "Thumper[143]" and waved goodbye as she and the robot were picked up by a much larger bot.

---

[143] So-named because it tended to tap its foot impatiently if the humans took too long to do something. She had developed an affinity for the small, hyper robots because she too had spent a lot of time tapping her foot, waiting for Howard to notice her.

"Launch Tetherball!" Ericka shouted into Thumper's ear, her words transmitted across the field to her small troupe of robots moving along the base of the stadium ship's walls where the force field met the ground.

Like medieval catapults, the arms of line after line of earthmover robots swung and threw their payloads up into the air. But this time they weren't throwing rocks, they threw Thumper (with Ericka clinging to his shoulder for dear life) and the rest of his team up, over and across the barrier wall of the stadium ship.

Miles of salvaged telephone lines and power cables trailed behind the flying robots as they flew.

***

Gary ducked under Bee Bee's arm and clung there as the fragments and gravel (that is to say rocks the size of Volkswagen Beetles instead of buildings) rained down from the stadium force field. Bee Bee kept one arm up to protect them and ducked the larger stones as it drew nearer the point where the force field met the ground. Bee Bee's kept its troops moving, drawing as close to the edge of the energy field as it could without getting fried by the electricity arcing off of it.

Peering up from the robot's rusty armpit, Gary could see the crowds of the ever-changing felt-forms watching the fray, though whether they were spectators or combatants was difficult to say.

Gary felt like a character from one of the Roman epics, waiting in the sand of the grand arena for Caesar to raise his thumb and decide his fate. *Spartacus* or *Gladiator*, though his mom wasn't supposed to know he'd watched the last one -- except neither Kirk Douglas nor Russell Crowe had an army of iron automatons watching his back.

He hoped it was enough.

The line of robots following Bee Bee into the fray spread out along the burnt line of soybeans where the force field met the field and waited for the signal, arms raised to fend off the falling rock barrage that had now been joined with strange orange projectiles thrown by the weapons WARD's space marines were setting up along the ridgeline above the battle.

He hoped they didn't get in the way when the dessert course arrived.

"*We're ready!*" Ericka's voice squawked from Bee Bee's speaker.

Robots all along the line took up the slack in the cables they had been carrying and started to fall back toward the center. Around the entire circle, other robots did the same as on the far side of the stadium ship, Ericka and Thumper leading the way.

***

Howard stood atop the head of his general, heedless of the death rays and flying stones as he directed the battle as best he could. He wore the old copper waste basket as a helmet, the flimsy plastic pirate hat still glued atop in all its crushed and cello-taped glory. His wrench was shoved in his belt like a sword and the slimy copper crown hung from the end.

Ericka's plan worried him, but even with the WARD batteries adding their weight, the alien force field had held. Half his robots lay broken on the field and his builderbots were struggling to keep the remaining troops upright.

Every time the general moved beneath him, Howard felt the crown swing and thump against his leg, a reminder of what awaited the planet if he failed. Howard especially hated the part where he had to watch his friends ride into the thick of the fight without him as he and the bulk of his remaining troops completed the rest of his plan.

He'd never had close friends before who weren't mechanical. And though he worried about Gary, the thought of Ericka in harm's way froze a part of his chest he'd never been aware of before. His hand still felt warm where she had gripped it after the coronation.

"*Now! Now! Do it now!*" Ericka's frantic shout carried to every corner of the battlefield through the general's cellular connection and Howard had no more time to think.

Gary and Ericka's troops threw more and more lines over the

walls of the ship, driving broken stumps of telephone pole into the hard Missouri granite, to tie them to, grabbing and re-tying cables as they snapped.

As Ericka had predicted, the automatic functions that kept the alien craft centered in the force bubble kicked in and the ring began to dig into the ground, forced down by the glowing web of super-heated cables forcing the alien craft to land.

They would never hold if the phone didn't... The General's head started to ring. Howard grabbed the handset and raised it to his ear.

"Operation Cosby is ready to go, your majesty."

Howard smiled.

"Fire."

***

On the far side of the United States, deep underneath an extinct volcano in the state of Oregon, the final phase of Howard's plan clicked into place.

In the chaos following Howard Carter's escape, WARD had been inundated with forms and IOU's from tractor dealerships, car dealerships, supermarkets, and Popsicle factories across the central states. Amid the general mayhem, the secret base had also begun to receive tractor trailers loaded with sugar, dry milk, and corn starch along with tankers full of various artificial flavorings, mostly pistachio.

With everything else going on, it had seemed the least of Howard Carter's pranks.

No one thought to look in a cookbook and ponder what those ingredients might make. It was too late now. Robots scavenged from the remnants of the WARD army had loaded the ingredients onto the shuttles, already aimed at the battlefield where earth's future hung in the balance.

When all was ready, one of the flying cats brought a phone to the pink felted pig creature they had adopted. Among the magic marker scribbles adorning its arms was a telephone number, a direct line to the mind that used to belong to the Dread Pirate Robot.

Howard picked up on the first ring.

***

Out beyond the orbit of Mars, just shy of the left turn at the asteroid Albuquerque III that would take you to Jupiter, lurked a worrisome mass of asteroids known as the Apollo Cluster. This clump of space rocks were worrisome because their orbits pass inside of the orbit of Mars and occasionally go careening across Earth's path with the haphazard abandon of deer crossing a dark rural highway.

The occasional collision is inevitable.

A 2002 report prepared by the RAND Corporation explored the idea of using earth-based rockets to make this sort of thing happen on purpose, using smaller members of this wandering tribe as weapons[144]. If one of those rocks were brought to earth, even a small one could strike the planet with the force of several nuclear bombs, but without all that pesky radiation.

If only they could be aimed...

Skillion's boffins watched the public reception of this idea carefully and were relieved when most commentators and policymakers dismissed the idea as unfeasible.

Unfeasible, at least, for conventional forces fighting conventional wars.

WARD had never been accused of being conventional.

With the help of scientific delinquents from Arkham Tech, Skillion and his people launched one of the most curious and most successful of all his projects for WARD. It was so successful, it had been a challenge to keep it under wraps. The next decade was spent paying off members of the mission team to keep their mouths shut and bribing astronomers to look the other way.

Literally.

Skillion's call had been to his accountant: Stop the

---

[144] True story. The section of the report is called "Natural Meteoroids As Weapons" and is part of a larger report called "Space Weapons, Earth Wars."

payments.

It took ten minutes for the accountants to rout the order from WARD headquarters to the various offshore banks where the clandestine agency hid its billions. A minute later, perturbed astronomers and journalists were on the phone with editors, blowing the lid off the whole operation. The world woke up to the presence of an alien fleet overhead and the bizarre counterattack already underway in the skies.

Meanwhile, in the Apollonian Cluster, automatic systems awoke, made calculations and fired their rockets, sending half of the smallest stones in the cluster spinning out of their natural orbit and toward the besieged pale blue dot of Earth.

39. Irresistible Forces

One of the oldest thought experiments in physics is what would happen if the unstoppable force met the immovable object. The experiment has been kept in the theoretical realm by the simple fact that as far as anyone knew, while a number of immovable objects had been invented or discovered, there was a dearth of truly unstoppable forces to oppose them with.

The science directorate of the Nictos Empire had equipped their wandering Viceroy with what they called an Infinite Mass Immovable Energy Field. The simple force bubble the alien had engaged protected him from the force of the kick from Howard's robot, but it meant being flung through the air in the direction of the kick like an extraterrestrial soccer ball.

Embarrassing to be sure, but a proper IMIE Field took time to set up and build to full power. If the alien had time to engage the IMIE field, the general's iron foot would have crumpled while the alien stood majestic and unaffected as the emperor intended.

The problem with the immovable is that you can't move it, and being unable to move around put a damper on the viceroy's style. Who knew that a kid like Howard would turn on him so fast?

As the alien picked its way out of the rubble of the hotel where it had landed, it concocted elaborate lies to tell its bosses in the Planet Conquering division about why it had let its guard down. It eventually decided to claim Howard had possessed some sort of brain-control, super-science deviltry it couldn't be expected to anticipate in a human.

Obviously, the feltform sent ahead to reconnoiter was to blame for not reporting this ability on the part of the humans.

As it popped its green head out of the rubble, it spotted

several human adults head toward it down the street. The viceroy dusted off its glimmering robe and engaged the full strength of its IMIE field, just in case.

It sent out a wave of thoughts ahead of them, ratcheted it up a notch.

This time it would cow their primitive minds into submission by sheer force of will.

"BEHOLD, HUMANS! YOUR NEW OVERLORDS HAVE ARRIVED!"

The IMIE field shattered and the alien went down on its skinny little butt to lay stunned on the pavement, wondering what happened.

Funny thing about the laws of physics -- some of them are laws and and some of them are more like guidelines. Little did the alien realize but it had just witnessed the first date between the immovable object and the irresistible force.

A second date was not to be encouraged.

As it lay hovering on the edge of consciousness, staring up at Howard Carter's fuming mother being held back by both of her husbands, the alien couldn't help but think: *Well. I guess that answers that question…*

***

As the burning streaks of inbound missiles were sighted over the battlefield, Howard gave the signal for his forces to break off their attack. Every remaining robot moved to the perimeter to help Bee Bee and Thumper hold the stadium ship down.

Confused, the feltforms gathered in the mud and trampled soybeans, regrouping among the broken fragments of tractors and trucks to watch the earthling army run away. The earthling strategy made no sense and they watched as they struggled to keep the mother ship grounded.

It was only a matter of time before the viceroy returned and the captain went to full thrust. The ground underfoot was already heating up from the friction of the forcefield and the substrata of granite.

If the captain cut in the engines, even if all the robots on the field piled on, they wouldn't be able to counter it.

What was the kid thinking?

They looked to their leaders for orders, but without the viceroy, they weren't entirely sure if they should destroy the human army or humor them. How do you counter an attack that isn't an attack? Humankind's defender was a child and he was fighting like a child.

The airwaves were clogged with news reports and frantic cries.

The humans were waking up to the invasion already underway and their real military would respond soon. Subjugating the humans was supposed to be the job of the truant king. If they were going to conquer the planet the old fashioned way, it was time to be about it already.

Scout ships were reporting skirmishes with aircraft dispatched from the nearby airbases to probe the alien lines and there were inbound missiles confusingly packed with foodstuffs instead of explosives or fissionable material.

The feltforms were becoming unnerved.

These humans were weird.

They looked up in wonder as the missile-borne foodstuffs burst open overhead and it began to snow cornstarch, powdered milk, and sugar. Before they knew it, there was a foot of white powder on the ground and still the missiles burst overhead and tons of the stuff fell into the center of the stadium ship.

"Now!" Howard's voice echoed across the field, echoed by a thousand speakers mounted on the thousands of remaining robots, all of whom grabbed their lines and began to run clockwise around the field. At the center, the feltforms stood watching as the mesh of cables fused by the electrical field began to drag the stadium ship with them in ever faster circles.

In 1687, Sir Isaac Newton was the first earthling to observe that once you set something in motion it tends to keep going until something stops it. This preservation of momentum is what keeps the earth spinning, and on a smaller scale, Howard's small army of robots did the same thing to the alien ship, kicking the dry powder up into a blizzard of milk fats and starches in accordance with the directions on the package.

Soon, the bowl formed by the stadium ship and the rubble kicked up by the force shields digging into the ground (not to mention a couple hundred broken robot chassis) was a white-out of spinning powder. The alien ship wasn't terribly put-out by the spinning and the captain saw no point in stopping it. The feltforms at the center of the field could see on several wavelengths of light, so they too saw no reason to stop the curious behavior either.

When Howard first pitched the idea, the felt pig creature had predicted the alien's reaction - or lack thereof - with perfect accuracy. They would never know what hit them. As if summoned by the thought of it, the phone on the side of the General's head rang again.

Howard picked it up and the piggy voice had good news.

"Phase two is overhead."

"Thank you, my friend." Howard smiled. "We're ready for a little rain down here."

***

High overhead, a flight of B-3 "Aurora" stealth interceptors out of Hall's Air Force Base closed in on what they had thought to be more inbound alien aircraft. As they drew within sight, the radar signatures resolved into physical objects visible from the cockpits.

After a moment's discussion between pilots and navigators, they called home for instructions. A fleet of milk tanker trailers were in flight on a course and bearing that would deposit them into the midst of the alien landing zone.

The generals and politicians watching events unfold from a bunker deep underneath Omaha looked at one another and shrugged. They had bigger fish to fry. The order came back to the Aurora crews.

Let them fly.

It's telling that with all the strange events unfolding in the skies over earth, somehow a flock of migrating milk tankers seemed positively normal.

***

Throughout the early years of the 20th century, anonymous scientists labored heroically in secret laboratories, experimenting with blends of sucrose, casein, and polysaccharides. At stake was no less than the future of their world.

Their work was often overlooked, and did not reach the height of its potential until the results were put into a sort of cryogenic stasis and impaled on a stick. The scientists didn't know they were engaged in weapon's research that would one day save the planet.

At the time they just thought of it as instant pudding.

***

It wasn't until the milk started to fall that the feltforms and their alien overlords began to get concerned. The gelatinous sludge quickly weighted down their appendages and soaked into their felted skin. The spinning of the walls of the stadium and the heat generated by its friction also began to hydrolyze the dried milk fats, proteins denatured and tangled, coaxing the gelatinized starches into a thick green soup that bore a distinct scent of pistachios.

By this point, Howard's iron and steel robots were clinging to their lines not to keep the ship spinning but to keep from getting dragged to the center of the whirlpool of congealing pistachio pudding.

Howard had successfully bogged down the enemy forces (along with much of his own, actually), but he wasn't done. As the speed of the spinning ship reached its peak and the milk began to rain down, it was too dangerous for Ericka and Gary to remain in the thick of things. They had each in turn patted their mechanical steeds and shot above the fray on the recharged rocket belts Howard and Deeds had used to escape from WARD five days before.

From his vantage point on the ridge where Sunshine Rock no longer stood, he could see the two hovering figures aim their water pistols at the green mess of floating aliens and robots below and fire.

The stench of ammonia overpowered even the smell of the pistachios.

Howard laughed and pounded on the shoulder of the general as he watched the spinning ship slow and then come to a halt, arrested by the world's largest frozen pudding pop.

That's when he remembered that he'd forgotten to call the Guinness Book people.

Oh well. You can't think of everything.

***

High overhead, beyond the range of all but the most powerful earth-based telescopes, the rest of the alien expeditionary forces turned from their contemplation of the planet below to face a new threat.

A barrage of rogue asteroids was inbound on a collision course.

That they had been set on this vector by artificial means was irrelevant as the ships were faced with the prospect of dodging objects larger than they were. While Skillion's asteroids were small for asteroids, that's a relative measurement. For even the largest of the alien fleet, it was like trying to dodge a building as it falls on you.

In the first minutes of the meteor shower, half the alien fleet disappeared.

By the third minute, the rest had turned tail and headed for Jupiter.

The battle for Earth was over almost as soon as it began.

***

The alien stumbled to a halt in front of Howard as his mother finally released her grasp on the flap of skin where its ear would have been if it had been human. She had hauled the alien viceroy into a nearby car and held fast all the way across town and down the trail to where Howard awaited them.

Its glassy black eyes stared past the boy king out across the frozen lake of green pudding. The glassine surface, kept frozen by WARD marines armed with the squirt guns Howard had provided, was dotted here and there with tiny heads or outflung appendages of the robots encased in the massive pudding pop. The ship remained half-buried in the dirt and stone, still hovering in the center of its force field but frozen to the ground by a thousand tonnes of pistachio pudding.

The viceroy knew that its fleet would not be coming to its rescue, driven into retreat by the human race's apparent ability to control the flights of their local asteroids -- an ability that they were not supposed to have.

Something somewhere had gone seriously awry.

It turned to survey the smug and angry faces of the people who had defeated it. The Carters watched the alien with stony silence and the Deeds family looked alternately bored or distracted. The alien thought it detected a certain amount of sympathy in the faces of the men and women of WARD -- a kinship wrought of having been bested by an eleven-year-old perhaps.

The future Howard, Ericka, and Gary took their places a pace behind their younger selves. The Garys and Erickas flanked the Howards as they stared down the alien invader. The elder Howard spoke first.

"You are not welcome here and we will not be joining your empire this time."

"You think it will be that easy?" The alien was so irked it forgot to engage its thought-speech device. "Your tricks may have caught me off-guard, but more will follow. They will not land as I did or try to get you to surrender, they will bombard this planet from space until it's just another blackened rock hurtling through space!"

"They are welcome to try," young Howard said. "But if they do, I will be here with as many of myself as it takes to send them packing again. But I don't think they'll be here any time soon."

"And why is that?" the alien sneered. "Because we're scared of a boy?"

"Because you're going to have your hands full when your feltforms refuse to attack us." Howard had the pleasure of seeing real fear and confusion on the alien's face. "Igor?"

One of the WARD contingent stepped forward and set the small creature it had been holding on the ground in front of the viceroy. The creature uncurled and stretched and continued to stretch, unfolding from the small rodentlike creature into a tall piglike thing adorned with magic marker scrawls and doodles.

The viceroy barely recognized the felt form it had sent to reconnoiter in advance of the invasion. The thing had obviously gone native.

"You have much to answer for!" the Viceroy snapped.

"No. You did not do your own homework before sending me here, so I think it shall be you who answers for these events." The creature smiled at the Viceroy. "This planet has a culture devoted to puppets. They allow them to teach their children and to entertain them, but also to walk among them and live lives of their own! If you had only watched the news feeds, you would know this!"

"Preposterous!"

"And they have *cats*!" The felted hands grabbed the Viceroy's stooped shoulders and shook him. "Do you know about the cats? Creatures devoted to curling up in warm places and nesting in warm fabric? Soon feltforms throughout the galaxy will be demanding cat companions to share the dark watches of the night!"

"You have been driven mad by this place."

"You sent me to explore this planet's time stream to find the most clever and ruthless individual ever to exist, so that I could track them back along their timeline and guide them to become a king you could manipulate," the pig creature said. "And I did. She stands over there with her twin brother -- the woman in manacles and a gag."

The alien stared for a moment at Cat Deeds and then back to its wayward minion.

"And what happened?"

"I watched her defeat you and then be defeated and overthrown by a man who was far cleverer, someone who would do anything for his friends, someone who valued the robots and artificial life forms he created to help him in his rebellion." The felted creature waved a paw at the Howards. "I flagged down a passing freighter and took them around the sun and back in time, but I lost track of the young Howard before he got embroiled in your arrival anyway. By the time I caught up with him, you were too close to wave off."

"You think he values his toys?" the Viceroy cried. "Look at them! He froze them in pudding along with all your brethren!"

"But he did not kill them," the felt pig countered. "He has mastered sucrose fusion but did not use it to build weapons, he came here in good faith to play your game. He even tried to talk you into playing a proper game, but you turned the hand of violence against him. He could have destroyed you, but he froze you instead."

"That is irrelevant."

"It is perfectly relevant, and it is the tale that is being carried among my people back into the far reaches of the empire." The felted pig released its hold on the Viceroy and stepped back. "It's how he defeated not only you, but the entire empire."

"Your fleet is gone," Howard stepped in. "It's time for you to go too."

Everyone waited with bated breath as the Viceroy contemplated the bare toes sticking out from under the ragged hem of its robe. Finally, it nodded.

"Release my ship."

"I will go along to see to it that this emissary brings the true story back with him to the empire." The felted pig stepped up to stand next to its former master. Howard gave the signal and Old Suit passed the order to his men to allow the ship and robot armies to melt.

Howard felt a twinge of regret.

He had succeeded in saving the world and possibly even toppling a galactic empire, but he couldn't help regret seeing the pudding melt. The Guinness Book people had informed him that it didn't count for the world's largest since he hadn't thought to put it on a stick.

Just his luck, really.

Epilogue: All Good Things...

The scent of pistachio still hung thick in the air as the kids and Doctor Deeds stood in front of the pig creature in the shadow of the hovering stadium ship. Deeds snapped his fingers at Igor and the young technician dug a folded piece of paper out of his back pocket and passed it over.

Howard smoothed the page over his leg.

"We contacted the Muppet people and on short notice, they gave us this certificate for you to take with you." Howard passed the wrinkled certificate to the pig creature with as much gravitas as he could muster. "It names you as a member of the fan club."

"You just have to write your name in the blank at the bottom," Gary said. "Ericka has a pen if you want to do it now."

"What is your name anyway?" Ericka asked, digging in her pockets for the promised pen.

"We don't have names, just designations." The pig creature whispered as it stared at the name and seal of King Elmo, prince of monsters and puppets. It couldn't believe it held such an important document.

"You should have a name," Howard said. "What name would you like?"

The pig creature was silent for a moment as it contemplated the decision. Finally, it took the pen that Ericka held out and scrawled "Douglas" at the bottom of the page. They didn't ask. It was a fine name for an alien felt pig/robot/puppet thing and they all took turns saying so.

"Maybe if you come back, maybe we can arrange for you to meet King Elmo in person," Deeds offered.

"Thank you." Douglas bent down to pick up the two winged cats Deeds had already given it and clutched them along with the rumpled certificate to its heavily-illustrated chest. Without another word, it dematerialized and followed the light path up to the waiting ship.

The three kids and the mad scientist stood waving until the stadium ship was out of sight[145] and then turned to meet their time-displaced doubles. There wasn't anywhere for the Deeds family to go - their time line was erased and gone forever, but the former king and his two friends were headed back to their time to see what waited for them[146].

The parting was a bit awkward and less teary than seeing Douglas off, but honestly, Howard and the others were glad to see them go. Their constant stream of advice on what was important and how to live out the rest of their days had quickly gotten annoying.

As they stepped through their portal into the unknown future, Howard and the others felt only relief.

The city of Sedville was coming back to life as the residents who had fled began to return, eager to pretend they had been there all along for the news crews that had converged on the town in the wake of what was coming to be known rather unimaginatively as wardgate.

Old Suit hadn't bothered them since the defeat of the alien invasion, an action he had been spectacularly unsuccessful at claiming credit for. Doctor Skillion's asteroid bombardment and Howard's pudding gambit had been trumpeted as heroic, while the rest of the WARD effort was overshadowed by the size of the bill presented to congress for all of the machinery Howard had scavenged on his march across the American West.

---

[145] Which took nine-tenths of a second. You don't cross interstellar distances at visible speed or you'll never get anywhere. You might as well try to swim to Jupiter.

[146] Both Garys had been a little disappointed when their future selves hadn't evaporated as soon as the alien ship was defeated and Cat Deeds was captured, effectively stopping the events that would have resulted in most of the key events that created their timeline. The Howards found this hilarious. The space time continuum just is not as good about tidying up after itself as it is in the movies.

By the end of the day, WARD's clandestine coffers were empty. Because the plot had been hatched during the Polk administration, most of the government was able to pretend they didn't know about it and the controversy soon died out in the wake of the new understanding of the universe and our place in it.

About the time Old Suit began to despair of ever seeing an end to the congressional hearings, he was asked to retire. He was only too glad to retreat from the spotlight to live out the rest of his days on a little ranch outside of Yellowstone where he insisted that everyone call him Jim and wore a cowboy hat with an enthusiasm that bordered on the fanatical.

The one person Old Suit might have successfully blamed -- Doctor Catastrophic "Cat" Deeds, Dean of Mad Science for Arkham Tech -- disappeared in a spectacular jailbreak with a young grad student and former WARD double agent known as either Kevin or Igor depending on whom you talked to.

Howard returned the Dread Pirate Robot to his old body (newly refurbished) and the old robot quickly found work with a local railroad where it happily wiled away its time playing chess and keeping trains from running into one another. Bee Bee disappeared one night, but if you want to find it, just follow the crop circles and rude suggestions that carved into the landscape.

People might change, but robots are admirably consistent.

Howard and his parents and friends returned to their lives as best they could. It wasn't easy to be a sixth grader and the Defender of Earth at the same time, but Howard was up to the challenge if anyone could be.

He certainly didn't have to worry about his name being remembered as a mummy finder anymore. He had written his own page into the history books and from now on kids named Howard Carter would have to explain their connection to *him*.

As for the future that awaits them or what their future selves found when they stepped across the decades?

Well, that's another story all together.

THE END

312

Thank you for reading this Crooked Cat book. If you have enjoyed it, we and the author would appreciate a review.

Please browse our other releases to find similar reads:
www.crookedcatpublishing.com

CPSIA information can be obtained at www.ICGtesting.com
Printed in the USA
BVOW11s1505071115

425661BV00001B/3/P